The Prophecy

Book Two

B.D LeLiever

The Prophecy
Copyright © 2015 by Breanna Dawn LeLiever

Publisher: LeLiever, Breanna
Stirling Ontario, Canada

Cover Illustration © by Breanna LeLiever
Cover and Interior Design © by Breanna LeLiever

All rights reserved. This book may not be reproduced in whole or in part without written permission from the publisher, nor may any part of this book be reproduced, stored in a retrieval system, or transmitted in any form or by any means, electronic, mechanical, photocopy, recording, or other, without written permission from the publisher, except in case of brief quotations embodied in critical articles and reviews.

First Printing September 2015

Written, illustrated and designed in Canada. Printed in the USA by CreateSpace, on acid-free paper. Distributed by Amazon.com.

For a list of retail outlets that carry this title, please refer to
www.theamityblade.com

This book is dedicated to Daniel Campbell, the finest talent of the arts ever to overlook my training.

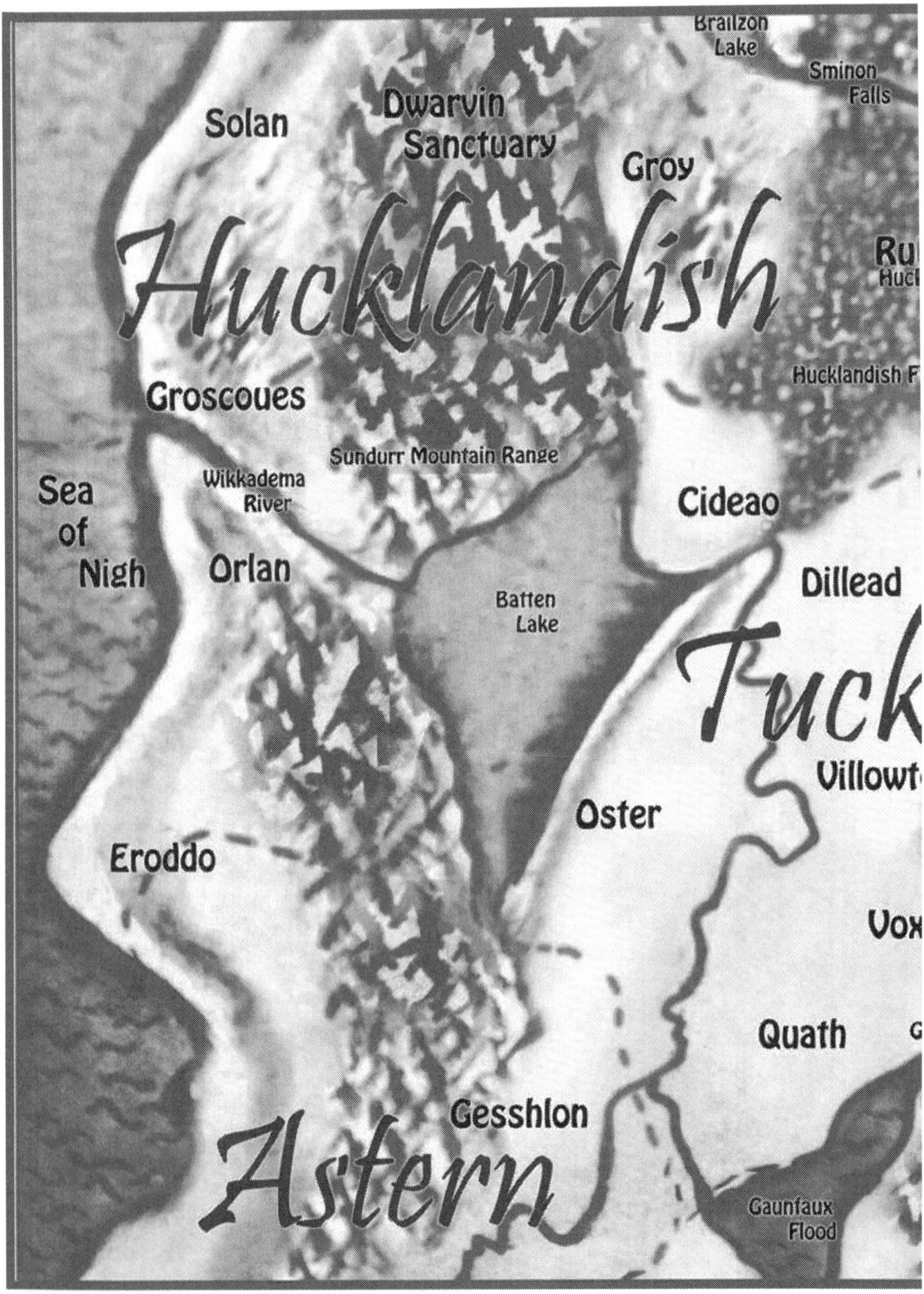
Brailzon
Lake
Sminon
Falls
Solan
Dwarvin
Sanctuary
Groy
Hucklandish
Hucklandish F
Groscoues
Sundurr Mountain Range
Wikkadema
River
Sea
of
Nigh
Cideao
Orlan
Batten
Lake
Dillead
Tuck
Villowt
Oster
Eroddo
Vox
Quath
Gesshlon
Astern
Gaunfaux
Flood

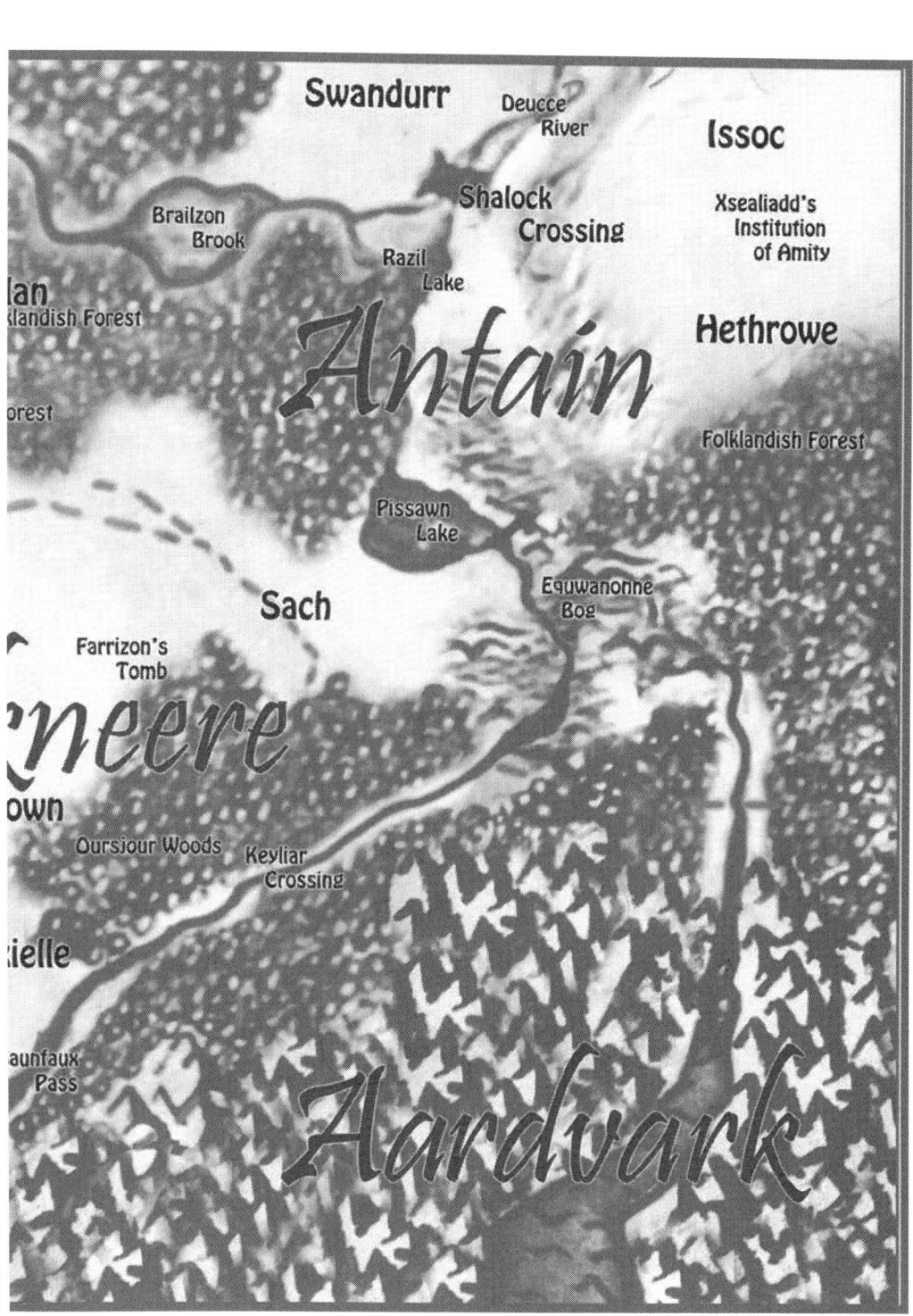

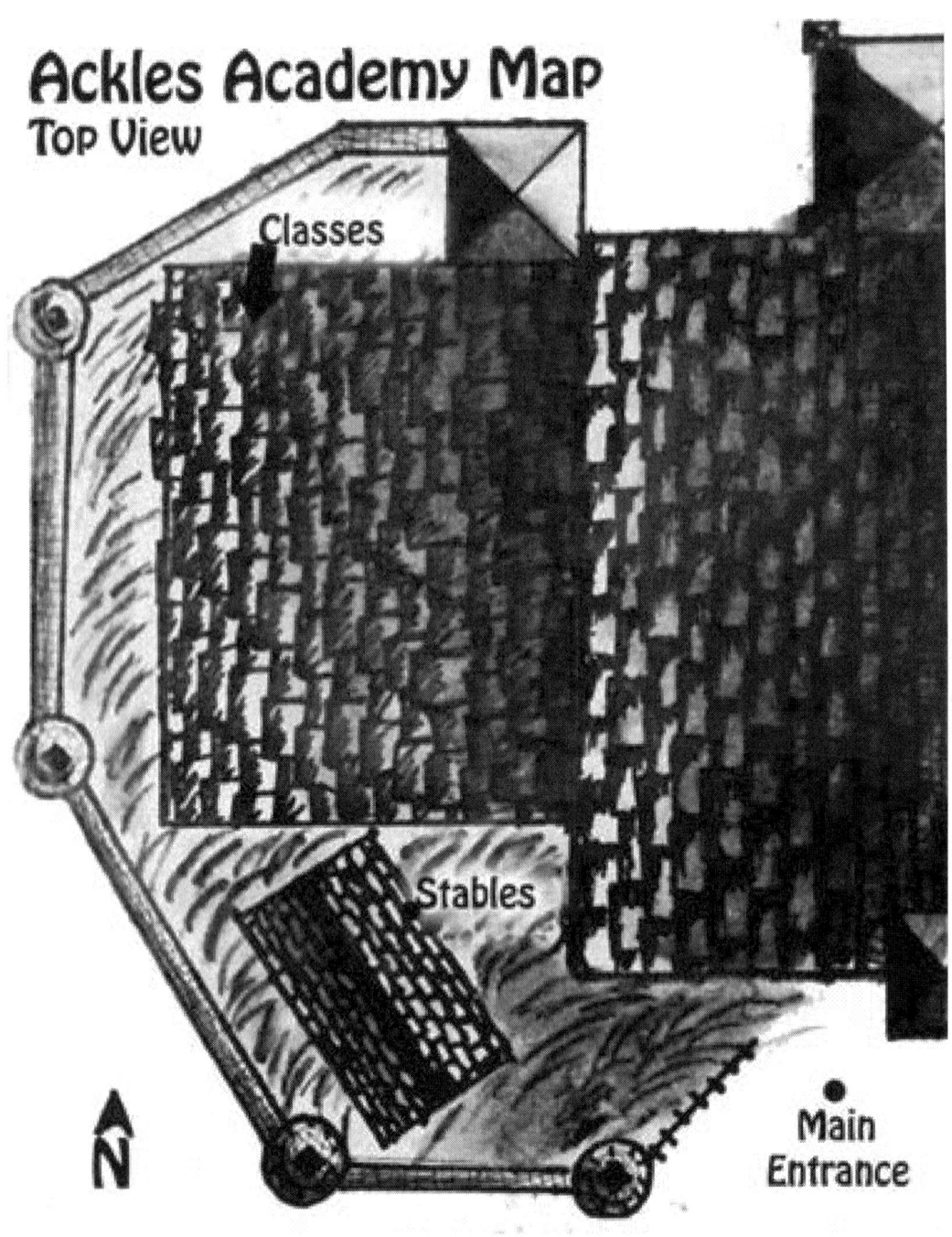

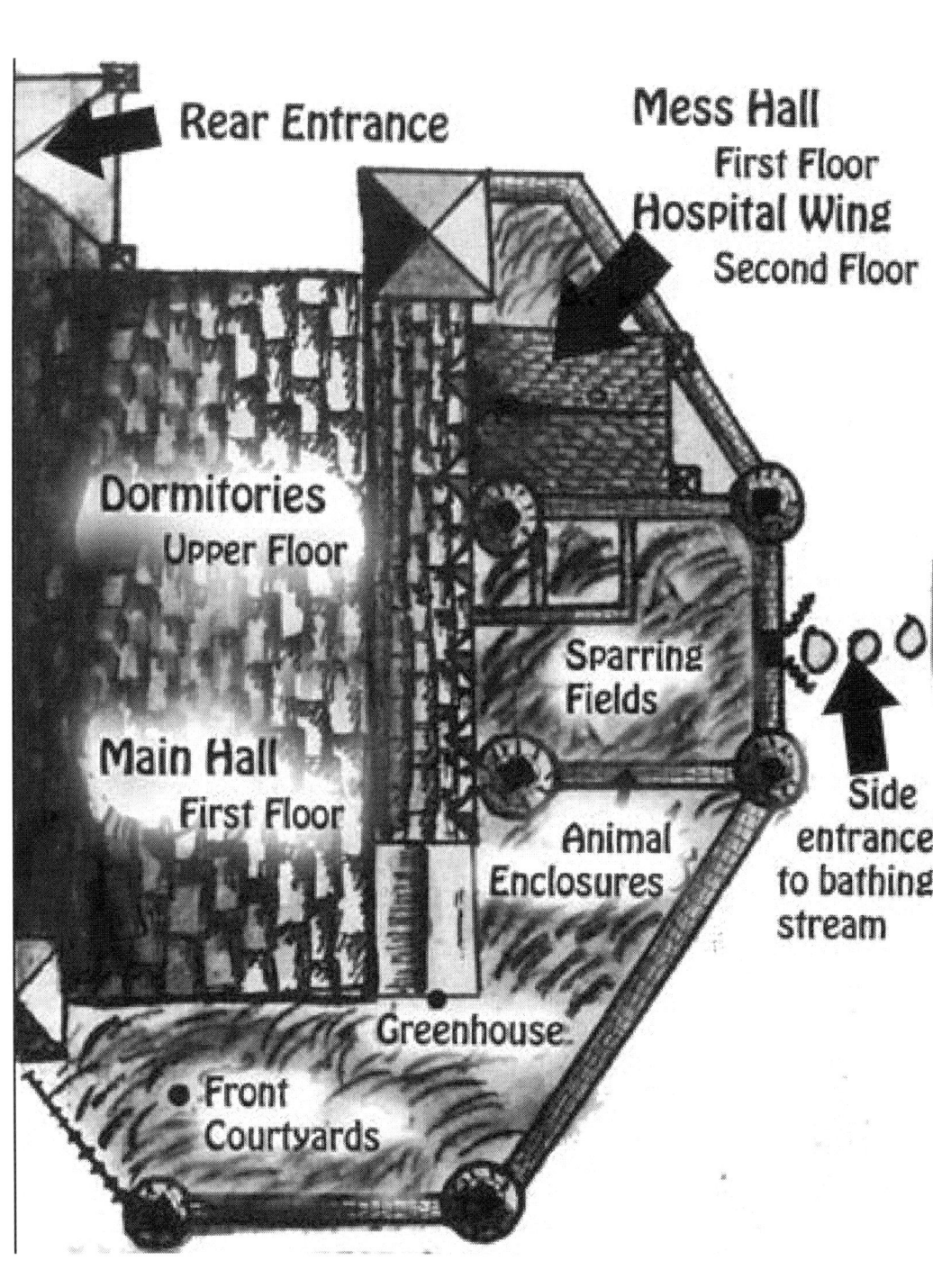

The Prophecy

Book Two

Chapter Index

Synopsis
1

Chapter 1; Conferences
12

Chapter 2; Training
24

Chapter 3; A New Beginning
31

Chapter 4; Soul sucked
40

Chapter 5; Fulfilled and Bereft
47

Chapter 6; The Crown
59

Chapter 7; Lost
68

Chapter 8; The Hero Unveiled
79

Chapter 9; Hamman
89

Chapter 10; Travel
98

Chapter 11; Scorch
108

Chapter 12; The Alpha King and Queen
125

Chapter 13; The Promise
136

Chapter 14; Accusation
149

Chapter 15; Black vs. White
159

Chapter 16; Quath
172

Chapter 17; Wagons
182

Chapter 18; The Prophecy
187

Chapter 19; Sardon
210

Chapter 20; Oaths
218

Chapter 21; Carddronnea Castle
224

Chapter 22; Black Tongue
235

Chapter 23; Enslaved
244

Chapter 24; Queries and Responses
251

Chapter 25; Captured
258

Chapter 26; Unfinished Business
268

Chapter 27; Fugitive
277

Chapter 28; Racing for Answers
294

Chapter 29; The Siege of Ackles Academy
303

Chapter 30; Disjointed
319

Chapter 31; Flying to Sach
329

Chapter 32; The Truth Comes Out
331

Chapter 33; Confrontation
339

Chapter 34; Homeward Bound
349

Chapter 35; To Sundurr We Fly
359

Chapter 36; The Cure
368

Chapter 37; Normality Faltering
374

Chapter 38; Identity Theft
378

Chapter 39; Tales Worth Telling
392

Chapter 40; Trainings and Tongues
407

Chapter 41; Happenings and Telling
417

Chapter 42; Obligations and Festivities
426

Chapter 43; War is Coming
434

Chapter 44; Party Crashers
438

Chapter 45; The Raising of Blades
444

Chapter 46; Captives
453

Chapter 47; The Proposal
458

About the Author
467

Synopsis

The blade passes hands once again, but this time to the hands of shadow as the Occluder's minions capture the blade and its carrier, an elvish prince named Athrin... or so they thought. Hivell, Athrin's travel mate aborts the mission.

Miles away, Ian is recruited by an elvish beauty, Valquee, to learn at an academy; his sister vanishes as Ian is taken, joined by a friend, Florian. Meeting many on his travels including a shorble named Bashlay, Ian is soon found to be entrapped in a dwarvish cave. By this time, Florian was taken by Hivell and Valquee imprisoned. On their travels Ian learns that the Occluder to be the Dark Lord and loosely that he contributed to the Great War. Soon Ian manages an escape. Continuing south, he bumps into a Golden Dragon which carries Ian to Villowtown. Tired, Ian rests in an alley and when he awakens from strange dreams of a shadowed dragon, he meets Teargo the elf who offers to escort Ian alongside Thyle, his student, to the academy.

Continuing south, Ian learns on his travels, that the befoullers were once forest folk elves who were relabelled when they followed the Occluder's rule thus soiling the elvish name: they were banished to form their own tribe.

As lessons ensued within the academy walls, Hivell discovers that Florian is actually Ian's sister Florence in disguise.

Thyle as usual has once more disappeared for his own business, something that caught Ian's eye. Meanwhile, three third year students depart to rescue Valquee. On the way back to the academy, a rider crosses their path and is repulsed at their ignorance for failing to notice she needs elvish medicine. Whisking her away, the students return to the academy empty-handed.

Ian soon rejoins a weak Valquee and they share what has occurred since they parted. She eludes that she's not the only one who thinks Ian is "special" but doesn't elaborate. Ian asks about a war at the dwarven sanctuary; the dwarves were fighting snorgs. Valquee tells him the war at the shrine was a result of the blade being threatened. She is more concerned with why a dwarf would challenge an "invincible" snorg. Ian also is curious about them "fighting on the other side" as he didn't see a battle. Valquee eventually admits to Ian that he is not supposed to know about the blade on school grounds.

While studying for midterms, Ian realizes that his Rukkian translations of individual snippets of text together begin to tell a story. Learning it to be a passage from a book "The Fall of Farrizon; Legend or Myth", a tale about the rise of the Dark Lord and his dragon, Ian was eager to locate a copy. Valquee told him it was pulled from the library shelves as it didn't fit the curriculum.

They visit Xsealiadd whom Ian remembers from Villowtown. In his hut, Ian grows curious about a large elegant hourglass; Xsealiadd explains how his soul flows through the sands and when they cease, he will perish. He tells Ian his spirit was put into the sands after a soul sucker stole it. Xsealiadd boasts he's been finding ways to slow the sands and has lived quite a while now. Death has been after him but he has been living on for a lesser significant though he won't disclose his name.

Valquee wants to thank Xsealiadd for his earlier magic curing her ailments. On the way they see a hooded figure approach Xsealiadd's residence and they follow him inside. The hooded figure wished for Xsealiadd to resurrect an Artani Boultier; Valquee, who sat nearby, swore she knew that name from somewhere. While there Ian finds and acquires a copy of "The Fall of Farrizon; Legend or Myth."

On the way across the academy grounds the hooded figure reveals himself as Rennaux to the spirit of Artani and he wants Artani to train the Niteshade he couldn't train in life: the dragon spirit in the lower dungeon which guarded the... he broke off and would not say what or whom. He tells Artani that the dragon is gaining power at an astonishing rate and must be trained to control it.

Still in Xsealiadd's shack Valquee tells the wizard "they're coming", something Xsealiadd grew distraught over saying why can't Death leave him be... After "looking into the matter" Xsealiadd then elaborates saying it is growing in strength, increasing in power and will soon gain potency to pass to our world: he still can't find a way to slow the passing of dimensions. Curious Ian demands an explanation. Xsealiadd tells him all things not meant to be forgotten, overtime, grew lost. The same cataclysm that sunk our world thousands of years ago is stirring. Again those same lands were threatened by that—A light bulb turns on as Xsealiadd adds "I think I just accelerated the downfall of the peace folk lands as we know them." He then questions Valquee about Artani.

During midterm break, Ian convinced Valquee to read him the text "The Fall of Farrizon; Legend or Myth"; because of its material she had to read it off school grounds. The text contained a history of the Dark Lord; his rise to power and how he ensnared the people of his lands to believe they need an encampment to train an army. He soon discovered the dragon's loyalty to humans and with them the Dark Lord formed 'the riders'. This obsession consumed him. After stealing a dragon for his own, he treated it foully causing the dragons to rebel birthing the Great War.

Out of the shadows Xsealiadd formed the idea of the binding of peace, the making of the Amity Blade. The four races that made it were called the peace folk four. At the birth of the new moon the blade passed from one clan leader to the next, it has been that way since.

King Farrizon rebelled the ways of the others, he wanted no part of it; he still desired his rider and dragons. The peace folk repelled his encampment idea, they wanted independence. When purifying themselves on the peace blade, the four races purged themselves of evil which Farrizon, also known as the Occluder, absorbed. Since he was tainted, the darkness consumed him and he collapsed into the shadows.

Ian learned Artani was a dragon trainer who mentored the dragons and riders. He was sent to teach the Occluder's Niteshade. This is when the dragons, tired of being shaped to do other's will, rebelled. The dragons ate Artani to kill his knowledge of how to possess the dragon race.   Ian   soon figures out that Ackles Academy is a school of shadow though the truth was never admitted outright. Ian soon questions the vulnerability of the blade, worrying about it falling into the wrong hands during the elvish party.

They meet a lost dragon hatchling whom they take to the elder dragons of Gesshlon. Ian believes the dragon tried to embrace him as rider according to Valquee's testimony of how it occurs. Making an observation that the dragon looks like one told about in stories, she quickly changes the subject explaining how magic between dragon and rider works. Ian learns Valquee's a rider and meets Blazzan her dragon. Valquee converses with Blazzan who secretly tells her the dragon kit wants Ian as a rider. When Blazzan finds out that Valquee brought the dragon to them for care and upbringing he was outraged. At the Renaissance Party Ian talks with Belron, a human rider, about how humans are too stupid to ride dragons causing the party to chill. Rennaux sentences Ian to death by beheading. The next morning he finds himself in a guillotine when Othorrow, Ian's language teacher, admits to giving him a sneak preview of the book he has been accused of stealing and reading. All elves go against Rennaux's actions. Weak as he was, Xsealiadd emerges and shields Othorrow and Ian from harm forcing Rennaux to abandon his actions and release Ian.

After class the next day, Ian noticed Thyle to be sneaking off and made to follow. Thyle headed to the forbidden corridor, food balanced in his grip. Ian watched him vanish into a room behind closed doors. When Ian put an ear to the door, he could hear a ferocious monster roaring within.

Florian notices a herd of angered dragons circling above Xsealiadd's place. With a mighty roar, they ignited the hut. Evacuating the house, Xsealiadd extinguished the flames and cursed the dragons. The dragons were angered that Xsealiadd resurrected Artani Boultier as they killed him to mark their independence.

Ian meets Nighdrake the shadowed dragon from his dream in Villowtown. Unprepared to face the beast, Xsealiadd rescues him. They discuss Thyle visiting the dragon often for an unknown reason. The dragon, according to Xsealiadd, is there to "watch over the academy".

Ian began studying how to pass the shadowed dragon. He tells Valquee he believes the dragon is guarding someone. Valquee promised to teach Ian a spell to pass the dragon but warned about the horrors of penetrating a darkened mind.

Ian soon tries to pass the dragon spirit. Latching onto the shadowed dragon's soul, Nighdrake shares with Ian precious memories, a couple of interest include: Farrizon feels his body is failing and knows he is running out of life. He admits he still wants to build his encampment. The Great War was unfolding when Larke appears ecstatic that he found a way to preserve himself for immortality as he rips off a scale from Nighdrake. Nighdrake confides to Ackles how Farrizon tortures him again and blesses the day Farrizon falls so he can fly free. Ackles assures that day is close.

Passing the dragon, Ian confirms to himself there is an elvish prisoner in a far holding cell. As Ian departed the room, he and Thyle cross paths, acknowledging one another. Ian tells Valquee about the prisoner.

Thyle tells his father Rennaux, Ian and Xsealiadd know about the secret shadowed weapon and possibly the elf behind it.

Ian and Valquee go to rescue the elf...

Rennaux discovered the herd of dragons had returned. Mad at Thyle believing he told the dragons about Artani, he orders Thyle to resurrect a Rubén Hokant. Concealed under a hood, Thyle obliged. Rubén, Rennaux requests to assassinate Xsealiadd. Going to the front stoop, Ian caught a glimpse of a shadowed being prowling in the dark, sneaking towards Xsealiadd's hut. Ian tells Xsealiadd about the prowler with unknown intentions. Ian learns, Xsealiadd is shielding Magnon though he knows not why.

With an excuse for Ian's absence, Valquee prepares to disembark for Rulan to get medicine for Athrin: the rescued elf.

Xsealiadd grew certain he had learned a way to reverse the resurrection. He was just completing a chant when Rubén snuck into his hut. He managed to complete his chant and dissipate Rubén but it robbed him of strength. Xsealiadd recruits Ian's help to remove Artani.

Thyle discovers Athrin's been taken and tells his dad he knew Ian had been meddling.

Ian found and led Artani to Xsealiadd after being asked for aid in the matter. Xsealiadd removed him but this time the spell knocked him unconscious. Ian takes him to the nurses' ward.

Meanwhile, Rennaux pursues his search for Athrin and Artani; heading outside he sees an overly cheerful Golden Dragon flying acrobatics above. Rennaux learns the Golden Dragon's happy because Xsealiadd came through on his word and extinguished Artani. The Golden King learns that Rennaux ordered Artani resurrected in the first place, in the dragon's eye a fire of revenge burned. Angered at Xsealiadd for killing Artani, Rennaux burns down his hut. Upset that Xsealiadd's hourglass will burn, Stanzer, who again interpreted for the dragons, rushes in to save it. When Rennaux pressed Stanzer for the hourglass's importance, Stanzer said better off not to know.

Gathering Athrin and Xsealiadd at the nurses' ward, Ian and Valquee find Thyle, a bottle of poison in his grasp. Thyle grew surprised that they had Athrin, just as they were of Thyle having poison. Valquee drilled Thyle with questions who admits that dad (Rennaux) told him to poison Xsealiadd's remedies, and that he wants Ian dead and that he regrets not decapitating Ian in the guillotine. He also told Thyle to poison Athrin with Moribrandy as well. It was dad who asked Xsealiadd to resurrect Artani, to train the shadow dragon for battle and Thyle, under dad's orders, resurrected Rubén to kill Xsealiadd. Thyle admits Rennaux captured Athrin to gain the blade for the Occluder.

Their plans revealed, Ian and Valquee fly on horseback north to Rulan with Xsealiadd and Athrin.

Thyle experiences the summoning for the first time. He quickly grows crazy.

Ackles gets Nighdrake to collapse a portion of the Academy killing many including Teargo.

Thyle, now under the Occluder's order, demands the shadow folk do whatever they can to find Xsealiadd's hourglass. He begins to see just how terrible the summoning can be and decides he wants nothing to do with it.

In Sardon deep in the Occluder's castle, they have a meeting. The Occluder questions if Rennaux has killed Ian yet. Rennaux explains that he tried once which is the reason the shield charm first came to evolve. The Occluder orders Rennaux to kill Ian. Rennaux educates saying there is only one way to kill Ian and that is to kill Xsealiadd. After much encouragement to do it, Rennaux reminds those if he kills Xsealiadd the blade will shatter and it is only with the blade and it's forging would they have a weakness to control the peace folk four in the first place. They further debate if it is really worth killing Ian. Rennaux suggests if the blade is possessed by the elves during their Renaissance Day party they may be incapacitated, unable to protect it.

Stanzer flees into the chaos of the academy with Xsealiadd's hourglass. Eventually letting the Golden Dragon carry it away.

Under the order of the summoning Thyle was forced to observe the cleaning of the academy collapse, something that tore at his soul. He soon finds himself in a power struggle with a toran.

Fleeing, Stanzer gets hit in the head with a snorg's club, being knocked out, the hourglass rolls away.

On the forefront of Villowtown, Xsealiadd awakens and because his hourglass was jostled, remembers nothing of Ian (hasn't met him yet). Immediately concerned about the welfare of his staff and hourglass he eventually goes to buy a new staff in Villowtown; Ian begins to worry that Xsealiadd, being a year younger has caused the shield charm that kept him and Othorrow alive has been undone.

The snorgs tell Thyle they couldn't get the hourglass due to a golden dragon, Thyle, still under the summoning, orders the dragon dead and the hourglass recovered.

In Villowtown, Valquee learns of the Golden King's death and that the dragon poacher who killed him is named, Nalo Tyklonne. They gather the dragon remains.

Xsealiadd gets a series of visions on his travel to Villowtown which educates him that his hourglass has moved from a child thief to a rider and eventually into the hands of the lord of Hethrowe village along with a crown. He realizes these visions were his hourglass sharing with him, experiences. In Villowtown, Xsealiadd meets up with Sam, the owner of a store entitled "Craft" as he wanted to purchase a new staff but hadn't any money. Sam makes a deal saying, "a half naked child stole from me a crown. If you get it back for me, you can have a staff of your choosing free." He later reveals the crown to be Farrizon's first as he ascended the throne of Aardvark. Xsealiadd agrees to the plan, with a new staff in hand he heads north tracking the flighty child.

Also heading north in a chariot along the main trade's road of Ellezwrainia, Valquee becomes aware of a child tracking them.

A fellow named Fraxron watches a comrade die when the same child steals from him a sword. Valquee catches up with the child and shoots him in the leg with an arrow to slow the pursuit. The child dives into a hole for cover where Ian and the Fraxron lad (also chasing the child) follow. Ian later learns this underground tomb is Farrizon's.

Valquee, overlooking the chariot and Athrin, is approached by a band of snorgs meaning to do her harm. This is when Xsealiadd appears and obliterates the snorgs to save Valquee. With thanks, Valquee sends Xsealiadd into Farrizon's tomb to find and locate Ian and Fraxron who, by this point, have caught and secured the child thief.

All except Fraxron rejoin at the carriage sometime later, and they continue north. During their travels Ian becomes friendly with the child thief against Valquee's wishes. Ian learns the child thief is named Hamman and he is from Xsealiadd's Institution of Amity. Hamman now realizes the blade he stole from Fraxron was the peace blade. Ian learns, according to Hamman, Ackles Academy is one of shadow, and Hamman was surprised Ian couldn't learn the history of Ellezwrainia. Ian learns the Dark Lord tried to recruit Hamman, when he fled the Occluder killed his parents: "Most students at the institution are orphans." Angered that Ian and Hamman grow friendly, Valquee evicts the child thief from the carriage.

Approaching Rulan, Valquee teaches Ian elvish customs. Once in Rulan, he stops in front of a building where they unload Athrin whom Ian learns is the prince of Quadre. Athrin's father, Lord Guwhyon heals him.

The following morning they were going to visit the prince of Rulan when an elf meets them telling them that Teargo has passed and his last wishes were for Valquee to sing his spirit into the trees. Valquee was hit the hardest.

At the funeral, many Ian knew attended. After the service, Ian meets Athrin face to face and unconsciously, instinctively, Ian bows to Athrin who claims since Ian was the one who saved him, it is he that should bow to Ian. "Athrin embraces Ian so tight he felt to be Teargo, a lost soul entwined in a tree, awaiting life in the beyond, whatever that may bring."

Chapter 1
Conferences

Great droplets of sparkling water splashed from the thundering falls dampening hair, flesh, and cloth of all participants at the gathering. Many of whom Ian knew from his stay at Ackles Academy, and furthermore, from his travels abroad. He had, up to this point, enjoyed the training he had been receiving during his stay in Rulan, the elvish village. However, this meeting was putting him on edge, he disliked it greatly when his name kept escaping Lord Guwhyon's lips but even more so was the manner in which it was being used.

"Is it not obvious, the intentions of the academy? Ian was nearly slaughtered—" Ian shifted uncomfortably in his seat as his name was uttered once again. "To top the already soiled reputation, my son, dear Athrin, was being held captive after his insides were laced with poison. What does that tell you?"

"My Lord—"

"Please Florian, call me father, it is elvish custom as you know."

"Sorry father, but aren't you getting off the beaten trail? We all here, I'm sure, are familiar with the happenings at the academy and have formed opinions of our own. I mean look at what happened to dear Teargo and his death, I have much to say about that! What we really should focus our attention on during this precious time we have to spend together, is to see how it shall be proven, and furthermore, how to prevent further attacks on members of the academy."

"That is a difficult thing to do, which is why every student has a guide experienced in many areas of fighting and warfare. The most ideal solution would be to remove all who are shadowed from the grounds."

"But father, how is one to prove who has a tainted soul?"

"You can't, it was wishful thinking."

"Father—" all eyes focused upon Xsealiadd, Ian especially thought it was weird, the keeper of peace also using the form father; most often Xsealiadd was the one people referred to in this formality he is the wise old one.

"Yes Xsealiadd?" Lord Guwhyon acknowledged.

"Say for a moment, if you will, that a way was found to prove the tainted from the rest, what would be a plan to rebel? To my knowledge, none here know how to extinguish those in shadow. And if we were to strike a servant to the Dark Lord, I am confident that many shadowed, such as snorgs, would confront our doings and attempt, may I add successfully, to best us."

"You've raised an excellent point Xsealiadd, however, you of all folks, I would hope, would be pursuing the knowledge of how to remove a shadowed folk."

"I know my power is great, but you have apparently forgotten the sheer wrath that is the Dark Lord. But words of comfort I deliver to thee now, I have exhausted every means of information I've had at my disposal for a great long time, but I must say, none of which confesses any gathering of information on the subject in question. I am, however, still seeking a resource that will divulge such a telling and in the meantime, I am open to any suggestions."

"Have you not pursued the path of the black book?" Ian's face grew puzzled as he exchanged awkward glances with Florian who sat several feet forward from his vantage point. Florian shrugged in response.

Xsealiadd, however, grew very ugly. "Only a right fool would risk gazing upon the foul declarations of such a text! Have you not heard of the legends?"

"Legends are just that, stories, often tainted by the imaginations of the tongue waggers who dare utter their tales, how much is really truth?"

"No one knows for sure, and I have yet to unearth the raw facts of its creation and what black magic has interwoven its pages."

"Well as your specialty, Xsealiadd, I would assume you would spend every waking moment of your being with your grossly oversized snout buried in your tomes until the truth about the black pages is revealed."

"Do you think I spend every moment of my time smoking pipe weed and drinking in merriment, I have many matters clouding my mind these days. Besides, you wouldn't appreciate the effects simple pipe weed would have on an overburdened soul; I have cloaked myself in far too much magic over the years, and it has taken its toll. I feel it in my heart, my Craft is waning, and my crystals are flowing ever much quicker, if I don't slow, my time may soon arrive."

"That is because you are too foolish with your Craft, you abuse it too much!"

"—please, enough with your insults! I cannot bear them any longer." Valquee cut in jolting to her feet, she looked nauseated and not well.

"Valquee, my sweet Valquee—" Xsealiadd commented as he wormed his way through the rows of chairs and their occupants, leaving a cloud of moths hovering in his wake. A nearby elf, who had been standing the duration of the session, eyed Xsealiadd's vacated chair greedily before thinking better of it. Who knows what those moths might do?

Wrapping Valquee in a loving embrace, his body trembling with weakness, Xsealiadd spoke softly into Valquee's ear, however, if he intended his words to be private, he was unsuccessful with the over abundance of keen elvish hearing present at the gathering.

"I have known you far too long my dear Valquee, what troubles burden your already strained heart?"

"Oh father—" Valquee squeezed Xsealiadd much tighter to bring forth comfort. "My dragon mourns the loss of the Great King of Gold; his cries have filled my soul now for many of days. Too long have I endured his suffering, I feel the time is ripe for me to remain by his side during his time of great sorrow; help guide him until the sun brightens, bringing colour to his misery once again."

Great mumbling burst excitedly from the onlookers, their voices being of agreement.

"You're right Valquee!" Lord Guwhyon's voice arose above all else. "Too long have those dragons carried us through many of dangers, it is time we begin to return the favours. This meeting is adjourned, you have a week to gather yourselves, and any provisions you feel necessary to bear on your travels. All who wish to bring forth comfort to our noble friends will meet here at sunrise on the seventh morn! All riders must come!"

The candles spluttered weakly as they struggled to birth light and warmth into the dark, dank, cold dungeon full of misery and despair. The candles floated lazily, or so it seemed, high above the long table, illuminating the sallow faces of many men.

Interweaving his unusually long fingers, the Occluder signalled as is his custom that the meeting would soon commence. A nameless figure sat curled in a corner whimpering in the fetal pose but was paid no mind as the room silenced to an awkward pause. The Occluder ensnared the focus of all members involved, as he always had done, with not a word spoken. His voice was slimy and full of chill, matching the atmosphere of the gathering. And when he spoke, it was no louder in volume than the dim glow of the waning candlelight, their wicks soon fading from all existence.

"The blade Rennaux?" The Occluder began.

"What about it master?"

"Can I count on its presence during the festivities of the elves?"

"Oh, that—" Rennaux chuckled awkwardly. "My knowledge does not stretch that far my Lord, I will not know for some time."

"Well find out!" The Occluder screamed causing the candles to falter threateningly, his anger passing through the mental links of his servants causing them great pain. Thyle's hands immediately flew to his temples to shield him from the onslaught of the summoning, the mental link that ties his soul to the Occluder's. A gentle, yet firm hand grabbed his wrists, prying his hands free from his face.

"Lower your hands boy." Rennaux soothed, both father and son could feel the piercing glare of the Occluder's empty eyes burrowing deep into their hearts. Silently, yet obediently, Thyle obeyed, despite the fact that his head continued to pound with the Occluder's rage.

"Cano?" The Occluder broke the pregnant pause.

"Yes master."

"I want Nighdrake brought to me, here."

"B-but master, how am I to relocate your dragon of shadow? He is buried deep within the academy walls, he will not listen!" The Occluder's glare was so intense, it caused all who were present to cower, regardless that it was meant primarily for Cano alone.

"S-so sorry master for uttering such ignorance, it will be done despite my hearts plea otherwise."

"This session has expired, leave now!" The Occluder cut into the tension, his stare never breaking Cano's quaking frame.

There was a scuffle as all others stampeded for the exit causing the candles to fail completely, Cano didn't even budge. It was obvious he was meant to remain. The heavy doors banged shut on the behind of the last Carddronne as the Occluder's profile stood against a small windowed backdrop, the only source of light remaining. His presence was intimidating, even the whimpering creature in the corner brought Cano no comfort. The wait was long, but it seemed much longer through Cano's eyes. At last, the Occluder turned to him.

Thyle's breathing was strained as he ran through the maze of corridors trying to distance himself from the Occluder and Cano. Leaning against a cold stone wall in a hall three floors above the session room, Thyle clutched a stitch in his side which had pained him for a good portion of his run. All was quiet where he rested except for the faint screams of Cano, three floors below. Thyle sympathized with Cano, though hoped he wouldn't have to discover the sufferings he had endured, it would likely make him ill.

"I must get away from all of this, I never wanted to be part of it, I must fight the summoning. But how? No one, to my knowledge, has ever before successfully..." Thyle mumbled aloud. It felt nice to finally get a moment of solitude, his first since he departed Ackles Academy after his year end exams. Even at his trainings, isolation from others was rare.

'Occluder? Occluder?' He thought, trying to get a sense of what he could do, or moreover, how not to call the Occluder. 'Bouldar!' He thought, practically screaming the word in his mind. Bouldar was the word used to summon the Occluder. As Thyle was told, it was a second nickname to his being. All was quiet, teaching him it must be spoken. With a grin he tried many more times to mentally call the Occluder with no answer. Thyle quickly became pleased with himself, though it was a small bit of progress, it was a start nonetheless.

"Hivell! Hivell!" Florian shouted as he ran through the abundance of elvish folk. At last he found Hivell; it seemed to have taken forever. Seeing Florian's state, Hivell immediately became concerned. Florian was reddened in the face and his hands and knickers were soaked with blood.

"Florian! What brought this on?" Hivell dropped the provisions he was carrying and rushed to Florian's aid. He was in the process of packing last-minute necessities for the travel to the dragons. The sun was rising on the morning of the departure.

"Oh Hivell!" Florian cried, "I'm internally hemorrhaging!" Florian broke into tears. "I didn't know who to tell, I am so sorry!" He wept before flinging his arms around Hivell in a comforting embrace, coating Hivell's traveling attire in a layer of blood.

Hivell soon pulled away, he knew something about Florian no others did. Florian's actual name was Florence, known as Ian's sister. She had snuck into the academy to follow Ian into training, only to have been discovered by Hivell, though he told no one.

"Tell me Florian, did this happen when you were relieving yourself?" Florian nodded vigorously. "Then we shall converse in private." Wrapping an arm around Florian's sobbing frame, Hivell led him away from the bustle of activity.

"Please father, I wish to travel in the company of your people." Ian looked pathetic standing in full plated armour looking lost and out of place.

"Ian, my people are traveling by foot, cross country. Your humanoid pace would certainly slow us down, burden our progress."

"Please, I can go by elvlock, I could easily keep pace then."

"No horse nor elvlock would dare enter the realm of the dragon, though a dragon wouldn't dare devour a peace folk, horses make a fine exception; besides many are staying behind, you will not be alone."

"My place is next to Valquee, this is where I flourish, I thrive. This is where I learn. I wish to proceed with my summer training."

"We have many folks who would be willing to teach you here in Rulan, I can arrange immediately for your lessons to commence—"

"Ian!" Florian shouted as he darted amongst the elves. His clothes were fresh and his flesh was washed; he seemed much livelier, brighter, and more cheery. "Ian, I am staying behind, I am not a rider, and my place is not there, does this not sway your decision?"

"Though my heart is torn, it still draws me south to the realm of the dragons, I am in dire need of more adventure, and I wish to check upon the development of the baby Niteshade I brought to the dragons much earlier this year. Besides, you and I were never close enough to tie me down to one place. My heart likes to be free, to remain stationary for too long is to die inside." Ian watched Florian crumple to the ground in an emotional heap. Ian's heart was cold, absent of sympathy. Turning from Florian, he marched to Lord Guwhyon. "I am going and there's nothing that can stop me!" Making for the sleeping quarters to gather his meagre belongings, Ian bumped into Valquee. As he gazed into her delicate features, the usual onslaught of emotions overtook him.

"If you come, you will ride as far south as I see fit, then I will send the horse from you, from danger, back home. Come now, we go to the stables to saddle you a horse."

On the way to the stables, something peculiar caught Ian's eye; many elves were trying to restrain several distraught elvlocks.

"Valquee, what's going on there?"

"Well Ian, sometimes we get horses and elvlocks who have seen too much evil, they come to us from distant lands in order to be calmed, and trusting to us once more. In simple terms, they are basically getting trained, broken to take the rider and saddle. Do you want to try to get one to trust you?"

"No way!" Ian's answer never hesitated to escape his lips, but no matter, it was like Valquee never heard it anyway as she thrust Ian into the paddock to break an elvlock pony. It was there she left him with a smile as she vanished for the stables to choose an elvlock; one she knew would bear Ian well. Ian only had to struggle with the unbroken pony for a short while, just long enough to get a feel before a strong elf relieved him of the reins. By this time, Ian was already caked in mud from being dragged around the paddock.

The day had nearly broken when Ian was straightening his things in the saddlebag. He was perched astride a horse, none other than Shilow, the black and white Clydesdale he brought with him from his home village of Solan. Off in the distance, he could see Hivell wishing Florian a good bye, though their voices were faint, Ian could just make out their low voices over the din.

"...You know, I am a rider, I am bidden to go." Hivell rolled up his sleeve revealing the bite wound that tied him to his dragon, "I will return to gather you before the school year commences. That is a promise." He added.

"I know Hivell, I know you will. I trust you."

Ian watched as they parted company before staring onward into the greenish glow of the immensity that was Hucklandish Forest.

"It is time!" Lord Guwhyon announced from the head of the processions, and as one, the group began at a gentle walk.

"Wait!" Florian yelled from behind, halting their progress. "Ian, I want you to know before you leave that I am your sister, Florence Cosswell, I followed you to Ackles Academy because I couldn't bear being without you; by your side through good and the bad. I love you Ian, not only as a sister loves her brother, but as a daughter who loves her dad; you were always there when papa wasn't, and I would go to the ends of the earth for you; I would traverse the unknown lands with you to the realm of scale and tooth if I wasn't in such a dire state, bleeding from the inside. I will never cease my love for you brother, please come back for me. May the rain never hinder and may the wind carry thee forth."

Silence rose. Elves slowly continued on without a word, leaving Ian to sit and stare blankly on, too afraid to speak for he knew words would fail, and too afraid to look, for he feared he may cry for the love and devotion he shared with the one he was about to leave behind.

The Prophecy

Chapter 2
Training

Xsealiadd was there through it all, he witnessed the love Ian was turning his back from, as he alone stood just out of view. The time quickly approached when Xsealiadd too would part from Rulan on his own journeys to reclaim his hourglass and the crown, which he must soon return to Sam the storekeeper of a place named "Craft" a wizards shop in Villowtown.

In his heart, Xsealiadd knew his health was waning, this quest, if he was not with care, may claim his life. Time was beginning to quicken, each day like a mere moment, each heartbeat, like a pound of a drum beating ever faster beneath his breast. The world was beginning to brighten, like the blinding of the vision on a midsummer's day. The gods were calling, death lurking in the shadows.

"I think time is true for us to also part Xsealiadd?" Paddo soothed, trying to ensnare Xsealiadd's wayward attention. "Xsealiadd? Baljune and I are ready to leave Rulan, we are making for Hethrowe, you desired once to join company in our travels, is your heart still true to this choosing or have your ways blown a new course?"

Xsealiadd was slow to rouse, his mind still clouded with his troubles as he simply gazed blankly to where the presence of Ian vanished from view.

"Sorry." Xsealiadd aired weakly, his feeble voice cracking.

"It's time we go, head east to Hethrowe. We are no elves, we have no place here."

Xsealiadd stirred without an utterance, the pronounced limp on his right side seemingly to worsen upon each and every footfall. The escalating pain in his hip bothered him more and more each step as his reliance steadily increased on his staff. The cloud of moths he had left in his wake, growing as it had been lately in size and population, a sure sign that his time was near.

"Well, my sweet," An icy, oily voice filled the chamber. "Your training has been neglected since Xsealiadd murdered Artani; my beloved dragon trainer. Since I trust none other to the task, I suppose it must be I who will teach you in your morals and skills."

A roaring scream reverberated off of the stone walls as what looked like billions of tiny diamonds materialized then vaporized into the blackness as the dragon of shadow bathed the room in fires of silvery light. The blindingly white nimbus about the dragon flickered as it struggled to maintain its radiance with such compromised energy of the flame.

"Now, now, now, don't fret, don't anger, our time together will be joyous and full of merriment like it once was." The icy voice filled the chamber once again, lost by the resounding roar which overpowered all other acoustics in the room. Within this roar, were pain, anger and sorrow from a dragon that has tumbled into shadow long before his time. A life cut short by the very soul who promised him joy and happiness; the very being of the Occluder who had tortured Nighdrake in life, and wouldn't stop tormenting his shadowed soul in death.

"I understand you possess the ability to rob energy from creatures about you, as well from the light and warmth that bathes you, I can feel it in the air. It is proven to me furthermore, by that obnoxious glow that lines your profile. Your skills are honed, but are aging rapidly. Any spirit can do that, it's time you advance to the powers of today, learn what most can't. Seriously Nighdrake, you're a dragon and that's something special; as far back in history as I can recall, not a single dragon spirit remained on this earth, and that definitely is something unique. Of course, none of them were my dragon, Nighdrake, bound to me in life and, by my very own hand, in death; a dragon, never to break the bindings of dragon and rider. We may have been the last of the riders to form, but we are definitely the most potent. Nothing can bring us down, we will be bound forever."   An agonizing cry from the dragon filled the room once more. A spirit, any spirit, should be free not trapped in a void one cannot escape.

"Focus Nighdrake! It is time to harness your true powers, to be as strong as you are meant to be. Did you ever notice the ever abundance of energy out there? Far more than you likely ever imagined. What sustains the fires to burn? What causes the wind to howl, or the waters to flow? Think about it Nighdrake, you're pathetic! You need to ensnare this power, embrace it, use it for personal gain, without it you are useless!"

Nighdrake's endless howls drowned out all life causing the torches to falter.

"Very good, expect my return in due time, you'd better have made significant progress in your lessons." With a gust of wind which caused all torches to fail completely, the air grew still.

The Occluder was gone.

Travels were lonesome for Ian's heart cried, cried with love, cried with glee, cried with sorrow; he never before realized his sister loved him so dearly. Many days passed before Ian could, once again, face the world about him.

"So what is to be with my training?"

"There is no time for that, however, when you are ready, I am willing to train you on the run."

"That would be a marvel!" Ian grinned at long last.

"Halt!" Lord Guwhyon's voice struck the travelers hard. "These are elvish tracks, and they are fresh." He paused to survey his surroundings. "It is us, we have been here before."

"But in the history of our race, this has never before happened? How could this be? How could we err in such a blunder?" A concerned traveler voiced.

"A dark presence, a threat has been growing these past months, a sleepless force, birthed from the south with unknown intentions. The Occluder's spirit stirs in such a way none ever thought possible, all of you have felt it."

"How is this to do with us being lost?"

"Because there is something that's rousing as a result of such a threat, something that hasn't stirred for an age; the forest is awakening, it has long since begun, look before you. Do you not recognize such a majestic oak?"

"The Oak of Arkan!"

"Indeed, things are no longer what they seem. We shall rest here tonight." A couple of elves, without word, began climbing the oak, dropping leaves large enough to use as a blanket upon their assent. They never returned for a long while.

"Where have they gone?" Ian asked, nudging in the direction of the Oak of Arkan as he dismounted and picketed Shilow.

"They are going to observe the movement of the stars to point our way."

"Oh." Ian responded as he gathered a couple of the enormous leaves to use as a bed.

"Wait Ian, I think it's time we begin your training."

"Oh, okay." He was a tad surprised; he wasn't expecting this now as he was surely weary.

"I've prepared a simple but effective enchantment; I feel it'll do well for beginners, mainly because it's simple to understand, and enunciate with basic structure of the Rukkian language. Most importantly, should you be lucky enough to engage the magical effects of the enchantment, no harm would befall the creatures or earth. If spoken correctly, it causes all vegetation you can see to flourish and ripen. It is one of our favourites. Also, and I must warn this to your person, from this moment forth, we as elvish body will revert to our native Rukkian tongue to promote proper lessons on your behalf. With our language uttered in such abundance, your understanding of our tongue should flourish at an astonishing rate. Anyhow, here is the enchantment, see what you make of it." Handing Ian a rolled scroll, Valquee made to comfy herself upon a nearby granite.

Awkward, and with great discomfort, Ian unfurled the scroll. Great slanted, loopy script flowed gracefully across the parchment. Aligned with precision and grace, it was Ian's first major insight into the workings of the elvish culture. Upon this page was one of their greatest songs, 'enchantments' Ian reminded, as it was up to him to sing it. When it came to vocals, Ian's were sound, yet he knew words would fail at the very sight of such complex tongues.

Though his trainings were thorough, nothing had prepared him for the fluidity of such a piece. To complicate matters, elves were talking merrily in their native tongues, and those who weren't, were staring at him making the moment awkward. And unlike at last year's Renaissance Day party where Ian sang a Rukkian song by connecting mentally with Valquee to foresee the words before they were vocalized, here all minds drew blank. Ian had no choice but to embarrass himself trying to read such a text.

"Tilli ouda tilli, tun 'shouee unn vana..." he began. There wasn't any grace and flow like an enchantment is meant to be, but mumbles, slurs and stutters as Ian struggled with the complex piece.

"Vas eal eekaa." Valquee drawled upon concluding his dismal performance in the reading.

"Sorry?" Ian asked, they had only just started speaking primarily in Rukkian, and already, Ian hated it. To make it worse, Valquee didn't respond. It quickly dawned on him she wanted it to be asked in Rukkian. His mind raced as he sifted through his limited vocabulary.

"Parduzze?" He asked. In translation that was pardon, but he hoped it would suffice as he didn't recall the utterance for sorry.

"Read it again." Valquee smiled at his feeble attempt.

Ian was greatly unsure how many times Valquee made him read the charm, but each performance was as pathetic as his last. Finally, when he was so tired that he felt he'd never get through it even one more time, Valquee began to sing in that delicate, beautiful voice he had grown to love. Other elves quickly joined in. Soon, the entire house of Quadre was singing in perfect harmony the very enchantment Ian struggled to even pronounce.

There was no reading off papers, or stumbling of pronunciations. Words flowed together like wind through the leaves. It was exactly as enchantments should be. Flowers soon bloomed, trees perked, there was true magic woven throughout their song. Envious and angry, Ian booted over a cook pot with a grumble as he stalked to the solitude of a distant flourishing aspen. It was here where Ian's weariness took a hold as he soon drifted to an uneasy slumber filled with dreams of hatred, malice of a strange unexplained force, which grew ever more potent in these passing days.

Chapter 3
A New Beginning

Xsealiadd's steps grew laboured very quickly. His travels to Hethrowe took its tribute upon his already strained soul. Baljune and Paddo, being in their prime, were quickly shrinking from eye view as they conversed light-heartedly about merry things. That's the thing with humans, like the dwarves they are oblivious to the goings-on of the world's surround. Only the elves seemed to understand the strain the world was under; it was at the brink of disaster. Felt upon by the sensitive-hearted, any tenser and it would snap, causing those who concerned themselves with such business to suffer direly.

As Xsealiadd very well knew, things were beginning to come into motion that could not be undone. It was foretold deep in the under workings of one of the key ancient prophecies. Awaiting only the birth of a boy when the sun and moon collided, enlightening the glow of the halo which smiled upon the child who was foretold to shape the new age. Xsealiadd knew this child had arrived, he knew him by name, and as prognosticated, a great force had been stirring in the south, gaining strength at the passing of each moon, its intentions: to contradict the boy's efforts. Xsealiadd knew he would be unable to protect this child from harm for very much longer. Already he could feel his magic stretched thin, it wouldn't be long now.

Soon, he realized he would have to teach the child much of what he knew so upon his failure of heart, this child could stand upon his own feet, but not now. The child still had not witnessed enough winters; he didn't even yet know his fate.

With their conversations flourishing, Paddo halted.

"What troubles befall your heart?" Baljune was of great concern.

"Xsealiadd is fading I must bring upon him some aid."

Baljune also fell back as they waited for the shrinking gap between the travelers to perish.

"You look terrible, what bests you?" Paddo questioned an out-of-breath, weary Xsealiadd.

"My hip, ever since the last confrontation on Ian's behalf, my injury has greatly pained me. I feel it may never recover proper use. The tides of my soul are quickly carving a new path; I feel I shall refrain from traversing among such company for I feel I will quickly grow as a burden, hindering the speeds of thou feet."

"Oh, nonsense Xsealiadd! If you feel unable by land, we will go by sea, along the ever flowing currents of Brailzon Brook only to part ways at the peace filled port of Shalock Crossing."

Xsealiadd's lungs strained as he drew a laboured sigh. "It may be a better road, however, I feel threatened by the sheer power of Sminon falls. Far too great a traveler has been swallowed deep into the hungry grasp of her rapids."

"It is a risk I fear we must take, come, we will gather canoes from the elves."

Xsealiadd experienced great struggles as he cautiously lowered his feeble frame into the ever shakiness of the elvish canoe. Ropes were severed before the canoe was greedily swept up into the angry white waters. Baljune and Paddo strained against the forces as they battled the unrelenting powers of the currents. Great thuds sent vibrations up the ribs of the canoe as its white oak frame shuttered and splintered against each and every collision with stone both big and small.

Even elvish made canoes were not invincible. With a final thud water rushed into where it was not meant to be, soaking feet and food with its icy chill. The canoe crumpled under the water's wrath leaving its occupants and their things to be swept up in the choppy currents, and Xsealiadd too weak to swim.

"Xsealiadd!" Baljune cried, but Paddo was closer as he did his best to try to swim for the bank one-handed, Xsealiadd clinging to his other.

Resting felt soothing as Xsealiadd lay on the northern bank in the lush grass, his robes drenched. Ironically, this moment was the best he felt in many, for his moths fluttered to the wayside with the sudden soaking. In many years he had been unable to separate moths from being, even with much magic. With their growing abundance amongst his presence more and greater amounts of energy had been required to repel them, claiming their prize on his heart.

Paddo remained by his side, overlooking his progress, whilst Baljune did what he could to fish out a great many of their salvageable provisions. Far fewer than he had hoped were still in fit condition.

"Xsealiadd, Paddo..." Baljune began, "I have unfriendly news to deliver."

"What is it Baljune?"

"Our food supply has been cut short; we may only have enough to sustain us for a few days at most."

Stacks of texts mounted as Jeban scoured page after page in seek of valuable information. Though he didn't know it, he had succumbed to a summoning so vigorously, he had no clue that the Occluder had possessed his body temporarily and had claimed it for his own. It was no use regardless, for the information he searched on Xsealiadd's hourglass he failed to find. He was soon ready to expire his search. It was apparent, there was no book in the black land's vast library which contained anything on such a topic in question. Stacked three floors high, the library held great readings of all shapes and sizes.

Perched in the loft overlooking the lobby below, the Occluder, in Jeban's body, began to read. "In the year seven hundred twenty six of the current age, forces drew arms... blah, blah, blah!" He scanned, "I already know about my part in the great battle, but how did Xsealiadd come to be? Where did he get such ideas as the Amity Blade, and what about him? Oh if only I had a biography of the creep then I may learn something, but where can I find it?"

A great roar shook the walls from some distant chamber. A distressed Nighdrake grew frustrated with his appointed skills, they were difficult to master. "That's my sweet." The Occluder mumbled before vanishing behind a book once again.

Ian struggled profusely with the fluidity of the Rukkian tongue. Even still, he found he was already beginning to understand more and more words and phrases day by day.

"Quick Ian!" Valquee's Rukkian was graceful. "What is this plant?"

Ian strained hard to remember. "Uh, Shwakka?"

"Aye, could you tell me its properties?"

"Tell you about what, sorry? I didn't understand that last word." The language of the elves was a complex one and Ian tried his best.

"It, tell me what you know of the Shwakka."

"Hmm..." Ian thought hard, he knew this was all part of his training. "...Has seven purplish leaves that surround a central cluster of black tinted berries. The berries are highly toxic for consumption as it is, however, if you burn off the juices, small quantities can be consumed safely if dehydrated with proper care, for it is the juice that brings forth harm." Ian sighed, that was hard enough to remember, much less recite in a foreign tongue.

"And what else?" Valquee urged.

Ian's stomach plummeted; he could not remember anything else as he simply shook his head.

"You took a lesson with Sauvan regarding such a bush, did you not?"

Ian nodded his response.

"Well that day Sauvan touched on one further detail about the plant." Ian still could not remember as he shook his head once again, this time slowly and with care.

"On this bush there are grossly large thorns, do you remember the thorns?" Valquee urged trying to get Ian to remember.

That was the statement required to provoke the memory for Ian, his brain simply needed a little nudge. "Only appearing beneath the moon's gaze, or when the clouds hang low, the thorns are fatal if they prick flesh, safe they are on sunny days for they hide away, remember this and you'll do best!" Ian was thrilled he remembered.

"So tell me Ian, will the thorns be out today?"

Ian looked skyward. "I believe so, a bit anyway, for clouds blanket the sky veiling the sun's glow."

"Take a peek." Valquee urged. Ian looked with care, should he be wrong. He wouldn't want to get poked and risk death. Moving aside a cluster of purplish leaves to find a stem, a flurry of bugs exploded outward.

Ian was startled, the elves were scattering, enunciating different S.P.E.L.L.'s and enchantments foreign to Ian's ears. Shilow, who was picketed nearby, reared. Snapping his reins which were brittle with age, he fled. It was utter pandemonium.

Ian cowered, peering through the thick leaves of his hideout he recognized the insects from a description once given by Xsealiadd as a soul sucker.

Many of the elves had hidden themselves, others had placed magical wards about them to offer protection against the deadly insect attacks, there were a select few who unfortunately failed to do anything at all. They were targeted.

The attacks were gruesome, Ian couldn't bear to observe as he glued his eyes shut. He couldn't obliterate his hearing though, and the sounds echoing in his ears were revolting. It was everything Ian imagined war to sound like and more so; the hum of insects in flight, what sounded like deep thuds of stingers piercing flesh, the painful death screams of a falling man. Again and again he was forced to experience such nauseating sounds, praying each time that it was his last. When all, at long last drew quiet, Ian bravely drew gaze. Countless comrades had fallen victim to such heartless attacks, nearby elves were emerging from concealment, rushing to the aid of the fallen. Ian felt he should help but knew not what to do. Revealing himself to the others, he appeared with great concern. Valquee appeared from amongst the many faces. Worry was deep in her heart.

"Go Ian, there is nothing you can do, they were attacked by soul suckers. Their entire self being is gone, it's going to take many years to recover, and they will never be themselves again. Those bugs stole their soul, which is what they do, but it is still such a shame. There is so much for them to relearn, I doubt they'll ever be able to ride again." A solitary tear escaped Valquee's heavy eye.

Ian understood the fate of the fallen. Soul suckers were brutal creatures, sucking out one's soul until their very existence was foreign to them. The size of a domesticated house cat, the physicality appeared as an enormous mosquito.

Ian greatly pitied the victims; he once learned Xsealiadd, the keeper of peace, suffered the same fate. Luckily for him, however, a quick thinking friend was able to capture the insect and salvage much of the torn soul, giving Xsealiadd a head start at finding his identity once again.

The more Ian thought about it, the more he realized, Valquee was wrong, he could help. Ian was going to be that friend, he was going to run to the ends of the earth if need be to find the soul thieves and get the identities back.

Ensuring all eyes were occupied with the fallen, Ian secured his war axe and bow he received last year, to his frame before slipping off in the direction the soul suckers last flew.

The sun burned angrily on the nape of their necks as Paddo, Baljune, and Xsealiadd traipsed across the vast expanse of meadow lands dividing the Hucklandish Forest from Shalock Crossing, a nearly five-day stretch if traversed by foot; however, with Xsealiadd's pain growing more and more each passing day, their travels grew slower each heavy step trodden.

Their meagre supplies were being stretched to the breaking point leaving longer spans for their stomachs to remain void of substance. Xsealiadd's condition steadily weakened as his body cried for food, a growing concern for Paddo and Baljune. It soon was too much for Xsealiadd as he collapsed unresponsive, crumpling from exhaustion, failing from hunger. There was no thought, Baljune and Paddo sprang into action.

"Look, you're the better warrior, stay by him and care for him as best as possible, I am going to forage, many fruits flourish near the banks of Brailzon. I should only be absent one day, should I not return by five, go without me. May the rain never hinder and may the wind carry thee forth." Baljune blessed before sprinting south across the plains.

"To you also my brother." Paddo spoke softly thumping his breast, watching Baljune's retreating back.

Chapter 4
Soul sucked

Traversing through the overgrown thickets of Hucklandish Woods was exhausting as every branch seemed to hold Ian back. He wasn't sure how he was going to catch some insects flying freely, miles above the treetops, taking the elves lost souls to their nest. It didn't help either, that Ian could not see more than ten feet before him without his gaze being stolen by tree or bush. Though this was strange to him, it was normal life to those who had walked the soils of Hucklandish on a daily basis. It was around midday, Ian was sprinting as fast as the forest would allow, when unexpectedly he ploughed into something squishy, yet solid.

The thing grunted. Turning to face Ian, the thing had the body of a man but in place of legs, was an elegant, slender, horse's body.

"A-are you a centaur?" Ian stammered, "I read about you in a book once."

The centaur grunted. "What's it to you?"

"I-uh, mmm—" Ian thought hard looking for a pleasing response. The centaur, however, never bothered to wait for one.

"So tell me, what is a youngster such as you doing roaming in woods like these eh?"

"Oh I am not roaming." Ian answered quickly. "You see, I've been traveling with the elves, riders of the dragons when we were attacked. A great few had fallen victim to the dreaded soul suckers. I am trying to find the bugs to retrieve the lost souls."

"Soul suckers huh? Awful things. Well I'm afraid you're fighting a losing battle there sonny. No one has ever before caught a soul sucker and not a soul knows how." The centaur snickered at his own lame joke.

"Not true!" Ian retaliated. "Have you ever met Xsealiadd, keeper of the peace, he lost his soul to one of them, a friend captured the insect and trapped its blood in the vial of an hourglass. It can be done."

"A boy with hope, I like you. The name's Banthumn, Lord of the centaurs. You?"

"Ian, Ian Cosswell."

"Pleasure. Look, normally I am against this, and no one is to know besides us, but..." Banthumn gave Ian a peculiar look.

"Be our little secret."

"Good, hop on." Banthumn crouched giving Ian easy access to climb to his back. Clamouring aboard, Ian nestled himself comfortably behind Banthumn's withers, clutching his waist for added support. Rising to full height, Banthumn immediately began at a good pace.

"You see, normally it is not proper for centaurs to bear riders, however, my heart is for the elves. They have been our allies and friends through many hardships. I know every one of them like brethren."

"Oh, well I'm not quite that close, but I still feel I should help. How do you suppose we are going to do this?"

"Well, I thought, go to the nesting grounds of the soul suckers, find ones full of soul—" Banthumn paused once again to chuckle at his joke. "—then I was going to knock them down and bring them to the elves."

"I'm sorry Banthumn but I feel I must rip you from your happy place. I see potential problems, and lots of them. Firstly, how are we going to tell which have had a soul or not? Second, how do we know the ones who bit the elves really did go to the nesting beds? And lastly, even if they did and we were really fortunate as to find all the full soul suckers, how are we to know if it's the right souls? It could be a pig's, or a horse's, anybody's soul for that matter." Ian stopped. Suddenly the very thought of Shilow with his soul ripped from him greatly upset Ian. Unfortunately, he would likely never know what happened to his lost horse, but prayed deeply that Shilow did not fall victim to a soul sucker. What an awful way to live, with no knowledge of oneself.

"I greatly understand and feel your concerns." Banthumn shattered Ian's silent thoughts. "We truly are seeking a quill amongst a forest of feathers; however, I have some knowledge that may assist."

"Do share."

"When soul suckers consume a soul, especially from a grown man, they swell, not a lot, but enough. Also, when the soul sucker takes its fill, it will immediately return to the nest to share its feed with as many as it can when the catch is still viable. Your third concern is a very legitimate one, and that we can only see. Now strengthen your hold for my pace is due to quicken." Obediently, Ian ensnared Banthumn's midriff with a vice like squeeze.

Hoof falls grew in strength and volume as Banthumn began in a strong gallop through the trees and undergrowth. He eventually grew to a halt.

"Here, rub these all over you; I am going to do the same."

"What are they?"

"Poinsuckle, red the leaves are, but it's the smell that really irritates them."

"Irritates them as in makes them want me, or irritates them as in—"

"They will go nowhere within arm's span of the potent odour. It's a natural bug repellent. Remember we, if not careful, could easily be targeted."

"Right—" Ian sniffed hard. "Whew, potent is no understatement. Poinsuckle, I must remember that. Identified by a red leaf you say?"

"Notice the jagged edges, and the tree they're from has thick greenish wood with a green hued bark, take a good look at the graining on the trunk." Ian studied the bush hard; he wanted to maintain his training. When he was satisfied of his lesson, he secured his seating on Banthumn's back as they continued on.

The trees broke to a swampy clearing, riddled with hundreds of thousands of soul suckers big and small. Their larva and eggs bobbed about in the shallows.

"Oh dear." Ian cried simply.

"Well I did say we are seeking a quill in a forest of feathers."

"You meant that without exaggeration."

"Aye." They stared blankly at the swarm.

"You know this will take an eternity."

"Not if we work fast. Think of it this way. We'll take out a flourishing soul sucker population. Now Ian, tell me quick, how would you go about killing a mosquito?"

"Slap it!"

"Well it won't kill them, but it'll knock them out, give you a chance to check for swelling, if they are empty, kill them!"

"How?"

"Well, my eyes may have deserted me, but do you not have a war axe harnessed upon your back?"

"Oh, right. How will I tell swelling?"

"You'll know, but if in doubt, just ask." Banthumn replied before grabbing a plump straight branch to use as a club. "Oh, by the way Ian, it's best if you use something to whack them like a club, the handle of your axe for instance." With a wink, he charged into the cloud of soul suckers, whacking and killing to his heart's content.

The fifth day came and passed without return of Baljune. Paddo was filled with worry, but dared not follow for fear of meeting the same fate, whatever that may have been. Instead, Paddo chose to follow Baljune's final wish and carry Xsealiadd onward. At least two to three days remained for a reasonable paced jaunt; however, this was anything but reasonable as Paddo struggled under the dead weight of Xsealiadd's limp frame.

With great many recesses and recoveries, Paddo at last, had Shalock Crossing in his sights. Shalock was not worthy of the term a town, village, or even hamlet. Shalock was comprised of naught but two shops; a general store and a trading post. Any other structure was either barn, stable, or home. All of which were owned by the private folk. Shalock's sole and primary purpose was to control and command the gateways of the conjoining waterways. From past experiences, however, Paddo knew it had a healthy supply of food and friendly villagers, many of whom he knew by name, and would overlook Xsealiadd's recovery. What concerned Paddo most, however, was Annesthia, one of his closest and most loving companions.

    The door thudded on each bang of the heavy door knocker, rusted and weathered with age. Paddo could faintly hear the clatter of cookware and the patter of delicate feet. Annesthia was coming.

    The door swung open. "Can I help you?" She was flushed and frazzled, or at least her hair was, as healthy amounts of wavy, dirty blond locks had broke free of her otherwise tidy bun. "Oh Paddo, what troubles weigh your heart?"

    "Oh my lady, Xsealiadd has fallen ill under the burn of the sun; he needs care and a place to rest where watchful eyes can oversee his recovery in my absence for I have great business still to attend to in Swandurr."

    "Look no place further dear Paddo, but do tell me, did you not part with another?"

    "Baljune parted my company nine moons past; he went in search of food for we had nearly exhausted our supply. He never returned."

    "My heart cries great anguish for him but we mustn't dwell on things past, especially if they can't be altered to our liking. Now please, bring forth Xsealiadd and I will give him care." Laying Xsealiadd across an unused cot, Paddo stared blankly into his sullen features.

"You're a good friend Xsealiadd; this is where I leave you. Goodbye and good luck." Giving Annesthia a quick peck on the cheek side, Paddo departed the dwelling with only a single, solitary, stray thought about Xsealiadd and Baljune.

Chapter 5
Fulfilled and Bereft

Much to Ian's dismay, but to no surprise of any, there were far more than expected soul suckers.

"What do we do now?" Ian questioned.

"We bring the whole lot back to the elvish camp."

"How, there are so many, and they are so big."

"I call my herd, we carry what we can and what we can't, we pile on your bed roll, and you can drag it behind you."

"I can't, I left it at camp."

"Then we use your traveler's cloak."

Ian eyed it regretfully. "If I must." The thought of giant creepy crawly insects on his cloak repulsed him.

"You must. Now, when I call my herd I suggest highly that you keep off my back, make no mention that you were ever up there, in fact, it's best if you keep your tongue still."

Ian nodded obediently.

With one last look at Ian, Banthumn pawed the ground three times hard then bellowed a strange roar Ian couldn't imagine a centaur to make.

Within moments, it sounded like at least a hundred hooves thundering through the trees. Ian became surrounded far faster than he would've liked.

"Hello Banthumn, who is this fine specimen of a lad?" A shaggy-maned, black-haired centaur began.

"Ian Cosswell from Ackles Academy."

"And why is he within your company?"

"He is the bearer of terrible news. A swarm of soul suckers has bested some of our finest elvish riders. It was young Ian's idea here to go in pursuit of the thieves and bring their souls back." The herd of centaurs roared with laughter. Fuming, Banthumn pawed the soil hard, digging an ever deepening rut with all his antsy pawing. "Enough! Show your leader some respect!" The centaurs quieted at once. "Now, we have together, singled out those who bear a soul not their own. We are personally going to hand deliver these to the elves to see if they can salvage any of the poor soulless riders."

"Soulless, you're soulless, perhaps even clueless!" An anonymous voice from the herd mocked, whipping the whole group into an uproar.

"Silence! Who said that?" All remained quiet. One would be a fool to reveal himself to Banthumn after that outburst. "No matter, what I called you here for, are extra hands to carry the soul suckers." One of the centaurs at the front of the herd studied his ruddy, dirty, rough hands doubtful that they would be of any assistance.

"Now, I want each of you to grab two soul suckers, one per arm, and transport them to the elvish camp northeast of here. And Bracko, since it was you who insulted me, and I know very well it was, I am giving you the honours of bearing Ian on your back to the elvish camp!"

"What!" Bracko roared. "It is unfit for a centaur to bear a rider of any sort, much less human scum!"

"Bracko! One more outburst like that and I swear it will be your last, Ian is a finely maturing young man, and it will do you well to open your mind to his culture; besides, your actions are punishable and let justice serve, I feel the consequences match the crime. Now Bracko, hang your head in shame if you please, but you will bear Ian on your back and remember who the pack leader is!"

"Yes, Banthumn sir." Bracko mumbled as he lowered his pallid gray haunches for Ian to clamber on.

"Why doesn't he just leave the pack, why are they so faithful to your word?"

"Well Ian, the centaurs' hierarchy is a complex one, now hurry up and get on, and I strongly advise you to mind your tongue with him, he's not in the best of moods."

Frigid waters seeped into Xsealiadd's sealed lids, shocking his eyes into an uneasy consciousness. Eyes fluttering open, he frantically took in his surroundings. A rather thin, but delicate lady stood above him, ringing a cloth over his brow.

"W-where am I?" He jolted upright, absentmindedly fumbling about for his staff.

"Shh!" Her graceful, yet firm hand drove his shoulders back into the feather pillow. "You are in Shalock Crossing on July the twenty second if you care to know."

"How did I get here?" Xsealiadd meant to ask, except the words got discombobulated on his tongue, and instead he questioned who the lady was.

She smiled with care. "Annesthia, now rest."

"No! I really have no time!" Xsealiadd heaved as he pushed himself against Annesthia's firm hand. He still had strength left as he rose to his feet. "My staff, where is my staff?" Annesthia rushed to locate it. She helped Xsealiadd balance his weight upon it.

"And by the appreciation of my folks, a care package has been assembled with enough provisions to carry you to Hethrowe."

"I am grateful my lady." Xsealiadd breathed, already out of puff.

Placing the heavily burdened pack upon Xsealiadd's nearly nonexistent shoulders, she wrapped him in a quick embrace. "May the rain never hinder and may the wind carry thee forth."

"You as well, Annesthia, and thank you again, I am internally in your debt."

"Don't be silly, you have done too much for us already, we are simply paying you back." Xsealiadd didn't understand her meaning regarding his work with the Amity Blade.

With a nod, he stepped off the stoop, and with care, proceeded to Shalock's eastern gate en route to Hethrowe.

Ian was unaware just how much he was cared for amongst the elvish culture, Valquee and Hivell especially were scouring every nook and crevice for his whereabouts. At one point, Hivell even searched for Ian in a knothole, which caused Ian to snicker.

"Oh yeah, I'm not that good!" He smiled.

SLAP! It came from nowhere, as Valquee back handed him across the cheek. Ian's eyes stung as he flexed his jaw and massaged his face, he said nothing.

"Ian you fool! Where have you been! You've upset the entire house with worry!"

"I'm sorry Valquee, I just wanted to help I really did. We brought you all the soul suckers we could find who have feasted on lost souls. I hoped it would speed the recovery of the fallen riders. We just don't know how to match the souls to the man—"

"Oh Ian, you're a darling!" Valquee ensnared him in such a way he'd never been hugged before. "Never before did I think that you cared about my people like this. You are so, so—" but the proper words never came to her as she began to weep.

"You are a selfless, heartfelt, young man who is maturing into a man any woman would desire to court. Did you know selflessness is one of the most important traits of a great warrior, to think of others before yon self?" Hivell assisted Valquee as he held out a hand to help Ian off of Bracko, the centaur.

"Thank you Hivell." Valquee aired.

Touching his right hand to his forehead, breast, then lips, Hivell touched Valquee's lips before simply repeating: "He is a selfless, heartfelt, young man, who is maturing into a man ANY woman would desire to court." Giving her a wink, he went to converse with another.

"You!" Banthumn bellowed.

Hivell spun on the spot. "Oh hi Banthumn."

"Hi? I haven't forgotten. One day, you will repay me with more than a hi. I just haven't figured out how yet, but when I do..." he trailed off. Before another word, Banthumn dropped a soul sucker he still held and stalked off, his herd mates following suit. The pile of soul suckers grew on each deposit, eventually drawing all attentions.

"What's up with him?" Ian asked with curiosity.

"Oh, I accidentally shot him when I thought he was evil stalking me last year. Or tried to at least, he hasn't quite gotten over it—"

"Aah marvellous! Simply superb!" Lord Guwhyon cut in as he rushed to the pile. Closing his eyes, he ensnared a soul sucker in a strange way. "Leeran!" He shouted and tossed the oversized insect over his shoulder. Caught by another, it was then fed bit by bit to the fumbling Leeran.

Ian's stomach retched. "Could yon not at least cook it first?"

"No, it's the blood that embraces the soul."

"Oh."

"How did Lord Guwhyon know whose soul it was?"

"Any elf has the ability to sense others' souls, whether in the body or not. If we know the person whom the soul belongs to, well enough anyway, it is easy to identify it. Every soul has a unique rhythm that makes them who they are."

"Cool." Ian observed before drifting awry. Nearby other elves had joined Lord Guwhyon in matching souls to their bodies. Some that could not be identified were discarded.

Ian soon grew lonesome; being unable to help as he sat perched aloft a boulder observing the action. Day gave way to night before all were identified. Elves were scurrying about trying to rouse the fallen, not paying Ian any mind as he drifted into an uneasy slumber.

"Oh come on, you lazy granitual, wake up you lazy beast, it is time to deliver the Amity Blade to our friends, the dragons. At this rate, all you'll do is sleep until you turn to stone!" With a loud tremor which shook the cave, the beast placed one heavy paw before the other. Its pace was slower than methodical. This, naturally, drove the impatient dwarf, who rode astride it, crazy as he slapped the granitual's rump continuously. The brute grunted irritably before slowing its pace even more to a near standstill.

"Come on!" the dwarf shouted. "We have fifteen days to make a near month's travel. We are already pressed for time!" Doing something never before done in dwarvish culture, this brave and foolish dwarf dismounted the granitual and began running on foot through the passages of the mountains, leaving all protection behind.

Only once the dwarf dismounted, did the creature break into a sprint, outrunning the dwarf in question. This naturally spawned a dirty tongue on the dwarf's behalf as he muttered foul curses beneath his breath.

A granitual, is a rock-like creature that is built like a komodo dragon. They are capable of causing serious harm, but are often more curious than all else, wanting to learn as much of their world as they can. Though being smashed is the only way to actually harm, or more so kill them, they often pass into a wild state, where they turn into a hibernating rock. While in this state, they can be roused, but few can do it. They are a rare friend of the dwarves, who understand common tongue, but can also speak the stone beings native language, which is comprised of grunts and squeaks. The granitual is a highly docile and friendly species if they are not threatened.

A calling was echoing deep within the Occluder's heart, though it had no origin, the Occluder knew straightaway that his dragon, Nighdrake, desired his company. No one could share so much time with another and fail to recognize its plea for companionship.

With a great whoosh that roused a breeze colder than night's icy chill, the Occluder's spirit filled the great chambers in which the Niteshade resided.

"What troubles thou, thy sweet, sweet Nighdrake?" The Occluder questioned. With a flash of lightning, he was caught off guard so greatly that, his potency nearly vanished.

"You've been practicing well I see." The Occluder commented, deep in his soul a spark of energy ignited as he thought of all the possibilities Nighdrake was creating. That spark, just like all warmth and fires glow which was ever abundant in the chambers, was quickly stolen away; however, as out of nowhere, great droplets of rain fell as it splashed angrily against the cold stone floors. Joining this rain was an energy, the same that would be experienced before anything momentous were about to commence. That type of intensity that numbs the body and causes the heart to flutter. The anticipation and reaction to the moment unknown which births that unsettling uneasiness that no one seems able to escape.

Nothing but the rain could be heard, and it was a sound most deafening.

Out of the emptiness a voice arose, a voice of fear, of insecurity. Not heard much in this fashion, it was the voice of the Occluder.

"H-how did you do that?" A shaky uneasiness sliced through his usual cold, icy, tone. Nighdrake cocked his head puzzled.

'I have only done what massster asssksss.' Nighdrake's thoughts filled the room.

"Steal the power of others, yes. Never before have I experienced one able to control the elements." The Occluder was growing flustered.

Silence. Nighdrake was at a loss.

"That, Nigh, is your next task, figure out what you just did, and harness it!" The Occluder ordered trying to compose himself as he attempted to subdue his excitement. "Nevertheless, your craft is doing well so far. Call me when you learn anything new or if your task reaches completion." The air stirred and then stilled as the Occluder vanished from the room without warning.

Great shouting lifted through the trees as Ian observed the arranging of the elves. Some were gathering up provisions, some were weaving up gurneys, and others were tending to the weak; Valquee being one as she moistened a brow of one of the fallen with a dampened rag.

"It's such a shame really, with all the efforts involved, I still don't feel they will be recovered enough in time for the great rejuvenation of the dragon herd as they crown a new alpha dragon; not to mention the rejoining of dragon and rider." Valquee mumbled beneath her breath, unaware of any who listened with curiosity.

"I'm sorry, but what rejoining? I thought that the time of the riders was over." Valquee jumped, startled, nearly poking the eyes of one of the fallen.

"Oh Ian, I wasn't expecting— I mean, I didn't— oh, never mind. Let's just say, there was a prophecy once written long ago, have you not heard of it?"

"No."

"Well it has begun to unfold for the last decade or so now and I—" Valquee stopped abruptly. "You know Ian prophecies are not my area of knowledge. All I know is, it is expected to involve you, and because of which, I don't feel that I'm the best to tell you, perhaps Xsealiadd could—"

"If it's about me, I have the right to learn it!" Ian cut in with anger.

Valquee sighed. "I only said it is suspected to involve you, it is not known for sure."

"But I should still know!" Ian was irate. Valquee, however, remained silent as she dribbled water on the sullen faces of one of the fallen elves once more.

The time soon arrived when the elves progressed forth, luckily for Ian, travels were much slower as the elves took in turn the transporting of the gurneys. Ian quickly grew bored as he engaged himself in activities to entertain his travels.

Anything from sparring invisible foes to exploring his surroundings took to Ian's fancy. None of the elves seemed to notice him as he drifted further and further from the fellowship.

As he explored about, he had nearly overlooked it, crushing it into a thousand tiny gems of glass sparkling beneath the sun, spilling the contents of black across the landscape. It was during one of his moments of wandering, when he had discovered it; a tiny vial full of a mysterious black fluid, lying amongst the strewn tree droppings. Being curious as he was, Ian scooped it up. Pear in shape and with thousands of finely cut fitting facets, the vial sat just comfortably in his rough palm. Its contents sparkled like a black ocean beneath the sun. Ian stared mesmerized at the vial as its contents sloshed about within the vacated air space in its bottleneck.

'What is it, I wonder?' Ian thought as he scanned his surrounds, no one was about, though he could hear the tramping feet of elves off in the distance.

The cork popped out oh too easily as Ian took a whiff of the swirling vapours which rose for the skies. A strange feeling overtook him as he stood there quite foolishly. It was a feeling never felt before as he raised the vial to his lips. Before his brain could react to the hand's foolishness, the black fluid oozed its way down his throat.

The liquid was thicker than Ian expected as it took its time seeping deep into his core, burning as it went. The pain was unimaginable, like drinking boiling water that never cooled. Thick as tar, it stuck to flesh, refusing to be cooled or removed. Even after emptying his water skin, the pain remained.

Clutching his throat with a final scream, Ian blacked out, his body doing all it could to shield him from the agony. He was burning up from the inside.

Chapter 6
The Crown

Deceivingly solid, the stretch of meadows spanning Shalock to Hethrowe were unusually marshy and unstable as they were so close to Equwanonne Bog. The journey was anything but relaxing as Xsealiadd tripped and slipped encountering numerous snakes and alligators. The journey itself was wearing on his limp frame, and thrice Xsealiadd nearly became trapped in sinking sand. Unpleasant as it was, he was making good progress being only a couple days from Hethrowe.

It was around midday, two dawns following the departure from Shalock and the kind Annesthia, when Xsealiadd was beginning to fall into that false sense of security. Nothing had wronged him since early yesterday morn.

It was the worst slip yet as Xsealiadd, with his bad hip, stepped on a clump of grass which was not solid by a long shot. Like a hungry beast ensnaring its prey, Xsealiadd immediately began to be pulled deep into the bowels of the underground. Clutching his staff with all his fumbling strength, Xsealiadd closed his eyes and thought hard.

The magic he often wove was birthed from texts; incantations from literature and script, to recall one on the fly and recite it without blunders was very impractical, especially when so much Craft is practiced by someone like Xsealiadd. As well, most don't often seem able to think straight in times of stress. To play it safe from mispronunciations, Xsealiadd chose to plea for help from the gods.

To most, the language was foreign, but yet Xsealiadd rambled on. The earth was nearing his breast before he felt the tugging stop, the ground began to solidify, and he was soon able to pull himself free of the dirt, muck, and mire. Exhausted from the struggle, Xsealiadd soon collapsed on stable grounds, where he rested for many days following, consuming his rations to depletion.

Valquee knew that scream well, she'd heard it before.

"Ian!" she cried, nearly dropping the pack she had shouldered. It thudded heavily to the ground as she bolted for the trees in the direction of the utterance. Some fellow of an elvish kind followed fairly distant in her wake for she had a healthy head start. "Please be okay! Please be okay!" She pleaded as she prayed for Ian's welfare.

Her heart sunk, however, as Ian met her eye line all in a crumple. "Ian? Ian?" Deep in her heart, she feared the worst for that scream was one filled with pain. Hoping for the best, however, she approached Ian in five healthy strides, steps that in her heart, felt to take an eternity. "Ian? Ian!" She scooped him into her arms after skinning both knees on the sharp rocks, twigs, and pine needles. Her heart pounded beneath her breast as her hands danced wildly across his being, inspecting his welfare.

Her frame sagged as she allowed Ian to slide from her lap. She began to shake as she let out a cry of sorrow. Joining her side Hivell gave her an embrace of comfort. Her response was weak as her arms quickly fell limp; she just stared to the soil, silent tears seeping down her cheeks.

Hivell held his wrists to Ian's gaping mouth. "No breath. So he's gone then." This caused Valquee to wail in hysterics. Hivell squatted in silence as he gazed absentmindedly at Ian's presence, only then did he notice the unstopped vial in Ian's limp grasp. Picking it up with care, he observed the meagre drops in the bottom. "This may be useful." He mumbled before replacing the cork and pocketing the flask.

Silence hung amongst the travelers in respect of Ian's passing. All that was heard was the pained sombre tears of a hysterical Valquee. Out of eye line, Hivell, though close behind her, shed many soft silent tears of his own. Though he wasn't close to Ian, he knew him well enough, and Valquee was one of his closest clan mates.

Out of the mournful silence, a song arose; birthed from the lips of the elvish father, Lord Guwhyon, who hoped to sing life to a soul so lost. The song grew in familiarity to some fellow elves, which strengthened the melody with voice and heart of their own. Great time endured before the music died, once again all fell silent, including Valquee, though silent tears still fell.

"Though the time or place is not proper, what say we sing him into the trees?" Lord Guwhyon suggested, "For time is quickly passing and we are still needed by the dragons."

"No!" Valquee sprang to her feet startling all. "Not here, not now! He is to travel back to Rulan to be overlooked by our people, if time does not allow him to rouse; I will personally sing him to a tree when I return."

"Valquee, why this decision?"

"B-because, Ian o-once told me, he thought Rulan was heaven. And that he never wanted to leave." Another wave of emotion overtook her as she, once again, crumpled into an emotional heap.

"Very well, who will take him back? It must be one who does not need to fulfill a rider's task."

A noble, masculine elf stepped forth, "I would be greatly honoured to bear his body home." All emotions uncontained, Valquee had a complete meltdown.

"Thank you Spayuhddeus."

With a nod, Spayuhddeus embraced Ian, before drawing further from the travelers upon every silent step.

"Hivell, get her on her feet, too much time have we lost already."

"Give her time, please father."

Giving Hivell a look of don't-mess-with-me, Lord Guwhyon drew cross. "Don't disobey your master Hivell, now come!" The party began to travel on Lord Guwhyon's word leaving Hivell no choice but to rouse a distraught Valquee.

"Be strong Valquee, rise. I am here to help you bear this hardship, but please on your feet for those whom you love."

Her tears were ever potent as Valquee worked her way up a nearby tree trunk; she had no strength to bear her own weight. In her heart her dragon's cries were louder than ever as, just like she shared his pain, he shared hers. Valquee grew more aware. "Blazzan, I must get to him!"

"That's where we are going Valquee, to be with our dragons." Though Valquee's heart burned with sorrow, she walked as steadily as she could, though relying heavily on Hivell for support.

Nearly all strength had perished by the time Xsealiadd reached the gates of Hethrowe. Nevertheless, new vigour fulfilled his steps as he knew what he was there to do. Losing his hourglass naught but several month's past to a fellow named Stanzer, after his hut was burned to the ground while he was unconscious, Xsealiadd knew he would have to find it here. It was after discovering his soul, which flowed in the sands of the hourglass, could communicate visions of great emotion with him that he tracked the passing of his hourglass from Stanzer to the King of Gold. Only then to be stolen by a child who had the unfortunate luck of running into a horse and rider, who confiscated his treasures to return to the Lord of Hethrowe and it was there that the hourglass currently resided; and that was where Xsealiadd meant to go. With a gentle rap on the door of the Lord's humble abode, Xsealiadd waited tired and impatient. The door was answered by a guard who recognized Xsealiadd at once.

"Xsealiadd, Lord Danahi awaits, now come, I will show you the way." At once, the soldier started at a brisk march through the corridors, his footfalls echoing loudly, competing with the clank of his armour.

"Lord Danahi?" The soldier announced as he approached a large seating area.

"Yes?"

"An eagerly awaited Xsealiadd is here."

"Well, what delays thee? Bring him forth."

At that cue, Xsealiadd strolled in. Weary, he collapsed on the nearest chair.

"Sustenance! He needs sustenance!" Lord Danahi called, and immediately a servant who was nearby rushed from the room.

"So Xsealiadd —"

"—hourglass!" He cut in breathless, "Where's my hourglass?"

"Right here Xsealiadd." Immediately, Lord Danahi leapt up as he passed Xsealiadd his hourglass.

Embracing it, Xsealiadd immediately felt strength fill him again. "I have also come for another. A friend of mine, Sam, he owns "Craft", a store in Villowtown, he is seeking a very special item. My heart tells me I'll find it here." Xsealiadd refused to admit he once had a vision of the crown being placed here.

"What is this item you speak of?"

"It was a crown, a diadem if you will." Xsealiadd waited in excited silence.

"I do indeed have a crown on my being and would gladly pass it to you, as long as you promise to keep it in good hands." Getting up once more, Lord Danahi withdrew the crown and passed it to Xsealiadd. "So tell me, why is your friend, Sam, seeking it?"

"Well," Xsealiadd began by taking a long deep quaff from the goblet that had just been presented to him by Lord Danahi's servant; it was a refreshing, yet sweet wine. "Sam's heart is not by any means, pure. He has definitely had dark past. Spent many years tied up as a Carddronne, you know a servant to the Dark Lord. Worked up the ranks, he was always a hard worker, ended up being one of the Occluder's best men; got right up tight in his circle of loyalists. The Occluder had in him great faith, entrusted him with this crown. Eventually Sam got out, knew it was bad, still fights him to this day. These desires that the servants get to rush back to him and do his bidding, whatever you want to call it. Somehow he fights the urges; don't know how, especially since they've been described as overpowering to the point where you lose control of yourself. No one knows how, he was the first to break it. You'd think if he knew one of his men turned traitor, he'd have took his own crown back. Unless he didn't know! Maybe Sam pretended to be a servant, acting only when he chose; kind of as a two-faced servant or double-edged sword, working with and against the Dark Lord. That would explain his ability to keep the crown and have a chance to study it. Yes, this must be it—" Xsealiadd rambled on.

"You really know little of your friend here." Lord Danahi commented, taking a seat next to Xsealiadd, a goblet in his pincers.

"I only know what I am told. Anyhow, he wants the crown back as he is trying to understand why it is so important to the Occluder; for him to insist Sam never lose it and to guard it with his life."

"Well, this may be of absolutely no use, but when one is appointed a throne or a chair of any worth for that matter, it is only customary for that someone to receive a crown, which is normally forged by the dwarves using only precious metals. Along with the crown is a weapon, each town has one to represent their village, it is used by the king if ever in battle.

That's why on our flags, we have two unique weapons that cross. For instance, Hethrowe's weapon, my weapon, being Lord of Hethrowe, is the flail. The weapon of Antain is the composite longbow, so our flag has the bow crossing the flail to say, this is Hethrowe village from the realm of Antain, no one needs words otherwise..." Lord Danahi trailed off before realizing Xsealiadd had lost interest in the knowledge he already knew. "Is there a problem Xsealiadd?"

"You said something along the lines of all who receive a throne gets a crown of great worth?"

"That I did, what's wrong?"

"Do you by any chance have a copy of, "The Fall of Farrizon; Legend or Myth?"

"I do, and what an excellent tale it is!"

"Well," Xsealiadd grew impatient. "Can you get it for me?"

"Right!" And with a snap of Danahi's fingers, the servant left the room in a hurry, returning only when a copy of the desired text was in hand.

Xsealiadd leafed through the worn pages with a sense of urgency. At last finding what he wanted, he let the pages fall open. "'It is tradition'", he began reading aloud, "'when one takes the throne to receive a crown of great worth, one bearing a symbol of their realm if you will, carved, more often than not, in solid gold. When Farrizon rose to power, he became hostile to this tradition. Disregarding the diadem, he felt no longer king of his rightful realm of Aardvark, but a king of his own right. Disregarding all normal practices, he transformed himself as a shadow king, or king of evil, long before he fell from the throne, the crown also toppling from existence.' Danahi, this must be when he passed the crown to Sam!" Xsealiadd commented excitedly. *"'—the crown later reappeared briefly in the hands of a shopkeeper. Some insider's information once stated that before it resurfaced, it was defiled with blackened magic, however this is only to be believed as a myth'* — myth my horny toads!" Xsealiadd shouted as he sprang up unusually fast to his unsteady feet. "That is it! I must tell Sam, he will be so pleased as to have a lead on the specifics of the crown. Thank you greatly my dear friend." Xsealiadd exclaimed as he prepared for departure.

"Yes Xsealiadd, now, by orders of me, Lord Danahi, I request you to remain here for a couple of lie downs so you can rest and my men can prepare you some provisions for the next leg of your journey to Villowtown."

With a grumble deep in his throat, Xsealiadd flopped back down irritably; he just hated having to wait for stuff, even to rejuvenate. He wanted to get things done, and done now. Folding his arms, he gave Lord Danahi a clearly foul look.

Chapter 7
Lost

The potion burned from within Ian as he drifted to and from consciousness. The world was black. A dull twinge of pain throbbed in the pit of his stomach, just enough to keep him aware of his own presence. His heart pounded, crying, begging for the life that was ebbing, leaving his soul. He began to roll and writhe, his chest pounding. At last he opened his eyes. What he saw scared him. The world seemed to dance and swirl an angry balance of blacks and whites which introduced themselves in unwelcoming splashes. What Ian was experiencing was indistinguishable from a dream or reality. It had to have been a dream; the world was not like this, the world was sane.

What sounded like hundreds of voices far off rang in his ears, but they weren't normal, like hearing a social gathering through water. Smudges of blackened masses manifested themselves before him before vanishing into a nearly nonexistent background. The surroundings, in fact, seemed the only subjects close to normal reality. It was deprived of colour, as if someone sipped the pigments right out of the world through a straw leaving the surrounds blotchy and void of vibrancy. Its near colourless shades were easily distinguishable from the trees right down to a single blade of grass.

'This is a dream, a strange hallucination, that draught makes me see stuff.' Ian thought. His thinking, however, never stayed clear or sharp. Fuzzy to begin with, it trickled away to nothingness. Ian held on to it about as well as one can hold onto water in a hand.

'No matter, I will simply awaken from it — I hate dreams that don't make sense —' Ian quickly realized that there was a problem. He could not tell if his eyes were parted or shut. The masses before him, black as night, seemed to move about in a peculiar way. The more he focused and strained, the clearer he could see and hear them.

They were in a forest, that much was made very clear. Black tall masses were gathered about a small clearing. In this clearing, two waist high figures were hunched over a solitary mass.

"No breath," he could make out amongst the ramblings, "gone then," he also heard.

A thought struck him right then, and a scary one at that. "Gone then, no breath, dead?" Ian's confusion drove him crazy, until the inevitable, Ian searched himself. He wasn't there.

He stared to the clearing with strong focus, trying to make sense of what happened. He was looking upon himself, still and lifeless. Valquee was crying over his body. The other elves were singing what sounded like an enchantment; he wouldn't know he couldn't feel it, he couldn't feel anything. Reaching far to take Valquee's hand, he passed her right through. He had no body, it was only then it dawned on him, he truly was dead.

'How am I hearing, how am I seeing, how am I here when I am not?' Soon, those masses began to move and dance, and so did Ian though where he was and where he was headed, he knew not. Still, somehow or another, he began to move.

 Standing ten feet tall with relative ease the great beast known as a toran roamed the great woods of Hucklandish, one of the few evil still able to do so without ill effects from the elvish enchantments.
 Torans, next to snorgs were the Occluder's second most favourite species to act as silent observers to others' activities; and no wonder, torans were snorgs without the shadow of a tainted heart. This particular toran was sent to observe the passing of an elvish clan heading southward on foot.
 Torans walk rather erectly, disregarding the gentle curve of their spines which are forced into such a shape from their troll-ish cousins. Their humanoid features are what overpower their profile. Their body-built frames are coated with black hair, though thin it is, it made their pallid gray flesh seem darker.
 Their faces greatly resemble trolls with huge snouts and a jutting under bite which exposes their two lower fangs. They are coated with a wild hairy mane, which nearly masks their beady-eyes and pointed ears. The greatest fault of the toran is that they are easily distracted. This one for instance had been tailing a great black horse now for quite some time and had long since lost the trail of the elves.
 His footfalls remained muted as he crept with care through the great underbrush, keeping his target close. Drawing breath he nocked an arrow. An opportunity was about to present itself, one he refused to miss. As the tree split into a

great wide fork, the toran sighted in his target, with a great twang of his bowstring he snorted gleefully at the cries of the horse, once again his aim was true. Unusual it was for a toran to be so accurate on the bow, this one was very unique.

Entering the great clearing, the toran yanked his arrow free of the worn reins which held the horse pinned to a large tree. Immediately, the horse tried to bolt, but the toran held him firm.

"Oh you are a real brute aren't ya", such a shame really, someone leaving a fine specimen such as yerself to fend on yer own." The toran commented as he gave the great stallion a once over. Black the horse was, with white splashes on the tail ends and around the hooves, where great hair flared like bellbottoms. It's most unusual feature was the white blaze upon its forehead. This horse was surely a Clydesdale.

"Yes, yes you will do nicely." Before even the horse was ready, the toran had mounted its strong back. "Yuh!" The toran bellowed, and with a hard kick of its enormous heels into the horse's ribs, they took off at a healthy run.

Thyle had long ago lost count of the number of hours he spent poring over countless pages, countless readings in his quest to find past cases of any whom had broken the summoning. The only one that came close was an elderly chap named Sam Utie, who didn't exactly break it by the records but did somehow mysteriously fall from the circle of loyalists; the circle of the Occluder's most devoted followers. In his search, Thyle did learn a little of this Samuel chap but knew, at least for a couple more weeks, he would be unable to escape the watchful eye of his father long enough for the travel to Villowtown where Sam lived and worked.

    Waiting was the key for in about two weeks time, he, and several other local students from the academy would head to Sam's town in question to complete some school shopping. Though most had done this under the supervision of their mentors, Thyle had the unfortunate luck of losing his to the collapse of the academy late last year; this meaning he would have to prepare under the stern eye of his father and principal of the academy, Rennaux. It was then he hoped to slip away long enough to have a private word with Sam, for now, however, the anticipation was murder as there was nothing more he could do until opportunity arose for him to speak with Sam.

    Xsealiadd spent his days in eager anticipation, like a child he berated Lord Danahi with great pleas and begging to be released. What irritated the lord the most was Xsealiadd's redundant asking of questions like is it time yet? And, can I go now? Many other queries of similar fashion also escaped the wizard's lips multiple times and in multiple forms during his rest at Lord Danahi. It was this alone, though he'd never admit it, that left Danahi with the decision to release Xsealiadd.

    When the opportunity finally arose, Xsealiadd snatched it like a cat to a mouse, pouncing on it he nearly fell through the portal being in such a hurry to leave for fear of Lord Danahi's mind swaying a new decision otherwise. Stumbling over his own feet and staff on his departure, he left in such a scramble he barely breathed a word of farewell, let alone of gratitude in his wake before he was off.

Now almost three days later, Xsealiadd flopped at the breadth of Folklandish Forest, at last taking his first real break since Hethrowe after making up for lost time. With a meagre supper he collapsed utterly exhausted from his excursion as he, in no time, fell into a peace-filled slumber. The moon had swelled to an enormous blue, an unusual phenomenon in the summers of Ellezwrainia; this did not prevent Xsealiadd from sleeping in great peace approaching the wee hours of the morn. What did prevent somnolence, however, was when he was abruptly being shaken, rather roughly, by another.

"Xsealiadd, get up!"

'Whatever this thing is, it knows my name, this could be either really good, or really bad,' Xsealiadd thought to himself as he came to his senses.

"Hurry, we need to talk!" Xsealiadd squinted against the bluish hue that was cast by the overly radiant moon. Against the bright night, he could make out a slender, squatting profile with ease.

"Who is it?" He mumbled just pulling himself to a sitting stance.

"Etar, I am an elf from the forest. I am from the house of Branil, Lord Branil is my master, and it is him I serve. My home is the forest you see before thee, the wood of Folklandish. What business brings you to the turf of my folks?"

"I am merely passing by; I am destined for Villowtown to deliver a message and a treasure to an old friend there."

"I am glad to hear you mean no harm, to remain on friendly terms, I am an ambassador to my lord. Our goal is to bring down the Occluder in any way, shape, or form. My role was to complete an order by Lord Branil and gather information on the Dark Lord in question. Since we are conversing, do you have knowledge on such a gruesome topic?"

"Too much I'm afraid, but perhaps I can help, to which knowledge do you desire to know?"

"This is one of those situations where if I knew I would tell, do you know of anything that may assist in the Occluder's demise?"

Xsealiadd shifted awkwardly under the immense baggage, even sitting it was uncomfortable to bear.

"Tell me Etar, have you heard of the black book?"

"Only of it but that is all, how is it significant?"

"The black book is supposed to hold great secrets of the Occluder and is highly discussed amongst those who are truly devoted to destroying the likes of that man, or well, the Dark Lord. You know of whence I speak."

"Indeed."

"However, the book holds much power and magic. Rumours also surround it which claim if you read it you will get sucked into the shadowed world in such a way it would be impossible to escape. No one knows for sure because nobody has ever been courageous, or foolish enough, to attempt it. Its author, like so much about it, is generally unknown but many believe that it was written by some member of the Dark Lord's circle of loyalists. It is here we pause from the telling for a moment as I'd like to tell you a little secret. To go off the record, can you maintain secrecy?"

"Aye."

"I have been snooping on my own. The book, my reliable sources say, has indeed been penned by the Dark Lord himself. Also, those rumours are true for all but two people. First, the Dark Lord himself, which should be obvious, however, there is one other who I have found can read the text without harm to his being."

"Who?" Etar was growing rather curious very quickly.

"There is an ancient prophecy which has been unfolding for a decade or so now and each year that passes, it mounts concern, have you not heard of it?"

Etar shook his head.

"I shan't delve in too deep with it, however, it states one shall soon rise who will meet, and succeed in besting the Occluder in battle. This foretold is the only one, besides the Occluder, who can indeed read the text with no harm. Until this book is read, no one truly knows how to overpower the Dark Lord."

"And you know this foretold?"

"Aye. And it is for me to withhold until the boy himself is informed."

"Aye, I can respect that. Just one question?"

"Just the one?"

"If my lord asks, which he will by order, can I echo your words?"

"Only to him and him alone."

Etar nodded.

"You should also know, though the book has never before been read by a rebel to the Occluder, many trials have been tested to find his weaknesses. Though much has been found to slow and lessen Farrizon's being, none were able to successfully and permanently best him."

"Well thank you Xsealiadd and I am terribly sorry to have troubled you."

"No worries, no worries, it's a curious subject and not just for you, for all." Xsealiadd smiled awkwardly with a toothy grin as he attempted, haphazardly, to rise to his feet. The motion was in vain as his unbalanced provisions caused him to almost fall back over. He would surely have had it not been for Etar breaking his tumble.

"Xsealiadd, you are far too weary to traverse now, please rest."

"Nope, nope. I must go see Sam, too much time has already perished." Xsealiadd flailed his arms partly to gather balance, and partly to release his exasperation. This, naturally, caused a flurry of moths to erupt skyward. Etar eyed them with puzzlement. "Then please Xsealiadd, allow me to accompany thee onward. I may be of assistance yet."

"Well, only until Villowtown, after which, I must see if my duty will allow your presence. However, my concern presses with Lord Branil. Won't your absence be missed?"

"My orders were to gather the required information regardless the time it takes. Besides, you're a wise one with whom I feel worthy of immersing myself in intellectually stimulating conversations with, for I may learn much to aid my folks in besting the one with the shadowed soul."

"I appreciate your compliments, I truly do, but you don't have to aggrandize me; I care not if you accompany my travels, just don't you dare hinder them."

"Of course not."

Before Etar was ready, Xsealiadd was taking shaky, tender steps onward in which Etar rushed to pace for support and a fine opportunity for further conversing.

The bushes continued to grow disturbed as the beady eyes of the toran continued to track a slow-moving elf. Sitting astride the black horse he had wrangled earlier, he puzzled to know the goings on with this fellow. It was moving awkwardly for the grace of its species and would become easy prey. The horse whinnied with restlessness as the toran cursed beneath his breath. He was trying to keep in shadow to remain invisible; he did not need to be given away by a common equine. Ever so carefully, he began to keep a stealthy pace with the traveling elf. To, mostly, satisfy the horse's desire for movement.

The moment soon arrived for him to pounce. Springing from the thick undergrowth, the horse trampled the traveler from the backside, he never saw it coming. Ensuring the elf's death was certain, he snarled with disgust, he now realized why the elf's gait was awkward and ungainly. He was bearing another already dead subject; a boy, whose face appeared strikingly familiar to the toran.

"The boy I keep for master, as for the elf... I shall feed well this night." With a pleasured growl, he burdened the horse of black with both corpses before vanishing to the trees with his find.

"Come Florian, it is time I escort you to Ackles Academy." An elf by the name of Altane commented, Altane had been training and supervising Florian during his stay in Rulan. Needless to say, Altane had been greatly impressed with Florian's fluency in the Rukkian tongue.

"But what about Hivell? He was my mentor, and he promised."

"And he still is. He will meet you when you get to the academy."

"Oh very well, talk about a brief stay here though."

"Indeed, we often refrain from bringing students all the way back to Rulan for summer, the travels here to there are distant and stays between are brief."

"There is certainly no lie there." Florian chimed.

"I must warn you, I am required to halt our travels to pick up my student I'll be mentoring this year, he lives in Dillead."

"That is just splendid." Florian responded in such a way that made sarcasm questionable.

"Then we'd be off?"

"Indeed." Florian watched as Altane gathered their provisions and prepared for departure.

Chapter 8
The Hero Unveiled

The sheer elegance of Cideao had the ability to easily ensnare any whose gaze befell upon it. Even its sheer beauty, however, failed to best the misery-stricken Valquee who barely lifted her head the entire travels from Rulan, at least not since Ian perished anyhow. In fact, she had been so consumed with grief, she had lately appeared as nothing more than a growth; a parasite upon Hivell's shoulder as he attempted, as always, to bring forth comfort unsuccessfully on Valquee's behalf.

"Look Valquee, isn't she a marvel for sore eyes, we have finally arrived at Cideao, though we shan't stay long mind for our dragons are calling us more than ever these days." Hivell pointed out.

Valquee simply groaned, lifting her head long enough for Hivell to note her ever present reddened and puffy eyes. As usual, she had been crying.

"Tell me Valquee, you have lost students before, you have never been this pained for any of them, why here? Why now? I'm sure Lord Guwhyon would be pleased to set you up with a new student, the school year has not yet begun, there is still time."

"No!" Valquee roared before slapping Hivell on the cheek causing him to wordlessly massage the contact point. He waited in silence for an explanation, he knew it would come in due time.

"Look, I'm sorry, you didn't deserve that, you've been such a good friend in rough times. Students are my life, I love training them, seeing their faces glow to a new manoeuvre or potion. Like most, I grumble to a new assignment, but once I get to know them, I remember why I love doing what I do. You can't just replace a child, though with another, as none will ever be the same."

"I know, but why so many tears for this one?"

"This will probably sound terrible, but I do not grieve for Ian but for the hope he brought."

"Hope?"

"Indeed, do you remember the ancient prophecy?"

"Aye"

"Well," Valquee sniffed hard. "Ian was the boy foreseen to best the Occluder. I have always known this deep in my heart, but now that he's gone, so is the hope. A stiff breeze disturbed the air causing Valquee's heart to flutter as it became subjected to the uneasy energy all elves get when a storm is sure to brew.

"Do you feel that?" Valquee asked Hivell.

"What?"

"Storm surge."

"Oh, no, sorry." Hivell was confused. A storm surge is a term elves used to explain the edgy energy at the breadth of a storm. More times than not, however, the storm surges are felt by all the elves at once, this one was different. The surge ebbed as quickly as it arrived leaving only one other explanation; a spirit's energy. Valquee's eyes darted about widely in their sockets for any glimpse of a shadowed beast lurking with fell intentions.

"Ian?" Valquee tested.

Nothing.

"He's gone sweet." Hivell replied.

Valquee once again crumpled in anguish as she gazed teary-eyed at the elves flitting through the streets of Cideao, every member of the fellowship had a role in replenishing their supplies; and all went about it without word. Fortunately, Lord Guwhyon saw no reason not to excuse Valquee and Hivell from their duties provided the circumstances. Sitting Valquee down on the front stoop of the bakers, Hivell tried once again to comfort her with kind-hearted words.

"We all wish for the sun to shine out the purer, for a day to come when we don't have to fear someone in our shadows, for the world to once again be at peace. Every day passing we cry that shadows still poison our land, and hope tomorrow, just maybe, our prayers will be heard. Every notion we hear with even a thread, a glimmer of optimism in its words, we cling to like parasites to a host. And then we become sorely disappointed when we find it to be false information. Remember Valquee, just remember, whatever ups and downs, twists and turns life throws at us, there is always hope. As long as we keep believing, keep trying, hope will always remain in our hearts."

Valquee's tears gave way to a tremendous sigh. "Thank you Hivell, I will do my best to think of it as another bump in the road, and to look on the brighter side of life."

"I am not ashamed to admit we are all disappointed, we all pressed our hope upon this child. But how much truth are prophecies? Personally, I think that crazy kook Xsealiadd fills his head with so much rubbish to make himself seem wise. But that's what happens when you read too much; that man's nose, I doubt, barely sees the light of day buried amongst those pages, then here we are, looking up to him."

A weak smile broke Valquee's lips.

"Wow, a smile even, I haven't seen one of those in a while."

Valquee remained mute, in her mind she was more at ease.

Ian's mind screamed with anger. 'How could she not tell me? I have even asked her! Man they've got nerve. Believing I could save them from certain doom, putting all their faith in a child who can't even survive a potion, what fools!' His mind was a raging storm; winds swirled about him, emphasizing his mood.

It took Ian a moment to realize the wind wasn't caused solely by him, as a fog drifted into the area before tightening into a shadowed man. It was only then that Ian realized there were others. The more he strained his vision, the more profiles he could make out. They look so lively and normal, but how could they be? Just once Ian wished he could understand his world.

"Hello."

Ian gazed before him. A rather chubby, stout, dwarvish looking spirit, stared at him, though Ian failed to know why, he had no body to stare at. "I said hello, do you not remember me?" Negative energy overtook the ghostly dwarf. "Oh, silly me, I forgot you cannot speak yet. Fair enough, I will take your negative impulses as a no. Nevertheless, I am the spirit of your past, here to grant you leadership of Aardvark, to take over where the Occluder failed. Do you trust me?" Once again the ghostly dwarf was filled with negativity. "Then you are a wise one. Any, if not spoken in the language of the gods is one who lies, though not always. It's best to believe it and since few even know such a language of the lords above, few can thoroughly be honest, thus, our world is filled with naught but liars and deceivers. Ah! And there you have it, your first lesson under my guidance."

Uneasiness swept the air.

"I'm sensing a lack of trust. Atta boy, being cautious is a wise thing. No sweat, I just can't get past the lack of, well, you. A sign of a novice no doubt in my mind. I think you need serious help... look, I don't expect you to understand, just listen to me. You died. Somehow or another, I have no clue how or why because you can't talk yet, obviously, but you did. You are now in the world of the dead, the world of shadow as many prefer. You're going to be here a long, long while, so it's time you learned some of the rules. There's a lot to learn 'cause the rules here are very, very different. For starters, we have a body no more; we were ripped right from it. It is time you create the illusion of life. You need to sharpen your focus." The ghostly dwarf felt to be observed, he knew Ian listened, he knew he ensnared his interest. "Okay my lad, I fully understand where you're at, I've been there too, we all have. You're confused, disoriented, you're just trying to figure stuff out. Worst off, your focus is about as muddy as, well there's no comparison. I must say, though, it's the dirtiest mud I've ever seen. I'll surely tell you that, that's for sure. Your job now is to sharpen it. Flex your brain, concentrating hard on what you're seeing, hearing, feeling, and your presence will clarify. Sounds will become clearer, visions will brighten. Even your understanding of yourself will become realized. It's a slow process taking much time. Sorry, it has been so long I forgot. Time is not a thing to you, not yet anyway. This task I leave to you will make you tired as you push your soul to its utter limit, do not fret just push harder. It will pay off." With a wisp of smoke in the gust of the wind, the shadow dwarf was gone, leaving Ian empty and alone.

"Reading again?" Rennaux was annoyed.

"Uh huh." Was the only response he received, this irritated him further.

"You know, I don't know why you've been taking a sudden interest in reading, but whatever your reasons I don't have to hear them to know, I don't like them. You are my only child and I would hate to lose you behind some mouldy old book. What are you reading there anyway?" Rennaux asked as he snatched the text from Thyle's grasp. "Huh, S.P.E.L.L.'s of the Elite. Absolute rubbish! Son, why are you reading this, you're too good for it. You don't need a book to help you in the ways of magic! Why fill your head with such utter trash?"

"To relax." Thyle grumbled.

"Well boy, you better be with care, too much of this behaviour and you'll wind up like Xsealiadd, your nose between too many pages. I couldn't stand to lose you like that."

"You could never lose me dad, not when you breathe down my neck day and night barking orders at me. Reading is the only peace I have found over the past month."

"Yes Thyle, but I know you better than that; you're not an avid reader, so tell me true. What is this about?"

"It's...uh —"

"Yes?"

"It's nothing." Thyle replied simply as he folded the tome and tucked it from sight.

Rennaux rolled on his feet, it was clearly evident he wanted to argue, press Thyle for his goings on. Thyle was, once again, grateful for his luck as his father refrained from interrogation.

"Very well, before I allow myself scarce, Master Occluder requested all present in Sardon for an important conference. According to his words, this one you won't want to miss."

"Fine dad." Thyle resisted an eye roll with great might.

"Excellent, then we depart at midday."

"Fine," Thyle echoed, his head bent low to shield Rennaux's gaze from his over-energetic expression of irritated emotions. Hearing the door slam, Thyle at last, lifted his head to find the room void of activity. This pleased him, he enjoyed solitude. Opening his text, he leafed through the worn pages to return to his reading. Immersing himself, he continued his study on ways believed to effectively resist the summoning.

Amongst all her sorrow, Valquee suddenly grew very edgy and alert. Grabbing Hivell's arm, she shuddered.

"Do you feel that?" She was anxious.

"Indeed," Hivell responded ever calmly. He and Valquee were total opposites. She was always nervous and jumpy, and he tended to take things with serenity, always calm was his outlook towards life.

"The strain on my mind is shifting."

"Indeed, the dragons have gained control of the blade."

"So you agree?" Valquee drilled.

"Of course."

The greater portions of the elves were immensely edgy. Ready to spring into motion at a moment's calling. Camping south of Cideao, they lingered near the banks of Batten Lake, one of the most unusual lakes in all of Ellezwrainia.

Batten Lake is joined to the Sea of Nigh, the western ocean of Ellezwrainia, by a rather large tributary named Wikkadema River. Like the Sea of Nigh, it is affected immensely by the tides. When the tide is high, a normal traveler would take nearly two weeks to complete the passing around Batten Lake's banks on foot. Tides, however, affect Batten Lake so greatly, that if one was patient, when the tides were low, drifting out to sea, his or her journey could be cut nearly in half as they could cut almost straight southward along its lessened banks which was what the elves were attempting to do.

What made them most edgy was not the spur of the moment travels, but the lake's cycle. Six days it takes to pass from peak tide to peak tide. If anyone was to get trapped when the water swelled, the consequences would be utterly catastrophic. The waters of the Sea of Nigh are as chilly as ice; as the tide swells, water rushes through the Wikkadema River spilling into Batten Lake, bringing with it fearsome sea monsters which normally inhabit the western ocean. Something the dragons of Gesshlon failed to mind for as the tide receded many of these creatures become left behind on its barren seabed creating a feeding frenzy for the scaly reptiles of the sky.

"Remember my people! High tide will arrive shortly before dawn tomorrow, whoever begins to see even one drop recede to the sea, must rouse all immediately for then we sprint due south for Gesshlon. Do we understand?" Lord Guwhyon drew an affirmative from the crowd. "What a marvel! Oh, and one more thing. Be sure your provisions are gathered and packaged before you turn in tonight are we clear?" Again, many nodded in the affirmative.

Assuring himself all was in order Lord Guwhyon joined the gathering as they prepared for an elvish supper of great fruits."

A great cloud of fog condensed from nowhere. Swirling and dancing it began to take form. It soon became recognizable as the profile of the ghosted dwarf. "Hello my lad." The dwarf observed, searching Ian's silhouette, or lack thereof. The ghostly dwarf seemed impressed. "You're doing well, your apparition sharpens more, and more each day, I am beginning to see the condensing of fog as your mass grows tighter. Very soon you'll begin to notice fingers and toes binding to a uniform fashion. The last to form will be your breast. Do not fret; this is completely in the norm as your heart tries to resist your actions.

It will fight to remain free. I bet you're beginning to notice your world with more clarity, is this so?" The air grew light and warm. "I have the feeling of happiness and peace in my soul. I am a pleased entity. Keep up the positive effort." The ghostly dwarf's shadow began to dissipate to a faint mist, which in time became one with its surrounds.

Chapter 9
Hamman

Etar stood statuesquely in Xsealiadd's shadow, mirroring his stance, and had he known, his thought process.

To their left, the great trees of Folklandish and to their right, and creating a barrier before them, were vast expanses of Equwanonne Bog, which stretched as far to the north as it did to the south. Fortunately they were at the narrowest stretch, however, that did not help much as they struggled hopelessly to find a way across.

"You know the wonders of Equwanonne Bog, is that it is deceivingly stable." A voice rose from behind. Both Etar and Xsealiadd spun in unison, only to face a small, skeletal child.

"What is your meaning?" Xsealiadd drilled. "Equwanonne Bog is a vast marshland which spans as far as the eye can see, and it is very unstable."

"I wish to prove to differ; I have crossed these marshes on foot, safely many times to date. I have not tumbled to the waters yet."

Etar and Xsealiadd stumbled on their tongues, unsure of what to voice. "I - If you know a way across, we would dearly love for you to guide us." Xsealiadd stammered.

Placing his hands high on his hips, the child glared squarely at Xsealiadd. "Fine, but I can't go further than the western bank of Pissawn waterways. I have been sent on an assignment by one of my professors to locate and bring back an eggshell of a Whozalumn. I've been given a week to find one." The child rambled.

"Well, perhaps you should do what you're told." Etar ordered, causing Xsealiadd to give him a how-dare-you-ruin-my-chance-of-crossing look.

"It's okay, they have like, a momentous nesting ground near Hethrowe, it'll be a cinch assignment." The child waved it off.

"Okay." Xsealiadd stared, his eyes glued to the child.

"What, am I growing a second head or something?"

"No, there is just something about you, you look familiar."

"Well," the child began playing with Xsealiadd's sanity. "I am from Xsealiadd's Institution of Amity, your institution. My name is Hamman, I'm also well known as a child thief. Does this ring any bells yet?"

Xsealiadd shook his head slowly, and unsure.

"Okay, last year I stole a hoard of treasures from a bunch of people. Amongst it I stole an hourglass, your hourglass, from a golden dragon. I was ensnared and forced by a man to ride in a wagon in your company, along with an elf and a boy named Ian, of whom I grew quite fond. Do you know me now?"

Xsealiadd smiled with care. "Aye. Now tell me Hamman, can you show me the way?"

With an ear-splitting grin, Hamman flitted at an inhuman pace across the wetlands, Xsealiadd and Etar following as best as they could in his wake. In the waters, creatures such as snakes and alligators lurked, awaiting fallen prey, something Xsealiadd and Etar considered most concerning.

"The tide is sinking! The tide is sinking!" It was utter pandemonium. The elves were erratic, behaving as if the world was falling to ruin. Scrambling to gather their luggage and provisions, they began walking at a fair clip through the ankle deep, numbing waters.

Elvish riders wounded from the soul suckers, took extra care and time as their gaits were still shaky and unconfident. Many of the victims chose to crawl for confidence. For one who failed to understand the severity of being struck by a soul sucker, this would have likely been a scene of great amusement. However, there was no laughter here, only great worry and concern.

"How will we get all across in six days?" Valquee voiced her fears, the same woes which troubled many minds. "At this pace, they will be swallowed by the sea."

"All we can do is move and hope." Hivell comforted.

Though their pace was a healthy one, their travels were filled with much misery and toil; nearly losing a great few to the ever increasing quicksand of the lakebed was their first major setback as their entire travels were halted to rescue the fallen. Some were attacked by sea creatures which were lurking in the shadows or otherwise, beached on the seabed.

Also, because opportunity presented itself, a majority stopped to gather beached sea life for extra nourishment. The elves were more often than not, vegans; this, however, was a nourishing alternative to starvation in which they refused to pass up.

    Moons waxed and waned as the tide ebbed and then began to rise once again. The elvish time to pass the ocean floor was quickly deteriorating. Throughout their entire travels, the elves thoroughly enjoyed conversing and observing their dragons, which came and went by wing to the lakebed to take feed upon the beached sea life. This was a common occurrence which commenced every six days for the duration of the receding tides. During their travels, Valquee caught a glimpse of her dragon, Blazzan feasting on a Flipstar, an enormous-like starfish, which became trapped in the sand and met its untimely demise.

    Even Hivell was enlightened when his dragon, a female Earthinne race, named Emerellsse came swooping in low to send her regards. Unfortunately this happened while she clutched a floundering fish, which happened to wiggle free of her maw, only to be snatched up by an elegant Silverstream.

    It was, indeed, a pleasant surprise upon first introduction, the dragons flying en masse from their southern hold of Gesshlon, forming a "V" in the sky as they crested the mountain tops, only to bump into their elvish riders of whom they did not expect to make such good progress.

    During their travels across the sea bed, conversation between the dragons and riders flourished, however, a dark shadow of worry grew in the hearts of the earthbound elves as the waters quickly rose. Some of the dragons who had remained behind for a last-minute snack, had sensed the troubles of the elves, and most were generous enough to bring a couple stragglers with them back to Gesshlon, on their flight home.

'Sssseee you ssssoon!' Blazzan hissed to Valquee through their mental connection, before taking to the skies. With the dragons departed, the travelers had to keep strong pace as the waters were quickly growing upon them, luckily for the elves, so were the southernmost mountains of Sundurr.

At last reaching the southern banks of Batten Lake, the elves made camp, they were in dire need of a breather and nourishment.

"Are all here, is all okay?" Lord Guwhyon asked with care and concern.

Elves all around nodded their affirmative.

"Wait!" A voice arose. Their lord's heart sunk. "Where is Thayuss?" The elves began to search about.

"Does any remember him going forth with their dragons?" Many shook their heads.

"Only Dreal, Oshrine, and Trinaris who had accompanied them as to offer aid to those who required it, at least to my knowledge. They were the only ones that I know of which left on the dragon's talon."

"Then he should still be here."

"There!" Another shouted. The gaze of all followed his pointing finger. Far off on the horizon of the twinkling waters, a bobbing rucksack could be seen.

"But he is not there!"

"Are thou eyes with veil? No one could survive those waters. Especially not him, he could barely walk, let alone swim."

"Your progress is sound my boy, I see your fingertips floating before my eyes, clear as day. It pains me though to know the clarity you still lack. Unfortunately, I grow impatient, and we have a ways to go. I shall remain in your company, pushing you hard for the next few days; days which are growing brighter as your progress passes quicker than I had hoped, very good, very good."

Hanging in Ian's presence must've been a boring thing, for even the shadowed dwarf seemed pleased at even minor improvements. "—I see your face forming before mine eyes, and what a handsome face it is. Your mind must be humbled and sound." A swirling smile presented itself on Ian's disjointed features.

"Expressions even! Ha! We have made great progress! Good, good..."

"Well, I think our travels have reached a cessation at this point." Hamman commented.

"I thought you were going to lead us to the western bank." Etar challenged.

"I took you to the crossing to the western bank, you'll be able to cross with ease from here, besides you, I hope, haven't forgotten I still have that pending assignment beckoning my completion."

"Indeed you do Hamman, and I appreciate the assistance you have offered and dearly hope you care for yourself well."

"Thank you Xsealiadd for your kind words, and I'm sure I will." Before any realized what had unfolded, Hamman was gone, his profile vanishing in the distance, smaller and smaller upon each passing step.

"Well, Xsealiadd, I suggest we stop to rest and feed, that child moves at a tiring pace."

"I am in total agreement with you Etar." Plopping down on some mossy grass by the riverbank, Xsealiadd opened his travel pack. "Oh dear!" He worried, massaging his sunburnt brow.

"What troubles thee Xsealiadd?"

"My provisions are low and the distance I need to cover is grand, I feel I may not have enough."

"Well here," Etar started, trying to be of some help. "Pissawn Lake and waterways is known for its rich supplies of Pissawn fish, hence its name. How be I skewer you a few lunches worth and we could consume a fish fry?"

"That would be marvellous if you can do it."

"Oh sure!" Etar replied, before disappearing in search of a fair stick to use as a spear.

Hopping the rocks while stalking the Pissawn, Etar overlooked a rather slimy boulder as he slipped into the rushing currents below, the scream he uttered was pained as he vanished briefly below the surface; he was quickly being swept from sight. For an elder, Xsealiadd still embraced enough vigour to exert a spurt of energy as he, half hobbled, half sprung after Etar, following him closely from the banks.

Somehow, Etar managed to ensnare a fallen tree limb which overhung the waters; he clung to it for dear life. This gave Xsealiadd an opportunity to move in for assistance. Reaching his dragon staff far over the waters, Etar grabbed a hold. The moment his hands embraced Xsealiadd's staff, he felt them bind to it, becoming part of it, surely one of the wizards spells. Dragging Etar to the bank, Xsealiadd knelt by his side. His body was limp but he was still alert.

"What ails you?"

"My leg, it brings me great misery." Xsealiadd searched Etar's leg; it didn't take him more than a heartbeat to notice the femur breaking skin.

"This may be a great discomfort, try to remain still." Grabbing the injury site rather hard, Xsealiadd began muttering incantations below his breath. Beneath his hands, bones, tendons, muscles, and flesh began to mend, causing Etar to howl ear-splitting cries.

Things grew itchy briefly before all irritation subsided, even Etar who had practiced basic enchantments, was enthralled by Xsealiadd's handiwork. His leg did not even twinge with pain.

"Thank you Xsealiadd." Etar was grateful as a solitary tear stained his cheek.

"That's what teamwork is about, you watch my back and I watch yours."

"Indeed, well, perhaps we should continue on before more time is wasted."

With a gentle nod, Xsealiadd and Etar proceeded up the bank to gather their left behind baggage before crossing the waterway, this time with great care.

Chapter 10
Travel

"Our provisions have been exhausted; we will be unable to eat from now till Gesshlon. That is five days; our people will not make it. Perhaps we should go back to Oster."

"No!" Lord Guwhyon voiced his concerns. "Are you mad? It is a four-day journey back to Oster, why add such time to an already wearying journey."

"Fine, fine, but even so, at this pace our people still will be unfit for the daunting task. I guarantee many shall perish."

"You never know what the future brings, being so near the dragons, we may be able to call on them for aid."

"Our distance is still too great!"

"Now yes, but we shall soon be drawing much closer."

The elves bickered energetically.

"Very well." Lord Guwhyon cut through the din. "By my order, and going by the majority, we go forth and pray for mercy upon our hungered souls. We march immediately as quickly as our pace will allow. Remember, we are elves, built to endure."

With great grumbles and complaints, elves gathered up travel packs, bed rolls, cookware, and other necessities. Burdening themselves, they moved forward at a fair sprint.

"Your heart has, at last come home, blessing you with a solid presence. I know so, for your body is complete and your smoke brightens." The dwarvish apparition rambled admiringly. "—excellent, how is your hearing, your sight? Are they as sharp as your soul? Remember, you have a head now, you may shake, or nod it if you do so answer."

Ian nodded clumsily.

"Aah! Excellent! It is time we move on for you will no longer gain clarity through focus alone. We must introduce the second element; energy; power, fuel for the soul. It is only with energy that you will be able to complete your focus and be capable of speech and controlling your environment as you once did. Where do you get this energy you ask, I mean, if you were able? Well, from your world around you, it is there in abundance. Your problem is you need to learn how to embrace it. Have you ever drawn energy from something in life?"

Ian nodded a vigorous response.

"Well then, it is a start but it won't fare well for gathering energy in death. In death, you need a great deal more focus to get energy to heed your calling. It is something words always fail to teach. The only thing that will save you now is a solid understanding of what you're doing. You've done this in the living you say? Try it now in the dead. You must expand your parameters far and wide to stab into as much energy reserves as possible. Remember, whatever happens, don't give up. Good luck my lad." And with that, the dwarven ghost vanished into the wind.

"My Lord? Occluder? Bouldar!" The toran shouted with great might as he rode with a deceased boy astride an elegant black horse through the gates of Carddronnea Castle.

"What is it?" The Occluder's voice filled the toran's mind.

"I brought with me a boy whom you may recognize, but do not fear, he is dead I thought you may be pleased to gaze upon his face. Look through my eyes, see him now." The toran snarled as he positioned himself to stare into the boy's pallid face.

"Is that... Ian Cosswell? The boy whose life I've been after for over a year now?" The Occluder's voice filled the toran's mind. The toran could tell with ease, the Occluder was ecstatic though he tried to hide it. "No matter—" the Occluder pointed before vacating the toran's mind.

Something strange happened then the toran did not understand. The air grew unstable and cold then suddenly, the deceased Ian before him began to stir.

"Ian?" The toran was startled.

"No, Farrizon." The mouth of Ian formed the words rather robotically as the face of Ian gazed at the toran. The toran couldn't help but notice the body of Ian appearing to have been through a shredder. Gashes split the flesh, though no blood escaped for none flowed through the veins.

"Master?"

"Aye?" Ian's mouth moved as he leapt, haphazardly, from the saddle.

"Spread the word, I am to be called Master." Ian replied before vanishing deep into the keep.

"Absolutely!" The toran boomed overly ecstatic of the news. Hundreds of leagues away, the soul of Ian howled, pained as it felt the body's anguish. Thunder began to clap, rain began to fall.

"Ian?" Valquee questioned, in her heart she sensed his pain as her pace drew to a standstill. She and the other elves were still sprinting towards Gesshlon, though they were drawing weak. Elders were sacrificing their feed to the younger riders who they felt were more worthy of life. Some of the aged had fallen victim to starvation. Even Hivell needn't question Valquee for he too felt, faintly mind, Ian's pain.

"What do you suppose happened?" He asked Valquee.

"I feel it in my heart. Ian's body, wherever it may lie, has just been sabotaged."

"Please father, we are famished, we need rest even if we lack sustenance. We are wet and chilled to the marrow, our spirits are dampened, and we wish not to proceed."
Lord Guwhyon was unfit to handle rebellion from his people, for it seldom occurred.

"But I—" seeing their long faces, he sighed deeply. "Oh very well, rest your weary souls."

"Bless you father!" One shouted over the rain and bustle as one by one, elves flopped exhausted to the muddy earth. Resting felt wonderful as they drifted unintentionally into a hypnotic state; an elvish slumber.

No sooner had they drifted off, had they been roused once again by their lord. "Wake, hurry, for we are blessed!"

"What, what is it?"

"Food, not elvish food, but sustenance nonetheless."

"What..., oh you seriously think we should eat them, I've never seen beasts like them."

"No matter, they seem to be enjoying the rain. Wait until they surface than take a quick shot. Snap, done, feed. Get the point?"

"No, but they will!" An elf joked as he nocked an arrow fletched with swan tail feathers.

Twang, went his bowstring. "There is supper for whomever wants it." But none of the elves moved.

"Angels and devils! It is only an overgrown worm. Must I do all myself?" Lord Guwhyon complained as he pulled the worm from its hole, and pulled, and pulled, and pulled. The worm had to have been at least sixty feet long. Dividing it into manageable portions, Lord Guwhyon eyed his folks. "Light me fire, all of you, now!"

Some gathered fuel, others tried to birth flame. No matter what the role, however, all struggled with their tasks in the pouring rain.

The Occluder poked the head of Ian through the door to the chambers of the shadowed dragon, Nighdrake. Once the initial shock subsided, Nighdrake gazed curiously, almost lovingly at him.

'Ian?' The dragon's thoughts filled the soul of the Occluder.

"I'm not Ian you fool, I am your rider and master, Farrizon, I just stole Ian's body. How do you know who Ian is anyway?"

No answer came. Nighdrake simply howled in misery, and howled, and howled, and howled. In his heart he actually thought Ian had come to rescue him from the trap he was forced to live in only to find out that Ian had been slain and his body stolen. The whole duration of his mourning, Nighdrake caused the room to quake and downpours to fall, flooding the chambers.

"Shut up, you worthless beast!" Ian roared.

Nighdrake silenced.

"Your work is impressive, you have learned a lot, but I must tell you what I came here to say. I have other business I feel worthy of tending to, though you must continue to practice solo for a while. Just review and refine what I've taught you and you will do fine. I will see you later." Turning on the spot, the Occluder slammed into the wall expecting the pass through it. Remembering he inhabited the body of another he did his best to mask his blunder as he slipped through the door. Behind him, Nighdrake chuckled silently to himself.

The passing of the prairies seemed endless, when at last Xsealiadd and Etar reached Oursjour woods. As they plunged deep into its depths, it was hard to ignore the feeling of being preyed upon. Skin crawling and hair-raising, Xsealiadd and Etar scanned their surrounds. Being distracted, Xsealiadd stumbled upon a prodigious tree root.

Tumbling to the ground, his hourglass rolling away, Xsealiadd passed out. This was a side effect of the jostled hourglass.

"Xsealiadd? Xsealiadd!" There was nothing Etar could do, especially since an immediate concern which demanded his attention overwhelmed him as a gathering of befoullers surrounded them.

"What is a Folklander doing in our woods?" The befoullers challenged, their pallid gray complexion moistened under the blazing summer's sun. Etar did his best to talk his way out of the situation as, out of his peripheral, he saw Xsealiadd stir.

"Where am I? Who are you? What am I doing here?" Xsealiadd asked disoriented, his hourglass had made him a day younger.

"Not now Xsealiadd!" Etar mouthed as he did his best to talk Xsealiadd free of the situation. His success came at a terrible price. Offering his own blood in exchange for Xsealiadd's free passing, he proved to Xsealiadd his loyalty by paying the ultimate price.

"Etar?" Xsealiadd mumbled still confused.

"He's dead wizard! Anyhow, we have allowed you risk free passing for a limited time. You better hurry though, before we change our minds."

Without a word, Xsealiadd scuttled along, his heart shadowed from the loss of a loyal companion.

Ian's soul continued to drift as he did his best to recover lost time and distance. Though as a spirit he could travel, Ian was ignorant to know how to move quicker than molasses on a cold January's day. This meant it was a breeze for the elves to out manoeuvre him at any given moment.

"Very good, the world is chilling and your soul must be warming." The shadowed dwarf appeared from no place. Halting his movement, Ian nodded his ghostly head in response to the dwarf. Ian, however, was not concerned with the conversation at hand as he gazed past the dwarf far off into the distance.

"What is it, no, no, don't tell me. Let me guess, did you become separated from your fellowship? Do you wish to find them? I am right now, am I not?" Ian nodded vigorously. "See, that's just the issue, we spirits, we travel slowly, though you wouldn't think. Anyhow, if you pay me close attention, I can teach you a quicker means of movement. With it, you can remain by your companions' side, with ease. Are you in?" Suddenly, Ian's attention was glued to the shadowed dwarf.

"Well, okay. For starters, the main issue with normal travel as a spirit is that you fatigue with ease, your soul fades quickly, and it's hard to maintain focus. I know because every spirit is the same." The ghostly dwarf began to pace leaving gray smoke trails in his wake. "Today I'm going to teach you a little secret about spirit travel. There is a slow way to move, which I'm sure you have learned. That way is easy. However, and this is where things get really interesting. There is also a way to achieve fast movement of the spirit. This form of travel is so quick, you'll be able to out manoeuvre even the quickest beast, even the dragon on wing if you wish." Ian's eyes grew wide with excitement. "Let me demonstrate a fine example." Vaporizing into a cloud of mist, the dwarf condensed a minimum of a hundred feet ahead. With patience, he waited for Ian to catch up using the slow way. "Now, I'll show you if you wish to learn." Ian could not nod more enthusiastically as he approached the shadowed dwarven mentor.

"Okay, well, your soul desires to be free, right? It is simple enough really. Let your mind rest, stop trying to focus. I'm sure you're tired of doing so anyway. Holding your form is exhausting work. Just let go. Clear your mind of all clutter, think of nothing." Ian cocked his head puzzled. He'd never done this before. "Okay, try this. Imagine you are part of the wind, try to remember or imagine what it would feel like blowing against your cheek, stirring your hair. Then try to let yourself blow free, let yourself go." Ian's profile began to dissipate, fading into the world beyond. In the sky, rain began to fall as it rolled silently from the leaves of the trees. Ian's mentor was crying, tears of joy from the ducts he did not have.

"Beautiful my lad, simply marvellous!" Ian had vanished to the wind. Disappearing himself, the shadowed mentor reappeared near an oak. "Now focus all your soul on rejoining me here, now." The shadowed dwarf coached as he indicated a spot before him. Slowly, very slowly, a fog drifted before him. Falling low, it condensed to form a mass which took the shape of Ian, who portrayed his cloudy form.

"Oh bravo, superb!" Ian's mentor boasted as the wind surged, causing the leaves to rustle, which sounded like the whole forest was applauding Ian's efforts.

'It must be a fluke,' Ian thought. 'Trees can't clap.'

"Now all you must do is practice, practice, practice my dear boy."

Searching the barren landscape frantically, Ian saw nothing.

His mentor was gone.

Chapter 11
Scorch

The rain had subsided giving way to a healthy roaring flame as the elvish travelers roasted the worm in preparation for consumption.

The sun had sunk behind the Sundurr Mountains, giving them a mysterious, orangey glow. That is the issue with residing on the western side of Ellezwrainia; days are always prematurely cut short as the potent mountains swallow the sun like a hungry wolf consuming its nightly feed.

On the edge of the eyesight of the travelers, vegetation began to stir. Hearts a flutter with panic, many drew weapons unsure of what to expect. Breaking free of the overgrown tangle of enormous thistles was a beast no bigger than a pony though its profile suggested something more full and stout than a small horse. It was evident by its silhouette in the rising moon; its head was lowered to the earth as it seemed interested in odours permeating from the atmosphere.

Though its features were not yet clear, evidence of something strong and muscular was overwhelming. Upon each and every footfall, the beast's body rippled with strength. Faint tapping blended with the sounds of thump, thump, thump which echoed on each footfall of its enormous paws. Another sound also competed for dominance; the sound of something large being dragged. The most peculiar feature was the sparkles of blue which flashed before the moonlit sky.

Many elves grew confident they knew what the creature was, and that it meant them no harm as they lowered their weapons. Ones that were unsure lowered their weapons once the beast meandered into the dancing firelight. The creature was, at that point, confirmed as a dragon youth with unthreatening intentions. Sniffing about like a dog, its nose to the soil, the dragon located what it was seeking.

The smell of the cooking worm was so overpowering it drew the youngster all the way from Gesshlon, a still two days journey away. It was the fault of the elves, they were upwind. Before it could be stopped, the dragon had consumed the elves entire rations of worm before curling up upon their raging fire, turning it into smoulders.

With a few blinks of its enormous, orb-like, watery eyes, it tucked its head beneath one of its tiny, out of proportioned wings as it grew still. Just then the undergrowth roused once more. Immediately the elves readied their weapons to a fighting stance. A fleeting motion which was quickly abashed as the elves grew to a realization that it was their dragons lurking in the bushes.

One, a fire engine red dragon, which Valquee recognized as Blazzan, her dragon, slipped over and nipped the youth on the tail tip causing it to whine and turtle behind another of the great beasts.

'Pleassse excussse him he'sss jusssst a dissssobedient ssssquirt!' Blazzan apologized to Valquee.

"I am not upset by any means; he is after all a youngster."

'A foolissssh and dissssobedient one he isss.'

"He is so cute, who is he?" Valquee asked curiously.

'Hisssss name issss Ssscorch.'

"Scorch!" Valquee exclaimed watching the little one bounce about. Suddenly emitting a tiny sneeze which sent wisps of smoke furling skyward from his tiny nostrils, Scorch shook it off, before sneaking up and nipping at the heels of a bigger dragon. Again, Scorch earned, yet another, nip to the tail. "Scorch? You know, I really think you should have named him Smoulders." Valquee smiled.

'Well, you know, like all youthssss, Ssscorch'ssss ssssaliva hasssn't thickened to molten yet, we are making an effort to feed him firebane, sssstill, the little ripper doesn't take it well though."

A second dragon, a Silverstream nuzzled Blazzan. Valquee could hear complex coos and babbles as the dragons conversed in their native tongues.

'Oh yesss,' Blazzan began once again. 'Ssstreaksssss hasss jusssst reminded me, there'sss ssssomething we need to dissscuss. It'ssss about Ssscorch. We learned ssssomething about him, about hisss parentage.'

"What?" Valquee was curious.

'Nighdrake issss hisss father.'

"What! Well, will this affect him if the time comes for him to bear a rider in the..." Valquee glanced around, "...unfolding of the prophecy?"

'Well you know, the prophecccy thing hasss been unfolding now for well over a decade. The time quickly approachesss, ssso no, I do not feel thisss will affect the ssssquirt. All the sssame, however, I feel it'ssss bessst he issss not told until the clossssing of all eventssss for fear it may affect how thingsss come to passss.' Blazzan paused.

"Fair enough, so how do you know this?"

'You were alive when the firssst riderssss came to be, you were one. Nighdrake wass a brethren to usss, young and foolisssssh mind, much like Ssscorch here, it'ssss hereditary, like dad, like boy. I sssstill remember the day he russshed to tell ussss when the Occluder failed to sssee, that he impregnated the finessst female who'ssss sssscalesss glinted like sssparkle on the ocean. A Bluefrill dragon. Ssso yesss, before you asssk, Ssscorch issss a mixed breed. Part Bluefrill, part Nitesssshade. We acctually knew thisss when you brought him to usss, even hisss parentage, Nitessshadesss sssparkle purple beneath the sssun, hence the Acklesss Academy colourss. No purebred Nitessshade would ever glint blue like Ssscorch, it'ssss the only reassson we took him in. Ssscorch issss the only mixed bred dragon in our colony or ever in knowledge of our hisssstory; no one truly knowsss the hisssstory of a Nitesssshade. Poor Nighdrake had no other choiccce; he had to interbreed to keep part of him alive.'

"And his mother?"

'That Bluefrill wass Teargo'sssss dragon, hasssn't left her cave sssince the collapssse, sshe'sss barely alive, a dragon needssss to feed. Come, we will take you to her. Come Ssscorch, it'ssss time we leave.'

Scorch, however, as per his usual disobedient self, was not listening. There was nothing there, or so they thought. Scorch, however, knew different. The ancient prophecy stated that he was destined to bear the boy of the foretold in the battle of the Occluder, while Scorch bested his father. Though the dragon was young, he was not foolish and unwise disregarding what people thought. He knew he had to bite the boy to call him his rider, he just couldn't figure out how.

Digging and nosing the ground and air, Scorch searched frantically for a way to get at the boy when a great maw came seemingly from the skies. Picking up the little dragon of black, the great dragon turned southward to follow the herd, a wiggling Scorch clamped in its toothy, gaping grip.

Ian's soul had been materializing and dematerializing for hours before he at last spotted the elves at camp. A fire raged before them as they were preparing a great worm for feeding. The closer Ian drew to them, the better he could hear their merry conversations. He found Valquee and sat down beside her, kissing her on the cheek, though she would never know, he thought about how much he missed her.

Valquee quaked, her neck prickling. "Ian?" She grew quiet. Suddenly, something drew Ian's gaze as well as the gaze of all others, as elves everywhere sprang up, weapons readied. The bushes stirred and even Ian himself drew tense, though in his heart, he knew he couldn't be harmed. He worried for the others, others such as Hivell and Valquee. The creature stirred as it nosed its way into the fire's glow. It was hard to ignore the relief that washed across the elves; it was only a dragon hatchling, one that looked familiar. Suddenly, everything began to move and stir. The world became alive with colour, pictures, thoughts, and emotions. Even basic sounds, flowed seemingly from nowhere. Ian had no idea of the goings on. His eyes scanned for the source of the emotion, the buzz of energy that made even him antsy.

It happened so quickly, an entire herd of dragons exploded over the horizon and through the nearby trees, their scales aglow with every spectrum of colour's richly vibrant palette. Ian let himself absorb the world. The more he took in, the more he realized that amongst the colour, thoughts, and emotions, words were being woven into phrases. At that moment it dawned on him; he was hearing the minds of the nearby dragons.

One conversation was more potent than the rest. It was Blazzan, and he was talking with Valquee about the baby dragon. Ian gasped as he listened to what Blazzan had to say. There is such a prophecy that is still unfolding; Scorch's father was Nighdrake, the shadowed dragon Ian faced a year past. All of it was startling information.

Coming to his senses, Ian leapt back. The dragon youth was digging, clawing, nosing, and biting the very air Ian inhabited. Remembering he couldn't be heard, Ian did his best to ignore this unusual behaviour to eavesdrop on the remainder of Blazzan and Valquee's conversation. Soon, the dragons trickled off, the elves in close pursuit. Curious to hear more, Ian didn't even hesitate for a moment as he followed close to Valquee.

As per usual, candles hung lazily over the long table, giving the illusion of weightlessness. It felt very strange, especially for

Thyle to gaze upon Ian, a boy he attended class with as his master.

"Greetings." It was still that same icy voice emitting from a teenager. "I am sure you all know by now that I have embraced, and enjoyed the inhabitation of the body of a boy I have grown to loathe. This is not why I have called upon you today. Long ago, I have poured my heart and soul, as well as the soul of another's, my dragon Nighdrake, into two items, a crown and a scale. When these two objects are joined, we will possess power beyond any wildest dreams. With these trinkets united I will become reincarnated; I will look as I once did. For now, my happiness is true, but it will only last as long as this decaying body will allow; which is why I cannot remain with comfort. Therefore, I must excuse myself from my post as I travel to distant lands to find what I seek. In my absence, you will answer to... Cano, who'll be my first mate, congratulations Cano, you have just been promoted."

Nearby, Cano groaned with dread.

"Thank you, this meeting is adjourned; I will be departing upon a fortnight." Scraping his chair across the floor, the Occluder vanished from the room through the grand wooded doors. A concept so strange to him, for it had been a long while since last he owned a body.

The walk across the open plains from Oursjour woods was a lonely one without Etar. Nevertheless, Xsealiadd looked forward to reaching Villowtown and more specifically, Sam, the shopkeeper of "Craft".

Xsealiadd's loneliness didn't last long, however, as he approached the great trades road. People, horses, wagons and oxen, to name a few, came and went along the busy artery of Ellezwrainia. What surprised Xsealiadd the most, however, was when a carriage actually stopped on the roadside. Out of this carriage, an oriental chap gave Xsealiadd a friendly greeting. Next to him, his wife nodded, her lap burdened with a basket full of edibles. Being neighbourly, Xsealiadd approached the carriage side, only then did he recognize the couple.

"Hayashi, Ming?" Nodding with a smile, Hayashi leapt from the driver's bench.

"How Xsealiadd?" He asked, coming around his carriage and taking a wide breadth around his temperamental oxen. His and Ming's fluency in common tongue was, by no means strong.

"I am fine Hayashi, how about you?"

"Grand, superb. What an elder such you doing wander the lands Ellezwrainia?"

"Well, actually, I am trying to get to Villowtown."

"Hop on then, we pass to Dillead, trade grain, we drop you on way."

With grateful appreciation, Xsealiadd boarded the wagon, wedging himself amongst the sacks of grain as well, Hayashi's and Ming's two children.

"Ooh!" The young boy admired.

"What it?" The girl asked indicating Xsealiadd's hourglass.

"It is an hourglass." Xsealiadd responded as he wrapped himself around it refusing to budge, guarding it as a dog does a bone. It was obvious: this was going to be a long and weary ride.

"I see your focus and hard work has delivered great rewards, you have grown into a very handsome ghost. You are white, this is a promising sign; it means your heart is pure." Ian eyed the dwarvish mentor, peculiarly. "I have a few yes or no questions for you which I am curious about. To answer, simply shake or nod your head, okay?"

Ian nodded.

"Do you have a sense of self? I mean this as, do you know who you are? When you feel angry say, do you understand, oh, I am feeling angry now?"

Ian thought this was a rather foolish query, of course he did. He nodded vigorously.

"One more thing, do you understand or relate to the passing of time, as in, if I say you've been dead now for four weeks, do you understand this?"

Ian nodded again.

"Excellent, then it is time we move on. Time has come, for me to teach you basic communication one oh one. Not words, you are not ready for those yet, no. You are far too unstable to sustain sounds yet. Thoughts and images, this you can do. Do you feel the presence of my soul? You should be able to."

Ian nodded once more.

"Feel my energy, my vibe, and latch onto it. Do this similar to reading the mind of the living."

This particular skill came easy to Ian; he did it enough in the world of beating hearts.

"Good, share with me a memory, any of your choosing."

Putting as much power as possible behind it, Ian injected several potent pictures into the soul of his mentor. Firstly of him drinking the potion, the second of the pain and blackout he experienced, and thirdly of Valquee mourning his death.

"Hmm... so this is how you met your demise huh?"

Ian nodded.

The shadowed dwarf grew silent.

'Is it possible to speak with her?' Ian pondered, thrusting the question to his mentor.

"Her? Who's her?"

Ian reminded him by pouring images of Valquee into his mentor's soul.

"Oh dear! No, I don't believe so. It takes great power to push words and thoughts far across the barrier. This is something even I struggle with."

Leaves began to wilt and fall from above as nature cried Ian's tears.

Great time had passed before anyone spoke, and it was Ian who cut the silence, it had to have been. It was obvious the dwarvish mentor refused to utter a word while Ian was grieving. 'So I guess I will never speak to her again, huh?'

The dwarf's eyes brightened. "Not so, of course I am a touch optimistic."

'How do you mean this?' Ian grew excited.

"Oh, silly boy! Have you not questioned or even noticed why others in this world appear normal, full of colour and spunk, and you appear snowy white?" Ian shook his head. As he thought about it, he wondered why he didn't notice such a peculiarity or why he didn't even question it before.

'Why is that?' He thought hard, ensuring the dwarf would comprehend.

"To get colour in the world of shadow, you need to have your body, or at least have it in a deathly state." At first Ian was confused, after awhile, however, his eyes widened.

'Do you mean to say I'm not dead?'

"Not completely, no."

'I do not understand, my body is dead, I watched Valquee's mate carry it away.'

"Just because you have no breath, does not make you dead, and there is absolutely no point in me trying to explain something that'll make your brain whirl. Besides, I get around, your body never made it to Rulan. It is being used and enjoyed by another."

'Who?'

"The Occluder."

'How can this be, he's dead also!'

"Half dead like you. As long as his crown and scale are intact, he will live on."

'Oh.' Was all Ian could come up with, he didn't understand anything about a crown and scale, he'd barely heard of such a thing; as well, all this information came to him far too quickly for him to digest.

"You look confused Ian, so allow me to explain about the crown and scale—"

'I already know a bit about them, Ian admitted, memories trickling back to him.'

"Is that so? What do you remember?"

'I remember the Occluder had created a powerful S.P.E.L.L. and that all he needed was his crown and a single scale of his dragon, Nighdrake, to preserve it. This S.P.E.L.L., would reactivate and remain so, as long as the crown and scale remained united. This S.P.E.L.L. basically preserved his immortality. That is all I remember.' Ian informed.

"You remember well, if you'd like, I can tell you a little more, I have ears, I get around, I know lots." The dwarf enticed.

'Sure.'

"Okay well long ago, after this S.P.E.L.L. as you say, was cast upon the crown and scale, the Occluder held a very important meeting. During this gathering, he bestowed the crown and scale to two of his most faithful Carddronne's from his circle of loyalists. One of these servants was a fellow named Samuel, or Sam as many called him. It was Sam's role to safeguard the crown with his life; he was told, since it was the Occluder's first crown after being appointed the throne, it was of great importance. Sam knew the Occluder more than that, he wouldn't expend such a valuable slave on a worthless item; this thing had a deeper meaning. No matter how much Sam pressured the Occluder on its importance, no information was ever revealed.

Now, being a friend of Xsealiadd's, Sam, after finding a way to break from the Occluder's circle, began to investigate the meaning of the crown, even to this day, with so far, no such luck."

'How did Sam grow to be Xsealiadd's friend in the first place?'

"Oh, you are just so curious aren't you? Right full of ponderings you are. Sam was born to parents who believed solely in the Occluder, he grew up in a heavily shadowed background especially the fact that he lived out most of his youth in the shadowed lands. There he enjoyed hunting a great deal. As a teen he was sent to learn at Ackles Academy, it was there he got summoned, as well, learned about his fascination for magic—"

'—oh, what's summoned?' Ian had never heard of the term.

The dwarf laughed whole-heartedly. "To be summoned is to be called, nay, forced upon by the Occluder to be his slave. He basically breaks into your head and says: you're mine, anyhow, Sam's fascination for magic, that's where I left off... Sam wanted to excel in magic, so he came upon Xsealiadd who lived on the grounds in a shabby shack. Sam would always run to him with homework he wanted help on. It was then they began forming a strong bond. Soon, Xsealiadd began to trust him, and began to show him more and more. When Sam's parents found out who he had hooked up with, they were furious; threatened Xsealiadd's life and did all they could to try and stop Sam and Xsealiadd from communing. Soon Sam promised to cease his and Xsealiadd's friendship. During the summer, Sam accompanied his parents in their meetings with the Occluder, being a new rising Carddronne; it was often forced upon him. The Occluder had him do more and more tasks to ensure his devotion. Sam soon dropped out of school. Fulfilling the Occluder's pledge, he continued on as a devoted servant, whilst on the side he pursued his love for hunting, selling his meat to the butcher. It was around now he became a servant of the circle of loyalists; you know where the Occluder puts his favourite men. This is when he was bestowed the crown. Curiosity getting the best of him, he rekindled his relationship with Xsealiadd so together they could seek answers for the crown; as well, it was then Sam decided he wanted out, so he pursued that path, eventually falling out of the Occluder's circle of loyalist and from all existence, at least to the Occluder. Using his savings, he opened a magic store, the one you probably know, he called it "Craft". Using the tools and instruments he sold there, as well as his own knowledge of the matter, he began to try to unravel the mysteries of the crown. You'd think the Occluder would come looking for his crown by now... with Xsealiadd's help, Sam quickly excelled in the ways of magic and with ease, climbed to the apex of the magic triangle. Do you know the magic triangle?"

'S.P.E.L.L.'s stands for special practice of energy through life and language, a type of magic using your body to channel energy to do whatever the desire. Enchantments, is favoured by the elves as it controls nature using the Rukkian tongue. Of course, on the apex is Craft, which focuses on theory, books, and the heavens; to depict stories, fortunes, prophecies and of course, to recite, mainly from script, insanely complex magic; often in the language of the gods. Now tell me, how do you know so much about Sam and all?' Ian queried.

Ian's dwarvish mentor hesitated. "Because long ago, I was his friend not that he really knew much at the time. Ever since he broke his relationship with Xsealiadd at Ackles Academy, Xsealiadd had asked me to spy on him, ensure his well being. I was in his year. I followed him right up until Sam rekindled the relationship with Xsealiadd years later. It was during this time we grew close, though I never admitted it to him, or anyone for that matter of my watchful intentions."

'And the scale, what do you know of it?'

"Pried from Nighdrake's nose it was given to Rennaux after the Occluder defiled it with tainted magic. Rennaux was the Occluder's second man, probably still is. Rennaux promised to conceal it in a place no one would ever think to look. Said he'd tell no one of its whereabouts. Probably never did. Rennaux is one of those types who would take something to the grave; a grudge, a secret. Probably thought it was funny to not even tell his Master Occluder knowing him..." The shadowed mentor trailed off leading to a pregnant pause.

Ian seized the moment to ask another pressing query.

'If I am half dead, how do I return to the living?'

"I don't know."

'And why do I see Valquee as black, as black as a snorg? And that's another thing, why do I see snorgs as white, as white as myself?'

The shadowed dwarf tried to mask his confusion. "In this world, black masses are souls who are affected by evil. We usually refer to them as tainted souls. As for the snorgs, I have never heard of such a thing."

'Valquee is not evil, and not dead either!'

"I don't know, maybe it's a side effect of your potion."

'Most likely, have you seen one of the snorgs lately? They are all weird and stuff. At first, I didn't even recognize what it was, at least I'm assuming it's a snorg, but I still could be wrong. I mean, it shared the same profile and all.'

"Look buddy, you're really confusing me here. Your elf friend, she is as normal as they come, and snorgs are always shadowed even in the world of the dead. Their evil just runs too deep otherwise."

Ian was taken aback. 'I do not understand.'

"Nor I. Perhaps you should talk to a snorg, ask them how they see themselves, but I doubt you'd get one to talk to a pure spirit such as yourself, white ghosts are always pure." The mentor added quickly.

'No thank you, I just want to figure this all out, and if I can, find a way back to the living dimensions; leave this strange existence.'

"And I shall guide your hand on this quest, my dear lad."

"Grab some boats!" The Occluder growled in such a way the servants were amazed he could get Ian's voice to sound so vicious. "We head north!"

"Aye, aye sire!" A servant responded as he nodded at the gate guard.

Sardon's pier was more like a boat launch with barely more than a dock which spanned way out into Gaunfaux flood. Somehow or another, it was able to sustain fairly steady traffic to and from Sardon, and still maintain a healthy fleet of small boats. That fleet, however, was often exhausted once the Occluder and his men decided on a voyage.

"Master, I do not feel this to be a wise plan, observe the sky and sea, the waves are choppy and I fear great trouble and damage on the dinghies part."

With a sour look, the Occluder withdrew the dagger he had sheathed at Ian's side and stained it in one foul swipe with the servant's blood. Once again, he appreciated that he had a body, anyones body. It was something he had waited for, for a long while. The last time he remembered having one was over ten years ago, and he forgot just how handy and convenient it was, bearing stuff upon his person.

    Cracking his neck, the Occluder scowled. "No one doubts my word and lives!" With great cheers from his men, the Occluder sneered. "Well what awaits you slimes, breakfast!" Stepping aside, the Occluder allowed his torans to dog pile the deceased servant. Gore flew as they indulged in a feast they considered to be fit for a king.

    "I am terribly sorry you boys could not join in, it looks to be a scrumptious feast."

    With a great shrug of the snorg's broad shoulder, they, without order, began to prepare for the voyage ahead.

Chapter 12
The Alpha King and Queen

At last the elvish travelers caught up with the beasts of scale. It wasn't anything like the reunion Valquee expected. Barely breathing a syllable of salutation, she had found herself ducking, her head shielded, praying for life.

The moment their gazes connected, Scorch, the dragon youth, had charged right at her. Realizing they would collide, Valquee dove to the ground at the last possible heartbeat, missing Scorch's springing talon by a shorble's whisker. Upon landing, however, the dragon failed interest in Valquee, or any elf for that matter. Once again, it began nosing and digging frantically at a spot on the ground. Unknown to all, right at Ian's feet.

'Ssscorch! Sssstop!' A purple dragon hissed, dragging the youngster away.

'Viovess, leave the youngssster be. Can't you sssee he'sss jusssst horsssing about?'

'We do not horssse about, we're dragonsss!' A great white dragon stomped its great ivory clawed foot, leaving a great crater-like impression upon the soft soil, icy breath escaping the corners of its maw without intention.

'Ssssettle, Quartsssel, Viovess issss right. There'sss ssssomething there, I feel it in my heart, Ssscorch issss jusssst curious asss issss the ressst of ussss. Whatever'sss there, I'm sssure would appreciate ssssome ssspace.'

Valquee stared at the great hole dug by Scorch. She was quiet, her heart was crying with hope. "Ian?"

'I am here Valquee! Why can't you hear me?' Ian shouted with his mind and heart from across the barrier.

Sensing others were watching her, Valquee shook her head vigorously. "This is foolish," she commented before drifting away.

'No, no Valquee no! I am here, listen to your heart, it tells you true!' Ian begged pointlessly.

'Come, we gather for the ceremoniessss jusssst over this dune, many have already come.' The message spread from many reptilian tongues as the words touched both dragons and their riders.

It suddenly dawned on Ian, he was hearing all dragons. Their words, their thoughts, their world hummed with colour and emotions.

'Hey uh… um…' Ian paused; he never learned his mentor's name.

Materializing before him, his mentor was right on cue.

"It is true," he replied simply. "We have forgotten to exchange names. How silly of us. Grunkle, you?"

'Ian.' Ian thought simply.

"Pleasure." Grunkle thrust forth his massive hand. Ian shook it as best he could.

"What troubles your heart?"

'Sorry?'

"Well, you must've called me for a reason, other than to exchange names. Mind you I did thoroughly enjoy that experience."

'Indeed, I just wondered why I can understand all dragons while I heard none when I lived.'

"Oh yes, of course, I keep forgetting how little you understand of this world. In this realm, there is no ranking of smarts, intelligence. A flea is just as important, just as significant as a dragon. Here, we are all equal. You will be able to hear all, because all souls are free, free to think, free to feel, and even free to share. I should mention, however, there is a way to overcome this intelligence barrier during life also; it is, though, a great deal more difficult. Very few can do it, for its complexity is, as I said, extremely high. Ones who can are called great harkers. It means great listeners, one who hears all." Grunkle explained, seeing Ian's confusion.

'Oh—' Ian began, however, anything else he was about to say got lost in his throat. He was growing amazed at the population of attendants at the funeral. Men, and even dwarves, who were never chosen as riders because of their iron hearts were present. Ian recognized Belron, a human rider, and even Habber, a dwarf he once got into a spat with.

Ian noticed almost straightaway, Lord Guwhyon, the elvish Lord of Rulan, standing up front near a very majestic bronze coloured dragon, which Ian assumed, belonged to him as dragon and rider.

Clearing his throat, Lord Guwhyon began for the first time in months, in common tongue. "Greetings one, greetings all! This here is Auzze, she'll be your speaker this fine afternoon, I, Lord Guwhyon, will be her interpreter for those who are not great harkers." The dragon's voice swelled in his head as he began to translate. "Thank you all for bestowing so much support, we are honoured as a dragon race to have such caring riders willing to traverse across these great lands just to be with us; we are grateful. As you know, this is not just about a funeral of great sadness, but a joyous time when we bring forth a new and noble alpha king. Our dragon race have passed into the late hours of the night with little chance of subsiding, discussing which of our herd members would be worthy to bear the title of alpha king. Many names sprang forth from dragon tongues, and though all seemed worthy of the title, none, and this saddens me greatly to say, have, in our hearts, rightfully earned such an honourable title. When we thought we had exhausted all our efforts, one more name seeped into our ongoing discussions, one we could not ignore. This particular dragon had endured more pain, and more suffering through her lifetime than any dragon could ever imagine. Long ago, she had lost her mate and partner of life to a rider not deserving of the title. She watched as her mate slipped into the world of shadow, only to be imprisoned where feelings, thoughts, and words could not reach. During this time, the only one who stood beside her through it all was her noble rider, dear Teargo. Just recently, however, news had befallen our ears of this rider's passing. How much misery is one dragon required to bear?"

  Off in the distance, Ian could make out with tremendous ease, a noble roar filled with misery and pain.

  "This female who has endured so much is now left with only a son too small to understand, and a herd who would support her choices every step of the way. Ladies and gentlemen, please welcome and congratulate, Ocenna, our new alpha queen!" Stepping upon a mountainous cliff high above everyone's heads, and nearly all eye lines was the most dismal, scraggliest, pathetic looking dragon Ian had ever seen. At first he doubted it to be one of those noble beasts, but then it shook, its scales clanged together causing a great chiming, the scales shimmered and sparkled like the twinkle of the sea. It was obvious, the dragon was proud.

All doubts of this dragon's rule quickly ebbed as the gathering got swept to their feet with emotion. Somewhere amongst the cheers, Ian could make out someone muttering. "It's about time some good luck passed her way." And even he a ghost of shadow, could not subdue his emotions. Leaping high into the air, he made a great cheer of whooping, yes, he actually made a sound.

Ian stumbled, startled, 'how did I do that?' He questioned.

"As per proper tradition—" Lord Guwhyon's booming voice projected into Ian thoughts, distracting him from all else "Before she can properly be named alpha queen, we must receive a blessing from each of the pure folk four." Auzze was then joined by Ocenna who had swept to a stiff landing after descending from the cliffs above.

Auzze, bowed her scaly head in appreciation, and across the mental pathway, thanked Lord Guwhyon immensely.

"Auzze?" A gruff voice barked unintentionally. "I am an ambassador to the dwarvish tribe; I cross the lands of Ellezwrainia fulfilling orders of my king. When we received word of yon choosing a new alpha queen, the name we heard at first startled us. After a great meeting of the tribes, we saw no reason to reject yon decision of the new alpha queen. Please, my name is Gizmo, I am an ambassador to the dwarven tribes; I am here to deliver a blessing from the dwarvish clans five to the new dragon queen, Ocenna. May you become a proud ruler any dragon would envy and obey." Following custom, Ocenna, dipped her powerful head in acceptance.

"And lastly, from the men, I am Lord Danahi, lord of Hethrowe. I am here on behalf of all men to deliver a blessing to the new alpha queen. Your choosing is sound. Ocenna, you will grow into a fine ruler."

Great whoops, roars, and applause filled the air, only to be escalated when Auzze touched her snout to Ocenna's brow. One by one, the dragons followed suit, even little Scorch, who had to be lifted by the scruff by a full-grown just to reach, as during the ceremonial events, it was deemed inappropriate for the new king or queen to bow to anyone, including their children. When all of the dragons had touched Ocenna's brow, a small glittering gem formed between the eyes. As bright as a blue star, it almost seemed to float there.

Once again, Lord Guwhyon's voice sliced through the cheers as he translated Auzze's words once again.

"A new alpha queen is born!—" he was again cut off by more sound-splitting rejoicing. Giving up, Auzze stepped to the shadows, in her place, Ocenna stepped forth. Still, Lord Guwhyon had to speak.

From the other side of the barrier, Ian continued to observe. Mysteriously involving into a great harker, he was able to tell that Ocenna was speaking to Auzze, who relayed her words to Lord Guwhyon. It was a long train of interpretation, since she lost her own rider who would have done it for her.

"Firstly—" Lord Guwhyon began, "I apologize for my delayed words. Without my rider, a gateway to your language has been very difficult to me. Teargo was a fine rider, as fine as they come, but we shan't dwell on the past. He will forever remain my rider deep in my heart. With that aside, I have been chosen to rule based on my hardships. My dragons feel, since I've had it rough, I would be a better leader, that in my opinion, is not the best way to decide who shall guide them. A good leader is one who is strong, brave, and is pure to the, right to the core—" depression leaked from her every word.

Something out of custom happened then that had not been done before. Valquee, her eyes reddened, her body trembling, rose upon the great rock next to Ocenna. Tears were streaming down her cheeks.

"Why are you not these things; strong, brave, and pure to the core? Your purity runs deeper than most. You resist evil when it stares you in the face; you were strong to still be alive when you've lost so much; and bravery, I know none braver. You look around in the midst of the fray and you see your brethren falling and then you think to yourself, oh it won't be me. And it's not, the storm clears, and you still endure. Yet you look around, and all your friends fell at the hands of battle. You don't want to be there, you don't want to go on. Your loved ones hold your hand; give you a reason to live. Then when you finally heal and finally have moved on, when you think life is finally grand, they are ripped from your grasp. Once again, the sky darkens as you wish it were you, yet again your heart still beats to the rhythm of the wind. These wounds never really heal and to have to live through them and try to heal from them again and again, it leaves great emotional scars. You want to die; you don't want to go on knowing that all you've lived for is gone. Yet you still press on; not for yourself, but for those select few, perhaps the ones you did not even yet know, who will reach out a hand and ask for you to guide them. To live for that reason and that reason alone, means that you're the most selfless soul one could ever wish to know. We have one right here, one who has lost so much to live for yet endures. Lying so lost and alone, depressed in her cave. You have all made the right decision, you have asked for her to guide you and by doing so, have given her that small reason to live."

The atmosphere swelled with support. Ocenna lowered her great head in response. The noise ebbed to a pregnant pause. When she was sure all would remain such, Ocenna began again.

"It is true," she began, the words escaping Lord Guwhyon lips. "Every spoken word from this fine being. Any who have not experienced terrible loss cannot know what it's like, lying in a cave praying for death to take you, all hope lost. Moving on, it was one of the hardest things I've ever done but nothing compared to having to do it twice. I didn't know if I was going to make it through yet, you held out your hands and asked for me to lead you through. Without that, without a reason to go on, well, I would have given up. I was nearly there. So thank you all, for giving me a second chance at life." Ian swore this was the loudest cheer yet, but eventually, it too died off.

Ocenna still remained on her rock, looking vastly more proud than earlier, she finally appeared to realize that she had a purpose.

"As your new queen, it is my first duty to deliver more sombre news. The reason I have been blessed here today with such a calling, is because yet again, another has departed us. Let us pay tribute to the fallen king of gold."

"To the alpha king of gold!" Voices everywhere filled head and ears.

"The Golden King, his many years of guiding us, cut short at the hand of evil while trying to fulfill the plea of his rider. Though I feel it appropriate to pay respects to his memory, my heart grows saddened dwelling on his passing. Remember him for what he was, and respect why he left us. Do not burden yourself with tears of sorrow, he would not want this, no dragon would. Now, Valquee, do you possess the Golden King's remains?"

"I do." Valquee replied.

"Please, place them before me now." Stepping forth, Valquee emptied a bloodstained, cloth sack to the ground at the feet of Ocenna. "Thank you Valquee let the ceremony begin!" Ocenna remained silent and still. Yet, one by one the dragons, knowing what to do, touched their snouts to the remains. Upon contact of the first muzzle, a small drop began to form. Each touch made it grow and grow. The drop, which shimmered like a tear, encased the remains of the Golden King. The bigger the tear became, the more golden it had turned.

The last to have touched it, was Ocenna. With a delicate touch of her nose, gentle enough to not even harm a flower, the tear ascended. A vast bubble hung naught ten feet off the Earth. Opening her powerful maw, Ocenna bathed it in flame, soon, other dragons joined in the act.

The bubble grew to a golden hue as it rose higher and higher. All watched it ascend as flame died in Ocenna's throat. It was not hard to miss even against the blazing sunset of reds and golds. The glow that danced around it was eternal as all gazed at it with sorrow-filled hearts.

"Every dragon has a star, now his will glow forever." Lord Guwhyon interpreted for Ocenna. From somewhere deep in the crowd, a great wail filled the silence. A great nose was being blown like a trumpeting horn.

"It's such a shame seeing such scales go to waste." Gizmo, the dwarf, commented.

"Excuse me!" Ocenna was offended deeply.

"It's just, why would you send such great scales to the sky when they can be reused as armour to save the life of another? They would make a fine mail, strong and beautiful. Strongest armour ever made."

A nearby elf rose to challenge the dwarf. "That would be an insult to his life, to not let the traditions unfold."

"I still don't see the problem with saving the life of another. We could even make it for you." The dwarf struggled to mask the greed in his eye.

"Because, dwarf, the dragon scales are the most precious gifts the dragon could bestow upon a fortunate. They are meant to be given, not taken."

"But we would never take, well, we would after presenting a hefty amount of gold. Dragons always want gold for their hordes. After all, dragon scale armour is made by the rich, for the rich."

Ian thought this was ironic. 'Wouldn't the rich just buy their way out of battle so they need not fight?' Ian thought to himself.

A great argument broke out amongst the races, subdued only by Ocenna's threatening behaviour. "Enough!" She stomped her powerful feet. "We are fighting like we used to. None of us want to go back to that. Now, if you cannot calm yourselves, go home, but it would sadden me greatly to see you part, for as tradition goes, a great feast has been prepared to be consumed in the Golden King's memory."

"—and, to celebrate your new lease on life."

"Yes and that too. Now come, the more the merrier!"

Ian looked up to the golden bubble. It was high in the sky now, and it was only then that Ian noticed it was not alone. Many bubbles shining every colour of the palette winked with the everlasting shimmer of the dragons of ole, hanging high above to watch over their herds.

Tearing his attention away, Ian drifted solemnly to where the great festivities were unfolding. Great foods of all kinds were burdening down rows upon rows of tables. The dragons, being so vast, ended up eating over the shoulders of others. Depressed as he was for not being able to join them, Ian couldn't help but smile as he watched the little dragon Scorch bounce around like a dog with too much caffeine.

Seeing Ian's long face, Grunkle dragged him wayward. "I think it's time that you learn to speak."

Chapter 13
The Promise

"Okay Ian, speak!" Grunkle ordered abruptly. Ian was surprised at Grunkle's sudden outburst. Nevertheless he chose some words with care and sounded them out. A soft whisper of a voice erupted before becoming lost into the wind.

"Ah ha! See, no sound. You need sound boy, and sound births with energy. Energy disturbs air which vibrates, conducting your voice, to me ears."

"You're nuts!" Ian aired pathetically.

"Sorry, what was that?"

Ian only shook his head.

"Do you know what a spirit is made of?"

Again, Ian shook his head.

"Energy, energy you need to charge as charged energy makes noise, a hum mind, but it's a start."

"How do you charge it?" Ian aired.

"Absorb as much energy from your surrounds as you can, store it deep in your core until you can't hold no more, then let it explode to the world beyond."

In no time, Ian had the world humming a merry tune.

"Great now it's time to put the two together. This time when you release your energy stores, speak. The energy will disperse slowly, mixing with your whispers thus creating a voice.

I must warn you though, this voice will sound nothing like what you're used to, it will be foreign and sound much different to your ears."

"Why do our voices sound different? ...Hey wait a moment, I'm actually talking!"

"Very good, your voice is different because it does not come from your heart but from the air you move."

"Oh, fascinating!" Ian drew quiet and observant. Before him, Valquee was stirring amongst the flourishing crowd of eating folk.

"Ocenna, you do not have to speak just listen to my words for I have something to say. Please do not get an interpreter, I wish this to be confidential." Valquee provoked the scraggly, blue beast.

Rousing from the feast, Ocenna turned her tail and walked away, Valquee's heart sunk, she felt alienated. She soon realized, however, this was not the case as Ocenna observed her with care from about one hundred feet away. Valquee then understood, Ocenna was allowing her a moment with the two in private. Valquee rushed over, she didn't want to take more time than she needed.

When she got within range, Ocenna took her great powerful wing and draped it over Valquee and herself like a massive tent.

"Wow, you really do respect privacy don't you?" Valquee was awestruck.

Ian who listened from the other side of the barrier, could not hear. Making a quick decision, he materialized right into the tent with Valquee.

"First off," Ian heard Valquee start, "I appreciate you taking precious moments out of your celebrations to allow me a couple of words. This is certainly a sorrowful thing I must tell." Ocenna dipped her great head in assurance.

"When I gathered the organs of the Golden King, I learned a bit about the one who killed him; his name is Nalo, and he belongs to the dragon slayers of Aardvark. I'm sure you feel the same as I about his doings, and like I, wish him justice. I have been thinking. I wish to avenge his death. Yessiree, I wish to march straight into the heart of Aardvark, to Sardon's front gate if need be to track down this slime and be done with him. I'm sure you can relate to my burn for revenge. Since my child I was supposed to teach is dead, I have no more obligations to fill, so what better purpose than to spend my life avenging the Golden King."

"Valquee, no! Do you have a death wish? Don't go to the shadowed realm. Not with ten thousand could you survive his wrath." Ian pleaded uselessly.

"...I have a death wish Ocenna; all I live for IS gone. I am going to ask one favour. Should I fail to return, only then can you tell the others where I've gone. And should I fail to return, I want Hivell to sing me to the trees. He'll know what by that is meant. Oh, and congratulations again on your new lease on life, you will become a fine ruler, if not already. I promise to avenge the Golden King's death. On this, I vow with my life."

Ocenna nuzzled Valquee affectionately before releasing her to fulfill her pledge.

Waves ripped at the hull of the tiny dinghies as the Occluder's servants battled the rough waters.

"This was a very unwise idea; whose plan was this anyway?" A servant complained as he threw his weight against a straining oar, his muscles in his neck and arms bulging.

Ian, whose body was stolen by the Occluder, snarled. "Well it was my idea so does this mean you're calling me stupid!" The Occluder growled.

"No, nope, absolutely not!" The servant puffed hoping to spare his life.

"Well then put your back into it and stop whining!" The Occluder ordered.

"Yes master." Pushing the oar against the swirling currents, the servant strained as the little boat was blown wayward on a new course, colliding with a boulder.

CRACK! It was an ominous sound.

"Uh master?"

"What!" The Occluder roared.

"I have just snapped an oar."

"Well that was smart of you wasn't it? Get paddling! This boat shant move herself!"

"Paddle? All the way to Villowtown? With what?"

"Your head? I don't know, find something! Blasted slimes! How thick can you get? You don't know how close I am to chucking you to the sharks about now. No! Not to Villowtown, to shore! Fools!" The Occluder was in a rage. "Got to make a new oar somehow!"

The servant opened his mouth before quickly shutting it again. He hoped the Occluder failed to spot the action as the slave quickly decided against telling the Occluder that there were no sharks in these rivers, the water was fresh and shallow.

Pulling to the shore, the Occluder, and his men formulated camp. "Now cut down trees! Burn fires, carve spare oars and for gosh sakes, someone make me supper!"

"Yes master!" Servants replied as one, before quickly consuming themselves with work.

"Grunkle, who is Nalo? I understand he killed the Golden King and that he is a dragon poacher who works in shadow, but who is he really? I mean as a person." Ian questioned.

"I - I don't know, the name rings a bell but no. But I mean, I should know him, why can't I remember; I - I did know him, I know I did, why can't I remember?"

"Relax, you don't know him, you don't know him."

"But I should know him, it's like knowledge that should be there but isn't, you know what I mean?"

"No not really, no."

"Oh, okay. Anyhow the more I ponder about it, the more it angers me that I've forgotten. I do know, however, that Nalo belongs to a guild."

"A guild, what's its name? Where does he attend it?"

"Again, don't know and don't know. Wish I did though, I wish I did."

"Do not anger yourself, I was just curious." Ian comforted, seeing Grunkle's frustration.

Off in the distance, Valquee was flitting between shadows, keeping away from activity, remaining unseen. Her primary focus was to get away before any realized what she was doing.

At long last she slipped away unnoticed; a fully laden travel pack was strapped to her shoulders along with her bow and quiver. The arrows themselves were a strange sight, for during the time at the dragon gathering, Valquee had spent time and care swapping and gathering arrows; which looked as unlike one another as possible. This, unfortunately, required her to swap a great few from various tribes of men and elves of distant houses where markings were different. This strategy, she hoped would keep the servants of Sardon questioning her origins.

Ian could not bear to see her go and, without warning, began trotting toe in toe with her. When her pace quickened, Ian focused on materialization and dematerialization strategies to keep up.

Much to Ian's dismay, an unforeseen problem arose. Scorch also had managed to break free of the dragon herd and was following Valquee and Ian's shadow to Sardon.

Though Xsealiadd thanked Hyashi and Ming immensely, in his heart, he was grateful the trip was over. The carriage stunk of mouldy clothes and stinky feet; the road was bumpier than he remembered, of course this could be due to the lack of padding on the seats, including his, as well the bumping of his wearing bones.

Not to mention Hyashi's and Ming's children: Squirmy, squirrelly, and rambunctious as children often are, they drained Xsealiadd of every ounce of energy he possessed and still he had to find a way to protect his hourglass from being jostled. Nevertheless, due to their kindness, he had made it to Villowtown in at least half the time.

Though his anxiousness to locate Sam was overwhelming, his hunger was more so. It, therefore, took little self convincing to recess and replenish from his travels.

He seemed very out of place, wandering the nearly deserted streets of Villowtown, searching for a place to rest. Coming to a halt before the most neglected, dilapidated, building imaginable, Xsealiadd readjusted his pack. Above the door, a faded sign hung rather pathetically and crooked. If one was to strain their vision, they would come to the realization that the sign read, "The Dragon's Cavern" and beneath that, in flaking gold lettering, barely seen to the eye: "Inn and pub, travelers welcome" was also written.

For Xsealiadd, however, there was no need to read such signage, he knew the place well. Parting the creaking door, Xsealiadd was faced with a rickety flight of stairs, which he knew would lead to the lodges. Instead, however, Xsealiadd took a sharp right into the pub. Though it didn't seem so outside, it was fairly busy within these walls.

Broxxan, one of the town's famed storytellers was working the rounds tonight; he had the crowd in an uproar as he concluded a great story of ole.

Xsealiadd eyed him with caution as he shifted for a barstool. Flopping down on a high stool he watched the bartender dart from customer to customer. Grabbing dusty wine bottles, the barkeeper poured wine into the grimy glasses.

The pub itself was once an old library which went out of business as customers shunned its material. It had been boarded up for eight years until about six or seven years ago.

It was a rainy summer's day, the streets were quiet. In fact, the only sign of life was that of an elderly wizard who, in only a few hours would be the new owner of the abandoned library.

It was the first day of autumn where we return to Xsealiadd who we find drinking away his troubles. His heart calming, everything was easing rather well for him. It was turning rapidly into one of those days when everything is going so well that it is believed, falsely, that nothing can go wrong. And why not? Xsealiadd had worked hard, hiking across the countryside just to get here. He had his hourglass, as well, Sam's crown, for the moment, few troubles weighed his shoulders. Apparently, however, Xsealiadd had forgotten just how common disturbances were in this pub.

Daydreaming about days gone by, and concerning troubles he'd soon have to address, Xsealiadd gazed dreamily at the bartender; not realizing that someone had been prodding his shoulder.

"Xsealiadd? Xsealiadd?" The dry, husky voice barked.

His senses returning, Xsealiadd suddenly realized that he was being poked. He spun on his stool, nearly upsetting his tankard. There in front of him was an elder, a parchment in his hand. Wearing a black hooded cloak, his black beard nearing the floor, the veiled man hobbled close to Xsealiadd. His crooked nose, mirroring Xsealiadd's in appearance, barely came above Xsealiadd's heaving breast.

"Xsealiadd my dear friend, my voice is wearing and the crowd desires more, why don't you tell them of the prophecy of hope?" Xsealiadd grew angered. "What? No how've you been? We haven't crossed paths in an age! Though your hood veils you from eyes a prowling, you can't fool me! I know who and what you really are, Broxxan the storyteller. If this is what the people see you as then why don't you tell them? You seem to have it all figured out." Xsealiadd swivelled away but for only a flash before he grabbed the rear of Broxxan's tunic. Once again, Broxxan acknowledged his presence. "And I was never your friend." With that, Xsealiadd swivelled his back to the storyteller the last time.

Xsealiadd tried his best to calm his person as he drank deeply from his tankard. It was unsuccessful. Broxxan had upset him too greatly. Swivelling about, he acknowledged the crowd and Broxxan who began the telling of ole.

"Long, long ago, long before the time of the Great War, and even before the birth of the Occluder, a prophecy was written, a prognostication which will shape our years to come. This prophecy states at the time of the great alignment of the stars and planets, a child will be born..." Xsealiadd shook his head with disgust. "The child they named Ian and on the moment of his birth, any who saw him, bowed to his being. They were so proud being blessed, at last, with hope—"

"Rubbish! Utter and complete rubbish!" Xsealiadd fumed flying to his feet, his stool toppling over with a clatter. "If you desire to tell a story of such great importance please get your facts straight for I can't take it any longer!" Xsealiadd paused, panting with fury. His shoulders were held back unconsciously and all eyes were upon him. "No one truly knows the forming of the prophecy, it was written long before the ages as we know them in a language foreign to us. Deciphering it alone was nearly impossible for the script was penned in a format which has grown extinct. In this prophecy, a boy born to the shadow and purity would emerge when shadow and light clashed in the skies. During this time, a halo appeared as the light soon prevailed. The prophecy also stated that this child's name would be Ian, his parents had no choice. Ian. Ichor for the blood of a God, your blood. A for atonement, sent by the gods to make the Occluder of shadow pay for his wrongdoings, and, N for necromancy; manipulating the shadows of one like the Occluder for the purpose of shaping the future using magical means.

"The magic is there, I feel it in my heart. This child is the only one who can do it; he must impale the Occluder upon the blade of Amity."

"But how? The Occluder is dead!"

"Not even I know, it's no matter anyhow, for the child himself has recently passed into the shadows. He has been murdered. I heard it recently in the telling of the gods. Though I do not understand, the prophecy is still in motion. If the boy was truly dead, it should be coming unravelled."

"You say I'm full of rubbish!" Broxxan snorted irritably.

Xsealiadd, weary as he was, seemed to drift across the pub in two great strides. Grasping the storyteller at the front of his cloak, Xsealiadd stared into the shadows of his eyes. "At least I know what I'm talking about." With a great throw, Xsealiadd had Broxxan to the dusty floor. His profile, like many of the footprints, we're clearly definitive in the film of dust coating the planks. Needless to say, it had been neglected and was in dire need of cleaning, not unlike much else in the pub.

With a great snort, Xsealiadd exited the pub, his tankard left barely touched in his wake.

The camp the Occluder's men birthed was rough and haphazard, perfecting its details was relatively low on their priority list.

"Where is my supper? I am absolutely famished!" The Occluder, still inhabiting Ian's body, was being very sour. Sitting on a log clad entirely in dragon scale armour of black, which once were owned by Nighdrake, he observed his men like drones to a queen.

"Master, if you continue to eat like this, you shall have none left." The servant rebutted foolishly. To worsen the matter, his stomach chose that moment to belt out a great growl of protest. The servant grinned sheepishly as he realized the severity of his blunder.

The Occluder scowled greatly.

"Perhaps it will be a good thing if I starve thee of thy rations as to starve out the idiots. You must apparently be reminded, you are my slaves. You do as you're told. No matter, in a few moments there'll be one less mouth to back talk and to feed. Who here is willing to roast me my most palatable feast. One I've longed for, for over five hundred years?" The slaves cheered. "Aah, excellent. Roast 'im!" For the remainder of you, stoke me a fire, hunt me game for our travels, cut meat, make oars, come on chop, chop!" All of a moment and activity exploded about the camp. The Occluder observed them dragging the unruly servant away, screaming and protesting.

"You would think they'd learn what comes of back sassing my rule. You've learned your lesson, haven't you slime?" The Occluder turned to a nearby servant who was slaving away at cutting branches for their fire.

"Oh yes, absolutely!" The servant replied without hesitation.

"Good, and don't be so peppy."

"No sir, I mean, I'm sorry sire..." the servant scuttled away before the Occluder got any ideas.

By morning, the Occluder had the fleet once again at sail. The weather had grown fair over darkness giving way for a smooth voyage north; it wasn't a long one, however, as the closer they drew to Oursjour woods, the shallower the waters became. Soon enough, the dinghies were scraping sand and stone.

"Master, our boats cannot proceed they are taking too much damage, we must bank them high beyond those clusters of trees."

"Who labelled you boss!" the Occluder flustered, his dragon scale armour clanging against Ian's body.

"No-nobody sire."

"Exactly, I'm the boss here, and we dock when I say we dock... okay! Bank them!" He ordered, after a rather large scraping emitted from the dinghy's undercarriage. Hauling the dinghies ashore, the Occluder took a great sniff as he gazed about.

"Okay, we proceed on foot; there is no time for stopping we are already behind schedule."

Groaning as one, the slaves burdened themselves with provisions as they proceeded along the tree line of Oursjour. Curious eyes observed them from the branches as they passed the domain of the befoullers. The Occluder soon found his route obstructed as strong, able bodied befoullers barred his path.

"Who are you and what be your mischief in these parts?"

"My dear friends, do you fail to recognize your own king and his men? I know I look different in a foe's body, but look past that, whose soul do you see?"

"Our apologies sire, perhaps we can assist, to what business drives thee?"

"We are trying to pass to Villowtown in warp speed. What would aid me are strong sprinters."

"Alas, we are as you described, it would be an honour to join yon company."

"Indeed, we're pushing through the night." The Occluder's men exchanged glances of nerve.

"Very well." The befoullers snorted, tightening their gear. "And so we'll be off?"

Offering his affirmative, the Occluder ordered his men forth.

Chapter 14
Accusation

Thyle was utterly dumbfounded at the looks he was receiving; the worst of it was he had no clue why.

"Thyle!" A booming voice reverberated down the hall, startling any who had listened. Thyle froze in his tracks, he knew that voice, it was Eemile, the warden of Ackles Academy, someone whom no one ever dared to cross. "Here we are, barely past the start of the year's announcements, and word has reached my ear that you have slain a fellow student over a scuffle!"

"What! Who?" Thyle couldn't believe his ears.

"Oh don't you dare pull idiot on me, have you not heeded, or even heard the whispers that hang in your wake? People want you gone. A good warrior is one thing, a cold blooded murderer, is quite another. You know the proceedings? I must take you to the principal for an accusation as severe as this."

'This won't be so terrible, dad will get me out of this.' Unconsciously, Thyle must've been smiling as Eemile grew even more cross.

"—and don't you think for a moment that you're going to enjoy this. At this academy, we believe the punishment to match the crime. Now, in you go!"

Realizing where he was, Thyle scuttled through the propped open door. "Hi dad—Cano?" Rennaux's office was as Thyle remembered it, except in the big principal's chair of wood, was not his dad, but Cano, another servant of the Occluder's.

"Thyle, what a pleasure!"

"Where's dad?"

"Got held up in Sardon doing the Occluder's bidding."

Thyle stood in silence.

"So can I help you Thyle?"

"Eemile sent me here because I am being accused of homicide."

"Did you?"

"What?"

"Did you kill this person?"

"I, uh—well, I... I really don't know. The last thing I remember is studying how to, uh—well I was doing some reading before I was overwhelmed with—" Thyle glanced around. Seeing Eemile by the door, he chose to play it safe. "I was overtaken by a cold, icy, voice. I blacked out and when I came to, I was mumbling out halfway through the school's anthem this morning after breakfast."

"Aah, I see, well, I'm no detective Thyle, but I'd say you did it."

"Huh? Why?"

Cano simply glanced down at Thyle's entire profile. Following his gaze, Thyle jumped, startled. His school uniform had been saturated in blood.

"Eemile, can Thyle and I immerse ourselves in a private discussion?"

"Absolutely!" Eemile responded, he however, failed to move.

"That means I wish you to part also."

Leaping with surprise, Eemile scampered, awry, vanishing from view.

Cano waited for Eemile's footfalls to recede down an adjacent corridor before deeming it safe to proceed in discussion.

"The Occluder's getting out of hand again, isn't he? Using student hands to extinguish others. It's no good; here you are, absorbing his wrongdoings."

"So what? No punishment?"

"No. But I'm afraid your life will seldom be a gathering of fruits for the next while at this academy. My advice is to lay low until things recede. Also, tell no one you've received no punishment for your crimes. There are few who truly understand the summoning."

"Yes Cano." Thyle paused. "While I have you here, can I question you on a troubling matter?"

"What is it dear lad?"

"You know that name we must say if we want the Occluder to answer us?" Thyle tapped his temple. "The same word he uses to control us with the summoning."

"What about it?"

"Well, in all my reading, not once did I see mention of that being his nickname. I thought the Occluder was his alias for Larke."

"What's the concern Thyle?"

"Well, if it's an epithet, why would he use it to summon us? Do you think, maybe, it is something else? I just don't understand if it's his other name, why does he call us by it?"

Shifting uncomfortably, Cano scanned the surrounds tensely. "Close the door and sit."

In a flash, Thyle obeyed.

"What I am going to say is strictly between us, do you understand me?"

"Never parts from the room," Thyle responded nodding vigorously.

"I think it's a spell."

"A spell? What makes you think this! In all my readings I never came across such spell, are you sure?"

"No, it is only a hunch, however, when I was a bit younger, I was interested in complex magic, and uh, I did some reading myself. You may want to look into advanced Opthopathy studies; it may give you a little better understanding of the finer nuances of such craft. Now, this conversation is over and nothing has been said, right?"

"Yes sir, thank you again." With a great bow, Thyle drifted through the door and down the hall.

'Opthopathy huh? Of course, why did I not think of that before? Ha Opthopathy, think, I just made a joke! Good one Thyle.' Deep in thought, Thyle continued en route to the library to pursue research on the subject in question.

"Go, shoo! You shant be here!" Valquee was growing irritable towards Scorch, who, was not only trailing Valquee, but was sniffing her belongings, stealing her food, burying her cloth, sleeping upon her flames, and when she snapped, her temper raging, she flung rocks at the dragon youth; who happily retrieved and returned them to her with a generous coating of saliva, his scales shimmering and shining with pride.

"Oh, you stupid dragon!" She fumed. "It's hard enough tramping across the plains sunburnt and thirsty. I don't need you to slow my pace!"

Scorch cocked his scaly head, he did not understand.

"I'm sorry Scorch; I keep forgetting you're still a hatchling. Here..." Squatting low, Valquee unfastened her shield she carried on her travel pack and threw it like a Frisbee. Emitting a great plume of dust, Scorch tore after it across the desert. "I still don't see why you find me so interesting to follow." Returning moments later, Valquee's shield in his maw, Scorch dropped it with a playful gleam in his eye. "Oh no, Scorch, try not to put so many holes in it see, don't sink your teeth in it because then it won't bring halt upon a whole slew of arrows, and that's not good." Scorch lowered his head shamefully. Across the barrier, Ian was laughing in hysterics. He never realized a dragon youth was so full of play. Embracing the shield which was now coated in a healthy film of dragon saliva, Valquee threw it skyward. Observing it fly heaven bound, Scorch awaited it to return to the soils before, again, taking off in a cloud of dirt to retrieve it.

"Hmm," Valquee thought aloud. "Doesn't know anything about flight yet, huh?"

Florian watched in awe as his long blade passed in rhythmic fashion across the whetstone. Wok, however, was too simpleminded to grow amused in such a fashion.

"So where's my first lesson Hivell?" Florian queried with wonder as he received his sharpened blade.

"Intermediate level defence against rebelling forces. You train with Magnon this fine day." With a grumble, Florian and Wok drifted with their mentors in toe to the courtyards.

"Today—" Magnon began, "we're going to learn about jousting. Does any here know what jousting is?"

There was no reply.

"What was that, I couldn't hear you over the onslaught of knowledge? You bunch of thickheads!"

Students exchanged nervous glances during the brief pregnant pause. Even Florian, as knowledgeable as he was, was unable to recall the definition of jousting. Though, he was sure he had read it once.

There was an onslaught of emotions pouring from the mentors in such a way Florian quickly formed the notion that whatever it was, jousting couldn't have been good, for every knowledgeable adult was raising noise.

"Magnon you can't, they're too young for that!"

It was only then that Florian realized that the, normally, loudest protester was absent from the group. Valquee and, likewise Ian, still had not returned from their travels.

"Hivell, Valquee and Ian, where are they?"

"Oh dear Florian, you do not know?"

"No."

"Ian has died, and Valquee has vanished. We lost her somewhere around Gesshlon."

"Oh—" Florian grew silent, "excuse me please." And with that, Florian excused himself from the class.

"—Jousting, my class," Magnon cut in, "it's where you and a partner sit astride elvlocks and try to unseat each other, or knock each other off if you prefer, with great spear-like weapons called lances. Now, I know we have never covered the lance in class, but they are rather straightforward to use. Here, allow me to demonstrate how to properly handle such a fine weapon." Taking the lance, Magnon thrust it at whomever was in reach, causing a fuss.

After a few quick demonstrations, and many heated arguments, Magnon had wrestled the students into pairs and assigned them each an elvlock, an elvish horse.

Many struggled with this class, but none quite like Wok, who continuously lost control or fell off his elvlock long before he was meant to. This only resulted in a Wok tantrum, a scary outburst of emotions which grinded the whole class to a standstill.

"We are tired of this sprinting; we go no further until we retain a breather!" A toran snarled. The Occluder had been over exhausting his servants for several days now in an attempt to reach Sam for his crown. The Occluder's men, however, had been forming great protests in retort.

"Fine, breathe. But remember, if you come to look for me, you won't find me, now, are we clear?" The Occluder flashed his blade. "Now tell me, who here has still strength to endure?" The Occluder questioned.

The befoullers raised their hands as one, to them, sprinting was the norm. They, however, were not alone. Joined by the entirety of the snorgs, and some rested torans, they traveled on, leaving the weary to remain and no doubt, lose touch with the fellowship.

The gates of Villowtown were almost within arm's reach by sundown, this, however, did not urge the travelers to bring halt as they pressed on through the final night.

When they eventually arrived through the town's gate, which was just being shut for the night, the first man they saw next to the gate guards was a rather heavyset, moustachioed chap; wrapped in a warm tunic he set the street lamps aglow with a great torch.

"Blasted wind!" He could be heard muttering, "I just can't keep these things alit!"

Trying to be neighbourly, the Occluder nodded Ian's head in a friendly way. As his Carddronnes passed in his wake, they mirrored his actions. It was doubtful, however, that they were seen, for the chill permeating from such abundance of evil, had froze the firelight into oblivion.

The Occluder didn't need torchlight, however, as he was able to find his way to the "Craft" store with ease.

Parting the door with much strength, great honking met his ears. The Occluder snarled as he searched about for the source. Nestled in the corner was a goose, honking a great tonne of racket.

"Quiet you!" The Occluder howled as he tore after the waterfowl. Flustering with fear, the goose bolted, flying, flapping, running, and most importantly, making the Occluder's presence known. Upon every wing flap, some other precious item met its demise upon Sam's wooded floor. Great colours of smoke billowed from the shattered vials and some item was broken that caused it to snow in the back corner.

A great rumbling of footsteps resounded from the creaky floors above as Sam thundered down the stairs that led to his abode on the floor above. Middle aged in appearance, Sam was dressed in a nightshirt and cap, both in disarray. In his grasp, he clutched a short bow at the ready.

"Who are you, and what business do you have in my shop!" He yelled at the shadowed profiles.

"It is I, the Occluder; I come in the body of another. I wish words with you."

"Prove it!" Sam yelled, raising his bow to a firing stance.

"Bouldar!" The Occluder yelled.

Immediately, Sam lowered the weapon. "My apologies master."

"My visit here will be brief, for I am in need in other places."

"Okay."

"My crown, where is it?"

"The crown, uh, what crown... oh, the crown, ha that crown, it uh, it was stolen along with a plentiful amount of my finest treasures. Like one of my own inventions, a potion which swallows light; I really worked hard on it too, such a shame really, I only had the prototype."

"Stolen! By whom?"

"Never knew his name, he's known around these parts as the child thief. Has wild eyes, minimal clothes, and looked like he was starving. But that, that was at least five months ago now, he'd be long gone." Sam refused to tell the Occluder that he sent Xsealiadd in seek of it.

"And you haven't bothered to go and seek it?"

"How can I, I've got a shop to run you know? Family business, I'm the third-generation now!" Sam lied; he opened the shop several years ago when he escaped the Occluder's grasp.

"Are you trying to tell me, that your stupid shop is more important than your master?"

"No, nope, absolutely not..." Sam trailed off, seeing the Occluder approach in a rage. "Master?" Without a word, the Occluder grabbed Sam across the brow, it was like a knife being driven into Sam's thoughts, his dreams, his soul.

"Listen up men!" The Occluder ordered, his eyes were closed as he observed Sam's mind. "The one who stole my crown ran north, Sam also asked Xsealiadd, a dear friend of his, to track it down for him at the price of a dragon staff. Very well..." he mumbled. With a quick incantation, Sam crumpled to the ground, lifeless. "Okay men, let's go!" Swivelling on the spot, the Occluder came face to face with Xsealiadd, who stood framed, dumbfounded, in the doorframe.

Chapter 15

Black versus White

Valquee's thirst was overpowering as she crossed the open plains spanning from Gesshlon to Gaunfaux flood. Almost, it seemed, each day Valquee passed by a tributary of Batten Lake; small streams and rivers which flowed water clean as crystal. Once her thirst was severe, it took nothing to ignore the warnings in her heart, Valquee banked the stream. Filling her waterskin she drank it in great gulps. The water was like liquid ice, most importantly, it tasted funny. She'd forgotten how cold and toxic Sundurr Mountain runoff could be. Toxic, for the dwarves mine so many metals often traces leach into the water, tainting it for consumption. Cold, for the glacier peaks of snow.

Her temperature plummeted. Next to her, Scorch, who was guzzling the water by the wagon loads, began to quake with cold.

Struggling and fumbling beneath the alpenglow to start a fire, Valquee, at last, got the conditions to cooperate. A fire was born, only for Scorch to lie on it and snuff it out.

"Oh S-S-S-Scorch!" She quaked, her fingers blue. "N-n-n-now look w-what you've done!" Scorch hung his head shamefully. "S-s-s-stay there to b-b-block the wind and t-this time, don't lie on it once I get it a-aglow."

It was much easier this time to ignite a flame, with the grass so dry, and the wind being shielded by Scorch's bulky frame, a fire had roared to life. Much to Valquee's dismay, they were not going to go anywhere for a couple of days.

At last, Xsealiadd made it to "Craft", Sam's magic store.

"Ian? No, it can't be." Xsealiadd shook off such a notion. "Ian is dead, and he certainly wouldn't be with a band of snorgs, befoullers, and the odd toran... Who are you?" Xsealiadd asked concerned.

The figure he thought was Ian, cackled a high pitched, icy, poison of a cackle.

'I know that voice.' Xsealiadd thought. "No, not you, please tell me it wasn't you who killed the boy." Xsealiadd was in total shock.

"Fool! How can I kill a boy you've had so strongly shielded?"

Xsealiadd realized his own blunder. "Then how did he die?"

"I would think you of all people should know, the way you monitor and resurrect the dead."

"Death..." Xsealiadd snapped back with an insult "is something, nobody understands more than you."

The Occluder snarled. "How dare you!" He lunged, but quickly aborted the attack. "Wait, you have my crown!"

"Crown, no I don't."

"Don't lie, I sense it upon you, you are concealing the child thief from my vision."

Xsealiadd couldn't believe his luck, 'how could anyone be so stupid, nobody could conceal a child thief upon their person.'

"Give me the crown!" The Occluder ordered.

"I am not your minion!"

"Give it to me now!"

"Never!" Xsealiadd howled.

"Blundah outartoe!" The Occluder yelled, as a spell flew towards Xsealiadd causing the crown to fly out of his provisions. However, quick thinking, Xsealiadd belted out an enchantment of his own causing the crown to freeze in place, just out of the Occluder's reach.

It was unavoidable, a full on battle was about to ensue; wizard versus wizard, good versus evil, and with a battle like this, only one could win.

Standing statuesquely, the great sun scorching her face, Valquee gazed at Gaunfaux flood, her quest at a standstill. Sardon stood beyond Gaunfaux, a water body so vast it would take weeks to go around, Valquee had grown very unsure how to cross it.

The great circle had traveled a fair distance across the sky and was descending so low towards the mountains, it seemed they were threatening to swallow its light forever. Great halos of orange light swelled around the peaks of Sundurr before Valquee, at long last, decided on a course of action.

She would head to the village of Quath, to purchase a wagon. As long as Scorch cooperated, she'd have him pull the wagon to the shore. She would use it as a boat from there to bring her to Sardon.

Spells flew and items shattered, both Xsealiadd and the Occluder grew angry. Occasionally Xsealiadd would grab items from shelves to aid in his magic, weaving Craft the Occluder neglected to use to his advantage.

"You cannot win Xsealiadd!"

"Perhaps, perhaps not. Alas, I shall make your task difficult nevertheless."

The Occluder snarled as he grabbed something from the shelf and hurled it at the wizard. Capturing it with a quick, bony hand, Xsealiadd blew on it, causing it to erupt as a giant cougar leapt from within.

The feline charged, knocking the Occluder, in Ian's body, asunder. Xsealiadd stepped over his foe, his dragon staff was lowered to the throat. Xsealiadd gave the Occluder his entire focus as he ignored the chaos strewn about the floor, as well, the cougar pacing the realm. Out of his peripheral, he caught movement from one of the Occluder's men.

Out of reflex, he immediately reacted. His staff was raised, and he was ready to strike. All was still. Dust danced in the air as the silence was ear-splitting. Tensions were so tight, they could snap at the slightest disturbance.

Out of the moment, an uneasy, shrill voice broke. What it said was utter nonsense to most, but Xsealiadd knew, he understood every word.

His eyes widened, though he had no time to react, it was done faster than it had started. The air swirled angrily as, one by one, the Occluder and his men vanished into the wind. As for Xsealiadd, he remembered nothing more than being slammed into the breast with a hefty weight. His world grew fuzzy as the dusty wooden floor rushed up to greet him. Seeing swirling pictures of great callused hands reaching out, blackness at last took him.

Valquee couldn't believe her gaze, the last time she laid eyes upon Quath it was a peace-filled town, abuzz with activity. It was nothing like what she remembered.

The sky was an angry green, the ground was saturated with muck and mire, buildings were flattened, and livestock were running loose. It was utter devastation. Snorgs traipsed through the streets, holding spears and dragging clubs. It was definitely in the hand of shadow.

Faces kept peeping out windows, faces riddled with fearful expressions. Valquee was just trying to gather her bearings when a child fled through the streets. Valquee tore after her, Scorch at her heels, nipping them playfully. Valquee ignored him; she was too focused on the child ahead. Grabbing the child's scruff, the child yelped with fear.

"Ssh, I won't hurt you. I just want to know what happened here?"

"It used to be paradise, a peace-filled sleepy place, until the Occluder's minions came." The girl panted.

"Why did they come?" Valquee questioned, but the child had vanished. Her footprints in the mud suggested she bolted for an alleyway through two nearby shops.

Valquee wanted answers as she made to follow the child's tracks, on the way seeking others who possessed the information that she desired.

Nearby, snorgs assaulted Scorch about his presence in their town, apparently believing he could tell them. Scorch was scared, his world was filled with black and he didn't understand why he was in trouble as he snapped unsuccessfully at the shadowed apparitions of the snorgs.

Valquee maintained a healthy pace, seeking her answers. A moustachioed man opened his door to fling out some slop. Valquee rushed to his stoop only to be contaminated with filth, she didn't care. Her yearning for information was her only priority. She barged into his abode.

The lady shrieked and dragged her children into a room at the back of the house, slamming the heavy door in her wake. Valquee could hear a board being set across it on the other side. They had barricaded themselves in.

The moustachioed man charged her, the cookware he held in his embrace he was swinging wildly like a savage beast. Bits of food were being splattered about the room. The last thing she remembered was the smell of a brewing stew before she was hit upside the cranium with a heavy cooking pot. Her entrance would likely not have been so severe, had she not drawn her dagger before kicking in their door.

Outside, Scorch howled with agony and rage.

"What has happened to this place?" Ian echoed Valquee's very words; he had never before seen such a dismal town. Next to him, Grunkle shrugged pointlessly, both were at a loss. It seemed, Valquee was too as she had just pursued a child for answers, as if a child would know much.

"You know what Ian?" Grunkle cut the uneasiness. "I believe the time is sure ripe to teach you one final useful thing."

"What is that Grunks?"

"Manipulating things. The ability to, you know, pick up a rock and throw it. To swing a sword, you can do all this when you are dead too you know? To make it even better, you've already mastered the hard part; manipulating energy required for the task. You do the same thing as you talk. Pick up that stone!"

Many short tempers, and raging thunderstorms later, Ian kept the stone focused in his palm.

"Wonderful, now throw it." Ian did, but for some strange reason, the stone remained stuck within his palm.

"Cease the energy field encasing the pebble." This stone fell from Ian's hand with a small plop. "Fair enough, well, goodbye for now."

"Wait!" Ian was startled. "What do you mean?"

"Ian, I have taught you all I know. Practice, you can do it solo. There are many others who need me, please, let me be with them." Turning his back to Ian, Grunkle's form began to fade before clarifying once again. "Just one more thing Ian, should you ever find yourself facing a barrier, one such as a wall or closed portal, it is best if you just materialize onto the other side to save your sanity." Grunkle glanced to where Valquee just disappeared into someone's house. Ian followed his gaze.

"Well, good day to you."

"Wait! And if I ever was to find myself in a predicament where I won't survive alone—"

"—just call, I'll always be listening." With a smile, Grunkle's profile faded to a gentle mist, which was quickly engulfed in the angry, green sky.

Suddenly, Ian felt entirely alone, Valquee had vanished, seemingly for a while behind closed doors. Grunkle had disappeared for good, and Scorch, Scorch was… Ian searched about, he could hear cries of misery, and they sounded suspiciously like a dragon's.

Ian followed the cries.

"Hey, stop hurting my dragon!—my dragon? Where did that come from?" It was time Ian tested his newfound skills. Picking up a healthy sized stone, he launched it at a snorg. It passed the creature right through, that didn't stop the snorg from feeling it though. Shaking its head stupidly, causing its bat-like ears to flap, it searched about for the source of the rock's appearance.

Ian materialized elsewhere. "Shucks! I can't believe that didn't work." He mumbled to himself. Picking up another stone Ian grew an idea. "Foomantacilla erezaurantzé!" He shouted, heaving the pebble at its target. Again, nothing happened. "I wonder why I can't do magic? I guess you must have to havea periatti gland to weave spells, and since I'm dead, I can't. But wait a moment, the Occluder is dead, and he can still do magic, I don't understand." Ian was lost in thought, which, perhaps, was a bad thing as a band of snorgs barrelled upon him, leaving Scorch a moment to recover.

Ian grew to his senses at the last moment. Materializing out of harm's way, he'd bought himself several moments which he chose to scream at Scorch. "Run Scorch, run away! I don't want you hurt!" Ian shook his head as he materialized elsewhere. 'Oh it's no use,' he thought. 'Scorch can't hear me.' As Ian let the thought pass his mind, he looked over, there was Scorch bolting for his life. Ian once more, removed himself from harm's way.

"So he can hear me! I suppose this makes sense. Being a great harker and hearing them, why couldn't they hear me?" All at once, Ian released focus. It was all he could do from becoming harmed by the snorgs. He felt so lost and alone, stuck in this shadowed world, constantly having to defend himself. He was even beginning to grow desperate enough to want to speak to one of the snorgs, which had just tried to kill him, that was if he was alive.

The snorgs stood nearby, searching the ground irritably, nearly forgetting what they were searching for. One by one, they drifted off, their attention span onto something new. Ian waited until only one remained.

"Wait mister, uh..."

The snorg grew suspicious as he tried to search for the source of the voice. "Aak, he finally said at last, my name is Aak."

"Aak, huh? Well, how do you do? Please do not fear me for I mean you no harm." Ian remained an invisible fog to the eye, only projecting his voice into the shadowed realm. "I am just curious, and puzzled to know, how do you project yourself into the world of life, the world of normality?"

"What's it to you? And where are you anyway?"

"Don't you worry about that, I just want to know, because I'd like to do it; I'd like to project myself into their world to see an old friend."

Aak snarled. It was clear he was irritated. "You have to be potent enough to pierce the barrier!" And with that, Aak the snorg, vanished with an unusual pop.

Xsealiadd awoke to a moistened brow. Staring down upon him were his good friends Hayashi and Ming.

"My dear friend." Hayashi sympathized, wringing a dampened rag upon Xsealiadd's forehead.

"No, no stop honey, you do too much! Too wet." Ming criticized, before whisking away the rag and basin.

"We watch whole thing. You hurt."

Xsealiadd grumbled, he was woozy and his head hurt. "Yeah, yes I hurt. The Occluder cast a spell, and made me fall and I've bumped my head." He explained.

Hayashi grabbed Xsealiadd's head on both sides at the temples, and kissed his brow. "There, Hayashi kiss it better."

"I'm afraid—" Xsealiadd began trying to pull himself to a sitting stance. "—magic doesn't quite work that way."

"Oh, magic not working?"

"What magic?"

"Magic, black magic."

"Oh, the Occluder's magic?"

Hayashi nodded his head vigorously.

"The Occluder's magic worked wonders, exactly as he had planned it."

"Then what magic not work?"

"I said, the rules of magic don't allow a kiss on the brow as a cure." Xsealiadd grabbed an invisible head, and kissed it on its invisible forehead. "That," he commented, "it doesn't work in my world, and I'm sorry, sometimes I wish it did."

"No, no! Fine." Hayashi responded.

Ming then broke the conversation as she rushed into the room with some soft feather pillows for Xsealiadd to prop his stiff back upon.

"Thank you Ming." Xsealiadd acknowledged, adjusting his pillows. As he was shifting about, his blanket slid off, just as Ming was re-entering with a pot of tea; to worsen the situation, Xsealiadd himself had just realized he was in the nude as he snatched up the blanket.

Ming smiled, but otherwise brushed off the awkward moment. Acting as if it never occurred, she placed the tray of tea cups, saucers and a teapot between Hayashi and Xsealiadd, pouring them each a mug of piping hot tea.

"So, uh, where are my things?"

"Gone. Shadow took—"Hayashi made a grabbing motion before sipping deeply from his mug. "Aah, lady talent, certainly strong on tea."

"What about my clothes?"

Again, Hayashi made a grabbing motion as his mouth was, once again, preoccupied with his wife's brew.

"And my hourglass?" Xsealiadd questioned, dreading the answer. For a third time, Hayashi's nimble hand swiped at the air.

Xsealiadd gulped, his heart seemed to have become lodged in his throat, Sardon was one place he would be unable to go after, and retrieve his hourglass. This didn't mean he wasn't going to try.

"Clothes Hayashi, I need more than flesh where I'm going!" Immediately, Hayashi leapt up and exited the room.

Outfit after outfit Xsealiadd tried on, none seemed to fit for they were all much too small. Growing impatient and frustrated, Xsealiadd finally just rolled, ripped, and tied the blanket that veiled him into a quilted toga; though he looked foolish, his appearance was a surprising improvement from before, given he had no moths and tatters added to his attire.

"Thank you for all your assistance, but I must be off."

"What about eat?"

"No, no you've done enough, really. Honest."

"You must eat when travel, here." Ming quickly prepared Xsealiadd a travel pack of her most palatable foods; rice filling up the majority.

"Thank you, again, I am forever in your debt."

"Travel in wagon."

"Sorry."

"Hayashi take you in wagon."

"No thank you."

"No, really." Hayashi insisted.

"I can't." Xsealiadd protested. "Really and truly."

"Why?"

"I don't want to offend you, but your children tire me, I am an old man see."

"No, no, no! I no go. Hayashi take you. I stay with children." Ming explained.

"Oh—" Xsealiadd was surprised, but mainly felt greatly of guilt. Next to him, Ming and Hayashi nodded encouragingly. "—okay, but only as far south as Voxille."

With a great surge of excitement, Hayashi grabbed his traveler's cloak off the mantle before making for the door.

"Bye Xsealiadd, happy travel!" Ming blessed.

"Going to Sardon, is not a happy place, or a happy travel for that matter, but I will take your blessing to heart. Thank you Ming." With a great slam of the door, Xsealiadd was off into a future unknown.

Chapter 16
Quath

The Occluder could feel the eyes of his Carddronne's on him, people who looked up to his ways. He couldn't fail, not now. This battle, however, was draining, pushing his magical powers to their utter limit.

He dared not admit it to anyone, especially not his foe; his magical power was on the brink of failure, it had sustained too much use, too much strain. He had exhausted all spells, even the petty weak ones, which deemed useless against a wizard so strong. With no magical use left, he grabbed an item off the shelf, something, which at a quick glance, reminded him of a snow globe. Using Ian's strength, he whipped it hard at Xsealiadd.

The wizard faltered for only a moment; however, his reflexes were too sharp. Catching the item in flight, like a cat would snatch a mouse, he blew a gentle stream of air over its smooth glassy surface.

Even the Occluder, though he concealed it well, couldn't believe someone, anyone, could perform magic so potent with such little effort. Obviously there was an area of magic the Occluder missed.

His eyes widened though he did his best to shield his fear from all knowledge once he saw what pounced out of Xsealiadd the elder's palm. A cougar of immense size was bounding towards him. Correction, make that bounding right at him. The Occluder ducked but it was too late, great paws of immense strength caught him square on his breast. He went down. Though his dragon scale armour shielded Ian's body of all major harm, it still couldn't prevent the wind from being knocked out, leaving him limp and lifeless.

He had no choice, he had to get out, he knew, in his mind, all his strength had parted, this fight had to cease. There was only one way in his heart, he knew to get out without his weakness becoming detected. He must drain a victim of energy to gain enough power to move his entire circle of followers. It would not move them far, but far enough. Drawing upon Xsealiadd's strength, he moved his men across town.

The Occluder opened his eyes near the stables which wasn't too bad for one with failing magic.

"Come men, we gather horses for we must flee this town. Do not rush quick, I have one, a befouller I have left behind, he will meet us here shortly."

"What has held him up?" A servant questioned curiously.

The Occluder rose to his feet, or at least tried to as his legs gave out. Too much strength had he lost in the battle. Xsealiadd had gained much strength since their last confrontation, even with the Occluder possessing a body. This was what made him lose so badly, though he failed to realize it. It takes a much greater amount of energy to move a body than it does a spirit. Bodies move slower than souls, making it harder to dodge, as well as giving the foe a target.

The Occluder panted as he tried once more to rise to his feet. This time two nearby befoullers rushed up to support him beneath the armpits.

"It is honestly not any of your business what orders I provide my servants, however, to satisfy your curiosity, I will tell. I left a man behind to gather up Xsealiadd's provisions. He possesses a couple of things of interest which I'd like to have for exploration of magical means."

"Thank you master for your kind response."

"Yeah, yeah, yeah, now get me astride a horse will you? And what are you slugs waiting for, why aren't these horses saddled and you mounted? Hurry up, I have not all day!"

"Yes master!" And with a flourish of activity, all got down to work.

Valquee parted an eye, everything felt odd, she was unsure exactly why; it was strange like a dream. The world was fuzzy. Trying to clear her mind she attempted a sitting stance. This was greatly difficult as her hands were bound.

"Where am I?" She mumbled, her words were slurred.

"You reside in my abode though your welcome has long since perished." The moustachioed man grumbled with an accent sharp in his throat. Wringing a cloth in a basin, he made a move for Valquee's brow which she effortlessly rejected. With a quick nervous glance to the man's wife for aid, she noticed her belongings propped against a far wall. His wife was no place about.

"What's happened to me, I can hardly think?" She shifted slowly in discomfort, her whole body ached, and heaviness hung upon her every fibre.

"We had to drug you to subdue your violence, my wife misjudged and gave you too much, you nearly perished."

"Oh, my violence?"

"You kicked in our door, a knife in your hand. You meant to murder us!"

"Oh, did I? I'm sorry. I just, I just didn't expect the town to be so, uh, dismal. I'm an outsider just passing through." Valquee couldn't help a quake as her eyes flailed wildly in their sockets, her pupils unnaturally large.

"Drink this." The moustachioed man's wife responded handing Valquee a thimbleful of a coloured liquid. Valquee eyed it with a suspicious gaze, or at least, studied it with the blur of her vision, her symptoms seemed to worsen.

"W-what is it?" She slurred. Her head unsteady, threatening to spill the few precious drops of fluid.

"Calabar bean extract." The man replied with nerves.

"The Calabar bean?" Valquee's world began to spin. "Does it not contain the toxin, physostigmine?"

"You're a smart girl." The moustachioed man smiled from beneath his fringe.

"Physostigmine's poisonous, it can kill."

"If taken in excess, yes."

"I'm not taking that!" Valquee set it away using both hands without a choice due to their bindings.

"The physostigmine toxin—" The moustachioed man began, picking up the thimble, he held it within hands grasp of

Valquee, "—is also used as an antidote when too much atropine pumps in thy veins."

"But I didn't take—" Valquee grew still. Giving the man the dirtiest, sternest glare she could muster with compromised senses, Valquee swallowed the lump of nerves from her throat. "P-please tell me you didn't. Please?"

"Belladonna, we administered it as an attempt to sedate your fury."

"My fury? What are you, witch, and warlock?"

"No I make shoes; Arienna was a housewife, until the king took control, forced her to study as a healer. She learned all herbs and their uses."

"Well, you certainly have a ways to go." Valquee snorted at her ignorance. "—but I'll give you this, you are learning."

The moustachioed man scowled.

"So why'd you bust through our door first off?"

Swigging the small thimbleful of physostigmine at long last, Valquee came around. Luckily things such as ailments don't affect elves the same as man. "This town, tell me and I'll leave in peace. What did the Occluder want with it; it is obviously his work out there."

"I - I don't know!" The man was frightened by Valquee's sudden burst of authority. "He wanted some black book, said he needed to refer to an ancient spell. Said he wanted to release magic that had been cocooned far too long. Wasn't even the first time he came for the book either. Sent a servant this time, wasn't even here to look for it himself. The servant pounded on our portal, he wasn't much to look at. Dark hair, brown eyes, and a full build, real husky on the shoulders. He was mangled, scars all on his face. They weren't normal scars either, black as night they were. He wore armour of black dragon scales and a peculiar emblem here." The man signalled within the premises of his navel. Grabbing a quill and parchment he uncorked a bottle of ink. From behind him his wife emerged without his notice, she unbound Valquee's wrists, evidently trusting her.

With his quill loaded he began to sketch. "It looked like this." He was not a great sketcher but his message was made. Sketching an outline the general shape of a man's torso, pinched unnaturally at the waist and very broad shoulders, the shape reminded Valquee to have been severed at the biceps. Upon where a chest may go, was blocked in a letter "A". Under the horizontal cross of the "A" were two inverted triangles. Those he shaded in. One more block "A" he drew very small as if surrounding the torso's navel. Even before he was part way done, Valquee recognized the symbol as that of Ackles Academy; she should have, she'd seen it enough. When the symbol was looked at as a whole, it formed the face of a shorble, in particular, Ackles.

"A student from Ackles, but it couldn't be, it sounds like you described Ian, but it can't be, it just can't. Please, may I look into your mind to what it is you saw?"

"Why?"

"Because the student I believe you've described has perished to my understanding, though I expect his body to have been sabotaged. Being a close acquaintance to this young lad, I would dearly desire confirmation either way. I miss him dearly, to see that he endures would be a blessing beyond all else."

The moustachioed man grew nervous as he exchanged uncomfortable glances with his wife. To be of support, she nodded and embraced his hand and seated herself by his side, preparing for what was to come. No further words were spoken as Valquee allowed her mind to plunge deeply into his. For a moment, their thoughts merged as one.

The taste of salted pork was thick on her palate. Her moustache quivered as she shovelled food in hungrily, a dash of pepper tickling her sinuses. Withdrawing a stained kerchief in dire need of a wash, she rubbed her bulbous nose before replacing her hanky in a breast pocket. Next to her, a dainty lady who she had known as her wife... his wife, ate peacefully next to her, Conversation was scarce as she asked her wife in a thick accent what troubles befell her that fine day. Only petty talk endured.

There was no warning as the door leading to their kitchen came flying from its hinges birthing tremendous splinters. Behind it, a distraught youth and two snorgs appeared. "—Wait a moment!" Valquee sharpened her telepathy. "That was Ian! But no, how could it be, he's dead!"

The moustachioed man could feel Valquee's presence vacate his mind. Opening his eyes, he saw her crumple to the floor in shock, withdrawing herself entirely from the man's thoughts.

Her body shook from head to foot as she lay sprawled on the floor.

"My lady?" The man was concerned, all anger had ebbed.

"Ian." Valquee whimpered the single, solitary name.

Great time passed as Valquee found herself calming with a tankard of ale, an effective nerve tonic favoured by many. Valquee nearly embraced the brew, slumped round shouldered on the rugged chair, a blanket wrapped upon her shoulders.

"D-did you say this Occluder came before for the same reason?"

"Yes."

"Do you remember the reason then why he wanted the book?"

"I think the same, said something about a dragon though I remember not what."

"When was this?"

"Few months ago, perhaps."

Valquee nodded. "Just one more thing? Why do you think he would target this town specifically?"

"Because the last chap to have read the book lived here in Quath, fell to shadow after reading it, Charon I believe they called him. After which, he threw the book into a foundation of an old fallen watchtower just north of here. The Occluder wanted that information alone."

"Wait a second, how can he throw the book into the foundation after he collapsed into shadow, that just makes no sense."

"Well from my understanding," the moustachioed man began, "you don't fall completely into shadow, not right away anyhow; the fellow looked quite normal afterwards for a great time. Then for some reason, something caused him to at last collapse permanently into shadow though I don't know what. Obviously he is not here to ask."

"Oh, I see... wait, when the attack here on Quath came, who exactly did the Occluder target?"

"Well, I thought you just had the one question."

"Sorry."

"It's okay. When he came, he wanted to see me and basically attacked any who got in his way or refused to tell him where I was."

"What would he want you for?"

"Because I was a friend of the one who fell into shadow. He wanted to press me for information on where my friend hid the book."

"And did you tell him?"

"Yes..."

Valquee grew disappointed.

"I'm sorry okay; I just couldn't bear to see any more get hurt."

"It's fine." Valquee did her best to brush off her negativity. "I just worry what he might do now that he has it, that's all."

"I understand your worry and I share it also."

Once more, Valquee dipped her head, she did not feel up to pressing the chap for more answers. "Thank you. Do you know any here who would be willing to sell me a wagon?"

"Few are left in this town, most are gone, fled from fear however most have given up on their property. Many have been destroyed. I'm sure if you find a wagon intact you can help yourself, it won't be missed. But how do you expect to pull it? No livestock has survived in this town, ones that did have scattered, fleeing with terror."

"Don't worry, I have a way." Valquee smiled weakly. With a nod and a quick gesture of gratitude, she ensnared her belongings and excused herself from the premises. The moustachioed man and his wife pressed their faces to the window like so many other fearful ones in this town; for them however it was to ensure Valquee's safe departure.

Chapter 17
Wagons

If someone were to question, to this day Ian was doubtful he could tell any how he escaped the grasp of the snorgs. Last he remembered he relaxed strain on his heart, hovering as a fog. This was how he spent yet another sleepless night.

Ian missed sleep, to close his eyes on a feather pillow and let dreams ensue. Above this he missed human companionship most, to sit down with, say Valquee, just to talk about his day and problems he faced. Loneliness wasn't his most pressing issue right now, it was worry. Ian had been observing the portal where Valquee had vanished behind earlier that day. Still to this moment, no activity was detected as far as Ian could tell.

Light had died. Night began to pierce through gaps of the high buildings and worry was beginning to ebb to panic, that's when Valquee emerged. She appeared exhausted and shaky, something was wrong.

Ian refocused his form close to, but not barring her way. He unfortunately learned that lesson rather unpleasantly as, more than once, people had passed him right through.

Whatever had ailed her, however, never seemed to slow her pace as she slipped between shadows and structures, evidently seeking something.

She took a brief pause near someone's barn and paddock. Something of interest must've ensnared her eye.

Her pace healthy, Valquee walked with intent ever deeper onto the barbarian landscape. Amongst the brambles was a wagon, rotted and in ruin, one wheel had abandoned its home upon the structure, the other, so rusted, it had seized up solid to the frame.

Valquee tried her strength as she attempted to manoeuvre it. It failed to budge. She panted, her body growing limp, her breath laboured. She was not incapacitated long, she birthed a secondary idea.

Checking the wind she smiled with pleasure, its direction must've pleased her as she, with haste, concocted a fire. Retrieving a great portion of fleshy edibles from her travel sack, she threw it to the flame. Ian soon learned her plan, as, across the wayward fields and fences in ruin, across the discombobulated untamed grasses, a creature was stirring, bounding forth in their direction. Ian had seen that stride before, he knew those contours; it was Scorch, zeroing in on a late day meal.

Valquee waited until the dragon was in close proximity before snatching the cut of meat from the blaze. Dangling it enticingly for a moment from the end of a charred skewer, she flung it beneath the upturned wagon.

Scorch dove, like a frightened child beneath the covers. She must've thrown it far beneath for Scorch had to burrow his muzzle deep under the buggy. It's what she wanted, his shoulder blades glancing on the cart's frame, Scorch pushed hard, causing the coach to ride along his scaly back.

Great snorts echoed from the carriage's chamber, Scorch must've claimed his prize. Minutes passed, the dragon began to back out, this wasn't what Valquee desired as she tried all she could to drive the dragon forth or more preferably skyward. Unfastening her pack she waved it desperately near the dray's rear where she knew the hatchling's nose had been. The dragon continued to reverse, Valquee was downwind. With a stomp of frustration, she rushed to Scorch's scaly rump and gave it a hard kick. The dragon youth squealed before cowering scared beneath the wagon. He was frightened as he caused the wagon to quake.

"Just flip it over dude and she'll leave you alone." Ian voiced lazily. Great colours of reds and oranges filled Ian's heart as the lorry flew upwards and Scorch in the other direction, bolting fearful across the farmland.

The carriage came crashing to its side causing Valquee to utter an epithet which Ian guessed to be a foul mouthed Rukkian phrase.

"I still need you!" She bellowed but quickly brushed it off. She had a buggy to fix.

The ride with Hyashi was a great deal more pleasurable without his kids pestering the riders as they always did.

Pulling to the side of the great trading road, Xsealiadd and Hyashi exchanged fond farewells before Xsealiadd headed south, his toga bundled tightly around him with care. He didn't dare tell a soul his business. He was going to chase his hourglass to the ends of Ellezwrainia if he must but to let the enemy possess it was absolute murder on Xsealiadd's part. Though many spells and magic surround it, it would not be difficult for one as advanced in the magic triangle as the Occluder to unravel its magical puzzle.

The horses traveled hard snorting with exhaustion, on the brink of an all-out collapse. The Occluder didn't care, however, as he pushed his men, with urgency, to get home. Returning to Sardon was his all out priority; he wanted to unravel the mysteries of the hourglass, as well, find the scale: the other half of his spell, the key to unlocking his ultimate power.

They ploughed through the boughs and bramble that barred their way like water on rock. Though a path had been carved through Oursjour Woods, it was by no means wide enough, or stable enough to support both his men and horses; that doesn't mean he wasn't going to try.

It was like a snowball effect, one of the horses tripped in a gopher hole. With a great snap of a fetlock, the horse went down, too crippled, and too exhausted to move. Others soon followed until the ground looked like it was filled with a bunch of crying, writhing, on the verge of death creatures, which some were.

"Rise you beasts of burden!" But they didn't. The torans and befoullers raised a fuss, which naturally, failed to assist the matter.

"Please, we must rest, the horses are exhausted, and we must tend to those which are wounded." One of the befoullers interjected.

"We are not stopping for a beast of burden!" A toran rebutted.

"They are not beasts they are noble creatures, animals which are tired, and overworked."

"They are nothing but slaves lower on the power chain than even you and I, they are here to serve us."

It happened so quickly. One was upon another, swords drawn. Squires of the Occluder began to choose sides. When the dust soon dissipated, few had remained; those mostly were wounded and bloody from wayward slashes of weapons.

The Occluder swore loudly. Many of his men had perished, his horses were weak and battered from travel, and the one with a broken leg was unable to be saved, as with a great swing of the war axe that hung by Ian's side, the horse was relieved of its suffering.

"We stop for feed and rest!" The Occluder announced to a cheering following. Immediately getting to work, they began to prepare fresh horse for dinner.

Chapter 18
The Prophecy

Valquee swallowed her nerves as best she could as they approached Gaunfaux floods western bank. Slow and methodically Scorch strained and whined against the harness of the wagon pull; though Valquee knew it to be an act in an attempt to gather sympathy she ignored him in the complete. Instead, she busied herself with her straps and buckles though she established, many times, that they were sound. She had to busy herself with anything to keep her mind from straying to the task ahead.

It would be insane for her to not be with worry and nerves at the thought of proceeding into Sardon in search of one she'd never met. All she knew was Nalo was a dragon slayer and poacher, nothing more. The same unsettling questions resurfaced that had been resurrecting themselves over the last few days. Queries such as, how will I find Nalo? Also, how will I blend in? Just to name a few. Sitting in the back of the wagon listening to its squeaky wheel was driving her around the bend. She hated having nothing to do but think dreaded thoughts. More importantly, she hated to wait at the edge of the unknown in a way she could not escape. She knew, she promised to do this in a way oaths must be kept, but nevertheless, doubts inevitably flooded her soul. Sickening queries she was unable to subdue.

The wagon grinded to a halt before Valquee was even aware. Scorch stood knee-deep, his talons dug immersed into the silty lakebed, it was all he could do to keep himself oriented in the swaying waters. Meeting Scorch at his side, Valquee unstrapped the harness that connected him to the wagon as he made for the banks.

Scorch stood simply on the muddy shores, washing the grime from his scales, his great forked tongue slithering between his toes. Ian watched him groom and clean subconsciously when a thought struck him.

"Grunkle!" he shouted to the wind. Somehow, someway, Grunkle appeared before him within heartbeats.

"Yes Ian?"

"It is time. Valquee, once she leaves this bank, will be docking in Sardon. I would go with her, but I'm afraid Scorch will try to follow."

"He does seem quite fond of you, doesn't he?"

"Yes. Anyhow, I do not want Valquee to go solo. Even if no one can help, someone could at least tell me if she survives. So could you—"

"—go with her to the eastern shore? Absolutely m'boy, I'd be delighted to assist." Without another word, Grunkle drifted onto the wagon.

Valquee was growing impatient and cross. "Okay Scorch, your scales are gleaming, now push me into open waters." Scorch cocked his head; he was playing around, something that was most obvious to Ian. "If you push this wagon into the water, I will throw you a big hunk of food." Opening her pack, Valquee, once more tempted Scorch with a slab of meat. Scorch charged, bumping unintentionally into the wagon's rear, splintering its board and causing his brow to throb. He stood stunned, blinking profusely. He just couldn't believe a wagon to be so cruel as to attack him; after all, he was just a hatchling, and all he knew was play. The wagon dislodged from the mud and inched forth before settling again in the thick silt. Ian tried to urge him on by whispering into the stunned dragon's ear.

"Push her into the water. When the wagon is floating, you can get your meat." Though Scorch cocked his head, he did not obey. Ian sighed causing waves to ripple. Gathering energy from his surrounds, being careful to spare Valquee from exhaustion, Ian began to focus the power behind the wagon. Slowly, very slowly, it began to move.

Grunkle was elated.

"My boy, you've been practicing!"

Ian couldn't respond. Every ounce of energy he had was being channelled into moving the wagon. Grunkle began to assist; together the wagon began to move easier as it never had time to settle.

Valquee watched the wagon moving without reason. Emotions swelled within; puzzlement, fear, hope, and relief. Unsure of how it moved, great thoughts of doom filled her. Thoughts such as the Occluder's great spells were pulling her into his grasp, like what had happened to a dragon last year who spaced out and found himself near Batten Lake, but he said he had succumbed to an enticing voice; Valquee heard nothing but the whistle of the wind across the open waters. At last relieved she was moving, she grew hopeful at a fleeting thought of merriment that maybe, just maybe it was Ian's energy that guided her along.

None was more puzzled than Scorch as he couldn't understand how the wagon could move on its own accord as he sat poised, one claw-filled foot jutting skyward. His toes were splayed apart, his forked tongue dangling limp from his maw, he was awestruck.

The wagon was soon bobbing in the depths. It was then that Ian and Grunkle parted ways.

"Please care for her, she is my love, and I'd miss her too much if we were permanently parted." These were Ian's last words. With a final wave, Grunkle's profile weakened, though Ian knew, he would never part completely.

Ian stood motionless, for how long, he could not say. If his body and soul were united and one was to see him, they'd think he'd be daft as he stared blankly into the waters that swayed back and forth, back and forth. It wasn't the water he was staring at however, it was his reflection. Yes, Ian, bizarre as it was, was gazing at a face reflected in the waters, exactly as he remembered his reflection to appear. His darkened hair was a little out of sort, and he had dark rims around his sullen eyes, the reflection showed how he felt; so lost and alone. So consumed with himself, he neglected to see what Scorch was doing as he bounded playfully about barrelling over an elder, one of whom Ian never even heard coming. The old man groaned in pain, something masked by Scorch's great footfalls.

It wasn't until the aged chap dragged himself to the riverbank, to splash water on his face that Ian noticed him at his feet. Though the image of the man's profile was black, the same as Scorch's, his reflection clearly showed the face of Xsealiadd. Ian executed a leap, what was even more startling, was that Xsealiadd froze in mid-splash. He was simply staring open jawed, at the water. Clear as day, there was Ian, staring back at him.

He snatched at the water, it was just water. Looking to his side, he saw only terrain, and a small dragon naught fifty feet away gnawing on a dried out animal carcass. With widened eyes, he returned to study the reflection.

"Ian?" He asked, unsure if it was a spell. The reflection nodded. "How did you become a reflection?"

Ian acted out as best he could, drinking a potion and falling into shadow.

Xsealiadd nodded his head, he seemed to have understood.

"So you're trapped with the spirits?"

Again, Ian nodded.

"Listen!" Xsealiadd continued to shout pointlessly at the reflection. "I am going to do my best to pull you free of their dimension, however, it may not work do you understand?"

Ian once more affirmed.

Xsealiadd began chanting insidiously before thrusting his head and hand through the element.

"Take my hand!" Xsealiadd's head shouted hurriedly. Quickly, Ian obeyed, grasping the floating liver-spotted hand. An almost enlightening, airy, vaporous feeling overtook him, one he had felt before. He was being pulled through the realm.

Xsealiadd fell to the ground exhausted; the spell had greatly weakened him. After catching his breath, he seemed more eager to talk.

Ian's spirit, now visible to the eyes, sat crossed-legged next to him as he waited patiently for Xsealiadd to breathe.

"So what happened to you?" Xsealiadd began; he was still out of breath.

"I, uh, I drank some potion, it burned my insides, I convulsed, blacked out, and now I am here. I tell you though, some weird stuff I saw in that world. I saw people such as you and Valquee as black as a snorg. And likewise, the snorgs seemed godly, almost alive, almost floating. I see reflections as they should be and I could hear all thoughts including dragons—hey wait a second, I don't hear Scorch's thoughts anymore!"

"Scorch, is that his name? Well, to hear a dragon's thoughts, you have to be their rider, or, if you are unfortunate, such as me, to not have a dragon to ride, you could become a great harker; though I doubt you even know what that means. But if you would like, I could teach you. And spirits, they always hear everything."

"I do, you know that? I've learned what a great harker is. It's one who can hear all thoughts, provided the creature allows."

"Very good, I should tell you that I am a great harker, after all it is simply an advanced form of magic that I can show you, later. Scorch, right now, is trying to tell me he's hungry and he wants to bite you."

"Bite me!" Ian flashed the dragon a dirty-filled glare.

"He means to make you his rider." Xsealiadd explained unbuttoning his pack and tossing Scorch a generous portion of meat. "So why are you on this riverbank?" Xsealiadd tried to keep the conversation moving.

"I'm waiting for Valquee's return."

"Valquee? Where is she?"

"She is heading to Sardon to slay the one who killed the dragon of gold. His name is Nalo, do you know him?"

"No, she WHAT! Oh dear Valquee, no, I'm coming!" Xsealiadd leapt up, however, Ian forced him back down. He had great strength in spirit.

"Please don't Xsealiadd. She desires no one to know as she wants none to risk themselves on her behalf. Besides, I sent a secret weapon in with her."

"Really? What's that?"

"Grunkle."

"What's a Grunkle?"

"He's a spirit I met while under, he said he'd go with pleasure."

"Fair enough." Xsealiadd tried to relax a bit.

"So what brings you to these banks?" Ian questioned curiously.

"I am seeking my hourglass, again, as well as information about a crown once owned by the Occluder."

"You mean his crown and scale?"

"You know about them?"

"Why sure, I spoke with Nighdrake once, in a very strange way of course, at the year's end. He showed me a couple of memories about them."

"Are you meaning to say, that I have traversed the entire countryside of Ellezwrainia for answers I could've found on my front door stoop?"

"I guess."

"Well, what holds you? Spit it out boy! I would shake it out of you if I could!" Xsealiadd pressured impatiently.

Ian smiled. "Well," he began. "Amongst all his shaded thoughts and black colours, he shared with me this... He had found a way to achieve immortality." Ian's eyes were closed as he tried to recall the specific memory. "It was a rather complex S.P.E.L.L. He took his crown and a scale of Nighdrake's, and uttered a phrase of great complexity. After the S.P.E.L.L. was weaved, all that needed doing, was to unite the crown and scale and it would replenish their strength; give them a body, and provide immortality. The Occluder ripped off one of Nighdrake's nose scales, causing the dragons to rage, fires to erupt, and the Great War to begin."

Though he hid it well, Ian could clearly see tear stains on Xsealiadd's cheeks.

"Is that all?"

"No, when I was with Grunkle. He told me a great deal more on the subject." With great strain on his memory, Ian did his best to teach Xsealiadd the information. "There were other memories too, you know, of Nighdrake's?" Ian commented.

"Like what?"

"Just memories."

Xsealiadd sighed. "You know Ian, you should really share."

"Look! If I thought they would help you, I would. But they won't help you in your quest. Nighdrake shared them with me out of confidence, I do not know if he wishes for any others to know his secrets. Being as it is, I feel it improper to share someone's private memories without their consent, if you really wish to know, ask Nighdrake!" Ian grew short.

"You are an honest, sincere, respectful soul Ian. I honour that. Besides, I have more important matters I wish to discuss."

"Okay."

"Have you ever heard of the great prophecy?"

"I think so, but I'm not sure. Is it the one where everyone's counting on me?"

"Well, yes." Xsealiadd sighed. "And though I have told it many times before, I have never told it in full. I do this to protect you; you are the only one who will ever hear it in the complete. As I tell you, you will see why. And so I begin. The forming of the great prophecy was long before the ages as they are known to us in a language so foreign. Many hands it passed through the seasons. Yet none could decipher it for its script was dead. The prophecy fell to me, and in my great pleas to the gods, fate led me to a place. One I have never been before and have been only once since; a lost, desolate place, where I discovered a tome, still containing text of, at the time, a dying script. It provided enough information that I was able to loosely translate the pages.

"The prophecy begins by claiming a boy born to shadow, who I learned to be the Occluder, though none truly know. As well one born to light or purity as some may prefer, one with a pure soul. This child would birth when shadow and light battled in the heavens. A halo soon appeared in the midst of the fray, shining down upon the child's arrival. Light soon prevailed the darkness as peace soon filled the lands. This child, born over six hundred years ago, would be named Ian. Ichor, bearing the blood of a God. That is the "I". "A", represents atonement, one who was sent by the gods to make the Occluder pay for his wrongdoings. Finally, "N" stands for necromancy. One who manipulates the shadows of ones like the Occluder for the benefit and purpose of shaping the ages as we know them only to form a new age, with a new King of Kings. I should tell you Ian, normally, we have a leader who rules all else, King of Ellezwrainia. The last to have held that crown was slain by the Occluder. It was shortly thereafter, the Dark Lord fell into shadow. Since then, we have never replaced that king, Ellezwrainia has been leaderless. But that is okay, as we all agreed the next to get crowned such a noble position would be the one who slays the Occluder." Xsealiadd paused for questions; he knew Ian must have plenty.

"So, uh, I'm named after this hero, huh? That's cool!"

"Ian, you are that hero. All last year, Valquee's been trying to tell you..."

Ian grew still.

"There is something I should really explain. When Farrizon was king, he married someone whom he believed to be the most beautiful woman he ever laid eyes on. One day, she confessed to him she was pregnant with his child. After backhanding her, Farrizon said he'd kill her if the child was born and people were to find out. She was only supposed to be his servant." Xsealiadd explained. "Anyhow, with his permissions, she retracted her services as a slave and fled north. Settling as far away as possible in the peace-filled village of Solan, she met another, a saddle-maker, who made the finest she had ever seen. He agreed to support her and her child and raise it as his own. They fell madly in love and quickly wed. This saddle-maker adopted the boy upon arrival into our world, named by another, me, your Xsealiadd, as simply Ian. I just told you it is an acronym. Florence was later born to the pair, making her your half-sister. As you know, the prophecy states that the son born to Farrizon will defeat him, blah, blah, blah." It was obvious, Xsealiadd conversed this topic with too many.

"But my parents are normal humans, with a hundred year lifespan, how come they still endure?"

"That is only half true Ian, your mother is not normal, she is a goddess, the goddess of purity and love. She saw the wrath of what the Occluder was doing to such a peace-filled world. She couldn't bear to see it, such a beautiful place being destroyed by such an evil entity. Descending from the heavens, she personally exploited him; ensnaring him with her beauty she used him to create a being so powerful. She knew one day that this entity would best the Occluder; it had to be that way, half of the Occluder's blood flowed in his veins, your veins. But something happened then she did not expect. The Occluder found out her secret, and using dark magic prevented her from ascending back up to the heavens. She had no choice but to remain trapped in our world. Taking on a human form, she endured, raising her child, a god-ling. One who is half god, she prepared him for the day he was to best the Occluder. She met me, and in secret told me her story, her troubles, and that she found someone, a saddle-maker, with whom she had fallen in love. The three of us sat down, and had a great discussion. During this discourse, we all agreed, it was best that I keep this saddle-maker alive to give you as normal of an upbringing as possible. A heavyhearted decision, which they likely still feel was best."

"But when you die, they will too? Won't they?"

"Only your dad, the saddle-maker, whatever name you prefer. And not right off, the spell leaves him with enough time to set his affairs straight. Eventually, however, he will indeed perish."

"Would he know if this spell was released?"

"Yes, don't you ever wonder why he never seems to age? There is one more thing. Since you are the one who is to bring down the Dark Lord, it would be best if I teach you a great deal more, but that's not the only reason. In the last few months, I feel my life slipping through my grasp. I feel weary like too few men trying to shield too great a keep. As much as I hate to admit it, my time rapidly approaches.

"Problem is being peacekeeper, when I perish the blade will shatter, unless I bind another to it, by magic, to the title of peacekeeper. Since I know you must best evil as we know it, and I must teach you anyhow, I feel you the best choosing to guard the blade. If say, you agree, then when you take over as peacekeeper, you have a choice, you can take over the spell that keeps your dad alive, or leave it to perish along with him, you will have to decide."

"Whoa! Talk about information overload!"

"I know, take your time and digest."

Ian was still for some time. Finding his voice after his mind finished processing, Ian bombarded Xsealiadd with queries.

"This spell that keeps dad, well Gardo alive, does it affect the Occluder since he is my real dad?" That was one bit of data, Ian struggled to digest.

"Yes, it certainly does, to what extent even I'm not sure. The Occluder is dead, so I'm positive it doesn't prevent his age from progressing; however, I suspect it will surely interfere with his potency."

"How so?"

"Well, with such a spell active, it is likely, with the crown and scale unified I mean, that the Occluder would be more potent; thrusting his solid form across the barrier into our world, perhaps even more so in the dark realm. Without the spell, his body may only be shadow in our world, and solid in the black dimension. To be honest I really don't know, I'm only guessing on a gut here."

"And without his crown and scale?"

"Remember, he does not have those yet. So it would be as he is now, only shadowed in the dark world, and more so than not, without focus or form."

They drew silent for a long while.

"Xsealiadd?"

"Aye?"

"About my dad, the Occluder I mean, does anybody really know?"

"As far as I am aware, I am the only one. There is a reason I leave it out of my telling."

"Thank you Xsealiadd."

"Much welcome. When I learned it myself, I decided to keep it concealed to protect your reputation. Had people known, they'd expect you to do terrible things, take after your father. You'd never be trusted. You shouldn't have to live a false life you're not deserving of."

"And what about Gardo? I mean, he wouldn't know would he?"

"He knows you're not his, but who is your real father, no, he does not know. I doubt, your mother has told him. Heck, I'd be amazed if she told him she was a goddess."

"What would she have told him then, the fact that she's living all these years?"

"I told her to blame me, tell him that I inflicted a curse upon her and her unborn child to live a long terrible life. I must say, Gardo had a right fit when she said it."

"What about the Occluder does he know of me?"

"Well, he definitely doesn't know you're his son if that's what you're asking. Remember, your mother had you while in Solan with the saddle-maker, Gardo. I'm so sorry. I am so used to not using names in the telling of the prophecy: Gardo. She was already settled with him when you were born in Solan at that point, again I apologize—"

"Wait a second, how could mom have been with the Occluder, he's dead?"

"Your mom conceived you when the Occluder was in his prime, roughly six hundred years ago, like I stated in the original telling of the prophecy a few moments passed."

"This is not possible, I am not six hundred years old, look at me. I'm fourteen!"

"Nothing slips by you does it? No matter, I've been waiting for this observation to creep up for an age. I must say, you're a smart lad. I warn you though, get comfortable this will shock you. What I'm about to tell you will explain how you got that shadow scar across your heart. When you were conceived, the Occluder was nearly shadowed; his body was at a breaking point. Can you imagine how difficult it was for your mother, a goddess of purity and love, to carry a tainted child to term? Evil slows the development and makes it unable to deliver properly. It was Death's intention to imprison you within the womb until both you and your mother fell to his arms, met your demise. What he had overlooked was that gods and goddesses are immortal. You could never die, or at least your mother couldn't, something he should have known considering he's the god of the underworld; but she did get very sick. If it wasn't for my concern for your mom's well-being, and for the fact that we were close friends, you would be dead now. You were born under my eye, and when you were, I happened to look skyward. High above my head, a great halo shone down, I knew right then that you were the foretold. The boy, your mother, the goddess of purity and love created to best the Occluder. You were the portended: the boy of your mother's prophecy. Did you know she sent the message in the stars? That is how I knew; you were very ill, your mother also. Nobody, not even the goddess of love and purity could touch such evil, hatred, and malice without ill effects. Death was angry at your fate, and still, he greatly desired to best you for he is the one who birthed the Occluder; ever wonder why it seems every shadow folk seems to be after you? And I warn you, the longer you live, the more persistent they'll become. The last thing he wanted was for you to destroy his creation. Being who you were, I couldn't afford to lose you, not now, so I, like your mother, kept you alive but not without consequence. You have to understand Ian, a god-ling, someone who is half god, is not immortal, however their lives are long. You can die. That shadow scar on your breast was your father's mark."

"So if this is true, then Death is my grandfather?"

Xsealiadd laughed wholeheartedly. "I guess you can say that, yes."

Ian was quiet; he failed to make eye contact.

"What troubles you? I know this must be hard."

"I'm having a hard time believing you, especially since I'm fourteen."

"You are not fourteen, upon your birth I put a spell on you, one that slows your mind, makes you believe you're still a child; five hundred years now the spell has hung upon you."

"Well why did you put it on me in the first place?"

"I thought it would help you have a childhood. But I was wrong. When I cast the spell I made a fatal error. The spell I have enunciated improperly, since then, I do not know how to remove it. I have spent years, my life even, trying to fix this mistake, it haunts me every waking moment. Because of this, likely for your whole life, unless I can find a way to reverse it, you will suffer moderate mental retardation. You will always be behind for your age."

Ian opened his mouth, he was going to accuse Xsealiadd for being so stupid but thought better of it; Xsealiadd was hurting enough. "So this prophecy's been in play for a long time?" Ian asked, covering his actions.

"Since long before we were both born, but look on the light side, we are nearly as old as each other. Unfortunately, no matter how much training I bestow upon you, you will never be as wise. Hopefully together we can remove this spell, and that will change. Especially since, as I said, I doubt to endure much longer in life and wisdom."

"If mom's a goddess, is Florence also a god-ling?"

"Yes, your mother created her to guide you until your task is done."

Ian was starting to expect the unexpected, learning to not be surprised of what unknown foolishness would come from Xsealiadd's mouth next. "So how old am I really?"

"Seven hundred and twelve, you were born just after the Great War."

"Wahoo! So I do have a chance at Valquee after all! Man it feels great to be a ripe old age, though I don't remember it." Ian felt to be floating. He possessed a very warped view on life.

Xsealiadd smiled. "I am glad you see a glimmer of happiness in all this, though, in all honesty, I very much doubt Valquee to believe this any more than you did at the start; remember she knows nothing of your parentage only that you are the chosen one. She, like most of Ellezwrainia sees you as a young teenager. I must also say, living a long life is both a blessing and a curse; you spend your youth building your world the way you want it, and then in your aging years, you watch it being torn asunder. You come to a point in your life, where, as you look back you realize how very much your memories have faded through time. Remembering fond childhood memories becomes about as difficult as trying to contain water in cupped hands. No matter how hard you try, it seeps away. Then you look forward into no end. The worst of it all is the bitter sweetness of cessation. Every life I seem to touch has, in some way, perished before my eyes. Whether it is by the edge of the blade or by the endless consumption of time, all I seem to meet, perish. Now tell me Ian, do you really feel it great to live an extended life? Perhaps it is good that you believe to be younger than you are, but, perhaps, that may make your life seem that much longer."

"I grow to see your point, considering I only remember fourteen years of mine!" Ian grumbled. "...Wait a second, does this mean when I take over as peacekeeper, I will have to keep myself alive?"

"No, however if you do not break the spell, you will always seem to develop slowly. Consequently, you must also realize, because of your parentage, you are connected in strange ways to the Occluder. The stronger you become, the weaker he grows, like a see saw, you will always be at opposite ends."

"Could I ever kill him this way?"

"No, but you must also remain strong, he has much greater power than you, for now anyway. It would take nothing for him to best you. You must know this Ian. In the prophecy it is written that you must impale the Occluder upon the Blade of Amity. Though it isn't relevant, I was part of the prophecy too. It was told to me, that I who was to bind the races in peace during the Great War by means of a blade, when not all five races cooperated, a second prophecy was written to counteract the first. It is the second one that declares you the hero. You must beat the Occluder."

"That's all wonderful except for one thing."

"What's this?"

"I'm sort of trapped as a spirit."

"About that, honestly I've never heard of such a draught, however, I'm sure someone, perhaps Mme. Dumpling, may have answers."

"Oh." Ian grew depressed. "Let's say for a moment, I am willing to proceed with all this nonsense of yours—"

"—it's not nonsense my lad."

"—how am I to best the Occluder?"

"Well, stepping away from the prophecy, and just looking at the raw facts for a moment."

"Of course."

"The blade was made in order for all to contribute, when the Occluder failed to do so it left our world unbalanced, tainted with evil. He still has to make his contribution for the darkness to end. That is why it's your job to stab him with the Amity Sword. The sword has to pierce the heart of the evil lord of shadows with light, and only by a chosen innocent. That way, all clans will have contributed to the making of peace; the Occluder would have contributed with his life, obviously. The problem is that he is rarely in human form, as I explained earlier. If the peace treaty is successful, the innocent will become one with the blade. The blade will pass its power onto the purehearted who dealt the final blow. That innocent will then, with the aid of the sword, be able to control and manipulate all the clans, thus, automatically becoming the King of Kings. During this transfer of power, the land will balance all clans, including that of shadow. The world will be brought together to live in harmony, to coexist as one."

"And they lived happily ever after?"

"Well we can hope so, but I doubt it would work as so."

"Goodness gracious Xsealiadd, do you think we live in a freaking fairytale?"

"Far from it!"

"You haven't even told me how to best the Occluder yet!"

"I thought I did!"

"Yes I got it, we have to stab him, but how can you stab something that's not solid? You've said nothing, there's got to be a way! Am I supposed to bring the crown and scale together to give him a body that I can stab or something?"

"No, the crown and scale must eventually be destroyed. As long as they remain intact, it is a guarantee the Occluder will endure even if you stabbed him a thousand times. I suppose I should mention about the black book."

"What black book?"

"There is a book, believed strongly to have been written by the Occluder himself, I've been trying to track it down. Though most have a good idea what lies within its pages, none are ever completely sure."

"Why?"

"The book holds great power, used to keep the Occluder's secrets hidden. Rumours encase its pages, stories I have confirmed true, ones that claim if one was to read the book's gruesome script, they would be thrust into the shadowed dimension with no way out. No one has been brave enough to challenge these theories, to my knowledge, and can you pin them blame? However, in my readings, I have learned the spells he encased within the pages allow just two people who will be able to read his penmanship. First is the Occluder himself as I'm sure you guessed; second being you."

"What!'

"Being the boy from the prophecy, a foretelling I actually believe the Occluder to have learned, you are able to read his secrets which I believe will allow you to best him."

"What exactly do you know is in the book?"

"Nothing is certain, but I believe secrets of his fears, weaknesses, desires and strengths. You know, kind of like a diary, a journal. I believe it's a place where he spills his soul. If you want to know further, ask Nighdrake, I'm sure he'll help you out."

"Still at Ackles?" Ian never finished the query, he didn't need to.

"No, Nighdrake has been moved to Sardon."

Ian's heart plummeted. "Oh. So, uh, this peacekeeper thing, we should really discuss it before the sun completely perishes." Ian stifled an enormous yawn, more out of boredom than fatigue.

"What do you wish to discuss?"

"How do I become your next of kin?"

"Well, you basically give the affirmative that yes you're willing to take over peacekeeping duties then I swear you in as my predecessor with many complex spells; which you have to say a few funny words that will make it binding, then I begin your training."

"Training?"

"Foolish boy! We have six hundred years of magical material I have to teach you for purposes of besting the Occluder and being my heir to the blade."

"Oh well before I say yes to this, I have two curious questions."

"Aye?"

"How can you believe a prophecy which was written about me before I was ever in existence?"

Xsealiadd laughed a deep bellied laugh. "Oh dear lad, this is all so complex, all this is written by the stars, and in turn, your mother, who as far as I understand, formed the prophecy as it needed birthing."

Ian looked up with raised eyebrows, doubt in his eyes. Few stars, which popped out in the early twilight winked peacefully back. "Uh, huh. And, uh, so if I become the new peacekeeper, why are you protecting Magnon? Othorrow I understand, I mean he nearly gave his life trying to protect mine, but Magnon? He's just a crazy teacher who's lost his beans. I'm only asking because if I'm taking over your spells, I should really know what I'm doing."

"Indeed. I have been keeping Magnon alive and protected as he was once a faithful servant to the Occluder, in fact, the Occluder's best Carddronne, or follower as you may prefer. Magnon witnessed his corruption. Out of desperation to save his soul, the Occluder pleaded with Magnon to stop the breakdown of his body and soul by evil. Magnon, in all honesty, admitted that nothing could be done. Believing Magnon was false hooding him, the Occluder tortured him. Now insane, Magnon managed to flee as he searched for my aid to protect him. I am always singled out as I'm trusting, old, and wisest of all... well, almost all."

Ian cocked an eyebrow with peculiarity. "Very well then."

"Ian if you ever go back to that school, you'd better not peep a word of this to anyone! Any of it!"

Ian smiled mischievously. "Don't worry Xsealiadd, I won't." Ian affirmed cheekily, his profile fading.

"Ian, where are you going?"

"Don't worry. I'll be here when you wake in the morning. Don't forget, we have oaths to make." Before another word was breathed, Ian faded to a fog, letting his soul rest.

With a great scoff, Xsealiadd laid his head on his pack. Nearby Scorch rushed to shield the wizard from the prevailing winds. The dragon had only offered his protection because his rider to be cared.

Soft snores sounded deep in the chests of both scale and flesh as together Scorch and Xsealiadd welcomed in the night with peace-filled slumber, a long day, finally drawing to a close.

Chapter 19
Sardon

Never before had something disturbed her more than this. What was most troubling was how nervous she really was. Elves weren't supposed to experience fear; it's what separated them from humans. Perhaps Valquee had gotten it wrong, perhaps they were known by their grace and strength, to hide their emotions better than most; if either was the case, Valquee considered herself a disgrace to the race of elves. None of these were thoughts of comfort, which was what she needed most at such a time as this.

"Nonsense!" She yelled a little too loudly. "I may be elvish but I should have just as much right to fear or cry if I choose; it should make me no less strong!" Her chest swelled with a wave of confidence. "I'm me, and I will do all I can to fulfill my pledge, and if I can't, at least I know I tried my best." Valquee talked pointlessly to herself, trying to keep her mind from wandering to the suicide mission she had set upon.

Though she tried her hardest, it was impossible to ignore the vast stretch of Sardon that lay before her. Two watchtowers and a great stone castle greeted her almost immediately upon docking at the port; it was obvious, outsiders were highly unwelcome.

Her chest burned on every stroke of the makeshift oar and her biceps were screaming, pleading at her to stop. There was no way, she had to endure. Resting this close to Sardon in open water would certainly be a sentence of death; with so many eyes she would surely be seen. In fact she was surprised she hadn't been yet. Although, perhaps it was that twilight which had worked its magic as it often does, injecting its long, dark shadows across the lands. It's always twilight in this town. The Occluder keeps it this way as light often weakens his servants; he likes to keep them at their peak performance. It's strange really how that works, as snorgs and torans are blinded to nightfall. With such in mind, it makes watchtowers rather pointless when none are ever seen approaching. Nevertheless, Valquee was not taking a single chance, who knows what magic of black the Occluder has plagued the city with.

With a deep, almost breathless sigh, Valquee at last decided it was time to face the task ahead. She allowed her keen elvish eyesight to sweep the banks as she decided the best point of entry.

Directly before her was a series of lengthy docks tied together to make a small pier with one great walkout plank which jutted far into the waters to make for easy docking; coming as well as going. This pier, over the last few days, Valquee had observed to be buzzing with activity. Beyond that, it sloped upward on a healthy incline. A great ramp connected the pier to a picketed gate manned by two very dangerous looking guards. The gate joined two spans of wrought iron fences which flew both left and right, joining them to two massive stone buildings. A fairly decent watchtower stood to the southwest, at the right edge of Valquee's vision. Beyond that, buildings of great mass carved their way skyward disturbing the otherwise peaceful horizon.

To Valquee's left; the incline gave way to a craggy cliff which supported a great building adjoining the fence, and behind that, a second watchtower. Even more left was the great castle of Sardon, Carddronnea. The cliff fell to the waters as cold as ice. It didn't take a genius to establish, it would be suicide turning left.

To Valquee's right was what ensnared her attention most. At this side of the pier was a small boat house, no doubt holding supplies of Sardon. Next to that, at the water's edge, was a great cluster of trees large enough to shield Valquee from prowling gaze. The water's edge here seemed fairly flat, only beyond did it rise to a hill backed with a large structure.

'Aim for the trees and go from there.' This was precisely Valquee's plan as she adjusted her wagon accordingly. With care, she moored on the snowy, rough embankment. Caked with ice it jutted out behind the trees, frozen from evil.

Without pause, Valquee swung into the trees where she rested, her heart pounding, waiting for any commotion to ebb. Her patience gave way to hunger; she bore into a quick feed from her pack. It was here she would spend the night.

Valquee guessed it was the next morn, for it remained twilight all the time, when a barge drifted from the south. On it was a healthy load of grain, this was Valquee's moment.

Nocking an arrow, she pushed aside the great bushy boughs. Her shot clear, Valquee executed the young lady who stood at its front. A distraught middle aged man rushed from the cabin, babbling excessively... frantically. He drew great attention to himself. Left with little choice, Valquee silenced him permanently with another quick shot. The hillside suddenly became a buzz of excitement, people tried to see what caused the racket. Valquee couldn't, let them see the deceased upon the barge. With a quick thought she muttered several phrases beneath the wind; the craggy cliff on the opposing side of the pier gave way, taking a large portion of the structure with it. For a fleeting moment Valquee felt bad, she didn't mean for that much of the cliff to erode.

    Shadowed servants flocked to the damage like a pack of shorbles to a berry. Valquee had to keep them at bay if the next part of her plan was to work. Luckily the raft and the deceased still had not been seen. Valquee knew what had to be done. As quick as she could, she took off as much gear and cloth as possible; she was going to impersonate a barge worker. There was one more thing that needed doing. Selecting an arrow with care from her earthed quiver, Valquee began to massage the fletchings, this one shot mattered. The arrow had to be perfect for it to work. Great, complex incantations escaped her lips, as, beneath her gentle touch, the fletching began to curl oddly. Valquee executed a shiver as she clipped a cone shaped steel apparatus to her bowstring. A pointless device, as was the talent needed to operate it, according to the elves of Rulan. However, this was one of those times Valquee appreciated taking the time to learn to shoot an arrow backwards.

    Brushing aside the low lying boughs, Valquee balanced the arrow's tip in the inverted cone she had clipped to her bowstring. With the shaft perched uneasily upon her forefinger, Valquee aimed with care. The arrow clattered near where the servants congregated.

Spotting it, a nearby toran snarled. Picking it up with a great sniff he scowled.

"Ugh! A manly arrow, Hethrowe tribe but scented with honeysuckle and pine needles... elf!"

Valquee's heart sunk. Not once did she think of masking her scent.

"You can't fool us!"

"I saw it! The arrow came from that way!" Another added, pointing in the opposite direction of Valquee. She smiled to herself, her heart filled with satisfaction.

Slipping from the tree boughs, she executed a shiver as she slipped on the attire of the raft man to veil her goose bumped flesh. The bodies she heaved overboard, as well, she ensured any evidence of her origin of house was hidden away. It had nearly broken her heart to part herself from the necklace given to her by Teargo; the knot of Hucklandish. 'This...' she thought fleetingly to herself, 'I cannot bear the hardship of leaving behind. In my pocket, that's where it shall remain', and pocket it she did. Taking a final check all was in order, Valquee moved the barge forth.

Arriving off port she pulled up her hood to veil her ears so pointed. In her heart she longed for a helm. With a nervous hand, Valquee smeared mud across her face; she hoped it would subdue the elvish contours of her face and jaw.

Tying the great barge to the docks, Valquee clamoured ashore. Slaves tending to the rockslide suddenly gained great interest in her actions as they pierced her soul with suspicious glares. Luckily her hood hung low shading her face... or was it? With nerves, Valquee checked once more all was in order as she swallowed a sharp lump in her throat.

'Relax.' She soothed herself, 'just act casually.' The problem was, she knew not what casual was around here. 'Don't worry, you are not one of them, yet, you are a tradesman, at least by your outfit. Just whatever you do, don't act elvish.'

"Grain shipment" Valquee commented trying to keep her voice deep and husky, but convincing.

"You're late."

"Lost my oar a while back, hard to paddle upstream without one."

The servants flashed Valquee a glare of doubt and suspicion. "Well come on then, get up here and start unpacking!"

Shouldering a sack of grain, Valquee grabbed a folded bit of parchment she spotted at the last minute. Following the servants, she dumped the sack atop a pile of already stacked goods.

"Can you tell me where your shipment manager resides?" Valquee's voice cracked with gruffness.

A servant signalled the building nearest behind the trees. "Why?" He eyed her.

"I need a signature on the invoice to confirm the shipment!" Valquee waved the parchment over her shoulder.

The door creaked with weight and age as Valquee stuck her head through with caution. Assessing the situation with haste, she chose her next course of action. A single servant sat behind a desk, the entire office filled with books and charts which tracked the ins and outs; the movements of the shipments and supplies. The servant looked up upon Valquee's approach. She did her best to act casual.

"I need your signature on a shipping invoice." She grunted, unfurling the parchment. She had him trusting as he reached for his quill.

Coming around to his side of the desk she flattened the parchment. He was in a headlock before he could even see what the parchment contained. Withdrawing a dagger from a fold in her cloth, Valquee breathed heavy. The cold steel pressed just beneath his grayish chin. He swallowed hard. Soon, he began to cackle, black spittle oozing from the folds of his mouth.

"Answer only what you're asked and your life will be spared." Valquee was antsy; she had to make a conscious effort to deepen her tone.

The servant's eyes flashed dangerously as they moved wildly in their sockets. Looking out of his peripheral he could make out the contours of Valquee's features, there was something not right about them, though he was unsure what. He cackled more enthusiastically. Valquee ignored him. "I'm looking for Nalo, he's a dragon slayer, where is he?"

"And what would a barge operator want with a dragon slayer?" He challenged. Valquee pressed the cold steel of her dagger hard against his flesh causing a line of bloody droplets to appear.

"I'm the one asking questions here, so answer me!"

"I only answer to master!"

Frustrated, Valquee let the dagger cut deep, spilling his life and blood before her. Changing once more, this time to the cloth of a Sardon servant, she slipped from the building.

Sitting in the alley nearby, she thought long and hard. It didn't last long however, this moment of solitude, as a toran nearby entered the building from whence she came. Something unexpected happened then. That same toran emerged dragging the bloodied corpse.

"Who has been slaying for pleasure!" He bellowed loud enough, Valquee swore, for the whole of Sardon to hear. "Never are we to waste food!" With a gray, scabby hand, the toran reefed back the dead servant's head and began taking savage bites; soon, others joined him in what appeared to Valquee as a scrumptious feast.

It was nauseating, as her stomach retched she had to get out of here, and fast. Taking off in the other direction, she weaved through the buildings in search of Nalo.

Chapter 20
Oaths

Scorch roused first, giving way to Xsealiadd who had somehow in the night repositioned himself to lie across the dragon's scaly hide. It was the stirring of the hatchling alone which roused Xsealiadd.

The wizard's eye parted to Ian standing over him.

"Good morning sleepyhead!" Ian chimed.

Xsealiadd grunted.

"Why so grumpy on such a fine autumn day?"

"Leave me be Ian!" Xsealiadd stretched as he sat up.

"Okay, but I thought we were to fulfill some oaths today."

"Oaths?"

"Me, your peacekeeper in running."

It's like he just got a lashing.

"Studying six hundred years of lessons, that's no simple feat! I best start teaching!"

"Eat first, you need strength."

The wizard couldn't eat fast enough, his arms almost flailing as he shovelled his food down. Next to him, Scorch whined.

"I can't keep feeding you. You need to forage on your own." Xsealiadd's eyes widened. "You've never learned how to hunt live food, well it's about time you did. Ian, you move faster than I, especially shadowed, do you mind teaching this youngster how to fetch live prey?"

Ian smiled. "Anytime... come on Scorch! Come on!" Materializing across the plains, Ian searched for anything in motion. After awhile he spotted a rodent scurrying against the grassy stubble.

"Hey Scorch! You see that little scurrying thing over there yonder? Bring 'em here!"

Scorch crouched in anticipation, his tail held high like a kitty cat ready to pounce. He sprang into motion and with a great snap; he brought it to Ian and dropped it at his feet. The creature was still.

"Very good." Ian praised, seeing the wounded rodent upset him. "Now you eat that... and quickly."

Scorch cocked his head.

Picking up the carcass, Ian flung it to Scorch, who snapped it up and swallowed it whole.

"Very good, shall we look for more?"

About an hour later, Ian returned with a satisfied Scorch at his heels, Scorch struggling to waddle, his stomach inundated with nourishment.

"I think he's got it." Ian responded once Xsealiadd was in view.

"Excellent, now come, come!"

Ian rushed over.

"Now take my hand as best as you're able." Ian obeyed. "You are to declare your oaths. It will be in a foreign tongue but I will help."

Ian did his best enunciating the strange pronunciations of the language of the gods. After a great chunk of morning and strange words spoken, some repeated by Ian, others not, Ian was sworn in as the new peacekeeper; a faint tattoo, like scarring, wrapped its way around Ian's wrist, as if a rope was tied there permanently.

"What's that?"

"It's your binding, it is now official you're peacekeeper."

"Is this, like, my title, if I show people will they know its meaning?"

"Doubtful, any who swear a binding promise in the gods' tongue will have one; now, if you feel able, we will start your training straight away. I think the basics would be a good place." Xsealiadd began. "Energy, it fills our souls, it births the wind, it helps the fires rage, it causes the waters to flow it is amongst us in abundance. Everything we do requires its power, everything we touch either has energy or requires energy to work and, or to make. However you see it, this potency is very important to how our world works. Now tell me, how does magic work?"

"Energy!" Ian blurted out. "S.P.E.L.L.'s, special practice of energy through life and language. We utilize our bodies and tongues to manipulate or control what we want done using energy! It is power and makes stuff happen."

"Very good Ian, however, energy isn't just used in the practice of S.P.E.L.L.'s, it is also required to create Enchantments and the practice of Craft also. You must understand the differences of these three types and forms of magic. Would you care to guess?"

"Well," Ian thought hard, he didn't want to upset Xsealiadd. "S.P.E.L.L.'s focus on your body, you use your body to power your magic; with Enchantments you use your environment to make things happen and Craft you—" Ian broke off, he realized how little he knew.

Xsealiadd smiled. "S.P.E.L.L.'s is the basic magic, it teaches you basic theory and how to use yourself to alter something else. To a degree, all magic relies on your core to perform a spell and all are equally as dangerous, to others as much as to yourself. Why would it be hazardous to you Ian?"

"Because..." He paused. "If you don't know your limits you can kill yourself by overworking your periatti gland, the mechanism in your brain in charge of creating magic. Yours must be huge."

Xsealiadd's eyes twinkled. "No, see Ian it's not how big the spell is, it's how it can be performed with the least amount of energy. Moving something is easier than creating it. It's all efficiency, very crucial. Anyhow, getting back to your magic triangle, Enchantments you sing to nature, Craft you sing to the gods, and S.P.E.L.L.'s you sing to everything. There is nothing you can achieve with Craft that you can't achieve with S.P.E.L.L.'s or Enchantments for that matter. But it is very crucial that you master S.P.E.L.L.'s before you even think of advancing; because, despite what most say, it is actually easier to learn Enchantments and Craft with a strong basis of S.P.E.L.L.'s. Once you master S.P.E.L.L.'s I will teach you the language of the gods and as many scripts I can before my day. Once this is known, common sense will aid in weaving magic, and a strong passion to read will aid with the study of Craft; as I'm sure you know, reading is a healthy portion of such a study. Now I know you can't practice magic being a spirit. So tell me, what is the most complex S.P.E.L.L. you have ever weaved?"

"I felled a boulder from a hilltop."

"A S.P.E.L.L. which would've been easier done with Enchantments no doubt."

Ian looked puzzled.

"You see Ian, you can get by knowing one, but to know all, each has an advantage which will make your life easier; just like, something spoken in one language may be easier to state its purpose than to say the very same thing in another of Ellezwrainia's many tongues, you follow me? Now to make your lessons interesting, I won't show you the hardest S.P.E.L.L. I've ever weaved as I've created none hardest. I will, however, show you one with the highest ranked difficulty you can get... S.P.E.L.L.'s are ranked, just so you know, to help beginners protect damage to their periatti gland; however, in Enchantments and Craft they aren't, so you must take great care. Anyhow, about showing that S.P.E.L.L...." Xsealiadd grunted as he pulled himself up. With a slight limp to his gait, he walked knee deep into the water.

"Aquwenrian!" He bellowed. All at once the water began to explode outwards as it began to spin a raging vortex. "Oudaire!" He screamed as the vortex formed a great funnel, lifting him about twenty feet above sea level. His eyes sparkled, he was having fun showing off. "Fluzza!" He yelled over the roar of water, like thunderous water in motion. Out of nowhere, great fire sprang up, encasing both Xsealiadd and the vortex.

"Utole!" All at once Xsealiadd was lowered on the calming waters as the S.P.E.L.L. perished. "Remember," he smiled, "anything is possible given the skill."

Ian was awestruck, speechless. Inside he was screaming, he couldn't wait to get started.

Chapter 21
Carddronnea Castle

It must've been fate that drove Valquee to the pub. Be that as it may, being exhausted, she allowed herself a rest. The goers here were equally as shifty as those she had already crossed paths with. Rowdy and violent, it took nothing to set them off, a valuable observation Valquee took into account. Perched aloft a high stool she ordered "whatever on rocks" to the bartender; more concerned about what she saw and heard than what she drank, which ended up being something green and sludge-like poured over a handful of small pebbles. Apparently the bartender never had heard of ice being called rocks.

Observing her surrounds, Valquee educated herself as to how these creatures spoke, their body language, how they acted and behaved; as well, in general, what was proper in their culture. For instance, they slapped each other on the stomach as a greeting.

"Aye, aye maggoty brains!" One greeted and slapped another.

"Aye! Light blazin'?" He responded.

"Nah, shadows rule!" The first replied. It took awhile to realize, for instance, this was a toran's way of asking how the weather was, a familiar greeting as Valquee heard it echoed more than once.

'Man this'll be tough.' She thought. After hours of observing, Valquee gained enough confidence to question one about Nalo.

Slapping a passing toran hard in the abdomen, she hesitated as he turned to look at her.

"Aye, aye barf breath! Maggots in yer pants?"

"Bah, roaches in my soul."

"Aah, touché slum, beetles in thy bed!" Every eye turned to her. That must've been a bad, uh, saying. "Sun blazin'?"

The toran, like many others eyed her with peculiarity. The one before her thumped her in the head with his tankard, intentionally. Valquee had set him off. It must be their language; no one could ever figure what these sayings meant.

"A plague will shade your sacks!" This toran yelled as he thumped her again. Every blow felt like getting trampled by a horse, Valquee had no choice but to retaliate, torans were big brutes. With as much strength as she could, she hit him hard in the temple causing utter pandemonium, a bar fight greater than imaginable.

It was like a storm had come and gone, after twenty minutes of surviving blow after blow, every pub goer was great friends again; including the one she apparently insulted.

Yanking her up by the scruff, the toran slapped her stomach.

"What's burning buzzard brains?"

Now was her chance, she had to question him fast before she caused any more turmoil.

"Huntin' dragon killers, Nalo, I want his flesh!" Valquee did her best to sound like she wanted to feast on him because he was scrumptious. She was, however, unsure if her performance was convincing. Her heart quivered with nerves.

A corner of the toran's great mouth twitched, his great mousey yellowish-gray fangs jutting forth. "Well, y'know, Nalo breath aint the foulest, you may want a Dougan hide."

"Nah, my gut cries for Nalo flesh!" Valquee cackled falsely, her knuckles cracking beneath her fist clenched white.

The toran grunted. "What's say you earn your answer, always like new member!" He spoke rather loudly.

Another toran drifted over, and slapped him hard in the gut. "Yuh, we bros of de Banzil Guild. We're duh ones everyone speaks of. We're 'bout to shoot some sticks, face off and un. Five gold gets you playin' sharpest shots wins..."

"Yuh, yuh and dose answers, yuh?"

Valquee understood a minute amount of what they said but played along as best she could.

Reaching behind the bar she grabbed five Goldallions, it's the only thing "gold's" could be, and slapped them into the toran's gut. She couldn't just give them to him from her pouch, as she reminded herself; she's now hated and evil.

Through her helmet, she glared at him. "Let's fire sticks!" ...whatever that was. Valquee stifled a cough, talking gruff so much pained her throat.

"Sticks 'n' shooters o'er dere, five sticks per contestant!" A toran bellowed.

It turned out, sticks and shooters were arrows and bow something Valquee was good at but did not know if the torans were better.

Grabbing a bow and her allotment of five arrows, the first thing Valquee noticed was the fletchings were bent and crooked. She stood in silence, unlike all else, observing the first toran. Much to her pleasure, target shooting, according to this toran, was not their strong point. They seemed to have a strong arm, just not an accurate one.

Waiting patiently for her turn, Valquee caressed the fletchings, all the while muttering under her breath. Her incantations were Rukkian as she, with care, resorted to an ancient art form she'd learned in Rulan; how to properly curve the fletchings to cause the arrow to spin in a tight spiral, this keeping the arrow stable and on target.

The more arrows she watched fly, the more adjustments she made to hers. She was up next, it was only then did she realize there was one thing she failed to adjust. The bows themselves were not designed properly, their wood grains running against rather than with the natural bend of the archers pull. In all the cases she observed, this resulted in an under propulsion of the arrow or breakage of the bow altogether resulting in disqualification of that archer. If only the toran knew, and to think this whole time they thought it was their comrades over pulling on the bowstring, creating excess tension, in their view, trying to cheat. The bows, in simple terms, were designed for the users to fail. Even the ones that didn't break, as Valquee observed, usually shot way off target, falling far too short.

'Well this explains their inaccuracy, it's not lack of skill these torans suffer from, it's lack of knowledge.' Valquee thought. With one last minute utterance, Valquee whispered to the fibres of the wood that compounded her bow. Beneath her fingers, she could feel them bulging and twisting, smoothing, and bending, like little worms trying to find their place, she checked for last moment imperfections.

She was up now. Subtly swallowing a lump, she hoped she had adjusted everything right, she didn't want to lose. The money she cared nothing about, she was desperate not to lose her chance at some answers. She drew back to full draw. The bow creaked but did not break, nearby torans scowled. To ice the cake, her shots were effortless and right on mark. Others grew suspicious at her grace, nevertheless, a beefy, shadow scarred toran handed Valquee the pot against his own heart's desire.

"Yer question?"

"I want Nalo's blood, where does he linger?" She asked too proper and drew even more mistrust. The toran sniffed and gave her the once over.

"Dat honeysuckle and pine needles?"

"Uh, yah, I ate a woodland elf for lunch, saw her sneaking about Sardon, killed her, den got hunger." Valquee thought quickly.

The toran nodded, apparently in appearances sake, she presented normal as a toran, except smaller, obviously. Luckily for Valquee, the toran never questioned why.

She did her best not to let the nerves and excitement interfere and give her away; after all, she was already treading on the edge of secrecy, she had raised far too great a distrust.

Waiting with patience, she listened to what the toran had to say.

"See yur bites, fly guts! De dragon slayers guild hides, she's not want seeing. Master places great magic to protect herz great colony. Magic make you dumb, forget any you say or hear of de girl. Only two know her besides her flock mates an' dats master and his mate. Good riddance ta ya findin dem ta ask, dey stay in da great Carddronnea, innit she a beute?" The toran got distracted observing the great castle. When he turned back, Valquee had vanished.

    She looked stupid just standing there observing the castle, something torans wouldn't. It was then Valquee was struck from behind, another toran meant to murder her.
    "Gold glows in yer pouch!" Was all he said before Valquee had ended his attack. She watched him squirm as his nerves stilled. She stood frozen, too lost in thought to move.
    "Oi!" A voice shouted from behind. She didn't dare look she always seemed to find trouble. "You eat dat or die! I'm tired of food waste around dis town!" Cold steel met her throat.
    "Aah!" She screamed savagely cracking her knuckles. She dropped to her knees being careful not to injure herself upon his blade which projected itself into her personal space. Of course this was just an act, one she wished would end.
    Ripping a piece of flesh she held it between her teeth as she tried not to retch. Elves seldom ate meat if it was cooked, being vegan was her norm. Her commotion caused others to awaken their appetite as they swarmed in around her, tearing and ripping hungrily. When she was sure none were looking, she spit out the flesh and scrambled to her feet. Turning on the spot, she was confronted by the one who ordered her to eat first off. He made a move, Valquee took no chances. Knifing him she threw him to the feeding torans.
    One looked up, blood dripping from his chin.

"The beast was about to knife me!" She snarled before running away. Great stone walls concealed her as her stomach emptied its contents to the snowy, frozen ground.

"Oh this place, take mercy upon it. How can life go on this way, I can't stand it? I want this to be over, I want to be home with Hivell; I wish Ian to be alive and to be with him; I don't want to be in a place where no light shines down and people eat their own. I want to die!" Right there, right then, Valquee broke into tears.

A force from nowhere raised her up and guided her heart, enlightening her with warmth and hope.

She began to walk, though why or where she did not know. Down a precipice she trod that stood next to Carddronnea, the great castle, tripping and slipping all the way down. Once she was at the bottom she was faced with a courtyard before her and the great castle walls to her left. The only thing that broke the endless pattern of masonry was a small iron door.

Valquee's eyes wanted to, naturally, be drawn to the door. As she stared at it, the door began to open. Upon instinct, she took the opportunity and dove for it. The closer to the door she got, the more doubts clouded her mind. Perhaps this was a trick, but yet something in her heart told her to trust, and trust she did. The moment she was inside, the door slammed shut, plunging her into darkness.

The sudden loss of light had her fumbling about blindly. Beneath her fingers a cold metal handle she felt. Instinctively she pulled; the door obediently swung open, flooding light to where she stood. Both to her right and her left, great stairways rose, one to an arsenal tower and one to a siege engine tower, though none of this could be seen through the veiling blackness. The door she held open broadened to a great courtyard, beyond that, the upper bailey. She must've just entered the public entrance, to her knowledge of castles anyhow. Just beyond the next wall, a great keep rose from the middle bailey, it was there she wanted to be and it was there she doubted she could get to. She was, however, going to try. Slapping a passing toran in the gut as per custom, she eyed him nervously from beneath her helm.

"Beadle bronne! My bugs have wasted me; I need to plunk my boozat, where can I land?" The toran simply pointed and walked away.

"Figures I'd have to talk to a gate guard, I don't even know how to address them!" Valquee grumbled. Moving within earshot, she began to listen.

"Oh guardly one... famished me gut, slam me bugs!" One begged. This helped Valquee a lot as she watched the toran being burdened with a pathetic excuse for food. Valquee climbed the steep stone steps.

"Oh - oh g-guardly one... weary me soul, plop me a bed." Valquee stammered, fighting to keep the lump from her throat. With a scowl and a glare, he opened a door and administered her in. The great hall was spectacular and was greatly crowded as many villagers, some torans, and others of a smaller sort conversed energetically. Some sat on floors, others on stoops, and Valquee herself sat against a wall, removed from all as she observed them conversing.

After what seemed like hours, a great number of lightly garbed men came flooding from a great door opposite where

Valquee sat, each carrying several bushels of straw. Rushing back and forth, they arranged what Valquee recognized as beds or nests as they more closely resembled. With a great yawn, she clambered upon the nearest one as she tried to gain comfort.

    Her eyes just closed when a heavy boot stomped on her chest knocking out her wind. Scrambling to her feet she was, once again, knocked down by an elbow in the back. Rolling upon the landing, Valquee relied upon momentum to carry her to her feet where she readied herself for the next attack. Gripping the handle of her dagger in its usual fold of her clothes, she waited. The toran charged her, only to have a dagger wedged between his ribs. The toran doubled over allowing Valquee a clean shot to his gray, liver spotted back. He went down for good as Valquee kicked him aside, scoffing at his rudeness. For a fleeting moment she had forgotten where she was. More villagers charged her as she realized, even with the efforts, there was a shortage of beds. Torans, men, and whoever else roamed these quarters were fighting for a spot to rest. Well, no matter, if it was to cost her life, Valquee refused to lose her nest. Withdrawing her dagger from the fallen toran, she meant to take on all who challenged her without mercy; and that is exactly what she did.

    Her victory was savoured on a bed of straw as she pondered what to do next; she didn't cogitate long as the elvish sleep known as hypnosis overtook her consciousness as she lay there, eyes open, in a Zen-like state.

    A great horn tore through the chambers rousing all who slept. Valquee, however, was not one of them; she had been awake for many hours now on high alert.

Once more, a great rush of men poured from the opposing door to clean up the straw mess, this was Valquee's chance. Not one more night could she see herself surviving such chaos. Gathering up her straw bed in her arms, she rushed for the opposing door; no matter what it took, she would become a servant to this castle, at least for the time being!

The horses continued to struggle through the great Woods of Oursjour, many casualties did the Occluder lose in their previous fight making it very difficult to navigate through the thick forest growth. Great movement stirred up ahead, in response, the Occluder halted his men.

"Who goes there?" He bellowed, the voice of Ian filling with authority.

"It is I, Stanzer, a forest folk elf, here with my student. We are studying the life and activities of the Nugar Newt."

"Come out where I can see you, or I'll have my men stick you full of arrows."

Stanzer appeared from around a clump of trees, his student, he had ensnared around his shoulders.

"Ian?" Stanzer asked, his eyes widening.

"I am not Ian, you fool, I am the Occluder, and I demand the utmost respect. Restrain them!" The Occluder ordered as his men rushed forth to fulfill their master's request. After a tremendous struggle, both were bound.

"What do you want done with them sire?"

The Occluder thought hard.

"You! Do you recognize this?" The Occluder asked holding up an hourglass.

Again, Stanzer's eyes widened as he nodded vigorously. He could not speak for the servants had him gagged.

"Most excellent, he comes with me. As for the other one," the Occluder eyed the student with disgust, "kill him!" Jamming his heels hard in his steed's ribs he surged the fatigued horse forth, great screams hung in his wake!

Chapter 22
Black Tongue

It was developing into a monotonous rhythm. Each morning, Ian rose from the shadows and guided Scorch to the wilderness to help him learn to feed on his own. He was growing into quite a natural; Ian then returned to Xsealiadd who had fed and hydrated himself before training sessions began.

Returning to Xsealiadd from his morning hunt, feeling rejuvenated, Ian had barely gotten close to the elder before his next order was thrust upon him.

"You know Ian, I think I'm going to introduce something new to your routine."

"Yes father?" Ian responded. That was another thing he was growing used to doing, referring to Xsealiadd by his proper title of either father or master.

"I'm going to leave it up to you to start teaching Scorch to fly. To do this, you must take him out earlier each morning to compensate for the added time. You and he must be gone long before the sun has risen, even before the day breaks. You leave when the first splash of light touches the sky."

"Yes master." This did not bother Ian for he never slept as a spirit anyway. What troubled him most was how he could teach a dragon to fly, when he did not fly himself.

"Sir? —"

"—to fly is a natural thing for a dragon. I'm surprised he's not discovered his wings already. Nevertheless, do what you can to get him airborne. If he does it once, he should continue to try on his own; it's a natural curiosity of dragons. Though, just as a warning, this is not always the case."

"I'll do my best master."

"That's all I ask."

"Come on Scorch!" Scorch's eyes lit up, he wanted to play.

Ian drifted along, flapping his arms madly. Curious, Scorch stopped and cocked his head. Ian sighed exasperated, the wind whipping through the trees. At a loss, Ian approached the dragon, "Scorch, what are these?" Scorch spread his wings trying to figure out what Ian was looking at. "Did you know you use them to fly?" Once more, Scorch looked confused.

Ian's mind raced before he suddenly got an idea. Sifting through all his memories, he filtered out any where he was watching dragons flying. The time he was hanging upside down from the maw of the Golden King, the time he was watching Blazzan and the Golden King fly away. Taking these thoughts he thrust them at Scorch. Spreading his wings, Scorch flapped them several times in quick succession before tucking them neatly across his back.

Ian grumbled with frustration as he returned to Xsealiadd.

"How did it go?"

"Won't try getting airborne."

"Well, let me try." Xsealiadd replied, awaiting Scorch's return.

"Good luck."

"Mitubayie!" Xsealiadd screamed, thrusting his fingertips far into the air in the direction of where Scorch peaked on the horizon. The poor dragon was thrown skyward; he didn't even see it coming. Rolling and tumbling, he fell like a stone to the soft soil. He landed hard, right on his spine, his tail unfurling from the ordeal, his head flopping back, his tongue sliding to the side of his drooling, parted maw.

"Oh my! Scorch!"

"Just leave him be. It'll do him some good to rest for a while." Xsealiadd grabbed a healthy sized stick. "Well?"
"Never before have I observed you spar, nor can I envision you fighting in battle, are you sure you are able?" Ian aped his motions.

Xsealiadd scowled, "I have fought many battles young master Ian, more than you could ever know. Yes I am more than able to defeat you by weapon, even in my progressing age."

"Defeat me? Well aren't you arrogant!"

"It is not arrogance young lad, only knowledge in my abilities as well as knowing how you are trained; seeing that I have done a great portion of your schooling myself."

"Wonderful will be the day I can fight with my axe again." Ian voiced, disappointed at having no proper weapons. Even Xsealiadd struggled to do basic magic without his staff; it was just so hard to control.

"Wonderful will be the day we can access an entire arsenal of weaponry for you to practice with. And..." he panted, "... for you to have a proper trainer who can guide you with a great challenge."

"I don't know Xsealiadd, for an elder you have a fairly strong stamina, you were right, keeps me sharp if nothing else." Ian comforted as he readied his axe substitute.

"Are you ready Ian?" Xsealiadd smiled, his eyes twinkling like a loving father.

"Aye."

Allowing adequate footing, Ian raised his stick, he didn't know what to expect as he prepared for anything. To his amazement, Xsealiadd had not underestimated his skills as a swordsman, for he exploded into a flurry of blows. Ian barely stopped the one to his shoulder when another happened upon his side he didn't anticipate. It was his own blunder, he shouldn't have moved quite that way for it opened up a vulnerability to his ribs.

Xsealiadd glared, "dead" he said simply.

"I apologize father, I went to block your strike here," Ian pointed to his collar, "and I neglected to shield my midriff."

"It is good that you recognize your errors, how better could you have approached that?"

Ian thought for a moment. "Perhaps if I twisted my body this way, and lowered my stick, that would allow a wider range of protection."

"Very good, now, we try again."

Resetting to a starting stance, this time, it was Ian who exploded with a series of blows; which Xsealiadd effortlessly countered, this time across the back of all places.

"Dead." He commented pointlessly once again. "You know you have a ways to go right?"

Ian threw up his hands in exasperation; his stick flew from his grip which Scorch now alert, caught playfully. "Ugh! I know! You tell me every morning!" Ian was very frustrated.

"You practice strongly, and you lose well." Xsealiadd bowed as he tried to bestow comfort upon Ian. "Perhaps we should leave it here for today; I'm sure once Valquee returns she'll have no trouble aiding you along. Besides, we have much scripture to get through, which I believe is something far more important. Just, as usual, give me many moments to set up."

"Yes master." Ian responded. The moment Xsealiadd turned his back, Ian scowled. He was a sore loser. 'At least,' he thought 'I'm not a sore player; else I would have just let the blade pass right through me.'

Taking a great long moment of silence, Xsealiadd drew deep and regulated breath. "The language we are looking at today is a rather gruesome one. No one truly knows its birth name but it is known by most as black script or black tongue, can you guess its origins?"

"Aardvark?"

"It is not a kind or forgiving script but is one you should be familiar with, or at least recognize if naught else." Taking a stick, Xsealiadd carved strange etchings into the mud; it took a while as he drew at least a hundred of them.

It seemed to be the way that many of his lessons were going. After sparring, Ian would find himself facing a new language each day. At least once a week, he would be faced with the tongue of the gods; Xsealiadd's most important dialect which he wished to teach. At least Ian was familiar with it, though vaguely, as it was his mother's favourite one to instruct him. Not once either, did Ian find himself facing Rukkian. This was because Xsealiadd felt he had a healthy head start and the elves would train him further in such a tongue.

"The most difficult thing about black script, and there are a great few like it, is that there is no alphabet as you know it. Characters are used in place of letters. One character may mean one of several things, such as this one for instance..." Xsealiadd pointed to a rather squiggly one. "It can mean light, bright, or sun. The proper pronunciation for it is aukh. However, if I was to do this," Xsealiadd carved the symbol again in the sand, and next to it, drew a more linear symbol, "I would have just told the reader, I want the first symbol to mean sun as the second symbol here, unna, means sky, heavens, or atmosphere. Together, they tell the reader I want to say sun. You following me?"

Ian shook his head, more in an attempt to loosen the cobwebs than to offer a response. "And why must I learn all these scripts and languages?"

"My dear boy, it is very important you understand both what you see and what you hear, that way you can never be fooled in any language. As a peacekeeper, this is especially crucial. Also, should you wish to master Craft, which you will, magic reads from books; it is most often, not in the common tongue; you need to be versatile, understand all pens."

"Yes master, but perhaps, could you simplify your explanations a bit, it's making my head spin."

"I'm sorry boy. Black script is a complex one and is difficult to simplify, but I will do my best."

"Thank you master."

"My pleasure, now, just a quick aside, could you list one language we haven't touched on yet that requires characters not alphabets?"

Ian began to think, "Treall, no we covered it, Cusha, no that has an alphabet, just different, and we did cover it a bit. Hmm... I know! Primordial Graphemics! The language of the dwarves, one of mama's favourite languages, but in that one, bright just meant bright, nothing more."

"Very good Ian, yes, you've remembered. In just a few short days, I'll give you a refresher course on that one, but not now. Today we're going to memorize each of these symbols, their spoken names, and what they mean. Of course, I am talking in the black script."

Again and again Ian had to draw and say funny names and symbols. As per usual, Xsealiadd refused to recess until both were certain Ian had retained the lessons. Lunch came late that day as Xsealiadd's stomach protested to the hours of memorization he had to help Ian endure. At last, when the sun had made a strong decline towards the mountains did Xsealiadd finally eat. As usual, when he refreshed, Ian was left to go over all the morning symbols and memorization. As feeding concluded, Ian prepared for the next onslaught of knowledge. After midday meals, time was reserved in learning the spoken rules of each day's language.

Xsealiadd cleared his numbing throat, he had spoken too much. Here came his spiel, a bombardment of more data Ian was expected to absorb.

"In the black tongue rules are surprisingly forgiving. Words are spoken in combination of the common tongue, as in, you would say aukh unna meaning bright skies, bright heavens, or sunny skies or sunny heavens, blah, blah, blah; as opposed to unna aukh, sky sunny, or heavens bright or —actually that one you could get away with doing either, so it's not a good example, but you get the point. Whatever way sounds more proper to your ear is what you should use. The exception, of course, being if a certain rule forces otherwise, or, if it is more proper with script. You understand?"

"I think so."

"So, Ian, tell me something."

Ian knew what this meant, he was supposed to practice stringing together different words that he had learned this day, and tell Xsealiadd something in that language that made sense. He did this every afternoon until the sun died. It normally took that long just to say one simple sentence.

What he hated most, was when Xsealiadd said something back. He usually said it a bit too fast, though he didn't mean to, and he often used words Ian had not yet learned. Though Ian figured this was intentional to help him learn. Nevertheless, Ian closed his eyes hard as he processed all the information he had acquired that day to try to concoct a phrase.

"Bunna atché rukkulz—"

"No."

"What?"

"You learned that yesterday."

"What?"

"Rukkulz, was jump in Treall, you learned that yesterday."

"Sorry!"

"Don't be, I understand how difficult this is for you. Please, try again."

Again and again Ian had to be corrected on words misused, or taken from different languages and like each day that passed, he struggled through a basic conversation.

"—very well done today Ian, very good." Xsealiadd cut in, halting his teachings for the night. The alpenglow was strong against the Sundurr Mountains as the world was on the verge of swallowing the sun, giving way to yet another dark and cold night.

Ian was stunned. He wasn't used to being halted in his lessons so abruptly. Xsealiadd must have been either really tired, or desperately wanted some thinking time. Either way, Ian was happy to cease the ache in his overburdened mind.

"Oh yeah Ian," Xsealiadd sounded from his sleeping stance, "tomorrow I teach you the forgotten language of the dwarves, which hasn't really been forgotten, you know. G'night." Faster than normal, great snores resounded from the shallow rise and fall of the elder's breast. Once more, as per each and every night leading up to this, Scorch shielded the elder from the wind, this time, using a massive wing which he had finally found a use for.

Chapter 23
Enslaved

The door burst open as Thyle sprawled in uninvited; across the room slouched across Hancer's cot, Hancer being Wok's dwarvish mentor, sat Hivell and Hancer both intimately engaged in what appeared to be a brutally close game of chess.

Hivell made a move, both not acknowledging Thyle's presence. "Knight to A five! Ha!" He mocked scooping up one of the black castles from where his knight currently resided.

"Aww shucks, my rook!" Hancer, groaned.

"Should've seen it coming!" Hivell grinned cheekily.

"Excuse me!" Thyle shattered concentrations.

"What!" Hivell replied more forcefully than he had meant to, he was simply too involved in his game. Hancer seized the moment to switch around the board pieces. Hivell grabbed his hand while in the process of replacing his fallen queen back onto the board.

"Can't do that!" Hivell warned.

"Says who?"

"Says the inventor of chess, it's been in the laws for hundreds of thousands of years."

"Well." Hancer scoffed. "I'm going to break dem dere ruddy rules and put dis here and dat dere..." Hancer rebelled, shifting every possible piece around that he could.

"You don't know how close I am to stabbing you at the moment!" Hivell couldn't stand Hancer's obnoxious rebellion.

"Oh, bloody booty!" Hancer yelled not even realizing it slipped out as he eyed the pot. Both had bet on their game and had confidence in their hand at winning. Hivell's wager was much more realistic than the greedy dwarf's of a meagre Brozan, the second smallest of Ellezwrainia's currency; however, seeing the dwarf's hand at cheating, his wager may not have been so far off.

"Don't even think of it." Hivell cut in gathering the coins and replacing them in his pouch. "Can I help you Thyle?"

"Um yeah, Hivell, since you have kind of taken over my Opthopathy lessons in Teargo's stead, I was wondering if you could answer me a question."

"What Thyle?"

"I was reading a text that one can hypnotize another while practicing Opthopathy, how is this possible? Can you tell me how this is done?"

"Thyle my lad, these are very, very deep questions about very dark matters, I don't feel it wise to answer that on school property." Hivell eyed Thyle suspiciously.

"Okay then, can you at least tell me how it can be prevented?"

"I have never heard of a way to prevent it. That's why elves shun the whole practice of it. But don't mistake me, I never once said there wasn't a cure, I just don't know of it."

"Do you know of any who might?"

"Xsealiadd is the only one that springs to mind, but he's out roaming the countryside right now."

"Oh," Thyle drooped depressively, "okay, thank you very much Hivell." He turned to leave. "Wait!" He paused. "Could you let me know if you see him?"

"Certainly, my dear Thyle." Hivell responded.

With a nod of gratitude, Thyle exited, his cloak whipping the corner in his wake.

A great pot soared through the air aimed at Valquee's person. Her lightning quick elvish reflexes allowed her to dodge it with relative ease.

"You slave! I told you to clean master's quarters!"

"I did!"

"Don't lie! There is a layer of dust blanketing stuff in there at least a finger width deep! Master will be returning home soon, I expect his quarters to be dirt free."

"But Master Udkaa, each time I try, I am whisked away by another clad in cloth as fine as silk. He says I'm not to touch master's things, that's what he says and I listen." Though this guy was bossy, Valquee thoroughly enjoyed speaking proper English with him. Nevertheless, the more Valquee reflected upon her situation, the more it puzzled her how she'd gotten where she had. One moment she was carrying armloads of straw about, hoping not to raise suspicion, the next she found herself to be taking orders from some manly looking Sardon slave, whom most would likely fail to recognize a burr from a beehive. As much as she hated it, however, she was one giant step closer to speaking to master about Nalo.

"Wretch?"

"Yes Master Udkaa?"

"What were your orders?"

"Yes Master Udkaa."

"Don't take the day either." Udkaa scowled, his expression riddled with the distaste which he normally reserved for anything of beauty such as flowers, sunshine, or serene peaceful seclusions. As Valquee was quickly learning, the only time a smile appeared was when either she, or another servant, did something of great stupidity. Exiting the portal, Valquee was forced to duck to avoid a goblet striking her in the head.

It was unusually quiet in the chambers today. Valquee's great footfalls echoed in the emptiness as she hurried through the winding maze of corridors which lead to master's chambers.

To the other workers of the castle, Valquee was known as just slave. Here, nobody cared who she was or where she'd come from, this did not at all mean she was going to let her guard down. In fact, the only one bothering to pay her any mind at all was Udkaa. And this was only when he was either insulting her or ordering her about. She liked it this way. It was a far greater improvement than life out in Sardon.

It was an improvement on more than one front as she was no longer forced to eat foul foods, and even if she didn't want it, she had easy access to master's chambers; if only master was there. Even this may be a good thing, his absence. She could not imagine having to clean his chambers with him in it, her heart was too pure. Right now she just needed to find someone here with the knowledge of Nalo.

It remained eerily still and quiet as Valquee approached the portal to the highly private chambers of her master.

Normally this room remained locked, if it was, she'd have to search the chambers for someone with a key. It was usually around now she'd be stopped by another, yet nobody so far had come.

Approaching the door cautiously, she noticed straightaway it was unlatched. Whoever was here before her forgot to set the key. Master's door was always supposed to be locked.

Nerves swelled within her as Valquee slipped inside. The chamber was vast; great tapestries hung from the ceiling to the floor with great coloured pictures of dragons embroidered, woven into the fabric. The largest one, spanning a great chunk of wall, had what Valquee recognized as Nighdrake, custom painted within its threads.

In the room's centre, a great four poster bed stood, dusty and virgin to an occupant, with a cloth of gold and silver hanging like a canopy above. For a bed, it was one of sheer elegance. Other furnishings were very minimal, often dark and weathered, they blended into the shadows.

The only thing besides the bed that competed for attention was the grand fireplace with its jutting hearth. Upon its mantle was what stole Valquee's gaze, a tattered book stood on display next to a great dragon egg.

'A dragon egg, why would he have one of those, and more importantly, where did he get it?' She thought as she let her fingers brush the egg's glassy surface. At first glance, it looked simply like polished marble; except to an eye that's trained, great veins of pulsating colour snaked their way across its shell like great tendrils in a web like fashion. This one,

Valquee could clearly see, was going to be an Earthinne for its veins were pulsing green as an emerald.

After a great time staring, Valquee tore her eyes from the egg only to be consumed by the book. Old and worn it was, bound in black leather. Unclasping the strap, she let it fall open. Its pages were yellow with age, and, as Valquee leafed through them, she noticed every page to be blank. "Odd." She commented. What was even more out of the ordinary was the strange pull, like sinew which held her bound to its presence. This was certainly a potential problem for voices had birthed in the near. She knew in her heart she must move along, however this strange vibe held her firm. A power like never experienced before, a warmth had her unwillingly entranced. She couldn't break her eyes from the ratty black leather cover. An unexplained tingling, almost like an unusual heartbeat, a tremor, resounded upon her finger ends. A peculiar beckoning sounded mysteriously, like an unexplained force encompassing the book. The dark magic was calling out to her, tempting her, urging her to read its gruesome scripts. She couldn't, she mustn't allow herself to succumb to its enchantments there was far too much at stake. With great effort she managed to break gaze from its cries before tucking it deep within her cloth; she meant to further study it later, and by study she meant to ask Xsealiadd.

Voices arose from nowhere, voices of great energy. Valquee whipped about knocking her helm askew. Straightening it frantically, her eyes flashed about. No one was there.

That was one thing Valquee hated about this place; how much sound reverberated, carrying itself to unwanted places. Regardless, Valquee could not subdue her curiosity. With care, she tiptoed along the vacated hallways in the direction of the chatter.

    The people were on the other side of the door, Valquee was sure of that. One of them even sounded mightily familiar. Placing a hand on the knob, she hesitated, this could get her killed. The curiosity was overpowering, and in her mind, it greatly outweighed any potential threats. Before she changed her mind again, she turned the knob causing the door to fly open.

Chapter 24
Queries and Responses

"Too long has it been since this sight has met my eyes." The Occluder commented as he gazed upon the massive wall of Sardon. A horn of mass bellowed from the deep and great drums which sounded from above, pounding out a rhythm for which the imposing gates swung forth. Beyond the wall, a substantial gathering of Sardon residents stood unusually elegant awaiting to greet their master.

"Yes, yes, I have returned and I hope I was missed. No need to answer, I can spot the liars!" He greeted. "Men, I want you to guide me home, too long has it been since I have humbled myself from within the walls of Carddronnea, I miss her so."

"Yes master." His servants replied in chorus as they walked alongside, guiding him to the great castle.

"The lost language of the dwarf is only irretrievable because in ancient legend it is said—" Xsealiadd's mouth froze and his face grew still.

"Master? Xsealiadd?" Ian panicked. Xsealiadd began to writhe and squirm as he screamed with the shrillest voice, like a dying man he felt. The pain shot through him in waves, each more intense than the last. It was a feeling like cold liquid nitrogen, pumping where blood should be. Xsealiadd gasped, his wind escaping his chest, he had felt this pain before; he knew it well.

Light began to swirl and dance before his consciousness until it blinded him entirely. He blinked several times trying to focus. He could hear blood rushing to his ears, but it sounded foreign, it wasn't his blood, the pulse pounded too rapidly; he could make out great voices amongst him, all chattering excitedly. One he thought was highly familiar, though he couldn't be sure.

His gaze lowered, and all at once he understood why he was there. On the table before him were his hourglass, his staff, the crown, and all of his other provisions. The men before him, torans mostly, were all greatly fascinated by the hourglass. Who wouldn't be? It was a fine piece of art, as well as his lifeline.

The door flew open and all eyes turned to the portal. In the doorway stood, what looked like a toran, only too small, its frame built more like a human's or elf's.

The creatures stood frozen. It didn't know what to make of what it saw.

"What are you doing here?" One of the torans snarled.

The creature in the door hesitated, almost as if it were analyzing its options. "What are you doing here and with the peacekeeper's things?"

The torans grew suspicious. "How do you know these are the peacekeeper's things?"

"Master told me he was bringing them. I wanted to see for myself." There was something familiar about the creature's voice which drove Xsealiadd mad, especially since he couldn't place a finger upon it.

"Yes, master sent them ahead of his fellowship; he wanted them to be safe here."

"Nothing is safe here with you two sliming them up!" The creature snarled.

The toran retaliated as before any were prepared, a great toran fight broke in that tiny room. Xsealiadd winced; several limbs were flying far too close to his precious hourglass.

"Behave yourselves all of you! Master has come, I hear him now." The only man present ordered. The torans quickly obeyed, and the creature, though slow to respond, got the message and stilled. "Now, I suggest you all go greet master like good servants, while I wrap these things up the way master wants them."

"Yes sir." The torans responded and lumbered from the room. The creature, however, didn't move, nor did, as no one noticed, a curious toran who stood just out of view.

"What do you want!" The man hollered. "Are you going to do as you are told?"

"No! You second in command?"

"Yes."

"I'm looking for Nalo the dragon slayer, from the dragon slayer's guild."

"And who are you to request such classified information?" The man challenged.

"I am a resident of Sardon dealing with a major dragon problem. I was just coming from Sardon's western flank where I was attacked by a ferocious beast of scale and claw. It caused me great injury and suffering and I want him gone."

"Do you know anything about the guild of the dragon slayers?"

"Yes, a bit."

"What do you know?"

"Just that if you tell me about it, I will forget. It's a form of magical protection."

"Indeed. And do you understand that there is only one way to break it?"

"I suppose, what is it?"

"You have to swear an oath in the tongue of black that you don't mean Sardon, nor its people any harm."

The creature thought about it long and hard. "Okay."

"Very well, just follow my lead." And with careful instruction, the man guided the creature through the oaths of the black tongue. The oaths drew to a close as the creature listened hard.

"Now, I'm only going to tell you once, so pay attention. Nalo is a member of the dragon slayer's guild called Tooth and Scale. They often hide out in a great limestone building, tall and narrow with iron rails and steep steps; it is located about three streets eastward of here."

The creature nodded, digesting the information as the man made to remove his helmet to scratch a spot on his jaw. The creature gasped, and so did Xsealiadd, beneath the helm was Rennaux, principal of Ackles Academy and Thyle's father.

The toran which stood in the doorway concealed from view had long since parted. Wanting to please its master, it decided it was to single-handedly take down the dragon before Nalo got there. Nothing anyone seemed to notice.

"What is your problem? I told you what you wanted to know now get out!" Rennaux screamed.

"You?"

"Yeah me, what?"

"You! Too much pain have you caused that school, too much have I endured your corruption, well not anymore!"

"That school, you? Who is under there really?" Rennaux asked curiously.

Removing her helm, Valquee glared. "The name's Valquee and this is the last time we shall ever meet!" Withdrawing the dagger that she kept concealed in the fold of her cloth, Valquee lunged.
"No Valquee, don't!" Xsealiadd screamed pointlessly for he couldn't be heard; only observe what he saw. "You swore in the black tongue not to hurt a member of Sardon, an oath I don't even know how to break, an oath that if broken could have dire consequences; I wouldn't know, I've never sworn or broken one…"

STAB! Rennaux went down, Valquee's blade in his stomach "…but, I suppose I'm about to find out." Xsealiadd added, life as he knew it was crumbling from around him.

Flipping her hair with pride, evidently unaware of the problems she had just created, Valquee gathered up Xsealiadd's belongings. Pivoting on the spot, she drew face to face with a scarred and mangled Ian.

The colour drained from her face, she saw it in the memory of the man of moustache. That wasn't the heart of Ian pounding in that chest.

Xsealiadd's world flooded back before him as he, once again, found himself lying peacefully on the banks of Gaunfaux flood, a frantic Ian by his side.

"Relax Ian I'm fine." He lied. "My hourglass was just calling me. It does this sometimes when we are parted, I will recover, honestly."

Ian eyed him with concern. The life that normally shone within the old man's gaze was gone. "Xsealiadd, I know you too well to know that not everything is fine. Tell me what you saw."

"Well," Xsealiadd thought about it long and hard, trying to refrain from the truth. "I just saw Valquee in Sardon." Was all he said.

"And..." Ian urged.

Xsealiadd simply stared silently.

"Come on, she means as much to you as she does me, tell me!"

"Oh all right, but not for that reason, just since you are the new peacekeeper, you need to be up on things happening. What I saw was Valquee walking in on a few servants to the Dark Lord observing and discussing the fate of my belongings, as you know, they were stolen from me. Anyhow, while there she tried to get information about the whereabouts of a Nalo, evidently a dragon slayer, using Scorch's life as a token to the information."

"I know the one, go on."

"Well, anyhow, one of the servants told her great magic surrounds Nalo's guild to keep Nalo and the other society members from harm. He also said that in order for this magic to be overridden, oaths would have to be sworn in the black tongue; which declares that you shall never harm Sardon or its people. Valquee swore to these oaths—"

"No."

"Yes. Then she found out the information and the man revealed himself as Rennaux. Angry, she killed him and made to run away with my belongings, only to bump into the Occluder inhabiting your body. My son, do you look terrible."

"What has happened to me?"

"He has bathed you in shadow scars."

"Do you actually believe she had to swear in the black tongue?" The question came from Ian's lips.

"No. Rennaux was never trusted; I think it to be a scam."

"As do I. And Valquee, what will happen to her now with the Occluder and oaths I mean?"

"I don't know Ian, I don't know. Your guess would be as strong as mine. You have to understand, though I can speak, read, and understand the black tongue, I really don't know the rules. If she swore in the language of the gods, nothing can unbind them according to any knowledge I possess. I neither know how forgiving the black language really is and I suspect nor does she, which is why I think she took a chance."

Chapter 25
Captured

"What were you doing in my castle?"

"Cleaning as I was told!" Valquee blurted, trying to keep any sense of emotion absent from her tone. Down in a dungeon she hung by iron shackles. Cold stone pressed against her skin bare. Clad in only a burlap sack to keep her covered, she quaked from the icy air.

"Don't lie to me!" The Occluder sneered. Taking a spear he rolled it hotly in his hands before, with a quick nod, he jammed it hard against her body, piercing her flesh. Valquee gave way to an involuntary scream of agony; she didn't know how long she could endure his torture.

A warm enlightening feeling filled her soul; she didn't know where it came from, but what a time to come.

'Come on Valquee stay with me, stay with me. There is still good in this world, though it doesn't seem so, and it's worth enduring for.' The thought pierced her mind, but faded in strength on each passing syllable. Across the barrier, Grunkle, a mere fog, struggled to communicate across the great obstruction, he was losing strength and fast. Then he thought about the poor girl that lay before him, being tortured and in pain. This reinvigorated his words.

Valquee's world faded from view as she slipped into an elvish syncope, a controlled coma, for a brief moment to stem the pain. Her world returned, but it was vastly fuzzy.

'Valquee,' the thought was weak, like a snaking tendril, it barely touched her mind. 'Don't give in to their madness. Do you remember that poem? The one sung by your kin and favoured by many?'

"Yes." Valquee panted, screaming into the void of nothingness, baffling the Occluder and his men.

'Tell me it. Tell me the poem now.'

"Akha unbane schkuze etam!" She bellowed, her chest heaving, she was hyperventilating as the spear, once more, pierced her flesh.

'Good, tell me more, come on!' The thought wavered in strength.

"I can't, I don't remember okay!"

'Yes, yes you do remember, I know it!' The thought brushed her mind.

"Just kill me okay!" She pleaded, nearing a breaking point.

The Occluder cackled, and the voice that touched her thoughts faltered.

'No. Valquee, my name is Grunkle, I am a good friend of Ian Cosswell, his soul still endures, he will survive. I'm not the only one who believes this. Xsealiadd has sworn in Ian's soul as the next peacekeeper. He's going to need you, so if you're not going to get through this for yourself, do it for him okay?'

Valquee whined and sniffled as the Occluder thumped her across the breast again with the shaft. "I will. I will survive for

Ian!" She bellowed. The Occluder cackled to an even greater degree, hitting her hardest yet.

'Now tell me that poem!'

"Akha unbane schkuze etam!"

'What's next Valquee? I want to hear more!'

"Akha unbane schkuze etam!" Valquee echoed the first line, her stomach being jabbed by the spear.

'Great, that's great! Repeat it as many times as you'd like just don't give in if that's what it takes!'

"Akha unbane schkuze etam!" Valquee bellowed again and again, upon each utterance, her strength growing.

"Very well." The Occluder sneered, after he could take it no more of her redundant repetition. "We will be back, you can mark my words."

'You did well Valquee, now, I'm going to find you a way out of this place.'

"Anything, anything." She mumbled her head lulling from the ordeal.

Very few times was Grunkle ever appreciative of being a spirit. This was one of those rarities. Able to drift between the thick walls and high ceilings, Grunkle acted as a silent observer, taking in the surroundings.

Poor Grunkle grew often so lonesome, being so used to aiding others. It grew to a weary, unforeseen time that Grunkle wandered that castle with its vast expanse of empty spaces and great shadows of darkness. Day and night he listened to the endless drivel, hoping to gather an idea for an escape. Days turned to healthy weeks, and though Grunkle learned loads of knowledge he never believed possible, none was of any use for which he searched: a way out.

There were times he wished he could call upon Ian to give him aid, yet he didn't dare leave Valquee's side to get him should another torture session commence. So here Grunkle was, a meagre existence in a grand castle watching people come and go, yet paying no mind. Opening his eyes one fine afternoon, after he accepted the daunting task of freeing Valquee unaided, Grunkle finally realized that each and every person that came and went, with the exception of the leeches, torans of the public who continually remained in the chambers leeching off the food and warmth, each and every person had a time and place. Times when cleaners swabbed the floors, times when the king, the Occluder and his second in running demanded meals, times, even when the royalties made their daily visits to the garderobe to pay their respects to the chamber pot.

"Chamber pots!" Grunkle exclaimed. "Waste has to go somewhere." Just then a shriek tore through the chambers, a scream Grunkle was learning well. "Valquee!" He yelled as he materialized his way to her dungeon hold.

Most fortunate for Valquee, the Occluder neither brandished a skewer at her, nor were his guards bearing one. However, the very sight of the Occluder was fearful enough. By the time Grunkle arrived, the Dark Lord was still cackling at her fearful outcry.

"Please, don't torture me again, I can't take it anymore!" She was ready to snap.

'Just hang in there Valquee!' Grunkle jumped in.

The Occluder sneered. "No? Well there's no need for that."

"Huh?" Valquee was surprised at the sudden change in disposition.

"Tell me, a while back you took an oath in the black tongue before one of my servants am I correct?"

"Yes."

"And did you not slay Rennaux, one of my most trusted slaves?"

Valquee remained silent.

"You don't have to say anything, I know you did, that's why you're here. If this be the case, then the ill effects of the magic oaths broken will be torture enough. Even now, as we speak, I can almost see the magical poison taint your blood." He sneered sadistically. "I'm surprised you are not already symptomatic yet. Then again, elves are very resilient, aren't they?" The Occluder slapped her hard on the cheek side. "Elves can withstand extraordinary things." His grin broadened as he unsheathed his dagger.

"No!" Valquee cried, and somehow, someway, the dagger caught flame, a flame burning so hot, the Occluder had to drop it as it burned to liquid metal and ash on the stone floor. The dagger had melted from the heat.

Across the border, Grunkle lay in a heap, his spirit so disjointed he feared he had failed Valquee in escaping. Never before had he performed that level of magic in death; he never knew the strength of power required; channelling that much energy had nearly extinguished his entity entirely.

'Valquee?' It was a long time before Grunkle could sustain a voice after rebuilding his spirit.

"Who's there?"

'It's me Grunkle, don't you remember? I'm Ian's friend.'

"Get away from me!" She bellowed, all in a panic.

'I think I have a way out of here.' He commented.

"Out of where? Where am I? Why am I tied up? Where is my shorble Scorch?"

'Scorch? Scorch is a dragon, not a shorble, and he is with Ian.' As Grunkle listened to such questions, he realized, this must be the effects of the magic ripping apart her memory. 'I've got to get you out of here fast.' Grunkle commented more to himself than anyone else.

There was no planning, Grunkle obliterated the shackles, grabbed Xsealiadd's hourglass and staff, and hoped that Valquee was not seen, as he tried to convince her to follow the voice in her mind; which proved to be a challenge as she continued to wail on about being tricked like this before by the Shadowed Lord.

'Look Valquee, I am not the Shadowed Lord! I am only here to get you out, now, turn right though this hall, once you exit the room. Good, now, I'm going in front to check for patrols, good...' Grunkle never worked so hard before trying to get someone, or something to obey. Several times he had to urge Valquee on with a push of energy to drive her forth. And on some occasions, force her into a room to avoid being seen by patrols. 'Do you see an opening to your left? I want you to go through it.' Grunkle ordered.

Valquee peered down it, her nose wrinkling. "It stinks."

'Yeah, I know,' Grunkle urged, 'but it's the only way out of here, out of torture, misery, and pain.' This must've sparked a nerve for Valquee wriggled into the tight spot.

Slithering towards the postage sized square of light at the other end, Valquee was surprised to see it drop straight down into the waters below; at least a fifty to seventy five foot drop. Along the bricks below, great stains of brown lined the smooth masonry. Whatever came down the chute was foul-smelling and acidic, something Valquee refrained to find out but suspected Grunkle already knew.

"How do I get out of here Grunkle? I don't want to be here when whatever gets dumped down the chute is evacuated."

'Well, you know,' Grunkle began, 'the water is quite deep here, and I assure you, there are no jagged rocks.'

"Are you suggesting I jump?"

'Aye.'

"I'll get killed!"

'No, hurt perhaps, but not killed.'

"And what about the towns' folk? They'll hear the commotion."

'Well, you can wait for the next cleaning, let the excrements carry you through, then nothing more than a large stool would be suspected.'

Valquee retched. "You know, I've had about enough of this filthy place." Before even Grunkle was ready, Valquee leapt. Even Grunkle had never seen such grace as Valquee's slim build held a streamlined pose.

'Valquee don't! You'll accelerate too much; the water won't be deep enough for that!' Valquee, however, wasn't listening. She was more concerned with making as little noise as possible upon entry.

Slicing through the icy waters with no more sound than a stone, Valquee splayed her limbs to slow her momentum just below the surface before pushing from the bottom of the lakebed. She seemed more comfortable in the water than a fish, though even she felt the effects of the chilling, glacier runoff. Nobody could survive there very long. She let the strong current guide her as she drifted just below the surface. She meant to arrive at the same place that she had entered Sardon; next to her wagon which still lingered by the clump of trees.

Hiding in the trees, Valquee camped with no inkling to move, all her provisions were with her, including her unspoiled rations, and Xsealiadd's hourglass and staff. Nobody seemed to notice them at the base of the tree.

A stiff breeze stirred causing her to quiver. Though chilly, the air was warm in comparison to the waters. Before even thinking, Valquee dressed in her elvish clothes as she wrapped her traveler's cloak tightly about her as she tried to ward off the cold. This provided a little comfort against the breeze, but she still longed in her heart for a nice warm fire.

She was close now. Too close to seeking her goal, all she had to do now was move. She had more common sense than that though; she knew she must wait for things and that would take time.

What troubled her heart most, however, were those bouts of confusion. Unexplainable they were in her mind and crippling as they destroyed nearly all sense of self. The worst of it was they had been growing more frequent and more severe over the passing days.

'Valquee?'

"Yes Grunkle?" She whispered in fear of being overheard.

'Will you be resting here a while?'

"I will be Grunkle."

'Then will you pardon my absence as I seek help for your confusion?'

"Thank you Sir Grunkle." Valquee smiled, she was blessed to have a friend like Grunkle, though she knew she would never see him.

As lazy as a summer's breeze blows, Grunkle drifted off, soon to be appearing next to Ian.

Ian leapt up at once. He was in the midst of reviewing last week's language before beginning to learn new characters and symbols. "Is she with you? Do you have her? Is she here? How is she? Where is she? Why isn't she back yet?—" Ian's bombardment of questions never ceased.

"Relax dear lad, I'll get to it? Actually, wait a moment Ian."

"Yes Grunkle?"

"It is time that you do me a favour. Can you please ask the wizard if he knows a cure for confusion and loss of self awareness?"

"Yes Master Grunkle." Ian replied, repeating the question for Xsealiadd.

Xsealiadd's face grew sullen. "Oh, oh dear, so the black tongue is much like that of the gods. If you break an oath, you will lose self-awareness, eventually slipping into a zombie-like state. This is not good. I know of only one cure and that is to surrender yon self to the gods; something most fail to understand how to do. However, if you can do basic magic, there is a different spell that can slow the process. Now if I teach you that, can you tell me all that has happened?" Xsealiadd asked, speaking to no one in particular.

'Yes.' The thought filled both Xsealiadd's and Ian's head.

"Excellent, tell away." Xsealiadd urged.

"—hey wait a brief moment, I thought you can't talk to the living!"

"I can, but it's excruciatingly difficult." Grunkle explained to Ian alone, before telling of all that had occurred since Valquee had left shore.

Both Ian and Xsealiadd were a great audience, gasping and cheering at all the right moments. When Grunkle finished, even Xsealiadd began to cry.

"My dear girl!" He exclaimed before at last teaching Grunkle the proper enunciation for the spell at hand.

With a quick 'thank you,' Grunkle dissipated into a stiff wind as he joined Valquee by her side.

Chapter 26
Unfinished Business

There was barely a greeting before Grunkle was blurting out those funny phrases. He wanted the spell to be executed before those strange words were forgotten.

Valquee stared into emptiness, her body numbing. "What have you done to me?"

'I've slowed the effects of the magic until you can return to Xsealiadd for a full reversal.'

"Xsealiadd?"

'The wizard peacekeeper, he's with Ian right now.'

"Oh." Valquee drew silent. She didn't want to overspeak for fear of being heard.

Sitting quiet as a mouse, poised upon a great pine bough, she waited for the next raft that would guide her into Sardon to finish uncompleted business with Nalo. She planned to use the same techniques as before. They worked once right?

Hours had passed before Valquee finally caught her first glimpse of a barge, it was empty of cargo. It must be a slow day for deliveries. Flicking away the dirt she'd been scratching from her cuticles, Valquee drew to her feet, her back arched; she stood tall like a hawk eying its prey.

The barge drifted inland, and with her vision obstructed by a cluster of tree branches, it wasn't until the raft drew close that she realized it was driven by a snorg. This wouldn't do for the plan to work; she needed someone with a body.

Pulling back the tree boughs, Valquee observed through a small opening, her elvish attire allowing excellent camouflage. Her eyes flashed wildly, her every sense on high alert. The snorg was banking the barge; something had caught his eye, something moving in the trees.

Jerking his head to the foliage, he stared, his gaze drilling into every shadow. Whether he knew it or not, he was staring right at a concealed Valquee. He began to move to the trees, intent was in his eyes. Valquee shrank back. Cloudiness flooded her mind she was all of a sudden lost and alone. She began to panic, whimpering like a small child. Not knowing who you are, where you are, or what you're doing in a place so foreign is a scary feeling.   The snorg began to charge, he was running straight at the trees, his raft left abandoned on the bank.

Something distracted him as he drew to a quick halt. Searching the air like someone trying to focus on a buzzing fly, he grew irritable.

"Grrrrowrrll!" He snarled before he had tumbled face first into the snow, correction, he was pushed face first into the snow, but by what? His great shadowed fist flew through the air, a great white swirl erupting amongst him. His shoulder dipped as he fell to his knees. It was indeed a strange sight. Something even stranger happened then that no one expected. A strange vortex swirled about him, black swirled white, white pivoted about black. The more that happened, the less black there seemed to be. Things began to brighten as the blackness dissipated. The white fog soon cleared, and the snorg was gone.

Valquee blinked hard several times trying to bring focus and sense upon her being. The cloudiness in her mind was also leaving; she had survived another of the oath's magical attacks.

'Are you okay Valquee?'

"Yes, what happened back there?"

'Oh, that, I just extinguished that snorg, I think he saw you.'

"Thank you Grunkle." Valquee whispered, a single solitary tear escaped her eye.

'Do you think you're ready to proceed?'

"Yes Grunkle, I think it's time."

'Okay, here's what I'm thinking...' Grunkle began, giving Valquee his input of what he thought to be a worthy plan.

Valquee nodded her approval. "Oh wait, Grunkle!" She called as she felt him exit her mind.

'Yes Valquee?'

"Just don't hit him in the stomach; he'll think you're his best friend or something."

Across the border, Grunkle nodded something Valquee obviously couldn't see.

A band of torans and men stood coagulating just amongst the port gate. All were chattering with merriment when the one near the middle stumbled forward for no apparent reason, all pandemonium unleashed. The toran that was hit spun around, glaring at the one behind him.

"What chu do dat for!" he bellowed, inches from the other's face, black spittle flying in great wads.

"Do what?"

"Don't chu play dum wid me! I don't like bein' pushed!" He screamed, slamming his massive fist square in the other toran's chest. He stumbled back several steps to maintain his balance, ploughing into the one behind him who fell over.

"Hey!" The third toran yelled, getting to his feet and brushing snow off his pallid gray flesh.

"You scum pushed me over!"

Needless to say a raging fight ensued, one in which, inevitably, there would be casualties as blades were being drawn.

Grunkle remained in the seclusion of the evergreens by Valquee's side as the fight unfolded.

"You're a great help, thanks Grunkle."

'Anytime.'

The fight only lasted a handful of moments, when it was all said and done, as predicted, several casualties scattered the bloodstained snow. However, being in a land of hungry carnivores, they didn't last long either as the carcasses were recycled for others' nourishment. Eventually filtering off, the men of Sardon left but an empty shell of bones and cloth in their wake.

"This is almost too perfect." Valquee replied, leaping up from the tree. She was going to get the clothes to wear as a disguise.

'Stop!' The voice was a forceful one between her ears. Valquee, so stunned by the potency of the order, froze at once. 'Too great of a risk would it be for you Valquee, sprinting across no man's land. You would definitely be caught; you would definitely be seen. Please, allow me to bring them to you. I can do it quick and unnoticeable.'

Valquee sighed, "Fine," she replied. In a flash, the mangled pile of bone and cloth began moving toward the evergreens, seemingly, upon their own accord.

The moment fate would allow, Valquee put as many clothes atop her gear as possible to veil her elvish attire. This time, when she left Sardon, she meant not to return by any means. Things she wasn't burdening herself with, she threw into the concealed wagon banked on shore. This was her way out, and out quickly was her intention.

Her pack slammed to the wooded frame of the wagon with excess force, more than she was intending for she was almost heard.

Stilling until the commotion ebbed, Valquee sprang into action. Climbing the fence just out of view, once again dressed like a toran, Valquee headed to the location described to her as Nalo's hideout. Luckily for her, the streets seemed abuzz with energy. Torans rushed here or there, snorgs performing great gruelling tasks, and even some men passed her gaze, burdened down with supplies and records.

The further from Carddronnea Castle she drew, the darker the ever pressing twilight seemed to become, until it was an almost claustrophobic feeling in the air.

A Sardon night had nearly broke when Valquee, at last, pinpointed the location she believed Nalo's guild was being held. If nothing else, the building matched the description with its limestone face, it's narrow towering frame, and steep stoop clad with iron rails.

Valquee observed the premises, questioning her reasoning doubts flooding her mind. This place didn't feel right, though nothing in Sardon did. For a place that was supposed to be hosting a conference, it was awfully quiet and dark. As Valquee climbed the steep stone steps, she pondered. This place was not silently stygian, it was deserted. A building with a layer of filth as thick as this had not seen activity for at least a decade. That was the rational affirmation of things. Of course, Valquee had to work hard to remind herself, she was in Sardon and in Sardon things don't always operate in the norm. A sure sign of its eccentricities being that it always remained dusk here, the world perpetually seemed to be bathed in green.

Extracting the dagger she kept sheathed at her side Valquee placed a hand on the large brass handle with care. Her palm emerged grimy. With a quick wipe on her slacks, Valquee turned the handle. The door creaked open, causing dust to billow and swirl all at once. Rays of green light pierced through the cracks between the slabs of aged wood which veiled the window panes. This place was eerie and neglected and was one of those buildings any sane person would desire least to be in. From what Valquee interpreted, however, Nalo was far from sane; he had to be, any with guilt, remorse, or a conscience, could not slay a beast as noble as a dragon.

Dragging the lone wooded chair from across the room, which scraped away dust trails on the floor, Valquee propped open the heavy door. For some reason, this offered her minimal comfort, knowing she had a way out; she was not completely encased with insecurities.

With care and extreme caution, Valquee slipped into the next room, her every sense on high alert. A tiny squeak caused Valquee to falter, it was only a rat. It was especially difficult to ignore that burn in her stomach, that uneasy ball of energy all elves experience when something wasn't quite right.

SLAM!

Valquee leapt from her skin before darting, dagger at the ready, towards the source back in the room she had come. There was no one there, though the door had shut and the chair was returned to its original location. Valquee was not alone; something was in that building with her.

A quick whoosh ensnared her senses as she jerked her head towards the disturbance. She was lucky, the arrow that was shot had missed her by a shorble's whisker as it impaled itself in the heavy wooden door she leaned against. The resounding twang was distracting as it quivered in its target to absorb the energy.

Valquee's gaze darted about, seeking the archer. There was no one to be seen, however, a cloud of dust swirled unusually just beyond the next portal; something had disturbed it.

In her heart raged a battle as Valquee's every sense, especially her common one, screamed at her not to go on. She did what she could to ignore them as she moved rather robotically into the next room. Valquee's heart pounded out a rhythm she was sure all could hear, though she hoped otherwise. Her eyes were wide with fear as she swallowed the lump in her throat.

Though she heard not a sound, her neck began to prickle. Jamming her back against the wall, she closed her eyes and voiced a quick prayer. She never was sure if a god existed, nevertheless, it felt good, the feeling of someone higher up guiding her.

Standing before her was a flight of rickety stairs which she was nervous to trust; to her left, a great hallway which split into several other rooms on both sides. What frightened her most was the portal to her right side. Someone could easily sneak up from behind and come through that doorway.

'Next time,' she berated herself in silence, 'trust your instincts, go against a wall where none is at your back.'

She grew intuitive, listening to every sense. If only she could hear the heedless warnings being screamed at her from the barrier's other side. Grunkle could see something Valquee couldn't, a soundless foe ready to pounce, lurking in the depths of the ever abundant shadows.

A deafening scream filled the air as a sharp pain seared in her right shoulder; Valquee had no time to react, no time to comprehend. Stunned with pain, she went down, defiling all elvish instincts to stay on the feet. "On the floor, that's where the enemy wants you." One of the first lessons in elvish training, and on the floor is where Valquee resided; crippled with pain, her senses numb to all else that moved.

It seemed like more times than once that fate had shined down upon her, for the figure coming towards her faltered, pushed by an unforeseen force.

Valquee breathed heavy as she sat slumped to the wall. Something brushed past her, for cool air tickled her flesh. Slowly, carefully the dagger was drawn from her wound and was tossed aside, wayward into the shadows. A burning sensation, neither hot nor cold overtook the wound. Valquee could feel the bulging and easing of muscle tissue and skin, she was being healed, but by whom, and why?

"G-Grunkle?"

'Yes Valquee, it is I.'

She breathed a sigh of relief, but it was short-lived.

The figure emerged from the shadows, clad as black as night; in his hand he gripped the dagger, Valquee's blade, which was lost in the commotion. Slowly, the figure raised his hand, the knife held aloft, ready to strike. But Valquee didn't see it. Her body on the mend, she was exhausted, her head lulled forward.

Grunkle, trying to rebuild his energy reserves from healing Valquee stared, his ghostly eyes flying wildly from the shadowed figure to Valquee. The figure was still drawing closer, the distance between him and the fallen elf ever decreasing. She did not see, her eyes swollen and out of focus. She didn't notice the danger. Exhausted, Grunkle tried to warn her, but he didn't have a voice, nor a thought, he barely had a spirit, he was weak.

It was impossible, nothing was working. Grunkle had no way to prevent the inevitable.

Chapter 27
Fugitive

It was intuition that stepped to the rescue as Valquee's neck prickled, her skin drawing taught. She looked up as the blade was coming down to greet her in a surely unfriendly fashion. She somersaulted, just clearing the dagger's path of trajectory

"Who are you?" She screamed, restraining the blackened figure.

"W-what's it to you?" The figure was scared, though he tried to subdue it.

"I am on the hunt for someone." Remembering she was concealed beneath a toran's helmet, she quickly added, "Master is seeking the blood of whomever let the intruder into the castle, he sent me in search of the follower with a single name. So tell me your name, servant, else master won't be pleased."

"N-Nalo, the name is Nalo."

"All I need to know." Valquee chimed, and with a quick motion, she snapped his neck. "That," she added, "is for the Golden King's death." Reclaiming the dagger, she cleaned the blood stains on her cloth before tucking it away and exiting the premises.

Valquee couldn't remember running so fast before in her life, although her existence was long, and her memories feeble.

For an elf to sprint as fast as she, it was only a matter of time before she ensnared unwanted attention as she began to gather suspicious followers.

Reaching the iron, picketed fence, she cleared its height with barely a workout. It was easy given the excessive momentum she had built up.

"Hey!" A gate guard yelled, clearly suspicious as he fumbled with his keys.

"Oran guarlé furuntee ashmine!" Valquee screamed as she leapt the distance from the hillside to the wagon. She was clearly high on adrenaline. The hillside gave way to the sea behind her, leaving her wagon to float amongst the deepening waters.

Fumbling for the oar which was wedged amongst Xsealiadd's hourglass, staff, her pack, bow and all the other things she had left in there from earlier, Valquee did her best to make a quick getaway. Getting the paddle in the water, she scrambled to get her wagon into open seas. Behind her, many of Sardon's men crowded what was left of the bank, watching her escape. Others were prepping boats as to draw closer the distance between their fugitive and themselves.

Valquee nearly dropped the oar as a fit of confusion overtook her. Breaking the oath of black twice had resulted in double the consequence. And what a time for it to strike too, for the men and torans of Sardon had just gotten a boat into the waters and were speeding towards her.

Ian's conversations in every language he'd been learning had been steadily improving. Currently, he was struggling to read a lengthy passage Xsealiadd had scribed into the earth.

His eyes fluttered closed as much as open as he concentrated on the particulars of the pronunciations. The language of the gods was very fussy in terms of one mispronunciation could bring down the mountains; luckily, however, Xsealiadd felt him not yet ready to chant a spell. Opening his eyes in the middle of pronunciations, something flitted in his peripheral.

"Xsealiadd look out!" He screamed instinctively.

Xsealiadd leapt to his feet, he had no weapons on his person. If it weren't for Hayashi and Ming, he'd have no clothes either.

A hooded toran with a sword charged, but not at Xsealiadd, at Scorch, who was fondling a rotted carcass in the grasses nearby. This may have been a good thing for he was the only one with any defence. Also, since he was trained to slay any that moves for feeding, he knew straightaway what to do. However, Scorch was still a hatchling and had never truly killed anything that could fight back, leaving Xsealiadd concerned of injury.

"Watch this one Scorch he has a claw of his own."

Scorch cocked his head.

Xsealiadd swiped at him as if he had bared his own set of hooks before nodding in the direction of the approaching enemy.

Scorch crouched low, his haunches high, his tail pointing skywards, it was quite a sight. Scorch charged, wisps of smoke furling from his nostrils. Leaping, he barrelled into the figure and with a great howl he rolled several times before stilling several yards away. As for the figure, his blade was gone and he was trying to rouse, he was shaken, flattened by the dragon youth. For a human, being trampled by a dragon, even one as small as Scorch would certainly have resulted in death, but torans are bigger, stronger, and meaner than a man, which is why Scorch lay in such a predicament.

Xsealiadd pressed a naked foot to his breast. "Undrakka adomiebay!" He bellowed, the toran stilled.

He didn't stay down long for this hooded toran had magic of his own. With a bizarre twist of blackened words, Xsealiadd was thrown at least twenty feet. Landing hard on impact, he groaned with pain.

The hooded toran however knew a losing battle when he saw one. Scrambling to his feet he fled west to, no doubt, return to Sardon. As Ian watched his retreating back, he noticed something he hadn't before, the toran clutched what looked almost like a wand in his hand; Ian had never seen anything like it.

Xsealiadd was slow to rouse, but once he did, he turned his immediate attention to a whimpering Scorch; Xsealiadd was naught two feet from the dragon when a fit of pain overtook him. Crumpling back down to the ground he began to writhe and squirm.

Ian watched helpless, "Oh no, not him too, again!"

Xsealiadd stilled as bright white light flooded his consciousness only giving way when new surrounds met him. He was watching a great wagon float upstream, in it, he recognized the face of Valquee, but there was something not right; she was dazed and confused, disoriented even, she was suffering from the magic poison.

Behind her, three boats paddled with tremendous strength and speed, their riders, torans. Xsealiadd begged for her to come to, for the boats were nearly upon her. She must've heard his plea, for she suddenly came around. She muttered something strange, though Xsealiadd never heard what. The water churned and soon, great waves propelled her forth. Seeing an inlet, she nestled in a cave.

She was preparing to sleep that night as she extracted a bed roll. The pursuers, apparently did not see her leave over the sizeable waves, for they sailed right past; heading upstream to the great forests where many who ever escape Sardon go to hide.

Xsealiadd observed many things being wrenched from her wagon, including his staff and hourglass, which quivered in her grasp. And as the vision was fading to reality, one more thing he managed to glimpse; a great unusual item which reminded him exactly of the wand the toran had held in his presence only moments ago; only this one bore more elegance, and if Ian were to see it, he would surely question why Valquee harboured such a shadowed weapon; Xsealiadd questioned the very same thing. Even Valquee appeared puzzled at this find; she must not have known it to be there.

At last the vision perished and Xsealiadd found himself to be laying on the muddy soils of the banks of Gaunfaux flood naught two feet from a still crying Scorch.

Xsealiadd crawled to his side. Lifting up a great front paw, he saw what pained him. The great blade used by the assassin was buried deep in a small gap between Scorch's maturing scales.

"Now, now." Xsealiadd turned inward, speaking to Scorch in his mind. After some time, he made to remove the cutlass, chanting funny phrases with his free hand resting on the dragon as the sword was drawn from the wound.

Ian quickly realized Xsealiadd was healing the dragon as he worked to prevent any loss of blood. As the blade exited the flesh it took with it a small scale, the size of a saucer. With a small yelp, Scorch nosed the fallen scale before licking where the wound had healed.

Xsealiadd's eyes widened with surprise. Though Ian heard or saw nothing, he guessed Scorch and Xsealiadd to be conversing in private.

"No, no certainly not, I'm not deserving of such a fine gift." Ian grew cross. "Are you sure young one? ...Okay then." And Xsealiadd gathered up the scale and tucked it away.

"Xsealiadd, I want you to teach me to be a great harker. So I can speak to my dragon too!"

"Your dragon?"

"Well you said he was going to bite me didn't you?"

Xsealiadd laughed wholeheartedly. "I did. Your dragon was just telling, no, insisting I take this scale as a gift for all I have done for both him and you."

Scorch cooed with contentment as he sniffed the blood on Xsealiadd's robes with concern.

"Oh I'm all right little one," Xsealiadd comforted. "We should really keep this." Xsealiadd drew the sword in close.

"I don't know if I want a blade stained with the blood of my dragon."

"Normally Ian I'd agree with you, but right now this is all we have."

Ian was silent for a long while, not knowing of what to say. It was then Scorch came over and nuzzled him affectionately.

"So when can I learn to become a great harker?" Ian asked, trying to ignore the crunches and smacks Scorch executed as he nibbled on his earlier carcass.

Xsealiadd laughed again. "You want to learn that badly?"

"Yes, I'd love to speak to all dragons, and flies, and roaches." He added quickly.

Xsealiadd grinned broadly. "If you really want to learn, I suppose I can teach you. Come here boy and we'll get started."

Joining Xsealiadd, Ian sat cross-legged by his side, his back turned to Scorch and his disgusting antics.

"So what was that vision about?" Ian asked curiously.

"That was just our sweet, sweet Valquee."

"And..."

"And she's coming home."

Ian whooped with glee, but quickly settled as he was anxious to become a great harker.

"And you know, Ian? I saw that dragon slayer coming for Scorch I just didn't want to frighten you. It would be terrible to lose your dragon before you get him, don't you agree?"

"Oh stop it!" Ian smirked, punching Xsealiadd on the shoulder.

Shifting to gain comfort, Xsealiadd gave Ian the eye. "We best get started for being a great harker is a difficult thing to learn."

A familiar scene was unfolding in the dungeons of Carddronnea naught a mile from where Valquee was concealed in a cave. Candles hung almost floating as per usual, several heads were seen above the long table. At the head of the table a scarred fading Ian sat, his fingers merrily touching at the tips as he waited for the meeting to commence. His breath hung heavily in the air, condensing in the cool chill the dungeon always provided.

"Everybody here? Good, good. This meeting will be brief for I must fly again."

Several staged groans erupted from a number of his Carddronne's.

"Thank you!" He slammed his fist hard against the table, "...For that false, heartless farewell!" He was irate. "This meeting has been called for one reason only. Within the last while, two of my most prized servants have been killed by a fugitive."

"Don't worry master. We have men hunting her down as we speak."

"Excellent! And when she is caught, which she'd better be, bring her here, dead or alive, I don't care! Anyhow, because of these great losses, I need a new principal for Ackles Academy; and since Cano has been doing such a fine job up until now, congratulations Cano, you have just been promoted."

Further down the table Cano groaned.

"I know, I know, everybody hates work, but it must be done! I also need someone to monitor the movement of the Amity Blade. Let me know the moment you discover if it will be in Rulan during their midyear festivities. Let's see, hmm... you! You will do fine for the job Largo."

Largo shifted awkwardly.

"None of this is troubling me at the moment. What does, however, is losing Rennaux. At the loss of him, I have forfeited valuable information; for he concealed an item of great worth. With him gone, no one knows where it is for he took the information on its whereabouts to the grave. I shan't, however, be surprised, suppressing this secret was a promise he made to me. He failed however, one crucial task. And that was to tell me where my item is!" His nostrils flared. "This is why I will be departing soon, I must seek it—" he froze, a thought had struck him. "And I know someone, who just might know its whereabouts. Spread the word, I depart sooner than I originally expected. This meeting is over!" The Occluder fled from the room, toppling his stool on the way past.

"Speaking of answers." He spoke to himself on the way through the corridors, "it is time I pay some good friends a visit, starting with Stanzer."

Stanzer didn't know how many stabbings, pokings, and proddings he had endured of the Occluder's great spear, his favourite means of torture. No matter how many more it would take, he refused to give in.

"No never!" He screamed. "I am the maker of Xsealiadd's hourglass. I'm the one who painstakingly gathered the crystals and allowed them to glow from within the bounds of the glass." He ceased speaking immediately, he had said too much already.

"What is it for exactly? And what spells did you put upon it?" The Occluder drilled, piercing Stanzer's flesh.

"No I will never tell! I made it for what it is and I'm not about to unmake it by telling! That is strictly up to Xsealiadd." He fell silent, now he'd really said too much.

It was this way he remained no matter the question that was tossed his way.

"Fine!" The Occluder barked frustrated. "I don't have time for this, if you won't speak, you die! Come boys, just leave him be, nature will take care of him, eventually. Just somebody, please, in a few weeks, be sure he's done. No food, no water either—" Then the great iron doors slammed shut as Stanzer heard no more. He was left, hanging by his shackles to bleed out from his wounds.

The magical rod Valquee turned over in her hand several times. On each pass, she grew more and more puzzled. A voice, faint and soft, she heard in her mind.

'You know, I nicked that from the Sardon folks. I overheard them speaking of its powers, it sounded useful.'

"Grunkle!"

'Yes?'

"What does it do?"

'Apparently it has the power to locate shadowed souls and has the magical ability to slay the corrupted hearts with ease. It will only target evil though.'

Valquee turned it in her hands once more. "Does it target shadowed beasts like snorgs do you know?"

'I don't know Valquee, I don't know. We shan't, however, be with great hopes in an uprising.'

Morning yawned before them as Valquee began to pack for departure. She paddled forth, her arms not yet recovered from the sculling yesterday as they screamed in protest. Nevertheless, she navigated on, her goings smooth, until an arrow whizzed by her ear nearly taking her with it; thank goodness for the torans poor archery skills.

Along the western bank where the tree-line strengthened, warriors from Sardon shot with purpose, meaning to bring her down. She gathered her bow and quiver. Shooting the men through the tree boughs with such accuracy, she could have shot a beetle in the blackness. One by one, they fell to dying screams as she brought her wagon up to an embankment.

Clamouring on shore, she began to unload her belongings. Pivoting on the spot, she meant to make camp further inland; something that would have to wait, for a band of Sardon folk anticipated her arrival atop the incline. It was an ambush, one she knew she couldn't survive; there were far too many.

"I'm sorry Nighdrake, sweet, this session will be brief. It just seems I have an unfortunate amount of dues to attend to. Let's see what you can do."

Nighdrake hesitated before he began to change the weather, causing it to rain, then shine, he made a river spring up from nothing, and then made it freeze as a blizzard slammed the dungeon, he also caused winds to roar which resulted in the torches to rage. With a great fiery sigh, he collapsed with exhaustion.

"Hmm, not very efficient I see. Well, I suppose it's time I teach you to use less energy for more power. See, I suspect your problem is that you are creating the wind, which would tire even me, and look at my skills. It is not your job to create these elements, leave that to nature, it's good at it. Your job is to tell nature to create the wind. That, understandably, will ease your workload, allowing you to conserve your energy. Now, I'll tell you a little secret, I've never bothered to learn such Craft, it was a waste of my time. I think, however, one of us should learn it and I'll leave it for you. I trust you to teach yourself such a skill in my absence. Now I must fly for my other errands beckon to me. I will promise to return when I can." Without another utterance, the Occluder had vanished from the room.

Florian was really starting to despise, "the pit." Week after week, he and his classmates climbed down into this sunken arena to face and test their skills with varying monsters. His stomach sat about as low as the pit's bottom as he, once more, met Orik, an assistant dwarf who aided in the study and defence of foes with strength.

When the students were on the battlefield and were unable to best their enemy, Orik's job was to offer aid to the professors to subdue and get the beasts under proper order.

The creature they were battling this time was a roaming herbivore rare to Ellezwrainia. At first glance, it would be likely mistaken for an oversized ram, with a shaggy pelt and spiralled horns, it turned out to be rather vicious for a leaf eater.

Covering these horns were elephant sized ears, which it used to fan itself cool, as well as a trunk of great strength. Its globe-like eyes were as bright as an owl and as keen also. It couldn't fly, but its greatest weapon was its ability to weave magic of great power.

"Remember!" Orik yelled. "Monsters, gods, and demons will, mostly take on a humanoid or at least, a relatable form. They will usually be distorted in form or power; do not let that deceive you. Find its weak spot and best it!"

"Find its weak spot; we'll be lucky if we find it at all!" A voice cut through the starlit blackness causing all to snicker.

"I'm sorry you have to fight night blind, but you need the experience, besides, it manoeuvres best during blackened hours."

"Yeah, that way it can sneak up upon us and kill us!" Another student joked. "Roar!" He added, and a great scream broke the night. He must've snuck up on a peer and frightened him.

"Relax everyone, remember it's a herbivore, it won't eat you." Orik advised.

"Yeah, don't worry folks, he won't eat you, only kill you." Another student mocked.

"Orik?"

"What!" The dwarf was growing short-tempered.

"Your advice stinks worse than a toran!" The class erupted in an uproar.

Only then did Orik notice Wok trying to beat the creature to prevent its escape. In his hand he held a great spear which he was whacking at the shins of the creature, the only thing that ten foot tall Wok could reach.

"Wok, Wok, Wok!" Orik rushed over. "You do not swing it, it is not a sword, are you stupid! It is a spear jab, jab!"

"Well, the fact that I've never used any of these weapons before in my life, yeah, I am stupid!" Wok grew cross. "Shows a reflection on you as a teacher now doesn't it?"

"I'm sorry Wok, it has been long since I was learning, I often forget what it was like." Orik apologized.

"Well, maybe this will help you remember!" Wok growled angrily, and conked Orik upside the head. The spear shattered as Orik crumpled. "Who says I have to jab?" Wok interjected. Nearby, the students roared with hysterics, everyone oblivious to the creature which was making an escape for freedom.

"—Ian?" Xsealiadd cut in. Ian was startled. He was in the midst of voicing a phrase from one of his many languages when Xsealiadd interrupted him. The only time Xsealiadd ever did such a thing, was when something serious was occurring.

"What is the issue Xsealiadd?"

"Trouble weighs upon my heart, worries that need answering. I want you to accompany me to where I go— oh, and Ian?" Xsealiadd voiced seeing Ian prepare for departure.

"Yes master?"

"I've got the blade, be sure Scorch travels with you, we'll need all the weapons we can get. I suspect this one's going to turn ugly."

"Yes master." Ian replied, curious as to where they were going. Like each time before this, he knew, he was soon to find out.

Valquee's heart pounded so loud, she feared it would break free of her chest. Of course this would never happen, however, that doesn't prevent one from thinking crazy thoughts when they fear for their life; which is what was happening here.

Being inundated with Sardon folk, Valquee was, literally, fighting for her life. She was beginning to feel she could not keep up with the vast amount of weapons being swung in her direction. In her heart she knew it was only a matter of time, she would dodge the wrong way, and the battle would claim her life.

Three great figures crested the hill, she couldn't bear to look, if she did, it would be her death sentence. This battle required her full concentration.

Great incantations rose above all else as, one by one, the Sardon folk fell dead to the banks below. Nearby, a great vortex of black and white swirled as Grunkle bested the souls of shadow.

At last all was quiet as Grunkle ceased his attack and Valquee was left standing in heaps of fallen soldiers.

Everyone exchanged glances of varying expression.

"Grunkle!" Ian broke the pregnant pause.

"Yes Ian?" Grunkle responded, though only Ian could hear, he was too weak to project his thoughts further into the world of beating hearts.

"You must teach me that swirling manoeuvre before I lose my shadowed form."

"Yes Ian." Grunkle replied, but quickly silenced as he observed Xsealiadd, who had rushed to Valquee.

"My love, tell me everything."

"Yes father," she breathed exhausted on the verge of collapse. She looked to Ian. "Somehow I've always known you've stayed with me after your tumble into shadow." She breathed her voice cracking.

"I would never leave your side my dearest Valquee, it broke my heart to do so on the shores of Gaunfaux flood, however, I couldn't risk the life of Scorch should he have followed me to Sardon. I remained behind only for him." Nearby Scorch cooed, proud of the love he already shared with his rider to be.

"That was kind of you." Valquee sighed. "Please gain comfort and I'll share with you my tale—"

"—not until you gain all the rest you need." Ian cut in, to a dark glare from Xsealiadd. "Seriously Xsealiadd, she is absolutely wiped, who wouldn't be after enduring for so long in such a foul place, you must let her rest. In fact, why don't you both rest until dawn? Scorch will shield you from the sun's powerful rays and Grunkle and I will keep watch."

Xsealiadd sighed; he was fighting a losing battle. "Fine, I'll trust you with this, don't let me down."

"Yes master."

Scorch rushed over, this was his chance to shine as he, also, grabbed a nap as he veiled Xsealiadd and Valquee from the daylight and enemy eyes, the only use he had for his wings.

The night was long as Ian learned many new manoeuvres from Grunkle, mainly the swirling vortex technique he used to best shadowed entities such as snorgs. When they were not training in attack moves, they were discussing their adventures amongst themselves. It was a night that they would describe as boarder line mesmerizing, one that everyone enjoyed as often as it would come, one where they couldn't remember ever sleeping so soundly.

Chapter 28

Racing for Answers

Dawn had not yet broke when Ian and Grunkle heard Xsealiadd's frantic utterings from beneath Scorch who, somehow, managed to sleep throughout the racket.

Forcing the dragon's wing up, he crawled out from beneath it. Valquee followed rather quickly in his wake. It was rather hard to make a noise like that and not rouse an elf considering they never knew somnolence as humans know sleep. Instead they drift into a semi-conscious state.

"What troubles thee father?" Valquee asked.

"You! In all this madness I have nearly forgotten to reverse your curse of magic, and here you are, slipping into darkness right under my nose. We can't have this, no we can't. Ian, Grunkle, pin her down! This one's going to hurt!" Rolling his sleeves, Xsealiadd dropped to his knees as Valquee struggled, maddened against the force of Ian and Grunkle. It wasn't the Valquee they knew for she would never fight her father. It must've been that corrupted Valquee from Sardon. Sure enough, their theory was proven as she yelled in protest as they pinned her down.

"Master says I am not to let you foul worthless scum tamper with his doings. I was a faithful servant, and he wants me bound to him for good."

"Well, he's not getting you! Too long have you been absent from my side!" Ian argued forcefully, holding her still.

Xsealiadd began pulling off vambraces, gauntlets, and her breastplate as he peeled away layers of armour frantically.

"What are you doing, slime!"

"Valquee, we need to reverse your corruption, your father needs to get at your heart. Don't you remember your father?"

"No!" She bellowed, fighting Ian and Grunkle's force with great strength. They struggled to keep her down.

Ian had never seen someone pull straps and cloth off as fast as Xsealiadd; he must really be in a hurry to finish the magic. Ripping open the last bit of cloth that veiled her breast, Xsealiadd froze falling to his behind.

"Grunkle, you didn't tell me this." Xsealiadd exclaimed awestruck. Valquee's entire body was covered in bruises and sores.

'I - I didn't want to worry you. Besides, I've been trying to heal them on my own, there have been just far too many.'

Xsealiadd didn't know what to say. After a great time he found his words. "W-what happened to you?" He asked with great concern.

"It's none of your business!" Valquee protested.

"Okay let's get this magic done with." Xsealiadd sighed. His ramblings were quick and breathless as he chanted in the language of the gods; his recovered staff held aloft in his hands. Ian understood perhaps one in every tenth word, which for a beginner he supposed wasn't bad.

Ian gathered the notion he was begging for purity and goodwill upon her soul; from what he could hear anyhow.

The shadows upon Valquee's heart began to lift leaving only a deep shadow scar across her breast as the soul Ian knew began to return.

"Oh Ian!" Was the first utterance from her lips, "I have missed you so greatly, please tell me everything, all that has happened for there is so much I wish to know."

"I harbour the same feelings Valquee, but I'm sorry to say there is no time, we must leave. We must fly now!"

"What is it Xsealiadd?"

"Last night—" he breathed as he scrambled around camp gathering all their provisions, "an oracle spoke to me in a dream. The message was disjointed and words were seldom, however, from what I gathered, Ian is returning to the academy; at least this is what the teachers will think. Your body has been stolen by the Occluder Ian, as you know, he is using it to do terrible things, you're slipping into shadow. But it is not you that greatly worries me. The Occluder is seeking something of great worth, something once protected by Rennaux. It is not Rennaux the Occluder seeks, though I don't know why, it is his son Thyle, he is in great danger. We must all be with great concern for if he gets his hands on this item he and Nighdrake will come back."

"—I killed him." Valquee cut in.

"Pardon?" Ian asked.

"I killed Rennaux, the Occluder must be seeking Thyle in hopes he has answers from his father's doings."

"Don't you remember me telling you Ian, Valquee killed him?"

"Oh yeah, sorry, I temporarily forgot."

Urgency was heavy in their tones as both Xsealiadd and Valquee hurried to get moving.

Their pace was brought to a standstill by the mere presence of a foreign beast.

"What's wrong with you scum! You cowards? Come on, I need to reach that academy!" The Occluder howled, kicking a nearby servant in the backside.

"Can't you see master, the strange creature that blocks our path? No one has seen it before and we don't know how to pass it. Everything we have tried so far has failed."

"Fine, fine!" The Occluder sighed, he was bested, and secretly he knew it too. Defeated he glared at the oversized ram with its shaggy pelt and spiralled horns. Its elephant ears flapped madly, it was agitated, its great trunk ripping leaves off of the trees.

"Where did it come from anyway?" A servant questioned before they all went to camp, out of ideas.

Xsealiadd was in such a rush to get to the academy, he barely noticed or cared what was happening around him, even when the befoullers from Oursjour woods blocked his path.

"Don't get in my way!" He ordered with urgency and force, and with one quick swipe of his feeble hand, the whole lot of them, and there had to have been fifty, fell to the wayside as Xsealiadd scrambled past. "I swear! If one more speck of substance bares my way, I'm going to blast it to smithereens!" He scoffed without slowing his speedy gait.

The men of Sardon had no greater ideas as they consumed their supper. The plan, however, did show up in an unsuspected form whilst cleaning their cookware. Clanking and rattling their cooking pots, the creature howled, filling them with great bundles of nerves. They silenced, and so did the beast.

Shrugging it off they resumed washing their pots in the stream. The beast began to howl once more. They weren't stupid, they figured it out. The clanking of the metal terribly agitated the giant animal. Taking great care, for fear of the monster turning on them, they scared it off as it tore through the trees. It was then and only then, that they noticed a wizard, an elf, and a dragon on the opposing bank of Keyliar Crossing, they moved at a strong pace.

Gathering up their belongings with haste, they meant to run parallel to the travelers on their side of the river, the south side, to observe their business.

It was only a matter of time before the wizard and elf noticed them. As a result, a healthy exchange of arrows caused several Sardon folk to fall; the elf was a very skilled archer.

Keyliar Crossing was just ahead, and it was clear that that was the elf's and wizard's destination. The Sardon folk prepared an ambush, it wasn't hard. There were enough trees. Still, it was a cold, rainy day. Breath hung in the air as bodies quaked from cold and drizzle seeping its way beneath any fold or covering of cloth that it could seek.

"Nobody moves!" The Occluder ordered as he stared over his shoulder in the direction his targets is would come. It was damp. Even he was chilled, yet he denied himself the luxury of warmth. It was crucial to remain still, maintain stealth as well to be ready. He had ambushed hundreds of times before, they were always the same. Different faces, same process.

A rustle of leaves sounded from behind as his men drew their bowstrings taut, they were ready. Closer still the footfalls were. They were nearly in perfect alignment for an attack. It was the Occluder that faltered. His hands flying up, he halted the entire operation. Bowstrings relaxed and everyone froze.

Oblivious to the ambush, the elf, wizard, and dragon strolled by. The Occluder swore he noticed the elf's eyes slide to his direction. Maybe she saw, maybe she knew they were there, though he hoped not. Waiting until they almost fell from view, he ordered his men to follow them, he meant to find out their business.

It was the dragon who confirmed their suspicion. Breaking from the rest of the party, he began sniffing and snooping about strangely. This was the Sardon folks' biggest fear; being discovered. They had to rid themselves of this threat. They meant to slay the beast. They didn't care.

Extracting their bows they readied an arrow. It was dusk, and an eerie twilight at that. This sky took on an appearance of an angry green, not a sound could be heard. To worsen the matter, the air was dead. Hanging heavy it carried the stench of Sardon folk to all whose nostrils it reached like a noxious fume.

When it came to the attack, only one noise was heard; the creak of the bows as their tensions mounted. With a faint whoosh of air swirling, the arrow flitted just past the dragon's peripheral. Scorch's eyes lit up. High on alert, he bounced through the trees with lightning quick reflexes; he snatched up the arrow in his powerful maw just as it was making its descent to the soft earth. With great pressure, as dragons often do, Scorch crushed the arrow to a fine powder beneath his teeth, so powerful, just as he would a bone.

Splinters flew as he spit out the rest just as a volley of arrows reared, their fletchings whizzing through the trees. Though Scorch was fast, there was no way even he could catch all of those arrows, there were too many. One had embedded itself deep into the thin membranes that made up the bulk of the wing tissue. Executing a yelp of pain, one heard by all, he gingerly pulsated, furling and unfurling his wing, trying to assess the damage.

Xsealiadd and Valquee rushed to his side at tremendous speeds. They took equally as little time to survey the situation. They first noticed the arrow protruding from Scorch's wing for he had to hold it strangely to keep the arrow from digging in and irritating more tissue than it already had.

A rustle barely touched Valquee's hearing. Her ears pricked, she stared off into the distance in the direction it had come. A faint movement caught her eye, she bolted, weapons drawn. Xsealiadd remained behind. He was carefully nursing the dragon's wound.

"Ian!" He whispered. Ian joined his side. "What would be the appropriate spell to heal this?"

As he was taught, Ian studied the wound, taking into consideration its size, and more importantly its depth. "Well, it goes into muscle and flesh but not bone, so..." he thought hard. "...Maybe the inar myer incantation."

"Very good Ian, now show me if you will, how this spell would be executed. Pretend to cast it."

Ian cupped his hands over the wound. Breathing heavy into the space between his forefingers, he recited the proper enunciations. His entire body felt to burn, his hands glowed white-hot as if an invisible man held the sun and all one could see was its glow.

Yelping, more out of shock than anything, Ian pulled his hands away. The wound was healed.

"This is crazy, I'm not, I mean, I can't— how can this be? Shadowed folks aren't supposed to do magic!" Ian was surprised. Looking to Xsealiadd, it scared him to notice, he was equally as dumbfounded. At last when words finally found him a great time later, and after opening and closing his mouth several times, Xsealiadd finally spoke.

"I have never heard of that in any case, a boy, with no proper training, according to Grunkle, able to properly perform magic without a periatti gland. The only other being the Occluder. It has been proven, also, that he has achieved it through black magic. If I were to guess, it would either be that, since you are his son, he passed it to you; his ability to conjure spells; disregarding the situation, however, I have never heard of magic being passed from father to son via birth. I contemplate, however, that it may occur, I don't know. The other option, and

I feel more likely the cause, is that upon your birth, when you nearly perished, when I touched upon you the spells that kept you alive, perhaps that day the gods gave you more than life; they perhaps, bestowed upon thee an undying energy that can be manipulated at will."

"Could I ever find the true reason as to why? Like why Grunkle was able to slow Valquee's curse in a magic which you passed to him."

"I'm afraid I don't know, but doubt is clouding any hope of finding the answer. As for Grunkle I rarely hear of dwarves weaving magic though it is possible."

Ian flopped to the ground, his mind deep in thought.

Her breath was slow and steady when Valquee finally caught up to the place where the movement was seen. No one lingered, all had fled. She knew this already, however, she just desired an affirmative.

She could tell they were the Occluder's men, mainly by their footprints pressed in the snow; as well as a familiar chill which hung in the air, the sign of evil afoot. Taking one final scan, she felt deep in her heart, the evil had fled, but only just recently. Satisfied all was safe, she returned to the fellowship.

Chapter 29
The Siege of Ackles Academy

"Okay, there's a lot to do so we best split up. I'll find Thyle, Valquee, you can replenish supplies, and Ian, well, you can stay with Scorch, keep him from mischief." Xsealiadd cocked a brow.

"No way, I'm going to see Mme. Dumpling. I want to see if she knows a cure for this." He gestured to himself, acknowledging his shadows. "You go Scorch, shoo, shoo! You shouldn't be here!" Scorch began to whimper and whine he understood he was not wanted. His thought pierced Ian like a knife. It was times like this Ian wished he had never became a great harker.

'A dragon and rider never part. I will remain by your sssside until the hand of death, at long lassssst, sssplitsss our bound sssssoulsss.'

"But I am not your rider see! No bites on my hands!" Ian flailed his hands irritably.

'Jusssst you wait!'

"Xsealiadd?"

"Yes Valquee."

"I've been sensing a fell energy stirring in our wake, I didn't want fear to taint your heavy hearts, but I feel it is best if we stay close."

"Are you sure about this Valquee?"

"Quite certain, it has been unsettled since before crossing Keyliar."

"Well then," Xsealiadd sighed. "I suppose we stick together."

"—my concern is how to hide a dragon that refuses to stay hidden?" Ian cut in.

"That, my lad, we'll figure out in time." The gates of Ackles Academy sprang into view, the scene that met them was nothing like what they had expected. The great gates were barricaded shut. Beyond in the distance, academy goers ran frantic like a colony of ants when their hill was destroyed. Something was amiss and the only one with the foggiest idea as to what was Valquee. Though she never shared her thoughts; she feared she'd be mistaken. Her self-confidence at this point was nearly nonexistent.

"This can't be good." Ian stared dumbfounded.

"We need to see Thyle! We need to stop the Occluder from gaining power and a body of his own!"

"I'm afraid even if we impeded him from retrieving the scale now, in the long-term we would be unable to resist his wrath. We as common folk would collapse beneath his strength."

Valquee grew angered. "Xsealiadd stop your pessimistic babbling and get us in there!"

Xsealiadd sighed. "As you wish." And with a great swish of his hand, the gates fell from their hinges.

They felt like outsiders observing a bad dream, not part of the panic but observing it far too closely. Inch by inch, they took careful steps, trying not to obstruct people's movement as they approached the academy. Much to Ian's good fortune, Mme. Dumpling rushed passed carrying trays filled with vials of what Ian recognized to be adrenaline enhancements.

"Mme. Dumpling, please!" Ian reached out a hand and with his own energy, stopped her in her tracks, her feet bound to the Earth. Her body swaying to dissipate the forward momentum, her vials rattling in their holders. She looked upon Ian and gasped.

"Ian?"

"Yes, do you see what happened to me? My body ripped from my soul, leaving me to be a wandering shadow. I need your help, what has this potion done to me?"

"I am sorry dear boy, off the top of my mind, I can think of none that would be so... potent." She replied seeking the appropriate word.

"Ian! There you are I can't believe I lost you." In amongst the chaos, Ian never realized he had parted from the others.

"Hello Angelidie!" Valquee greeted, being neighbourly.

"Hello Valquee." Mme. Dumpling replied, still unable by Ian's energy to move.

"Please tell me Angelidie, what evil has befallen the academy?"

"It is the Occluder's minions; they attack from the south, from Sardon. We must fortify our strongholds; reinforce them with men where age has failed."

"If I can be of aid in any way—" Valquee began to offer before Xsealiadd sprang from nowhere.

"Why do you two linger when there is much to do. Come, we must find Thyle, time has expired, the Occluder is here."

"I saw Thyle heading for his dormitory!" Mme. Dumpling shouted to Xsealiadd's retreating back, he was dragging Valquee by the scruff deep into the academy grounds.

It was like an explosion that ripped the grounds, thus spreading like a shockwave as men, befoullers, torans, and snorgs spread like a plague, burning buildings and challenging all who stood before them. Many were students, inexperienced against the skillful swordsmanship of the Occluder's Carddronnes. War had started before any seemed ready. Casualties began to mount as Ian stole one final, fleeting glance at the battlefield before the great entry doors slammed shut, it was a horrible scene to say the least.

The moment they entered the academy the atmosphere was significantly different. Outside was utter chaos and pandemonium, inside was nervous yet organized tension. Fighters were arranged in formations by skill, as well other, less important factors, ranks which quickly parted at the sight of Scorch. It was only then that Ian realized that outside were all the first years, sent out like pawns to thin the enemy numbers. The deeper into the school Ian went, the more experienced and aged the fighters were, until he reached the elite of elvish bowmen; who were also taking shifts to fire through the castle slits using great swan fletched arrows. Through the windows, Ian could catch a glimpse of the battle ensuing outdoors, archers shooting from rooftops, watchtowers, windows, and arrow loops.

Great trebuchets and catapults fired debris and dead bodies to the pressing army abroad, something their foes never reciprocated. This was something Ian thought rather suspicious, especially since they didn't carry much war equipment at all; it was only then that it occurred to Ian, the Occluder didn't want to fight this war. Those who were attacking, were emergency men drawn up at a moment's notice to aid in the academy's penetration, just so the Occluder could access Thyle and his answers. This was unexpectedly exhausting his energy and resource.

Tearing his eyes from the battle, Ian struggled to catch up to Valquee and Xsealiadd. Heavy breathing blending with urgent footfalls met his ear.

Nervous, and rightfully so, Ian spun around, a dwarf was running to him. He was bleeding profusely from a cut on his arm, and there were a few scratches still fresh on his face. His beard was soaked with a mixture of sweat and blood and in his hands he clutched a blood-stained war axe.

"I'm sorry." He panted, "I must make this quick for I am not even supposed to be here." He gestured the way he came. "Fighting you know?"

Ian nodded.

"Anyway, I accidentally overheard your conversation with Mme. Dumpling; it sounds to me like the Devigadora Draught."

"Sorry?"

"The Devigadora Draught, made by the dwarves of Sundurr, it is designed to send the drinker to the world of shadow to gain the ability to kill shadowed foes. That is why evil appears lively as good appears dead. This is so you can slay the right one, and you do see them this way don't you?"

"Yes! Yes!" Ian was ecstatic. "How do you reverse it?"

"It's best if you see the dwarves in Sundurr, they will know."

"Excuse me. Last time we were there, they treated us as foes because we didn't know how to gain entrance. How do guests visit their strong holds?"

"Just go to their gate and say ukh unnivye, it means, I am a guest, I mean no harm."

"Ukh unnivye, okay, thanks." Valquee was grateful.

A great bang ripped through the corridors, the grand doors burst open as shadows spilled into the majestic entrance hall. The inexperienced were overwhelmed as the Sardon folk broke what little organization they had.

A high-pitched voice rang loud. "Just bring me Thyle Holmes and none will get hurt, you are my students, I wish not to harm you." The Occluder attempted to seek Thyle's mind when a courageous, yet foolish student, challenged his blade, it was short lived.

"Well, I've got to go!" The dwarf commented before charging into the battle. Ian and Valquee sprinted in the opposite direction fleeing up to the dormitories, they had to find Thyle, and fast.

The door flew open.

"Xsealiadd!"

"Thyle!"

Introductions were brief; it was hard to dawdle with such a battle raging outside.

"Xsealiadd, can I ask you something?"

"Only if you let me say something first."

"Okay."

"The Occluder and his men are seeking you, entreating for your knowledge on the scale your father possessed. Why don't you flee, resist them, you know, for your safety?"

"Master would not allow me to fight on the side I wish. And should I flee, he'd drag me back. I've known they have been coming for a great time now. I hear them all the time, approaching." Thyle tapped his temple. "Master always harbours my mind."

"Can you tell us then, Thyle? Do you know its whereabouts... the scale I mean?"

"I don't know. I never have. I know father was supposed to overlook its safe keeping, though I never knew where he hid it."

"Fair enough, now to what do you wish to ask me?"

"Well Xsealiadd, I've asked the elves, they said I should come to you with such a query."

"Okay."

"Do you know anything about hypnosis linked to Opthopathy?"

The provisions Xsealiadd was embracing fell, scattering amongst the ground. "M'boy, that subject brings with it great trails of black magic and is only associated with evil."

"I just want to find information on it, not practice it."

"Well, in that case, legend has once said that a long line tied to master the art of what you seek from a book of blackness. Each had utterly failed with devastating results. The last who have tried it, cast away the text in the skeleton of an ancient watchtower. Recovered by its author the book had recently been hibernating on his mantle, however, sources tell me, it's on the move once again."

"Oh I hate it when riddles are your words! All I want to know is how it's done!"

"My dear lad, I don't know any of that black magic. I only read about it and find ways to guard myself against it."

Thyle's eyes lit up. "That's what I want, I want to prevent it! Can you teach me?"

Xsealiadd, who had just gathered his fallen provisions, dropped them again. "M'boy, have you finally lost your beans? That is insanely complex Craft it is, far too great for your level of skill and training."

"But—"

The dormitory door flew open as Ian rushed in. "—Xsealiadd we're running out of time, we must fly. The Occluder's men have nearly penetrated the inner keep."

"I'm sorry Thyle, I don't have the time now, I really must run." Xsealiadd called in response to the tugging, dragging, and ushering of Ian. "Where's Valquee?"

"With Scorch down the hall." Ian replied as he finally, at last, successfully managed to manoeuvre Xsealiadd down the corridor; just slowly as the wizard did his best to squeeze some last minute voicing contributions to his and Thyle's conversations.

"—just look up the Yotar theory!" Xsealiadd shouted over his shoulder. "This should help in what you seek!"

At last the dormitory door thudded shut, cutting off any dwindling conversation that remained between Thyle and Xsealiadd.

"Let's get out of here!" Valquee commented upon rejoining Xsealiadd and Ian.

"No! Not yet, we must replenish our food."

"There is no time!" Valquee argued.

"There is always time!" Xsealiadd rebutted, his stomach joining in the argument with a great gurgle of hunger pains.

Knowing Xsealiadd's stubbornness, Valquee finally gave in. "Fine, fine." She snapped. "But only if I can see the principal afterwards."

"What do you want to see him for?" Xsealiadd huffed from running.

"Oh just, it's not your concern." Xsealiadd eyed her peculiarly. "...Oh, as you wish. The whole reason we ended up in Rulan in the first place was to rescue Athrin after getting permission from Rennaux to go, for what he thought was my desire to be by my dying brother's bedside. My sibling perished after I left his side, something I still regret. Anyhow if you don't remember, I took you with us when we headed north to our elvish village."

The closer they drew to the mess hall and kitchens, the louder the clanging of swords and screams of people became. Veering down a side passage, Valquee did her best to guide Xsealiadd and Scorch away from the main battle. Ian started down this path but quickly grew sidetracked with a familiar face.

"Florian, Florian is that you." Dodging a couple of quick blows, Florian drove his blade into his opponent before glancing over. He had to steal a double take before he realized who it was.

"Ian?"

"Yes Florian it's me."

"Are you... dead?"

"Sort of, long story can't stay long."   An enemy confronted them, forcing Florian into a sword fight. "Well sorry Ian, our time is cut short but I must say all the things I said in Rulan I still believe it, every word." Florian garbled as he waved his blade insanely seeking an opening to slay his foe, all the while defending his person.

Seeing the situation hopeless, Ian simply responded, "I love you too, sister..." before drifting into the kitchens.

Valquee and Xsealiadd had just finished burdening down their packs with the stolen goods Scorch neglected to eat.

"So have you two any idea where Nighdrake's scale is at?" Ian asked filling in the tense, still atmosphere. It was awkward being in a room so eerily quiet with a battle raging on the other side of the mere three foot thick stone wall; recently repaired from last year's collapse.

"No." Valquee puffed as she heaved a heavy pack to Scorch's already laden frame.

"I hope we do soon, I don't want the Occluder finding it." Ian rambled when all in a moment, a thought struck him.

"Valquee, where is Ackles?"

"He's usually in his chambers three floors up, why?" She eyed him with suspicion.

"Long past Ackles used to be close friends with Nighdrake, perhaps he knows something."

"Ian—" Valquee was about to tell him it was a foolish idea when he cut her off.

"Hey, it's all we've got. I'll meet you back here."

"No, we meet you there, we have to go to the same floor for I have business to attend."

Ian had no idea where Ackles's chambers resided, though he prayed for instincts to guide him. Much to his luck, he bumped into Ackles pacing and padding the hallways, uneasy with the battle raging below. "Ackles, I bow before thee, do I have permission to converse with you for I can understand animals' thoughts." Ian sunk to his knees.

'Make it quick!' The thought busted into Ian's soul.

"Do you know anything about the scale taken from Nighdrake for the Occluder's personal use?"

'That very question is why there is a battle raging in my halls, if only people used words, answers would be found much quicker.'

"Aye."

'Because of your actions, you are far more deserving than any other for answers, which I bestow upon thee.'

"Thank you Bashlay— I mean Ackles."

'You know Bashlay do you? Wow, you are well-traveled. He is a good friend of mine.'

"I'm glad to know." Ian mentally logged such a fact.

'Now for your question. All dragons are uniquely bound to each and every part of their anatomy, just like any other. If you were to rip off something belonging to a dragon, it will feel phantom pains when it is gone. When it comes to a dragon scale, once it is removed from the hide, the dragon gets phantom pains; meaning it can feel where that scale resided at that moment in time. Nighdrake, to my knowledge, lost only the one. This is why dragon scales are such a noble gift. Once given to the receiver, the dragon will always sense its presence and thus, the whereabouts of the bearer of the gift. When you use this protection as a shield in battle, and it is subject to abuse with weapons, the dragon who bestowed it upon you will feel phantom pains as its scale is being attacked. Do you follow me?'

"Aye."

'If the receiver is noble enough, and they should be to deserve such a kingly gift, it is common for that dragon to rush to the person's aid on the battlefield.'

"Do scales grow back?"

'Yes, however, connections to the old ones never falter. In Nighdrake's case, he had lost only the one scale; however, he always sensed it to be on the academy grounds. This is all I know.'

With a great flick of his bushy pumpkin orange tail, he vanished around the corner, leaving Ian to contemplate his next move.

Valquee was like a battering ram, she wanted in the principal's office so desperately, she kicked the barred door until it splintered and crumpled beneath her elvish strength.

"Why are you not fighting with your people?" Was how she introduced herself to the new principal, Cano.

Cano scowled. "I will run my academy how I see fit."

"Oh yes and you're doing a tremendous job of it too." Valquee grew cross.

"What have you busted in here for, it must've been for something more important than criticizing my rule 'cause that amount of damage is hardly worth that." He replied eying the nearly nonexistent door.

"I want you to pass Ian Cosswell on his challenge that he embarked on late last year with Rennaux's permissions."

"Honestly woman, can you not see this is a bad time?" Cano sneered.

"Why you—" Valquee unsheathed her sword.

"Okay, okay, I'll pass him if it pleases you, there is no need for blades. Too much blood has already been spilt before me."

"You know, you're a slime. You are probably one of the Sardon folks that started it!"

"No, that would be my master." Cano rose from behind his desk, also withdrawing a tarnished blade.

"Valquee, come! Ian seems to think he has some knowledge of the scale's whereabouts." Xsealiadd poked his head in.

Cano leapt from behind his desk to the portal in two great bounds standing just out of swords reach of Valquee.

"Xsealiadd!" She mouthed to the wizard.

"I'm sorry but he'd have found out either way even if I called it you-know-what."

"I suppose, let's go!" She cried and both fled the room, Cano hot in pursuit.

Many halls, floors, and stairs they ran trying to break free of their tail. Eventually losing him in the fray of battle, they rejoined Ian in a deserted classroom. Quickly Ian filled them in on what Ackles had said before explaining his plans.

"... So I was thinking to ask Scorch here," he patted the dragon on his head, "...a few questions. Questions about dragons in general terms. Scorch, dragons are according to Ackles, psychologically linked to their scales, well, is there any chance you're linked, or even faintly sense another dragon's scale? I'm looking for a lost one. Your, uh, ancestor had a scale stolen and hidden somewhere on these grounds." Ian had to take care, Scorch was not supposed to know Nighdrake was his father.

Cocking his massive head, Scorch sniffed about like a dog seeking out its bone. In a wandering pass through the academy, out to the grounds, through the ebbing battle where Xsealiadd and Valquee escaped to the refuge of Xsealiadd's shack to gather forgotten and lost provisions which were salvageable from last year's fire. Scorch ended up leading Ian to the dilapidated dragon stables in the corner of the academy grounds.

Unlatching the wooded door, Ian pushed it aside. It was soft with moisture and age.

Into a stable Scorch led Ian, and as he surveyed it, he realized it to be the one from Nighdrake's memory. Trees were in the same place they were when Ian saw them in the dragon's mind and vantage points of buildings were exact.

Scorch nosed a corner where a great heap of rotted straw was piled high. Shifting and moving the hay bed, Ian extracted something about the size of a saucer, black and shiny; it was about an inch thick and highly reflective.

'How did Rennaux know this stable?' Ian queried before reaching the conclusion that Nighdrake must've shared his memories with more than just him.

He rushed from the stables, scale in hand, with Scorch at his heels. Barely exiting the stable doors, a frightful scene met his eyes. Naught fifty feet before him was an apparition; he was gazing upon himself, except more mangled and highly dressed. Scars cut their way across almost every inch of flesh, between many of the scars, great black of shadows were starting to show through. From what Valquee had told him, this was the Occluder destroying his body. It sure felt this way as the air was cold and any happiness he felt was robbed from him.

The Occluder had not noticed him as he ordered foot soldiers about. At last noticing Ian's spirit, more crucially, the scale he possessed, the Occluder lunged, making a grab for the one thing this battle was all about: his scale. Ian was quick as he jerked the scale away and disappeared amongst the warriors, Scorch following his lead.

Ian was halfway to Xsealiadd's shack when a force caused him to freeze still.

"I hope you're not making off with my scale." An icy voice chilled his soul.

'Scorch! Take it!' Ian thought hard.

Reaching to Ian's frozen hand, Scorch embraced it in his maw.

'Take it to Xsealiadd!' Ian thought again and envisioned the hut before him. Scorch bolted, Ian could feel the hold on him ease. The Occluder meant to take the scale from Scorch. It was Ian's turn.

"Andromodaylee!" He screeched. The Occluder's body tumbled to the ground. Barely rising to his feet, Ian struck him with another spell causing blades that lay around him to surround his person. With a great swish, the Occluder whisked them away.

"Impressive." He commented in that icy tone as he approached Ian's spirit. Ian faltered; he knew he would be unable to hold off the Occluder, he was way too powerful for Ian's skill.

Ian's mind raced as he attempted to form an effective, yet efficient spell. Under strain, however, all his lessons seemed to have been forgotten.

Fire sprang to the Occluder's hands with a simple phrase he threw great fireballs at Ian. However they meant to hurt, Ian didn't know, though he knew the outcome would be bleak. He tried to dodge when he felt a force pull at his scruff. His world flooded with great white light as he felt to be floating, enlightened with peace. He knew this feeling, it had happened to him before; Xsealiadd was pulling him from danger, or at least trying to do so. A great cry reverberated through the serenity and Ian's world collapsed around him. He was in a great forest, wherever it was, though it was not normal; it was like looking through a broken, splintered window; great shards of pure white light sliced the world into a bizarre, distorted nightmare; on the ground beside him lay Xsealiadd whimpering and moaning, half of his body was completely burned. Nothing had prepared Ian for this.

Chapter 30
Disjointed

"Xsealiadd? Xsealiadd? Oh Valquee, someone help!" Ian was in such a state, lost, alone, helpless, vulnerable, and scared, those were just a few of the many emotions that flooded his soul. He didn't know what to do or where to go for he knew not where he was. All Xsealiadd's teachings seemed to have left him back at the Occluder's side.

"Okay, think Ian, think!" He counted to ten. "Grunkle!" He shouted hopeless.

'Ian, where are you!' It was Grunkle's thoughts that pierced his mind.

"I don't—I don't know okay!"

'Describe it to me!'

"I'm in a spectacular forest surrounded by grand trees, but it's not normal, it's like a picture which has been shattered, broken, for great white shards pierce up everywhere!"

'White shards?' Grunkle repeated,

"Yes!"

'You're trapped halfway between the dimensions. You're seeing both dimensions simultaneously, but they're both broken as you are neither here nor there. Is there anything you have done lately that may have caused this?'

"Grunkle! What a foolish question! Yes I did something that may have caused it, well, not me per se. I was in a battle with the Occluder. Xsealiadd sensed I was in trouble and materialized through the dimensions to save me, but something went awry; I heard Xsealiadd scream and my world collapsed to this nightmare."

'Is Xsealiadd with you now?'

"Yes, but he's not responding, he's badly burned and won't stop moaning."

'Hmm, the Occluder must've attacked as you were passing through the portal. Xsealiadd, being the only one with a body, took the hit!'

"Can I heal him?"

'You could try, but it will likely fail you. The Occluder's magic is known to damage deeper than flesh.'

"Meaning?"

'He may be psychologically scarred or emotionally troubled, we don't know.'

"That can't mean good."

'No.'

"Look, could you find and explain this to Valquee? She'll have a sounder mind than I."

'Where may she linger?'

"Xsealiadd's shack."

'Okay. In the meantime, try healing him, you'll never know what will happen. Won't hurt that's for sure.' Grunkle's presence abated Ian's mind as he scoured the whereabouts for Valquee.

Ian waited in silence, his mind trying to choose the most effective spell of healing; there were so many to choose from.

Slowly enunciating a simple version of a healing spell, Ian waited as flesh knitted and merged. New skin flowed beneath his touch.

Xsealiadd's moaning had stopped; Ian had removed his physical pain. At least it was a start. The wizard was silent for a great amount of time as Ian sat over him, observing his progress.

Grabbing Ian's wrist unexpectedly, Xsealiadd began to babble. "I-I- I'm sorry dear lad, I tried to save you, I just didn't have the time." He tried to move but groaned with pain, "...or the strength. He hit me, he burned me."

"I know, I know, I do. Now tell me, what I can do to get us out."

"There is no hope, we have expired." Xsealiadd moaned.

"There is always hope, we have not expired until all is finished. As long as sands still flow in your hourglass, you will endure, now get off that ground and tell me, what can I do to get us out?"

"Hold my hand, tightly now, we can't have you slipping." Three times Ian felt his arm being tugged, and his body growing light and airy. Each time, he plummeted back to that same crazy, disjointed world.

"I can't, I can't, it's, it's just too hard." Xsealiadd moaned, his body growing limp.

"I know, but as a peacekeeper you've got to let me try."

"No, you are not ready."

So there they were, feeling hopeless and alone, Ian willing to try but Xsealiadd giving up. Something strange occurred then. Ian's world swirled, spun, and danced. Closing his eyes to as not be sick, he slammed face first, hard into the snow. The world, once he was brave enough to open his eyes, was back to what he had most recently deciphered as normal.

Valquee did not know how many times she cried their names and wondered if they heard. A normal thought to her lately as they were in a place even she did not understand.

"Ian!" She cried his name again. Turning on the spot, she bumped into Ian in question. "There you are! What took you so long, didn't you hear me calling?"

"—fool!" Ian yelled as he withdrew a sword. That was not the voice she remembered. She had forgotten in her stressed state of mind, that Ian did not inhabit his body.

"I'm s-so s-s-sorry m-m-master." She stammered.

The Occluder cackled, "I've got you well-trained. Now, give me my scale." He held aloft a hand.

"Never!" She yelled, and withdrew the only weapon she had in her possession; that little wand that targeted black hearts. She raised it high.

"How dare you use my own invention against me! Besides, it won't work, especially since I have this!" The Occluder withdrew a more elegant wand. Waving it around childishly, he began to roll and weave it between his fingers.

"What is that?" Valquee cowered back many steps; she was obviously fearful and rightfully so.

The Occluder cackled, a foul sneer was etched on Ian's face. He loved all this. "Same as what you hold. Except mine targets both good and shadow; whomever I wish. It can also kill the person fast, or slow, whichever my liking. It must be handled with delicacy, for it doesn't care whom it murders." The Occluder twirled it in a fancy manoeuvre. "And, this one overrides yours any given moment, yours was just a prototype." He let out another great cackle, before edging ever closer.

"Ne oka niagha oosha deno fuya!" Valquee chanted, not waiting for the outcome of this fight. Winds danced and swirled carrying with it heavy white outs. The world was quickly blanketed in snow; swirling, biting, chilling all flesh it touched. The blizzard waned, taking the wind with it. Once all was cleared, Valquee had vanished, leaving the Occluder in the middle of a winter land, not a soul nearby.

Whether Ian found Valquee, or Valquee found Ian, none would ever know, yet somehow, someway, their paths crossed. Ian, however, did not seem as happy to see her as she expected.

"Don't worry Ian, we will find Xsealiadd."

"It's not that."

"Then what?"

"I can't believe you lied to me!"

"What, I have never lied to you."

"You told my parents, Ackles just showed up. Well I was just talking to him. He didn't just show up, you brought him in to babysit Nighdrake, 'cause if you didn't, you knew the shadowed dragon could not be contained."

"I don't know where you got this illusion, but I didn't lie to your parents, we are forbidden to reveal unnecessary information to outsiders; I already told them too much, I was trying to do my job."

Ian didn't answer, though a nasty insult hung upon his lips, he chose not to utter it as to not spoil their relationship. Instead, he talked his mind off of it.

"Valquee?"

"Yes."

"Did you know that day you came to my house that you were picking up the boy from the prophecy?"

"I was fairly certain, yes."

"Oh, so how do you plan to find Xsealiadd?" Ian segued.

"Well Ian, it's kind of complex. You see, to pass through the portal as most call it, you don't really get lost as there is only one path that you might take; only one doorway that leads to shadow. Picture in your mind, as this is what works for me, a big city, crowded with people. However, for some reason, the city has a great wall that splits it down the middle. In this wall there is one doorway, which is always open, yet is monitored by only one guard. And people of the city use this gate regularly and constantly, however, that they have to be monitored by the guard to deem them worthy of passing through, this is exactly or at least close to what happens when you pass between the worlds. At least, that's how it was explained to me. There will be no finding him, we just have to get him on this side of the door, right now he's stuck in the portal."

It felt strange thinking of Valquee as Xsealiadd's student, yet it seemed her explanation of the dimensions helped Ian understand immensely. "Who guards this door?" Ian asked.

"Death, the underworld is his world; it is meant for people who have died. The shadowed realm is the portal that guides you there."

"Well then, that's certainly Xsealiadd, he died in good spirits and optimism. The whole time I was stuck with him, he insisted all hope in life was gone. He was giving up."

"Ian, listen to me, and you must understand because it's highly important. What you see with a black spell is not always what is real. It is common for them to leave psychological, emotional, as well as physical scars."

"So I'm told. So how do we pull him through the door?" Ian was growing curious.

"Using the oldest form of magic ever invented, so old, controversy still envelopes it to this day as many believe it to be unworkable. I, however, disagree. Not only have I seen it function with my own eyes, I have also used it on several occasions. You may want to pay attention to it as Xsealiadd will never teach you it."

"Why not?"

"He doesn't believe."

"Oh, and what channels this form of magic?"

"Like most, energy. What makes it unique is that it is not fuelled by a special language; it is effective in every tongue, like with all other known forms of magic. The thing that drives it is belief and intent. Feeling that in your heart, this is real, it can and will happen. That is what makes the magic work. It is not used very often, and is most effective when you feel strong faith deep in your heart. Now, watch how it goes." Valquee cleared her throat. "What power and hope has ever fulfilled me, let it fill the heart of the wounded, let him believe and to open his eyes. Allow him to see the path that is destined, carved before him. Let his heart be not troubled, but free of sorrow. Let him come back to us now, with a radiant heart and a pure soul, to live out the rest of his days in peace."

"It sounds like a prayer to me." Ian commented.

"What's a prayer?" Valquee asked confused.

"You mean you've never prayed to the gods before, or any God for that matter?"

"No, elves, only plea for fate to guide us, we have no gods. Though doubt always tries to claim us, we seldom fail to believe in naught but the raw data which has been witnessed time and time again unfolding before our gazes.

"Why... why do you not believe?" Ian was shocked.

"Laws of nature are absolute. Everything from the speed of growing grass to the speed that something falls; they are all absolutes of this world around us. Everything has a reason and a place, and each reason has an explanation. These interpretations, well they are consistent throughout. Of these descriptions, nothing explains gods, as religion wants you to believe they are there. A belief in gods doesn't fit with the rest of the natural rules, therefore, we elves do not believe in something that doesn't coexist with the rest of the Earth, it can't be true."

"Explanations, laws, can't... you're right about one thing, these are all absolutes. Incontrovertible logic, since when does everything in this world ever make sense? You must have a God!"

"No Ian, elves are too practical."

"Well, do you believe in energy, energy to heal, energy to kill?"

"Of course, obviously, I mean, given what we do, channelling our energy to achieve a purpose; singing to the trees to help them grow."

"Well why wouldn't that be a God? A God doesn't have to be humanoid, or elf, or dwarf, or whatever. Perhaps energy is controlled by God, who helps aid in whatever you need it for, and maybe you're just channelling God's strength for your needs. Remember, you have energy within you; it keeps you alive, keeps you breathing, and keeps the rhythm in your chest. How did it get there, you didn't sing that one there, I guarantee."

"Well Ian, ever hear of childbirth?—"

"That has nothing to do with it!"

"It has everything to do with it!"

"You and your logical explanations, if you're so analytical, tell me... how did the race of men, elf, dwarf, dragon, shorble, how did any of them begin in the first place; did they just spring out of the ground?"

"Oh Ian, stop! There's no such thing. You humans always cling to beliefs of weird and unexplained things."

"You say that, but tell me right now, you didn't give me a logical explanation to my question. I think, that you don't know, so I will give you another one, how did this world begin?"

"Alright! Okay! The truth is, you're right, I don't know." Valquee fell silent. The more she pondered the issue, the more she questioned it. 'What keeps rhythm in my breast? Where did we come from? How did the world begin?' Before rational answers were ever even remotely possible, an elders hand flopped from nowhere.

"Xsealiadd!" She squeaked as she embraced his feeble grip. She pulled hard, the more she pulled, the more of Xsealiadd emerged from nowhere. At last he lay exhausted in the snow.

"Whew!" He cried, "I was beginning to think I'd never have the strength to pull through! Ha, get it? Pull through? It was almost as if my strength got up and left me, probably for some younger, more handsome lad, like you for instance Ian. The nerve of it eh? Just getting up and leaving me like that!"

Ian and Valquee smiled.

"Good to have you back Xsealiadd."

Scorch, at that very moment joined the gathering, licking Xsealiadd with a thick slobbered, forked tongue, his eyes sparkled with youth and rambunctiousness.

"Good to see you too squirt!" Xsealiadd smiled, patting Scorch on the maw, he was still tired but improving.

Chapter 31
Flying to Sach

There was nothing holding him back, well, except perhaps Valquee, Xsealiadd, and Scorch, who moved at a snail's pace in comparison to Ian's quick and flighty movements. Right now, Ian didn't even care if they came or not, he just wanted to get to the dwarven sanctuary; he just wanted, once again, to be normal.

Ian tried to force himself to slow as Valquee and Xsealiadd, who were astride elvlocks burdened with provisions, and Scorch, who was talked into hauling a wagon of Xsealiadd's salvageable belongings, were far behind. They planned to head as directly as possible to the Sundurr peaks, something Ian questioned if it was even possible with the roughness of the land; especially around Oursjour Woods and Keyliar Crossing.

It was their intention to pass along the major trades road, the main artery of Ellezwrainia. Though their going was slow through Oursjour, nothing hindered their travels; this likely was because creatures, such as the befoullers, were already preoccupied with the battles at Ackles Academy. What caused the most problems were the Sardon folk, though cowardly, they were still a menace. Forced to partake in many unexpected battles with the soldiers of Sardon who had betrayed their master and fled, Valquee, Ian, and Xsealiadd were delayed in their travels for a great number of passing days.

Their provisions were nearly exhausted by the time they had reached the most northern point of Oursjour. Though they were all tired and dehydrated, Scorch was the worst. It took great work for he had to haul that immense wagon through such dense woods.

Sach wasn't too far off, perhaps, a two day travel. This wasn't what worried them; it was the alignment of such a vast city. Evil to the core, like many before it, Sach was once long ago a city which had reigned peace and serenity until the Occluder's minions runneth over.

Known to most, but never admitted, it was the Occluder's secret goal to overtake the entirety of Ellezwrainia, one village at a time. Should he ever get the blade, his task would grow easier; however, there were still those who would fight it.

In amongst all the warriors, Ian, Valquee, and Xsealiadd still found time to worry and wonder how such a magnificent dragon egg found its way onto the Occluder's mantle; a trouble which had burdened their hearts since Valquee had shared with them this telling days ago. Even in the disclosure, Valquee struggled with herself as she neglected to tell Xsealiadd and Ian that she had lost the black book of power; the Occluder's secret diary of weaknesses.

"This would make a fine tale for the storytellers someday." This was Xsealiadd's first comment. Ian's was more heartfelt as he became grateful of Valquee's safe return.

Chapter 32
The Truth Comes Out

They had reached Sach with heavy hearts. Famished and filled with dread, they all remained beneath a cluster of vast trees, each unwilling to go on.

"Well, somebody's got to go into the city and get food, I'm starved!" Xsealiadd grumbled hunger maddening his mind.

"It's not that easy father, we are all wanted, each and every one of us, well, except maybe Scorch. But we really couldn't send a dragon in to do our bidding. Could you imagine?" Valquee tried to lighten the tension. Nearby, Scorch cocked his head curiously.

'If Ian goesssss, I go.' It felt weird for Ian being a great harker. Though he heard Scorch's thoughts for some time, he hadn't quite gotten used to it.

"Uh, since I'm the most inexperienced, I feel I should remain here." Ian commented trying to talk himself out of it to protect Scorch.

"Nah ah! Don't think you can talk yourself out of this one!" Valquee cut in with anger.

"Don't forget Valquee, both Scorch and Ian are headed to fulfill the prophecy; both their lives are more worthy than ours, and if Ian goes, though he can't get hurt, Scorch is sure to follow. More importantly, we can't lose our peacekeeper; there would be nothing worse than the blade shattering... which reminds me. Thank the heavens I took just such a precaution."

"What precaution?"

"Just you never mind your meddling. It is complicated magical uh... stuff which I greatly expect you to not understand. All you need to know is Ian, being the chosen one, the rules of him being my predecessor had to be addressed quite a bit different than they were when I was in term."

"What? ...Wait a second, don't you start trying to talk your way out of this too. I am the most wanted and I have had just about enough evil for a long while."

"I am not talking about me."

"Well, you are peacekeeper aren't you, who else would you mean?"

Xsealiadd shook his head. "I am not the peacekeeper, not anymore! Have you forgotten Grunkle's words? I am just a feeble old man who plays with magic." He shuddered. This was the first time he even admitted it to himself. For over six hundred years, he wore such a title, and it had only been weeks that he had fobbed it off to another; it was something in dire need of adjustment.

"No, please tell me you didn't, please."

"I did Valquee, I know you don't want to admit it, but my time is nearing. Have you not noticed the explosion of moths, populating amongst my person?" Xsealiadd flailed his arms causing a flurry of moths to erupt skyward to demonstrate his point. "Do you not know what these moths mean?"

"No father."

"I am not your father anymore! He is, call me by my proper name; Xsealiadd."

Valquee looked over to Ian who shrugged hopelessly.

"No, nope! I can't do this, I am not ready. You're supposed to be father, the old wise one that all look up to." Valquee was frazzled. I simply can't run to a child whose wisdom is scarce when I need a spell woven or an old prophecy discussed, no, it simply won't do."

"I know this is hard Valquee, it will be slow and adjusting will take time, but we must all still respect the rules. Father was coined a term for the ruler of the blade, or peacekeeper by a name different, it was never meant to mean old wise one; people have just mishandled this term for years. Using it in its raw form, Ian is now father and you can still run to me for knowledge, for now anyway; until either I perish, or Ian gains enough wisdom to take my place, which one day he will certainly do."

"I am not a child!" Ian was growing agitated, being thrust into the middle of the argument.

"Ian you are fourteen, you are a child to my eyes!"

"Firstly, I am not fourteen and secondly, if this is such a battle, allow me to go and restock our supplies, I cannot get hurt and it will keep you quiet."

"You are not going, and this is a direct order from your master, Ian!"

"Yes sir."

Nearby, Valquee could be seen calming her nerves. "I'm sorry I lost my temper Ian, I suppose I should ask politely, what do you mean you are not fourteen?"

"Xsealiadd, perhaps you should tell her, she'll believe you more."

"Are you sure Ian, it is your deepest secret, kept hidden from all ears for your protection."

"I know master, I trust her, and I want her to understand the true me. But please, make her promise in the gods' language, that it shall never be revealed to anybody else. Even Gardo, my stepdad, doesn't know." Ian emphasized its importance.

"Stepdad?" Valquee questioned, but she was ignored, everyone knew she would find out soon enough.

"If you are sure Ian."

"I am."

"Valquee, please sit, this will startle you."

"From you Xsealiadd, I doubt it." She mocked, sitting beneath the trees, twirling blades of grass between her nimble fingers. It was obvious; she didn't know what was coming.

Xsealiadd began, as he did with Ian, recounting the entire prophecy without leaving out a single detail. By his conclusion, Valquee's jaw had dropped as she sat frozen, dumbfounded.

"Well you know," Valquee tried to speak, her voice cracking and unusually high. "We still have not decided who will get our food..." she trailed off.

"I will go." Xsealiadd leapt up. "After all, I am just a feeble old elder, besides, I'm sure your mind buzzes with questions reserved for our young father, thus, I'll leave you two alone."

"Wait Xsealiadd! Take Grunkle with you, he will offer protection in ways most cannot."

"That would be fine if he were here!" Xsealiadd gabbed.

'I'm here!' The thought filled Xsealiadd's mind. Ian, being shadowed, also heard it with relative ease.

"See Xsealiadd, I knew he'd come. Best you two be off." Ian ushered, urging them away.

Without a backwards look, Xsealiadd took several tender steps before halting. "Please care for my hourglass." He said simply before he continued northerly on his way, leaving Scorch, Ian, and Valquee in his wake.

"Well?" Ian began, waiting for the bombardment of questions, but none came.

"Shall we proceed around the city; wait at the northern edge of Sach's bounds?" Valquee talked herself away from the topic of Ian's parentage.

"If you wish." Ian responded, "But what about Xsealiadd, how will he find us?"

"Don't worry, he knows, we have formulated a bit of a plan."

"How? When?" Ian pushed.

"Well, that is for us to know and you to, well, not."

"Hey, but—"

"You know Ian, for a peacekeeper, you sure ask a lot of questions." She huffed as she heaved the hefty wagon to Scorch as she began to harness him in.

"Look, I'm still learning okay. I'm still the same guy you knew before I drank that potion. Still just as naive, still just as foolish. Thanks to Xsealiadd, a few things have changed, that's all."

"I'm sorry Ian, you're right, I shouldn't have mocked you." Valquee responded as she once more withdrew the tiny vial with a few meagre droplets of the mystery draught contained within. "It's pretty amazing really, such a simple little drink can muddle up a life so fast, but even more so, what amazes me is that we were able to find someone who actually knew the cure. And even more so, that you're not dead. My mind just can't grasp that. Here you are, shadowed, and yet you're not deceased. It's a strange potion really when you think of it." Valquee stared at the tiny vial in her palm, glinting like crystal in the sunlight. "Anyhow, we should really get moving Ian."

"Aye!" He replied. Ushering Scorch along, they took a wide breadth around Sach.

"Did you ever stop to think?" Ian rambled on as they walked with slow, methodical, care filled steps. "Scorch is Nighdrake's son, and is destined to best the shadowed dragon. And I am destined to best the Occluder and I didn't even begin to think that I was—" Ian glanced about with a shifty gaze. "His son." Ian added quickly, hoping not to be heard. "And to think, that I have to best him, a Dark Lord in whom people much wiser than me do not know how. It almost makes me wonder, have you put the two together because there's a certain third element, Xsealiadd and I have neglected to tell you."

"What?"

"Just think about it, Valquee, you're smart I'm sure you'll get it."

Valquee drew inward, lost in thought. Time passed, when she glanced to Ian.

"Okay tell me, I give up, I'm not getting it." Valquee scoffed.

"Really, an elf with your brains!" Ian teased.

"Just tell me Ian!" Valquee grew irritable.

"He's going to bite me!" Ian winked before dissipating into a fog.

"What! Ian get back here, wherever you are, I'm not in the mood for games!" Valquee mouthed, fearing to be overheard by unwanted ears.

Ian reappeared somewhere up ahead. "Aww, and tell me, what has happened to that sweet loving Valquee I fell in love with? Sardon folk steal her away? Tell me now and I'll head right back there to rescue that damsel in distress."

"Ian! Oh I'm sorry." She sighed. "I have been rather snippy lately, haven't I?"

"Aye."

"Well, I will do my best to soften my exterior. If you have been where I went, you would understand. If you didn't toughen up, you would never have survived."

"It sounds terrible, I mean, from what you tell me anyway." "Don't remind me!" She sighed, flopping near an unusually large dogwood for a quick mid-day break.

Though he didn't want to show it, Ian was nervous. Wagons and townsfolk continued passing on a path nearby. Surely somebody ought to see him, Valquee, or most likely Scorch sitting beneath the tree. If all three were lucky enough to escape notice, surely their wagon would give them away; it was only a matter of time.

Why Valquee and Ian then were so startled when it happened, no one would know. It was inevitable. A great merchant whose job was to be in charge of shipments going and coming from Sach was taking a wagonload of, what looked like weapons, along the main road when he spotted what he thought was an abandoned wagon parked just up a small hill. Pulling his carriage to the roadside, he crept up the slope with caution. Snoozing beneath the tree was the elf who had just escaped Sardon, of that he was sure. The face he knew well, for he was the one that had to watch her scream after aiding the Occluder in skewering her, something that deep in his heart troubled him greatly. Despite such, it was his duty as a loyal follower, a Carddronne, to give her up like any prisoner, to his master. Rushing back into Sach's borders, he raised the alarm.

Chapter 33
Confrontation

The usual environment was at play as the Occluder waited for the chatter to ebb. To portray his annoyance, he allowed his eyes to slide ceiling bound as he gazed pointlessly at the candles which seemed to float above, all the while, faintly aware of the rhythm his very own fingers were drumming against the grayed, aged, wooded tabletop.

At last the room silenced. Every Carddronne knew the expression painted upon the Occluder's face, and they knew it very well; he was anxious to begin.

"It seems lately, all of my meetings have been brief for I always seem to be flying to somewhere far away, a great distance parting me from my beloved Carddronnea. This time is exceptionally important, that wretch that escaped from here has been sighted near Sach, we have men attempting to subdue her as these very words fly from my lips—"

The room erupted in triumphant cheers.

"—No matter, this is not why we are here. In fact this is a highly unusual meeting as I didn't call it. Treggle heard I was to depart once more and requested an urgent gathering before I fly. So tell me Treggle, on which topic would you like to converse this session. Speak with haste for I am a busy man." The Occluder pushed.

Treggle was with great nerves. "I-I am terribly sorry for taking moments of your time master, it's just, when the elf was here she told Rennaux she was seeking Nalo as she had a dragon who had been bothering her at Gaunfaux flood's western bank. I wanted to impress you and take care of the dragon which I nearly did, except, when I was there I saw the spirit of the boy's body you inhabit and that wretched peace-loving wizard slime."

"Point?" The Occluder was clearly irritated.

"My point is, we both know that the boy is dead, it's just, last I remember, that peace-obsessed magic weaver wizard was protecting him with some spell, remember Rennaux tried to kill him and couldn't?"

"Get on with it!"

"How could the boy die with the wizard still breathing, I thought the elder was to perish first to break the spell—"

"—and the blade!" Another servant cut in pointlessly."

"Silence!" The Occluder ordered.

"What puzzles me master is why he is in the shadowed world? My Lord, could there perhaps be a spell or draught that could send him there?" Treggle raised a point.

"Oh there are, but I know of every spell or potion with such an ability. Also, I have spells to tell me if one is ever cast or drank."

"Then what could send him there and why would he be there?"

"Well either the wizard has lifted his spell, or someone knows a way to break past it and if they do, I want to find out who they are and above all, I want to know how it is done!" The Occluder slammed his fist hard onto the table causing a bruise to form on Ian's hand. Quickly and without notice, he shook it off.

"If it's any comfort master, the boy was likely killed by steel or some other horrible way that the wizard's spell can't protect from. It can't be any else!"

"Bah, good riddance of him! I don't care for this anymore. Actually, this is great news! Now I don't have to kill the peacekeeper and shatter my precious blade just for a stupid child. Speaking of the blade, has any found out if it'll be in Rulan for the festivities?"

"No master we haven't, but we'll do our best with haste to find out."

"I grow impatient."

"Yes sir."

The Occluder shook his head, he was obviously annoyed. "You know, this meeting is done!" Pushing his stool back so hard it fell with a clatter, the Occluder stormed from the room.

"I can't believe it!" Florian fumed.

"What is it Florian?" Hivell questioned, they were gathering in the dormitory lounge pouring over books and scrolls.

"Did you know, I was just reading about the academy's history and highlights, and it says here that they used trolls to cut down the local forest of Oursjour to fuel this place for heat and stuff?"

"Yea we knew that, why?"

"I can't believe they can get away with that! Not only is it cruelty to our local forests but it is cruelty to our wildlife and habitat too, poor things."

"Why do you care?" Thyle questioned from nearby through a mouthful of cakes he had stolen from the mess hall. Crumbs flew everywhere, mixed with spittle.

Florian flicked one from his parchment. "I think it's disgusting." He commented. "I think I should raise awareness!" Nearby, a great number of elves who had overheard nodded in agreement.

"Hey you've got my vote!" Hivell supported.

Right away Florian noticed Hivell to be crying. "What troubles you?" He asked.

"Oh, you're just like your brother, it must be genetic. That's the sort of stuff he'd do. But what can I say, like brother, like sister— I mean, oops."

Florian leapt up. "That was not the thing to say." He commented coolly before leaving the room. He couldn't help but notice all eyes to be upon him as the room was frozen with surprise and shock. Was there really a girl hiding out in an all boys academy?

"Hivell, may I speak to you for a moment?" Thyle at last broke the silence.

"Of course Thyle, what is it?"

"Do you remember I asked you about resisting mental attacks with hypnosis?"

"Yes." Hivell cocked an eye; he was a bit nervous where this conversation was headed.

"Well, when I spoke with Xsealiadd, he suggested I look up the Yotar theory. The problem is, I have looked everywhere in the library on the subject with no luck—"

"That is because the Yotar theory is vastly complex, eminently surpassing any student's skill level, at least any who roam this academy. We don't want students attempting to do skills beyond their limit." Hivell was cross.

"Could you at least tell me basically what this theory covers in general terms?"

"It is a theory designed to protect from mental attacks, the most common method used is to readjust the way your brain waves are fired. Put on a cover, mask your true self. This cover could be anything from you giving the attacker the illusion of having the brain of a horse right down to a gnat. This is used as a last resort and only if your defences are broken. You must sing to the gods to execute this portion to strengthen your defences. There is a simple spell which causes you to clear your mind, empty it of everything, and repel by projecting your emptiness onto the attacker."

"This won't work, the Occ—, uh, he would know."

"Yes Thyle, the attacker would generally be aware of your mental rebellion."

"Yes well, this is for people who are trying to probe my mind. I don't want to ignore his callings— I mean the attacks he thrusts upon me." Thyle corrected nervously.

Hivell gazed upon Thyle searchingly; he seemed confused, though, Thyle suspected it to be all an act. That was something elves were quite good at; leaving one unaware of what they did, and did not know.

"That is only the common variant Thyle there are others."

"Really, what are they?"

"I honestly do not know it is something elves don't normally study. We usually just practice the Yotar theory in its common form if we so desire protection."

Thyle slumped, disappointment seeping into his face. "Oh, okay, do you know of a text I may read on the matter?"

"I know there are such books out there, finding them may pose an issue. There is a store called 'Craft' in Villowtown— no wait, word has it that the owner has been murdered and his store closed, so that won't do. You could try Xsealiadd's hut, though after the burning, not much of his belongings remain—"

"I saw him empty his shack of anything with worth and value the other day, took it with him north to Rulan." Thyle cut in.

"Look Thyle, I'll keep my eyes and ears peeled. If I see or hear anything about a book that may help, or anyplace where you can access the information for that matter, I'll let you know."

Thyle drooped, sulking with disappointment.

"Hey now, don't be discouraged, I know how badly you want to get out of his circle, it's a terrible place to be. Besides, Xsealiadd has many acquaintances in the wizard community, I'm sure somebody will be able to help." Hivell comforted.

"You don't, you don't understand! You have no clue what it's like, coming around in the middle of Brewology with no idea how you got there; where you were before then or even what you were trying to concoct in the bubbling cauldron before you, or where even you are in the recipe. And then to look down and discover to your horror that you are drenched from your hair to your sock, in still wet blood. Having people stare at you when you walk down the corridor, yelling remarks and accusations to things you don't remember doing. No, you'll never know what it's like, which is why I want out, and now. Most importantly, I am tired of waiting for answers that I should readily get when I need. If I don't get out soon, it'll be my blood staining these clothes next you hear?" Without a further spoken word, Thyle vanished from the lounge.

It was utter pandemonium as many guards rushed out to challenge the elf and her dragon. Ian, they never saw, for in the past month, Grunkle had explained to him the theory of how to appear and disappear between the dimensions. To air on the cautious side, Ian happened to be lingering in the shadowed world where he was able to cause damage without being seen.

Valquee sprang into quick action, Scorch instinctively joining in, fighting always called upon a dragon's animal instincts. Behind the soldier's back, now there's where the real element of advantage lay. Picking up Valquee's small dagger, since she wasn't using it, Ian stabbed the nearest guard from the backside. The dagger found its way into a small gap between the helm and chest plate, right at the base of the neck. Being struck in such a vulnerable place, the soldier went down. His comrades reacted as they turned to face their foe; there was no one there.

This was Valquee's chance as she sprang into action, stabbing like a barbarian. The moment the soldiers turned their backs to the invisible Ian, he did it again. Grabbing the great dagger, he thrust it forth, falling another of Sach's great warriors.

Between Scorch's claws, Valquee's blades and Ian's stealth, they quickly dominated the battle, however, many soldiers still flowed from the gates of Sach all with intent to challenge Valquee and party.

Xsealiadd uttered foul words in one of his foreign tongues when Sach's alarm sounded; he hadn't even acquired food yet. That was a lesser priority now, however, as his primary focus was to get out before he was seen. It wasn't as difficult as it sounded for the city was in an uproar as many scoured the grounds for the intruder. Others were just trying to figure out what was occurring.

Xsealiadd purposely lost himself in the steady stream of people pouring from a western gate onto the major trade road. Forced to move with traffic, he found himself near the fray between Valquee, Ian, Scorch, and the folks of Sach; a fight where even common villagers brandished pitchforks and the like against Valquee, all voicing their disgust. Xsealiadd jumped in to assist, though Valquee seemed to have it beneath her control.

"So, how did it go in there?" Valquee asked curiously.

Xsealiadd sighed. "When I heard that alarm, I thought it was meant for me so I fled the city. I couldn't get any food or water."

"What did you get then?"

"You know, not a whole lot." He sighed.

"Well then I guess we shouldn't delay, else our hunger will set in." Valquee commented as she mounted an elvlock.

"Come on everyone, let's make haste! You too Scorch." She patted her leg to make the dragon motivate. A small growl escaped his maw as he rose to his talon filled feet, the wagon still hitched to his harness.

'Tell her to sssstop berating me. Thisss thing issss heavy and my sssscales hurt.' Scorch's thought interjected itself into Ian and Xsealiadd's mind.

"Later squirt!" Ian soothed, it's not too much farther.

Great wisps of smoke furled from his nostrils as slowly and methodically he placed one paw before the other as he trudged along.

The closer they drew to the woods of Hucklandish, the heavier the winds seemed to blow. The wagon rocked and swayed and threatened to topple. Not to mention the chilling temperatures, this froze the travelers to the marrow despite their layers of cloth.

"We can't go on like this! I can already feel my soul tiring!" Ian cried out of desperation. It was his job to keep the wagon from tipping, a task which drained him of his energy. "Grunkle, help!" He cried to the winds.

Grunkle must've appeared for the burden was lessening.

"I know Ian, Hucklandish Woods seems so near yet so far. Less than a day's travel yet I fear we will not make it. All my hope is ebbing." Valquee was as equally dismal as Ian.

"Oh stop whining the pair of you!" Xsealiadd voiced. Behind him, Scorch howled in misery. "You too, dragon! You're nothing but cowardly weaklings!   Ulhattarra boonge tuttarappe—come on Ian chant with me it'll make the spell that much more fulfilling."

Ian shook his head smartly. "I'm ought to anger the gods, not help us." He commented.

Xsealiadd shrugged before continuing his enchantment; the winds were lessening.

Chapter 34
Homeward Bound

It took a great amount of time, yet they at last reached the shelter of Hucklandish Woods.

"How are we to get the wagon in here?" Ian asked, curiosity filling him.

"We can't really, not without great difficulty. We use elvlocks; burden them down with provisions. Unload what we can in Rulan, resupply for the short jaunt to the Sundurrs from there."

"And what about Scorch, we both know he will follow me deep into Rulan's heart, what will the elves do or say?"

"Elves welcome dragons for the most part, remember we rode them for many years. Elves are fair we would never mistreat a pure folk in any way, even dwarves whom we despise so much. Scorch will be just fine in the realm of Rulan, just tell nobody that he wants you as his rider. I suspect some may find out but don't advertise it, okay?"

Ian assured his affirmative as both Valquee and Xsealiadd, burdened down the elvlocks and themselves with provisions, left the wagon behind.

"That wagon has passed a long way from the southern waters of Sardon, to the northern trees of Hucklandish, it has gotten me in and out of a great deal of trouble. It is old, rusty and on the verge of collapsing, it is becoming more and more useless by the moment and yet, with all that being true, I can't help but say that I'm going to miss it." Valquee commented, taking a final glance at the abandoned wagon, it was time they moved on.

The Occluder could not have been more grateful for the seclusion and concealment that day as he lay about his chambers licking his wounds.

"Why, why? My own academy, my own men, I train them for war, and they use their training against me." The Occluder was distraught.

"Well master you do tend to frighten people and cause havoc wherever you go."

"Shut up! I just don't understand. Why?"

"...Master, this came to us from the skies." A servant rushed in brandishing a homing pigeon in the Occluder's face. On its foot a tiny note was tied.

The Occluder bellowed trying to get his forceps on the tiny, dangling piece of twine which would unbind the scroll from the pigeon's leg, the bird lashed in panic and fear. Who wouldn't in such a close proximity to such an evil heart?

At long last after a great struggle, the Occluder finally got the note as he unfurled it gingerly in his sweaty palm.

The more he read of the sloppy scroll, the more cross he grew.

"What troubles befall our land master?" A servant queried curiously.

"That slime, you know that murdered Rennaux?"

"What about the wretch?"

"Well, says here, her and her accomplices have escaped the attack from Sach." Exchanging looks that clearly said you-know-what-I'm-thinking, they leapt up.

"I'll gather men and supplies!" The servant chimed, throwing the pigeon out a parted window.

"And I, I have some things to do." The Occluder declared as both he and his servant slipped from the chambers.

They couldn't move very far as a group of centaurs bared their way.

"What's your issue Banthumn?" Valquee asked to the alpha centaur. He stood boldest and noblest above all else.

"We have had enough of you elves passing through here without paying proper payment for shooting me last year. I said I'd come up with a way for revenge... this is it."

"We didn't shoot you."

"Hivell did and since he was an elf then your kind should, no, must pay!"

"Oh Banthumn, let it go it was an accident that happened over a year ago."

"Still, I want closure, I want justice, I want payment of something good."

"Well I can get you vast treasures from the great halls of Rulan, I'm sure Lord Guwhyon will agree."

"How do we know you'll keep your word and return? No, we want something right here, right now, or you shall not pass."

Desperate, Xsealiadd, and Valquee had offered nearly everything they carried with a great handful of exceptions belonging to Xsealiadd.

"Ian why don't you get Scorch to give a great scale to these centaurs." Xsealiadd suggested. "He seems fond of you." The centaurs eyes lit up with greed. Scorch, on the other hand, growled the idea down, telling Ian in a string of thoughts that they are not noble enough to deserve such a treasured gift.

Valquee and Xsealiadd were at a standstill as they pondered the problem, bickering amongst themselves. The moon had waxed and waned as they were well into midday on the second rising of the great circle, when Ian suggested a weird thought.

"They like to track and gossip do they not?"

Valquee nodded her affirmative.

"Well why don't I share with them Nighdrake's most prized secrets of himself and the Occluder when in their prime."

Nearby Banthumn shook his great head. "It's not enough, do you hear me!" He shouted at the party, he was growing irritable. It was only then a great idea struck Xsealiadd.

"On top of Ian's offerings," He began, "I'd like to heighten your senses to make tracking an easier task for you and your herd." Xsealiadd offered.

This tempted them greatly as they discussed the proposal between themselves. Eventually accepting, Ian flooded their heads with memories and Xsealiadd sharpened their senses. They in return allowed passage to Ian, Valquee, Scorch, and

Xsealiadd with promise to never hinder an elvish traveler again. They parted company as centaurs were staring at hooves or fingers, or rubbing ears and eyes, not believing what they heard, saw or felt. Heightened senses were something that would take great time for adjustment.

The Occluder slammed through the dungeon doors, no care of what was happening around him as he knocked a servant, whom happened to reside on the backside of the portal, to the ground. The Occluder barely paid him any mind as he concerned himself with the dragon, Nighdrake, who lay sleeping, well, as asleep as a dragon of death could be in the farthest corner.

"Well Nighdrake, show me what you've learned, show me how you manipulate the elements!"

Nighdrake arose, but slowly. With a great stretch and yawn, he lazily created various elements from a light Chinook, to a raging hailstorm, all the while, the Occluder grew fascinated, not by his skills, but by the power that coursed through them. It was a constant transferring of energy from the elements that were being created to Nighdrake who sustained them. It was this force that kept the manoeuvre in motion. The Occluder, being caught between these elements of energy, couldn't help but notice the surge flowing through his own soul. This made him remember those power hungry days.

"You know though Nigh, not everything has to do with energy." The Occluder tried his best to distract himself from the power swelling in his chest. "Mentally, there's great room for improvement also, manipulation for example. Have you ever tried that?" Nighdrake cocked his head, all elements in the room perished. "This is one of my favourite tactics as there's so much you can do with it. I, however, am going to teach you my favourite trick first, only because I can't wait. It's called the Bouldar spell, one of my very own inventions. It's how I ensnare and manipulate all my wonderful slaves. My little black book discusses all these theories and secrets plus more, all of which are true and I use. Do you know the beauty of it all? No one, other than me knows them because any who try to learn them will get sucked into the shadowed world and never return; isn't it marvellous? Penned by a prized servant, dictated by me, the servant was slain after the last character was inked. That way, I can ensure all information confidential. Ingenious don't you think? Now, where is my little black book for I'd dearly love to read it to my sweet, sweet Nighdrake?" The Occluder questioned the nearby servant who was still trying to get off the floor after being whacked with the door.

"Your black book that you have asked us to hide from everyone including yourself after we confiscated it from that elf?" He massaged his temple.

"You mean the one I told you to go and find! Why isn't it found yet?"

"I... uh... I, I don't know master."

"Well stop rambling and find it!"

"Yes master." The servant stammered before scurrying out the door.

"Well, Nighdrake, since my book of tricks and secrets is absent at the moment, you and I are going to focus upon sheer, crude, manipulation. The Bouldar spell is designed so that when the victim hears the word Bouldar, he or she feels compelled to answer it's calling; because if they don't, the spell will nag at them like a mosquito bite longing to be scratched. That victim shan't rest until they complete the task at hand, whatever I happen to appoint them to do with the spell. Most often, I am just too antsy to wait that long, so I make it happen instantly with just a simple matter of sneaking past their mental defences undetected and disabling their consciousness before they can retaliate. You'd be amazed just how susceptible the subconscious is. It'll be even easier for you, as, being a dragon speaking your own tongue they won't even hear you coming. And the best part about it is, just because you speak a different language, it renders the Bouldar spell no less effective. I'll teach it to you quickly now before I fly, but I warn you, it's going to take some time no matter how quick I make it."

    The Occluder could never remember teaching that spell, let alone at such a speed. Regardless, he was out of the castle and on the water before night had fallen, just the way he liked it. He had departed with about one hundred men as they headed north up the Gaunfaux flood waterways. The waters were churning with roughness and paddling had to be executed with care and precision. With frequent breaks, two days it took to cross north easterly, to the eastern bank further up the river. The weather never let up either once they were on land. Winds held steady bringing in a monstrous blizzard. But weather slowly improved once it passed, for behind it were milder temperatures causing drastic snowmelt; leaving the party wet and cold. Without any real choice, they were forced to spend a great number of days in camp beneath the woods of Oursjour.

Ian, Valquee, and Xsealiadd reached Rulan weary yet fulfilled. Immediately upon entry to the city, elves began berating Valquee as to tell of her travels.

"...Words have reached my ears that you have just come from Sardon after slaying Nalo the dragon poacher, are these tellings true?" An elf asked as they passed by.

"Yes, though it was meant to be confidential."

"What was Sardon like?" Another one questioned.

"...You seriously would be wise not to ask about that one." Valquee smiled.

"Were you able to find and kill Nalo?"

"Yes." Valquee breathed, getting a little annoyed. No one was supposed to know any of this.

"Did you survive?"

Valquee stopped in her tracks to acknowledge that asker. "What a stupid question, of course I survived, look at me I stand before you, but barely. It took great strength of others to pull me through." She commented at last acknowledging Xsealiadd, Ian, and Grunkle's efforts.

The asker lowered his hood.

"Lord Guwhyon! It's you!"

"Well, I had to attract your attention somehow and I know just how much you hate stupid questions. Now come to my place, I want to hear all about it, as, I'm sure you could tell, so do many others who live here in Rulan. And I'm sorry, I know you wanted this ordeal to be secret. Ocenna was just so worried about you she had to tell me, according to her anyhow. I think it was more an excuse to spread gossip. And, as usual, word radiated like a plague once it reaches elvish ears. I wouldn't be surprised if tongues of man are wagging right now either, they seemed pretty interested in the flying stories down at the dragon funeral."

Valquee put on a smile, her insides were screaming with rage.

"So hurry up, tell me everything as I'm dying to get the festivities in motion."

"Festivities?"

"To celebrate your survival and success in Sardon."

"Oh!" Valquee was surprised. "Well, I'm not exactly staying long, just passing through. I have to take Ian to the dwarves. Apparently it is believed they have a cure for that potion he drank a while back, you remember the one?"

"Aye."

"If all goes well, I shall only be gone a week, two at most. Then upon my return, it better be the best mid-year celebration I've ever endured!"

"For you Valquee, anything. Now, tell your tale, go on and spit it out!" Lord Guwhyon urged.

"No, you know what, I don't see it fair that only you should hear it. During the festivities in a couple weeks tops, during the time of the great feasting, I will recite my tale to the finest detail for the entire of Rulan to hear; until this time, even you shall wait in suspense." Valquee stood up, her stool scraping across the floor leaving scratches on the aged stone. "I depart for the dwarves with Ian at dawn, may my provisions be prepared. The sooner I leave the quicker I may return to tell my story. I cannot deny, however, the calling of my white linen sheets and fluffy feather pillow; I look forward to a peace filled night." She commented as she reached the door. "Oh yes, and the dragon that's been hanging around with Ian is not to be harmed, obviously. He's been following us since Gesshlon, in fact, if you could, make his stay as comfortable as you can. I suspect he will be parting with Ian and I at breaking dawn." With a final nod, Valquee left the lords abode only to try her best to weave between the curious elves to the peace filled seclusion of her own towering high, white home.

 Though Ian wished to be by Valquee's side, he knew his place was next to Scorch. Besides, Valquee would do well spending the night alone where all comforts would befall her, a place she knew as home. .

Chapter 35
To Sundurr We Fly

"We're not moving a step further until rest befalls us!" A servant protested not for the first time.

"Yeah, let's go to one of Oster's great parties!"

"Yeah!"

"We will not catch the elf when our guts are laced with ale and we don't know up from down. Besides, Oster is at least two days travel, one way, from here. As your master, I say you are not allowed to go."

"Well I'd say we go anyway!" A handful of servants disobeyed. This was all it took to set the torans off for they loved to battle, and battle they did. That's the thing with Sardon folk, no loss is really a loss for it would provide great sustenance in the days to come.

It was as the fight died that movement progressed without much hesitation. Food and supplies were gathered and men continued on foot, they were nearing their goal in just a week's time, the Occluder was confident he would ensnare his fugitive. In Ellezwrainia, however, he was oblivious to know, nothing was ever certain.

When Valquee arose, it was to many a gathering; preparing fond farewells to her once again. At the head of the crowd, the blackened scales of Scorch shimmered blue in the early dawn. Next to the dragon youth, a faint, misted profile was easily visible against the cold, crisp, morning air. That was the wondrous thing about Rulan, though the air chills, snow was never present. In fact, though it was late November, leaves still clung to the trees though their colours were extraordinarily vibrant; portraying every colour of the palette. Ian was exceptionally fond of the lilac tinged leaves. Commonly splashed with ruby edges, they were of awe-inspiring beauty.

After many acknowledgements of her clan mates, Valquee, at last joined Ian at the edge of their city. Ian never said much for he didn't want to embarrass himself in such an immense gathering of elvish folk and their keen hearing.

"Come quickly, for we shan't want to wait any longer than we must for such festivities!" Lord Guwhyon cried over the loud din of merriment.

Valquee knew these elves well, in her heart; she knew that this was just a transparent excuse to party. Though she couldn't understand why, for the Renaissance Day celebrations were not even a month away. The Renaissance or Rebirthing party was the elves' biggest event; for they celebrated the birth and rise of the new sun. It was basically their new year. During these celebrations they sang, danced and, drank Vegval; an elvish delicacy. It was a wine made from the leaves of the fallen trees and was aged no less than a hundred years, and through elvish magic, it was the sweetest wine ever to touch the palate. To make it even more special, it was only drank for these celebrations.

With a beaming smile and a quick elvish farewell she began to walk. Ian knew that gait, it was, I'm-in-motion-now-so-nothing-will-stop-me. Enthusiastically, Ian followed, Scorch in his wake, burdened down with tremendous baggage, Xsealiadd remaining behind in Rulan for rest and recovery of his weary soul.

"So how far is this walk from Rulan?" Ian queried.

"Five days for a slow walker." Valquee responded. "Enthusiasm and determination will get us there sooner." Without further ado they marched, ironically in silence. Eating colloiden rolls on their feet, they stopped to rest naught before sundown for their before bed feeding and rest beneath the stars.

Ian, though he never slept, happened to be resting in a hypnotic state when a voice pierced his defences. He recognized the thought patterns and immediately identified them as Grunkle's.

"What do you want Grunks?"

"Just to say goodbye for, well, probably a long, long time. Centuries, maybe even millenniums, who knows?"

"How do you mean that?"

"Well, you're going to get cured soon right? Well, I can't follow you into the land of life, I've been there already, I've spent my time. I must say, you will be missed."

"You too Grunkle." Ian commented, staring at the stars winking above.

"But don't get down, life can change in a twitch of a shorble's whisker, who knows, I may be back."

"You say it as if it were a positive thing."

"Perhaps, perhaps not, it depends." At least I know what to do now, thanks to you Grunkle, all I ever learned about this place was because of you. You're a great teacher."

"Yeah yeah, look, enough with these sentimental goodbyes, they irritate me so. Just don't expect me around any longer."

Ian's mind and body grew cold, empty, and alone, a sign of Grunkle's departure. He had really and truly left.

"What is the matter master?" A servant questioned concern in his heart.

"We're out of water and we can't go any further."

"What do you mean we can't go any further?"

"If you don't believe me, you try penetrating those woods, it cannot be done as far as I know by any evil soul. It is an elvish forest. I've heard they sing enchanted barriers amongst the tree and leaf so no foe can break through."

"So what does this mean for us?"

"It means we either have to camp around the forest bounds and hope that that particular elf reappears or we have to find a way to break their enchantments; either way we are running low on water and can't just sit like rotted toadstools all day."

"You want my opinion?" The servant questioned.

"Aye"

"We camp. Set out scouts for supplies and have watchers scan every inch of the forest boundaries, check every elf that goes in or out of that forest; find their business, where they came from and where they're going. She can't stay in that forest forever! You've seen her face, inject it into every servant this side of Ellezwrainia, someone's bound to see her."

"You know, I hate to admit it, but your plan is as sound as any. Mobilize it!" He hissed.

"Wait master! I have a concern; there is a fatal loophole in the plan."

"What!" The Occluder roared.

"As soon as you confront the elves, you'll reveal yourself to them, they'll know your location; they'll send men out, they'll kill you before you are ready."

The Occluder hesitated. "Then we counter with shadow, ready the snorgs, no one can better darkness!"

They had just come from Sach where a servant observed their fugitive heading due north, a ghost, wizard, and dragon, in her company. Following them as far north as possible, the Occluder received her last known location to be in the realm of Hucklandish; a woods which no evil could pierce. Much to the Occluder's dismay, she had once again slipped his grasp.

"You realize, this is twice now that that elvish scum has escaped my grasp. Her life hangs naught but by a thread. If I see her again, I will promise you, her head will be rolling across my floor. Do you understand me?"

"Yes sir."

"And if any of you are fortunate enough to lay your grubby little paws upon her person, you have my full permission to drop the head for me, just be sure to bring it to me so that I know it's been done; that she really is dead. That is your explict, and primary order, make sure it is followed above all else."

"Yes master!" The servant methodically obeyed out of habit before scurrying off.

"If it's the last thing I do, I'm going to get that wretched elf." The Occluder snarled to himself. "Of course I have said this about the boy and yet, somebody else has beat me to him—"

"Is there a problem master?"

"No, no not at all— wait a moment? Why aren't you at your station?"

Without another word, the servant scurried off leaving the Occluder in solitude.

Their travels quickly grew to a monotonous tempo, get up, eat, walk, eat, and sleep. Day after day it continued as such. The only thread of sanity Ian had was their reassurance that it was only a short, less than a week's, travel. About halfway through their forward journey, strange occurrences broke up their repetitive tasks. These being men dressed in black and shadow, all bearing the symbol of the Occluder, the stain of a dragon's paw blazing upon their torsos and gear.

It took great skill and stealth to avoid these men, something Valquee alone possessed but when accompanied by a clumsy dragon, all hope of speed quickly receded. The further along in their journey they proceeded, the more men and camps there seemed to be.

It was early morning on the fourth day, the Sundurr Mountains were near, when Valquee was sure she had been spotted. The party, clad in black moved forward, advancing upon her. She quickened her pace, Scorch matching her footfalls. The black travelers mirrored her actions, breaking to almost a run. Valquee growing to an elvish sprint, a pace which outstripped the shadowed folks. However, she had to exert herself twice as much for speed only came with ease when surrounded by vegetation, luckily, her stamina was healthy. Scorch, on the other hand, struggled immensely to even stay within the shadow of Valquee's wake.

Valquee sprinted without sleep that night, and when she finally did reach the eastern entrance to the dwarven sanctuary, she was utterly and totally exhausted. Scorch, however, was in worse shape. Falling further and further behind, he barely hung on the horizon when Valquee panted, uttering the instructed phrase to the stone. She was desperate and filled with worry. The evil entourage were nearly upon Scorch and she knew he couldn't fly away.

It was Ian who saved the moment. Using the tornado manoeuvre Grunkle had taught him, Ian swirled and danced, slowing the shadowed folk to a near standstill.

"Come Scorch! Come to Valquee!" Valquee urged. Though Scorch wished to stay with Ian, he seemed to understand the severity of the situation and rushed to Valquee straight away. She was so distracted by the situation she neglected to notice the dwarf standing framed in the parted cavern door.

"Can I help you?" The dwarf asked, his arms folded.

Valquee spun about, at last acknowledging the dwarf. "Oh, yes, uh, thank you—"

"You!" The dwarf yelled. Grabbing Valquee before she knew what was happening, she was dragged into the mountain pass, other dwarves pitching in. Their grasp on her struggling body was strong, offering aid. Being dragged roughly, deep into the mountain pass, Valquee was very vocal ensnaring Scorch's attention, he scampered after her frightened; he did not understand.

The great door of the mountains slammed shut on Scorch's tail. Letting out a yip of surprise, he slunk with great fear. The problem with this situation, poor Ian never made it through as he hovered outside the portal. At first he was distraught, but as his mind relaxed, it began to clear as he remembered Grunkle's instructions: 'if ever you find yourself facing an obstacle such as a wall or portal, it's best to materialize through to save your sanity.' Ian did just that, however, he decided it was best to remain invisible as he followed Valquee and Scorch through the dwarven tunnels.

"Master! Word has just touched my ear that the elf was spotted near Groy heading for the Sundurrs"

"I know I have just been notified of such using Bouldar."

"Yes, the wizard is not with them, he must've remained in Rulan."

"I don't care about him! Not enough, not now, it's the elf I fancy."

"Yes, about her, the word I received she was also accompanied by another. Upon a sourer subject..." The servant spoke slowly and with care as he chose wise words in an attempt to break the news softly.

"Which is?"

"By the time she was spotted, and our men mobilized, she had vanished deep into the Sundurr Mountain Pass."

"What! How can this be! My men are always quick to motivate!"

"Well, apparently they were drinking great tankards of ale, shipped down in barrels and casks from the great city of Groy. They were, in all honesty, a little groggy."

"What! I did not allow my men permission to drink. Send word to Sardon, we are mobilizing for war, three times is quite enough to slip my grasp! In the meantime, leave me be, I have some servants to punish severely." Before another word was spoken, the Occluder had vanished across the plains.

Chapter 36
The Cure

It felt very awkward hovering invisible in a dungeon holding cell, not being able to notify Valquee of his presence, yet lingering and observing her and Scorch sitting in misery.

To accentuate the situation, Ian was forced to listen to the sounds of battle, floors above, and feel guilty that it was the fault of himself and Valquee that the dwarves even had to fight the shadowed folk in the first place.

He was going to reveal his presence but decided against it, not yet anyway, until the fray of battle subsided. He wasn't as worried about Valquee this time as he was the last. He was here, and could go freely if he so chose, also, he was fairly confident she knew him to be there with her.

It was days later, once all returned to normal in the life of the dungeon caverns, he decided it was time to disclose himself. The cell door clanged open, as a great dwarf lumbered inside, bringing in the food that Valquee refused to touch as she learned her lesson last time. The dwarf turned to leave. Revealing himself, Ian barked at the dwarf.

"Oi! You!"

The dwarf spun around, acknowledging his presence.

"Hey! How did you get in here?"

"I am a spirit you know, and I request a consultation with your King. If you don't cooperate, I will find thy highness myself."

The dwarf sighed. "Fine, come with me."

Exiting the dungeon cell after the dwarf, Ian took one final look at Valquee before rounding a corner and vanishing from view. He had never before been in the dwarvish king's chambers or any private room of royalty for that matter, and was surprised at its sheer elegance.

Minding his manners, Ian did all he could to keep his gaze downward, despite the overwhelming temptation to look about; as, after all, it is considered highly disrespectful for one to stare upon the King without his permission. Something Ian had learned the difficult way early last year. And though he was granted permission on his previous visit to gaze upon the King, he was not shadowed then, and feared the King may not recognize him now.

"Your Kingliness, what an honour it is, having such a privilege to converse within your chambers riddled with such elegance." Ian spoke to the floor of polished marble. "My name is Ian, Ian Cosswell, though I have visited your sanctuary before, I have strong doubts that I have been remembered. I was a fool and a thief and such things are best forgotten against such a, being."

"Ian? Now I remember! You're the one who allowed foresight into an imminent battle, warning my people so that they were able to prepare. Again, though I have before, I thank you immensely once again."

"Yeah, that ability does surface from time to time. Though I have no idea what brings it on."

"Did I not grant you permission to gaze upon me then?"

"You did sire."

"Then why, pray tell, are you staring at my floor does its shine dazzle you, or does it need polishing, should I get a dwarf in here to get busy?"

"No Sire, your floor is fine Sire, in fact, it's quite beautiful. I mean, I didn't know if you would remember who I was, or more so for whom you granted such an honourable permission. I didn't want to upset you, or your clan mates by breaching those rules."

"You are very respectful to mind such manners, and a pure gentleman to obey the rules, however, I must say I only give that permission to a very select few individuals, it's hard to forget whom I have granted that privilege, therefore, I insist upon eye contact."

Ian looked to eye level. The King was much how Ian had remembered him, beardless, and lavished in riches far beyond Ian's imagination of what wealthy attire would appear. Then again, Valquee did tell Ian these dwarves were the most endowed in Ellezwrainia as they made the currency.

"So what troubles bring you before me on this, a fine day?"

"Firstly, I know your feelings towards the elves, however, I was hoping you could push them aside and allow my travel mate free, she did say she was a guest and you did let her in freely this time."

"You make a fine point my lad. Guards!"

The guards rushed in, their weapons raised, they were expecting trouble.

"I would like you to bring the elf here, but keep her bound just in case."

"And what about the dragon, sire?"

"Dragon?" The King, eyed Ian with suspicion.

"Sorry Your Highness, he has been following me everywhere."

"Bring him here also, but be sure to keep him contained."

This order, the guards must've misunderstood as once Valquee and Scorch arrived, Ian was horrified to see Scorch in shackles.

"Uh, your Majesty?"

"Silence Ian." It was almost as if he smelt Ian's accusation coming. "So what is your second concern as, usually when someone starts a conversation with firstly, other issues press his mind. Be quick for I have many affairs I must attend."

"Well, a dwarf once said to me that the symptoms I feel are a result of the Devigadora Draught, made by your clan." Ian commented.

"Oh really now? Do you see good as black, black as white? Do reflections appear as they should? What about when you drank the draught, what did it look like? Did it burn your stomach? How about when you first entered the world, did you have a body? Was your hearing and vision muddled, cloudy?"

Ian felt like he was with the medic undergoing an intense session.

"Yes, yes, black, yes, no, yes." Ian answered all the questions methodically.

"Well then, that definitely sounds like the Devigadora Draught. I'll tell you a quick bit about it. How it works, why it was made, that entire fun bit. The Devigadora Draught was indeed invented by our clan, it was created as the only known means of passing into the same environment as a shadowed figure, making it easier to contact and as we hoped, kill them. It works by separating body from soul, ripping one from the other. Though the body still is alive, it is dormant; it needs its soul to truly live. If somehow you are injured as a soul, when drinking such an antidote to reunite body and spirit, those injuries accompany you back within your body—"

"So this is what you meant when you said your men were fighting on the other side. It has puzzled me ever since you have said it last year, I kept thinking to myself, what does he mean? Now I know they were drinking the Devigadora Draught to best the snorgs!"

"Aye, the problem we discovered, is that this alone does not kill shadows, which is why we took a leaf from the elves basket and practiced archery. Why you ask, because we needed to understand how to properly throw our golden arrows, which I will get to. Do you know how life and spirits work?"

Ian shook his foggy head.

"The ba represents the personality, emotions, basically your whole being. The ba gives birth to the mahj the shadowed or spirit part of the being that lives on for all eternity. The basis of the being, the mahj is the foundation of life. When the person dies, so does the ba, the death of the ba births the mahj, our potion awakens the mahj from deep in your heart prematurely. If you don't take the reversal potion with you when you leave our world, and you don't have someone there who can send you back, it becomes far too easy to become trapped."

The King paused as he went to a cupboard Ian had never noticed before; it was filled with tiny vials, hundreds of them.

The King then selected three, two swirled with a silver fluid, one as black as charcoal.

"Lady elf, please pardon my absence for a moment. You two, keep an eye on them." The King gestured to Scorch and Valquee. Nodding their affirmative, the guards watched as the King uncorked the black vial, slipping the white vials in his pockets.

With a great sniff, the King gulped the black vial down in a great swig. Crumpling to the ground, his body stilled, but he was not gone, a clear ghostly figure stood, clear as day before Valquee. It was obvious he had done this before.

Withdrawing the vials of silver from where his pockets should be, he held them up. "That is the one thing that makes these special, they are built to travel through the dimensions," the King commented, "that is, as long as you remember to bring them with you: These are called Angellana; they are what will reunite spirit and body." Handing one to Ian, he simply said; "Be normal once more."

Chapter 37
Normality Faltering

Tipping up the tiny flask, Ian's world warped and skewed as it brightened. Suddenly the world froze as it felt he slammed into a wall of blackness and could go no further. It almost sounded as if voices were trapped beyond the wall, and when he looked down he saw himself, or at least his body anyway, one burdened with shadow scars sitting amongst the Sardon folk. Ian had no choice; concentrating with all his power he returned his spirit to the place in the dwarven sanctuary.

"What happened? Why are you not normal?" The King and Valquee asked in unison.

"I don't know. My world grew white, I felt light and free, but then I hit a wall of black and I found myself to be sitting amongst the Sardon folk—"

"Oh Ian, your body! Remember Ian the Occluder has taken it?" Valquee explained, realizing the complexity of the situation.

"What! Simply unheard of!" The King roared. "Have you ever heard of a wise one named Xsealiadd?" He questioned.

"Who hasn't?" Valquee commented, shifting awkwardly in her bindings.

"You need to seek him, ask him of your crisis, he may know better of what to do. In the meantime, I will give you another Devigadora Draught and two more vials of Angellana so that your elf friend can pass the barrier and give you the potion that will take you home. Please try once more when you feel confident your body is ready to accept your soul. Now, if there are any further questions ask away while time is still good."

"You say you designed these potions to kill shadowed folk? Well, according to an ancient prophecy, I am supposed to kill the Occluder—"

The King exploded in hysterics. "Seriously?"

"Yeah, I am being dead serious." The King chuckled, laughing off the joke.

"Oh, okay, in that case here's a bit more draughts to send you between the dimensions."

Ian eyed the tiny vial full. "You know, I was hoping to gather some followers." He commented.

"Well, in that case, you'll need this." The King handed Ian a folded bit of parchment. Unfolding it with care, Ian recognized it to be a recipe to brew, what he assumed to be, both the Devigadora and Angellana draughts.

"Uh, thanks." Ian commented, not knowing what to do with this stuff. "Look, is there any chance you could unbind the elf, I'd really appreciate her holding this stuff for me."

The King thought long and hard. "Well, alright, but no games." He replied nodding at a guard as he unfastened his war axe. The moment Valquee was untied she put Ian's trinkets in her pack.

"There is one more thing." The King began, eying her warily. "If you really are serious about besting the Occluder, you're going to need plenty of these. Unfortunately, I can only give you one for we have very few." The King replied putting on some snakeskin gloves, and selecting an arrow of gold from a quiver he had propped against a wall. "I will give you instructions how to make them, I'm sure the elves can help, they are arrows after all. The dwarves have been making them in secret for some time, however, in our hearts, we all fight for the same cause; so I guess the time is ripe to share our knowledge and as one rid the world of shadow once and for all." He eyed Valquee. "Elf!" He bellowed rather forcefully.

"Yes Your Highness?" Valquee replied, her neck growing stiff from staring at the floor.

"Please allow me to drop this in your quiver immediately." Valquee positioned herself so he could slip it in with ease. "Only use it for a shadowed beast, and listen up for this is very crucial. It will take more than one of these to bring down a single shadow. They work by absorbing energy from the shadow and when they consume all they can, they explode into a fiery rocket. And that's not even the important part, never handle one for they will absorb your energy and make you very ill. If you must handle them, never do it without gloves of a sturdy make. Oh and Ian, may the rain never hinder and may the wind carry thee forth."

"Thank you Your Highness." Ian bowed and began to back from the room.

Still looking down, Valquee approached the King, a few steps forth she drew. The King tightened his embrace on his war axe, elves and dwarves could never be trusted together.

"Look, I know you hate me and my kin and are angered at my presence simply because I am an elf. But bad blood aside, I would like to thank you for all you have done for Ian today, and to show my gratitude, I present you with a very special rock with great sentimental value given to me from a past student." Unfurling her hand she let the stone roll gently into the King's rough palm. It sat perfect in the bowl of his hand. He rolled it over several times in his grasp. It was the colour of cream and mottled with brown flecks.

"What's so special about it?" The king asked.

"That Master Dwarf, is called a geode. It may not be beautiful on its exterior, but just like some folks you meet, beings such as most elves, you have to look beneath the surface, and then, therein lies the beauty."

The King's eyes twinkled as he bid them a fond farewell, eager to crack open the stone.

"Where did you get that?" Ian asked curiously on their walk out of the caves.

"Like I said, a past student whose brother gave it to him. The brother, to my understanding, moved away to open a business as a pest controller specializing in gardens. The pest he deals with most would likely be a Greeg, an ugly, bald-headed, knobby-kneed, uh, thing. As tall as your foot is long, it likes to burrow beneath garden plants and feed on their roots destroying precious growth. To remove them, you must bop them on the head when they pop out of the ground before confiscating and removing them, usually they come up after a rain. They surface so they don't get drowned you know?"

"Wow, you sure know an awful lot about them."

"Yeah, it's hard not to, they are a public nuisance in Rulan. Why would they not be with all that wonderful food." Valquee rolled her eyes as she reflected on how annoying a Greeg could be. Smiling, they exited the chambers with light hearts.

Chapter 38
Identity Theft

It was utter chaos, so many men rushing about trying to fill so many orders. That's the thing with Master Occluder, when he wants something done, he wants it done yesterday.

In amongst the pandemonium a great rider, clad entirely in black astride a midnight horse with a diamond white on its brow and a splash of white on its tail and bell bottomed hooves, approached the Occluder.

Night had fallen by the time the rider reached the camp of shadow. Speaking before he was addressed, the rider rambled to the Dark Lord with urgency in his tone.

"Master I have hunted your presence as I crossed the entire countryside, over the fords and across the dells—"

"Hurry up, what tidings do you bring?"

"Knowledge has befallen me just a short while ago. The elves will possess the blade during their festivities."

"What! And it took this long for you to discover the true answer you... you useless, worthless... somebody kill him!" The Occluder roared so loud thunder clapped into the night.

A glint of silver in the dim fires light birthed the thud of a head as it departed the company of its shoulders marking the conclusion of the rider's life.

"And where is my army?" The Occluder bellowed out of rage. "They should be here by now!"

"Master, you have only sent for them two days past. It will be at least two to four weeks for your men to mobilize."

"What! The message should have reached them by now! Was the Bouldar spell not used?"

"No master, you sent the message along with a rider."

"What! Why wasn't the Bouldar spell used?"

"I don't know master, why wasn't the Bouldar spell used?"

The Occluder did not answer; instead, he stomped to his feet and departed from the camp.

"Master?"

"Leave me now!"

The servant scuttled away. Evidently the Occluder had personal business to tend to, though the servant was fairly confident as to what it was.

Great leagues away a fellow named Cano, whose job was to overlook the students of Ackles Academy, was sitting in solitude behind closed doors of his office. A great voice broke his mental defences and he knew exactly what, or rather who it was.

'Can I help you master?' Cano thought.

'Indeed. Post a notice for two students to fulfill their challenge. This is what I want it to say...' The Occluder's voice trailed on as he explained his wishes.

'I will get right to it master.' Cano chimed leaping up. He had a great job to do.

The Occluder did not just penetrate his mind but also the minds of many others in Sardon, giving instruction for armies to mobilize. He had a daunting task ahead, one he needed desperately to complete.

Thyle had his own troubles, trying to prepare for mid terms he was equally as anxious to resist the summoning.

Sitting in his dorm room lounge, his face in a book which discussed content of various potions and draughts and their effects, he was interrupted by Hivell.

"Thyle, you will be pleased to know, I've found you texts regarding that, um, theory you wished to learn about and a teacher willing to teach you."

"Really? Where?" Thyle's tome tumbled unnoticed to the floor, he was ecstatic.

"At Xsealiadd's Institution of Amity, it is taught as a regular subject there, they say they're willing to teach you."

"Oh, okay, thank you Hivell. Um, could you tell me where that is again?"

With a beaming smile, Hivell seated himself next to Thyle as he began to explain how to get to Xsealiadd's Institution of Amity.

Valquee and Scorch could barely move once they re-entered the realm of Rulan. So many curious elvish folk eager to hear the tales of their adventures crowded around, bombarding them with questions.

"Look how's this? You want me to tell you my tale?" Valquee fired up the crowd.

"Yea!"

"...And I want a party. So, what's say you set up the festivities while I find Xsealiadd and ask him a question. By that time, we should be ready to have a bit of fun."

The crowd cheered before dispersing. As they filtered off, the King, Lord Guwhyon, approached Valquee.

"In case you wish to know, Xsealiadd is staying in Teargo's vacated house."

"Thank you father." Valquee responded her eyes moistened with tears as she thought about Teargo's passing. Soon drifting her way through town, she made for Teargo's abode. Stopping outside a building a touch worse for wear, she knocked politely.

A voice rather familiar sounded from within. "Xsealiadd is away!" A suspicious look spread across Valquee's face. Knocking this time more impatiently, she was met with the voice once again.

"What urges you to rap upon my door? I am telling you clearly, Xsealiadd is not at home!" The voice from inside was frustrated, Xsealiadd surly didn't wish to be bothered. But this was an emergency, according to Valquee anyhow, thus Valquee knocked, no, pounded on the portal. There were no manners in it this time.

She never even heard him coming, yet, the door flew open with such force it knocked Valquee in the face as she stumbled backwards off the stoop, landing hard on the lawn. It was there she lay, still and resting, trying to mask the pain. She couldn't, however, conceal the blood trickling from her swollen nose.

Xsealiadd's head poked through the opened door. "Well, I'll be!" He exclaimed surprised. "Why might somebody be snoozing upon my lawn? Oh goodness me, Valquee, is that you?" He rushed to her side, her nose continued to bleed. "Valquee what has gotten into you to make you want to disturb me so, uh, urgently?" Xsealiadd interrogated as he healed her wounds.

"Oh Xsealiadd! It is Ian, the dwarves gave him a draught which was supposed to reunite soul and body, when Ian took it, he couldn't join his body because—"

"The Occluder is using it." Xsealiadd cut in.

"Exactly."

"Do you happen to have the text, 'Invoke and Purge: Body and Spirit'?" Xsealiadd asked.

"We may in our library, why?"

"Why else, Valquee? I need to purge the Occluder's spirit from Ian's body. I can't do it without the book. You expect me to have all these pages of incantations memorized! I'm only one man!" Xsealiadd barked.

"No, no of course not. Come with me and I'll take you to our library." Valquee interjected as they proceeded, conga-line, through the village.

"Come, gather round the flames for we must discuss the best course of action to break Rulan's defences. Now tell me, has any here been into Rulan in the past?" The Occluder questioned.

The only befouller in the camp raised his hand with fear.

"Aah, excellent! Come here sonny; sit next to me for I have much to learn."

Crawling over, the befouller sat next to the Occluder in the great circle which surrounded their campfire. The moment he sat, the Occluder beamed at him with an impish grin, Ian's eyes twinkling. "Now tell me son, everything, everything you know about the village, right down to the finest detail, right down to the individual leaf and grassy blade."

"You want my opinion of Rulan, what it looks like in detail? It has been over one thousand years since I have been there last; my memories of that place are surely dated. I will, however, describe it as I saw it on my last visit over a thousand years ago.

"The village is encased in thick forests with strong enchantments. Designed to keep those with a tainted heart out, they will repel you with great strength. If you dare penetrate the flourishing forest life, you will become swallowed deep into the trees, making you weaken, making you slow. This is no coincidence, this is their first defence. If you're not careful, becoming lost is a guarantee. Many centaurs roam these Woods of Hucklandish, excellent at tracking and knowing unfamiliar happenings, they are sly and stealthy. Being friends of the elf, if they see you, they will immediately warn the folks of Rulan. They are strong, quick, and nearly impossible to spot as they conceal themselves behind the dense thicket or else, dart from place to place. The only chance you have of spotting them is if they reveal to you their positions. Their numbers, however, are few and they likely will never challenge.

"Rulan itself is difficult to see. Buildings are hidden beneath the growth of trees which embrace them tightly. The buildings themselves are tall, white, and cylindrical, looking like tree trunks they are made of brick with plaster coverings.

"The paths throughout the city are narrow and winding, the width of a wagon at most. They, like so much around them, are blanketed by trees.

"The village in general topography rises in the west and sinks in the east, causing the great amounts of rainfall to drain to the nearby river. In the heart of town is where the elves like to coagulate to practice swordsmanship and enjoy great games of archery. The king's lair is northwest of the village's heart. It is here the blade would be held.

"Backing the village is a cliff, faced with stone and greens, it towers high. The river of Rulan flows from the north, carving a path over this cliff into a waterfall which bathes the courtyard for elvish meetings; located at its base on the western bank, in blankets of mist. The river is ferocious, but if crossed, you face Rulan's ultimate weakness. Standing at the cliff's edge on the western bank overlooking the city, one has a clear and easy shot, by longbow, to bury a volley deep within its bustling society. From this vantage point, you will be caressed by trees and become difficult to spot. From here you can see the king's lair, southwest of your position."

"And what about the elves, you were one once, what are your strengths, your weaknesses?" The Occluder queried, clinging to the befouller's every word.

"Our senses are sharp and our endurance is high, especially in Hucklandish where we can draw upon the energy of the flourishing plants and animals, just like they feed off of us. Still to this day, I feel that ball of energy fuelling my soul, the deeper into the woods I travel, the stronger I'd become; same as back home in Oursjour—"

"Are you trying to tell me that this whole time you and the other befoullers could have gone in those trees and captured that elf?"

"Possibly, it is difficult for one elf to capture another as we know each other's skills and tricks, we lose all elements of surprise. Besides, befoullers, as we are so called, are not welcome in Rulan, we would be massacred."

"Oh, anything else?"

"Of course! Feeding off the environment, this could also be a weakness for if you separate us from our nature, we weaken significantly. Our skills still hold strong but our speed would slow and our reflexes would grow equal to that of a man's. We are quick, agile, and we live by the trees, we know them well. We do better with ranged weapons and even in Hucklandish, can easily gain clear shots, yet our swordsmanship is no laughing matter. Our night gaze is strong but is no match for the dwarf. We also never sleep as you understand, but drift into a trance-like state for only a couple hours a night."

"And what of supplies, how does your city sustain itself?"

The befouller scoffed, he was disgusted. "It is not my city, not now, not anymore. Rulan is self sufficient with food and water. It is gatherers whose jobs it is to harvest and pick lush fruit and vegetables which are either selectively grown or flourish freely on Rulan's outer perimeters. They are then boiled, mashed, and made into elvish delicacies, or sometimes, simply eaten raw. Their main source of water is the river of Rulan. Fresh, clean, and cool, it is the finest water in all of Ellezwrainia."

"Armour and weaponry, how are they in terms of accessibility?"

"Aah, well there things change. The smith in Rulan, and yes they have one, orders his metals from the Dwarves of Sundurr. It is gathered and delivered by dwarves on granituals upon request.

"They use this metal for swords and mainly daggers. Their bows they carve from the trees after singing their obnoxious songs. Their armour and fletchings, at least the supplies to make them, are delivered to them by men, hunters of the north. They produce the leather for their armour, and feathers for the fletchings. Should they wear plated armour, which they have in the past, they also get the metals from the dwarves."

"Good, good, anything else you can tell me?"

"No sir."

"Then be gone!"

"Absolutely sir!" The servant responded, scuttling away leaving the Occluder to ponder the information he was just given, as well to plan his attack on the peace filled village of Rulan.

Ian, though shadowed as he was, followed Valquee and Xsealiadd into the elvish library. He couldn't imagine something so vast. The grand entrance had pillars flying hundreds of feet skyward, with intricate carvings about them they created the illusion of trees growing within the library itself. Looking up, the peak of the columns flared large and wide creating a realistic canopy which flowed, half painted, have sculpted, into the ceiling; which was detailed to appear like what one would expect to find in the forest canopy. The tree columns on the exterior walls also had branches that forked out forming rods to hang tapestries illustrating nature scenes, and the likes, and of course, to slice any wind attempting its way into the library's grand open windows. Four to five floors, Ian could not tell, overlooked the great entrance from the elegant balconies which accomplished a comfortable seating area on every level for extensive book reading. Straight ahead of them, a great spiral staircase wound and snaked its way to the upper levels.

On both their right and their left along the walls, great books, looking like they belonged to a large set, lined the portal. In the very centre of the entrance way, in the very middle of the polished marble floor, a round desk sat containing a single elf who smiled and nodded politely at their appearance.

"May I assist you?" She asked, seeing their approach.

"Yeah, we're looking for a, um, what was the name of that book again Xsealiadd?" Valquee began.

"Invoke and Purge; Body and Spirit." Xsealiadd replied.

"Well, we'll have to see won't we?" The lady elf from behind the desk, commented, rising from her seat.

Ian was surprised to see the lady go to the books he thought were encyclopaedias along the walls. Selecting one with care she let it fall open.

"How does she even know where to look?" Ian questioned, giving the lady a startle, she must not have seen him there.

"Well, she replied. Along this wall here are all the logs that list all the books we have in supply, and over there..." she pointed to the opposing wall, "...are all the logs of scrolls and other works."

"Oh. Sorry if I gave you a fright earlier." Ian apologized.

"No worries dear. Now, what was that name again?"

"Invoke and Purge; Body and Spirit."

"Oh yes, hold on to your britches a moment." She leafed through the pages. "Floor four, isle thirty seven, row ex." She replied.

"Thank you greatly." Valquee replied as she blessed the librarian with the elvish greeting. Taking her right hand, she touched her forehead, chest then lips before bowing her and her party off to the instructed location of the book.

"Aah! Here it is!" Xsealiadd exclaimed. "I'd know that spine a mile away!" Xsealiadd plucked the book of his choosing from the shelf. Ian, who had simply been staring awestruck, couldn't seem to tear his eyes off the towering high shelves.

"What's the matter Ian?" Valquee asked.

"Just wondering how'd you, how'd you get... up there." He pointed to the higher shelves.

"Uuda!" Valquee commented, and a ladder zoomed along the shelves seemingly from nowhere, coming to a stop before her.

"Oh." Ian replied simply.

"Will you two stop your blubbering and pay attention?" Xsealiadd grew impatient.

"To what?" Ian questioned.

"Do you want your body back or not?"

"Uh, yeah, sure."

"Then focus!"

"Wait, we're doing it here?"

"Here is as good as any."

"Won't it get messy?"

"Not with how I do it sonny. Valquee, please, cross the barrier and pass him the Angellana Draught now so he can come back on cue?" Obediently Valquee obeyed, drinking the Devigadora Draught to cross the threshold of shadow; experiencing all the same symptoms that Ian did except that she had a solid mass as Xsealiadd was fuelling her soul with energy and focus.

Once Valquee returned to the dimension of beating hearts, Xsealiadd began to read great passages from the book.

"Get ready Ian." Valquee prepped Ian for his task ahead. Clutching the small flask of silvery sparkly fluid Ian swirled it about observing the innocent appearance of the Angellana, meant to reunite body and soul. He uncorked it. "No, wait!" Valquee cried. "Wait for Xsealiadd to tell you when." She shrieked, she didn't trust Ian to not foil the plans.

Ian quickly noticed Xsealiadd to be repeating the same incantation again and again. On each utterance, he sounded more and more desperate, at last he screeched, "Now Ian! Do it now before it's too late, and quickly!" At that, Ian tipped the tiny vial, his soul disappearing from the library, going to join his body, wherever it was.

"What was that about?" Valquee asked, eying Xsealiadd with suspicion.

"You know that Occluder, he sure puts up a strong fight he does. It's not easy to get the king of evil to obey your magic."

They fell silent, both wondering what happened to Ian now.

It felt like a force had slammed against his backside and when he awoke, he couldn't help grow leery at the great number of eyes that bore into him from the others who surrounded the warming campfire.

"Master? Master are you okay?" Ian blinked several times, he was dazed and confused, and evidently, it showed.

'Why are they calling me master?' Ian pondered his thought processes were fogged, clouded by his ordeal.

"Master?" Another servant asked.

"Where am I?" Ian asked blinking hard again.

"Why, we're on the edge of Hucklandish, waiting for your army to join us."

"Army?" Ian was really confused. "What army is this?"

"The one you plan on bringing siege onto Rulan with."

"Right. Excuse me please." Ian got up from the fire and began to walk. He was in great pain and he didn't know why; nevertheless, walking was agonizing but as of now, he had to do it as he winced upon every footfall. His life seemed to depend on him getting away from these folks, whomever they were. Ian was sure of one thing, anyone who was discussing a siege on Rulan he wanted nowhere to be near.

Glancing around quickly, Ian established the Sundurr's to be to his left. Doing his best to keep them in alignment, he ploughed on, straight into the Woods of Hucklandish.

"Master you cannot go in there it will make you ill!"

Ian, his fog beginning to dissipate, spun around saying thus: "Master will do as I please! If any get in my way, mark my words, heads will fall!" And he stormed off.

Of course it was just an act, a distraction. As soon as the woods swallowed him from view, he dropped to the ground, tired and exhausted. He went no further, eventually even, he passed out from pain. This must've been similar to an elvish syncope, his body shutting down to shield him from the agony which coursed through him upon each and every heartbeat.

Chapter 39
Tales worth Telling

Ian parted his eyes wearily. The first thing he noticed was Valquee to be simply staring at him, her face distinguishable amongst the crowd of curious onlookers.

"What?" Ian asked irritable.

Valquee opened and closed her mouth several times before, at last, finding the courage to speak. "Never before has anyone I have ever met faced such great malice and survived with a pure soul."

"What?" Ian was confused.

Without further word, Valquee handed Ian a mirror. The room froze, not knowing what to expect. Slowly, Ian turned the mirror over and let his gaze fall onto it. His reflection stared back, scars sliced his flesh like a road map, scars as black as night.

Ian ran his fingers across his face. "What happened?" He mumbled.

"Shadow scars." Was all Valquee had said. Remembering what she had taught him about shadow scars, Ian searched his breast, sure enough, the scar he had since birth was there, bolder than ever. The more of his body he felt, the more scars he found.

"I'm crippled." He said.

"You have courage, more valour than most." Valquee commented. "Few could endure so much of his evil and survive." Ian gazed about. Amongst the faces, he could easily make out Xsealiadd, and, impossible to miss, Scorch. Many others, however, gazed curiously upon him.

"H-how did I get here?" Ian asked groggily.

"One of the Hucklandish centaurs found you lying in the forest; brought you here." Valquee explained.

"Hurry up and come to! You'll miss the festivities! And we'll miss our stories!" An elf near the back chimed.

"Braka! Don't be rude the boy's just waking up after being out of his body for months." Valquee silenced.

"What's all this about?" Ian asked.

"Oh they want to have a party to celebrate our homecoming and for us to tell the tale of our adventures; I told them I wasn't telling anyone until you were here and alert to correct any mistakes and to tell your tale from when you drank the Devigadora."

"Oh!" Ian was surprised. "I thought we were going to the academy so I could get a bit of my year's training."

"The Renaissance Celebration is naught but a month away. I feel it best we stay and celebrate, then go from there."

"Oh, okay. Wait! Valquee, there's something that just sprang to mind that I must say before it is forgotten once more. When I first rejoined my body, the Occluder's men were talking about the Dark Lord mobilizing an army, he plans on attacking Rulan. That is all I know." Ian warned. The entire onlookers gasped.

"Thank you Ian for that." Valquee commented. Around her elves began bombarding Ian with questions. "Please! Leave him be, he just told you all he knew, he just said it himself." Valquee protected. Ian swung his legs round to the bedside.

"Come on everyone, give him room and time to rouse. In fact, I will have him join you in the courtyard for storytelling when he is ready. Be there if you want to hear his tale." Valquee ushered everyone out.

The only ones who remained were Ian's closest companions, Valquee, Xsealiadd and Scorch, who came over to nudge him affectionately. Ian patted his snout several times before he was bitten unexpectedly, Scorch's sharp fangs piercing deep into his flesh.

Ian screamed in agony. Valquee rushed over, some rags in her hand, ready to bandage the wound. Nobody scolded the dragon, there was no need, they all knew it was coming it was just a matter of time.

Ian simply hoped no one heard him cry though his mind was clouded with doubt, who couldn't hear that. As he learned from Valquee, he expected word to travel fast.

Colours, emotions, and thoughts flooded into him. He had become a great harker for a while now and he could also penetrate the minds of any, including man, elf, or dwarf. This was different, still, from both of those talents. Ian could sense every feeling, every thought, every memory of the dragon who stood before him. He could feel Scorch's paw throbbing, absorbing Ian's pain through their mental connection.

Ian glared at Valquee.

"Why didn't you tell me this?" He asked.

"Tell you what?"

"When you become a rider, you don't just hear your dragon. You become one with him, every emotion, every thought, every feeling I now see the world in colour, colour not as I am used to, colour not as it is meant to be. Well, for instance, I now see you as pink. You don't just talk to your dragon you become part of your dragon!" Valquee grew sheepish. "What!" Ian drilled.

"In the language of the dragons, which you have just been introduced to, pink is the colour of love, purity being white, love being pink. You blend those two colours together and you get a dragons emotion. And the only reason I never told you is because I didn't think you'd understand."

"I may not have, but at least I'd be prepared. So does this mean Scorch loves me?"

"I'm sorry for not warning you, the answer to your question, no. Scorch does not love me, you do. You now see the world in the language of the dragons which is depicted by emotions and colours; both you and Scorch see everything differently as in, he may see me in a different colour than you depending how he feels about me. All getting bitten did was make you think like a dragon. Go on, ask Scorch how he sees me?" So, Ian did.

'She issss asss orange asss a carrot.' Scorch replied, his thought piercing Ian's mind.

Ian repeated this to Valquee who laughed awkwardly.

"Well now you know, he finds me palatable." Valquee smiled.

Ian gave Scorch a strange look.

"I am only kidding Ian, orange is the colour of playfulness and rambunctiousness, therefore, Scorch simply sees me as a playmate."

"Anyway, let's go to this festivity thing Valquee." Ian grumbled, it was clear he was not in the mood. "By the way, do you think any would notice this, perhaps I should get Xsealiadd or you to heal it?"

"Dragon bites don't heal, at least no spell exists to heal them."

'—just tell the ssspectators it wass an act of love.' Scorch interjected his thoughts crisp and pure, unlike before.

"—Scorch! That doesn't help!" Ian barked.

Valquee grinned broadly. "Welcome rider, to my world. You are the first of the forthcomings! You are much welcome." She mocked.

"Forthcoming? Why am I named that?" Ian was puzzled.

"Because we knew once the befoullers parted our company, the day would come that they would be replaced. Time was only the question." Ian gave Valquee a peculiar look. " We all knew war would once again befall our land, it must should we remove the wrong. We just didn't know when one would step up, rise to the task. With that the dragons solely understood that one day, once again, they would bear riders, it was forthcoming."

"Aah." Ian comprehended.

"Now come, our public awaits." Valquee led Ian to the courtyards for the great storytelling.

"Master! Master!" The servants grew worrisome.

'I am right here you slimes! I can only move so fast!'

"Where, where are you?" The servant questioned. A faint silhouette of a man flickered momentarily before him before collapsing once again into shadow. The Occluder did not have the strength to hold human form.

"But master, I thought you had a body, you went into the trees—"

'It was stolen from me, the boy, he must've come back to life.' The Occluder was outraged.

"That can't be! It's impossible!"

'Nothing's impossible! I swear if I see him again, I will punish him for his actions, it felt so good to have a body, I felt so alive!'

"I am so sorry you lost it sire."

'Silence! I don't care to be mocked.'

"I certainly wasn't mocking you sire, I was just—"

What he was, the Occluder will never know for he had, without warning, vacated the premises.

"Quiet down! Quiet down everyone!" Valquee began. "Now can all of you hear and see us? ...Excellent, now, let us start shall we? Since Ian began the adventure by dying, we should start with his tale. Remember Ian, everything except the rider business is fine okay." Valquee lowered her voice.

Ian nodded with nerves as he cleared his throat. "Hi, in case you don't remember me, my name is Ian, Ian Cosswell. I was very foolish that day when we were all traveling on our way to Gesshlon. I felt I was being ignored. I began exploring, drifting further and further from the party. I was wandering through the trees when I noticed something glinting in the sunlight. Curious I studied it. It was a potion of black. Uncorking it, I was bestowed upon an overwhelming urge, so I drank it down. It burned like acid. My world swirled and danced and I passed out. When I came to, everything was different. I saw pure souls as shadowed, shadowed as pure, reflections remained normal as did my world. Strangest of all, I had no body. I soon met up with a fellow named Grunkle, a ghostly spirit, who taught me all he could about surviving in a world of shadow; from how to keep a solid shadowy apparition to how to attack, even how to move quicker." Next to him it was evident Valquee sympathized as to the suffering he endured. "During this time I stayed with you, traveling to the dragon funeral, I witnessed the rising of the Golden King, as well the crowning of Ocenna. I even heard you all talk about the ancient prophecy; this angered me, I didn't like being relied upon; I even heard Valquee swear her words of revenge on Nalo beneath Ocenna's wing; how could I not, I was standing right there; Valquee do you wish to take over?"

"Well," Valquee began. "While at the dragon funeral, I promised to Ocenna in secret, as Ian said, to avenge the Golden King by slaying Nalo the dragon poacher. Nalo was the one who killed the Golden King. This meant heading right into Sardon. I snuck off, a dragon youth following, though at the time, I didn't know why. Why he followed, I later found out, was because Ian's invisible spirit followed me, the dragon sensed his presence and followed with curiosity. I went to Quath to purchase a wagon to cross Gaunfaux floods, but when I got there, I found the town in ruins; the Occluder's minions destroyed it seeking a book. I found a salvageable wagon which I used the dragon to drag to the waters. From there I used it like a boat to get to Sardon as I had planned. From the moment I arrived in the shadowed… realm, I had to sneak about. I learned, whilst in disguise, the only ones who knew of Nalo were in the Occluder's castle. Unknowingly, Ian had sent his shadowed mentor, Grunkle, to be with me. Grunkle helped me get into the Occluder's chambers where, on his mantle was a little black book. Having a fair idea what it was, I pocketed it, but there was also a dragon's egg on this shelf as well. I don't know, even now, why or how it had gotten there and am still looking into it, scouring for details. Anyhow, I came into contact with the Occluder's second in command who told me where Nalo was at the price of an oath in the black tongue. Though I swore to it, I never kept it. After I killed the second in command, whom I learned was Rennaux, I was tied up and tortured. Grunkle helped me out of there; I killed Nalo, grabbed Xsealiadd's hourglass which happened to be there, and fled. I met up with Xsealiadd and Ian near Oursjour then we came here, basically."

"Basically?"

"Well we did stop briefly at the academy. Xsealiadd wanted to talk to a couple people and it is there Ian learned of the cure to his swallowing of the potion so we just went to the dwarven sanctuary to help him out."

"Oh. And what were you doing when Valquee was in Sardon?"

"Well, I was waiting with the dragon on the banks of Gaunfaux for her return when Xsealiadd showed up. He told me about the ancient prophecy and being the one that must best the Occluder. After which he said my training wasn't adequate and he was going to teach me necessary skills to defeat the lord of blackness. He then went on further saying that since he had to train me anyway, he wanted to label me the next peacekeeper; save some training time. I accepted and swore the oaths, then spent the remainder of my time learning strange scripts and languages."

This sparked an outrage; it must've upset the elves. In amongst the chaos, Valquee caught Ian's eye.

"Come," she mouthed and led him back to her place. Xsealiadd unfortunately, got caught with questions and had to remain behind. Once in the seclusion of Valquee's sitting room, Scorch included as he was still small enough to fit through the larger of the doors, Ian became curious.

"What was all that?"

"Xsealiadd has been our peacekeeper for almost a thousand years as well as our first, they have trouble with change."

"And what about our feast?"

"Do you really want to feast with them?"

"Good point. Hey, in your tale you said you had the black book, where is it?"

"Well," Valquee sighed. "I didn't want to say this with Xsealiadd around, but when I was tortured, they had stripped me down to my flesh, the only covering I had was a burlap sack. When they had taken all that I wore, they found the book on my person and confiscated it. After much foul talk from the Occluder he declared he needed to find a new safe place for it. I don't know where it is now."

"Oh, hey if he took all your clothes how come you returned in what you left with?"

"You silly boy! Remember I was in disguise; I wasn't wearing my own clothes. You'd be a fool to walk into Sardon dressed as a forest folk elf. Now pipe down whilst I make us some blackberry tea."

Taking a seat opposite Ian at her small round table, loose leaf tea steaming before both of their noses, Valquee took a deep sip, her eyes closing as she savoured every smell, every taste, every bit of warmth that seeped into her bones; warmth that accompanied just such a drink. Though Rulan never had snow in winter, their cold months often grew rather chilly. On days like this it was hard not to appreciate the fine delicacy of an elvish tea.

Ian sat in silence, observing Valquee's beauty, observing her enjoy such a sweet simplicity; he never used to enjoy things the way she always did, but as the years were passing, he was beginning to appreciate the little things; such as a soft feather pillow, or a decent meal. The world that was being thrust upon him, he was beginning to understand, was quickly moving. He never knew from one day to the next when and if these simple pleasures would be denied to him; as he scaled rocky slopes or traveled across sun baked plains.

"You know Ian," Valquee began after several long sips in silence. "I really am going to have to train you in the ways of a rider but we'll have to do it discreetly. Most elves still frown down upon such times. The last time riders and dragons were one it was under the Occluder's rule. Most won't accept that times have changed."

"How do you plan on teaching me?"

"I don't know, perhaps away from Rulan, or during nights, I have not formulated yet a plan. I will say this though. Rulan's big celebration, you know the Rebirthing Party, is in about a month's time and I don't want you to miss it. So if you're staying here, you'll need a place to rest. Are you comfortable with me setting up the guest bed here in my house for you? If not I could make other arrangements because you know, sometimes staying with a female may be a little awkw—"

"Seriously Valquee I'm fine here, I in fact, really enjoy your company." Ian commented. The thought of spending a whole month with Valquee alone caused his heart to bounce.

"Well you know Ian, there is still probably a few hours until the daylight perishes. Our day has been too busy to start training now, so why don't we talk over tea?"

"I guess." Ian felt uncomfortable, he never talked over tea with a female other than Florence or mama, especially not one he harboured feelings towards. "I don't know what to talk about though." Ian mumbled.

"How about we get to know each other?" Valquee suggested. "I'm sure there is so much about me you want to know."

Ian grew tense. "Oh this is awkward." He mumbled barely above a whisper.

"Don't be shy Ian, let's talk like civilized adults." Ian jumped. He had forgotten just how keen elvish ears can be. He could feel his mental link with Scorch strengthen as he was recovering from his shock with Valquee.

'Ssshe'sss right you know.' Scorch interjected offering his support. 'If nothing elssse getting to know her may help you know if you truly love her. Sssshe could be an axe wielding maniac!' Scorch snorted, wisps of smoke furling from his nostrils.

"She is an axe wielding maniac, don't you remember she fought in the Great War, killed hundreds, thousands even I'm sure. Besides, you're a tad young to be giving dating advice Scorch!" Ian bellowed at the dragon. Once more a puff of smoke furled from Scorch's nostrils, he felt insulted. Turning his attention back to Valquee, he flustered. Spread across her face was a smirk of impishness.

"D-did I say that aloud?" Ian stammered.

"Perhaps one quick lesson before we turn more civilized." Valquee suggested.

"Oh! Okay, sure."

"Dragons can hear your thoughts just as well as you can hear theirs, especially if they're dragon and rider. Just something to bear in mind if you want to keep things, confidential." Valquee sipped her tea trying to ease the tension. "So Ian, what're your parents like?" She questioned, moving the awkward-filled moment along.

"I don't know my dad, I've never met him though he doesn't seem nice. Well I mean, I met him but briefly, you know my meaning?"

"I do. To me he will never be your father. You are too pure in the heart for that. I'm talking about your parents, the ones you grew up with."

"Well, my stepdad was a saddler, made the finest saddles in all of Solan. That's how I really knew him, by his work. As a father he was never really there. Whenever there was a problem, it was mama we ran to. When he disciplined, it was often a verbal as well as physical punishment; a good slap with an earful of screams. Perhaps it was good we never much saw face to face. When he'd come home, we'd be in bed. In my heart we grew up without a dad. The life I remembered with Florence was surrounded by love from mama. She was a wonderful mom. Let us get away with a great deal, but was firm when the need arose."

"And what about Florence... your sister?"

"She was stubborn. Made herself seem tough on her shell, but very sensitive. Often she would shut herself away in her room and cry in the night when she thought no one could hear. She's very soft and caring once you get to know her. She gave me this..." Ian clutched the necklace Florence gave him with a seashell on it early last year. "...The night you came to my house to pick me up and mama told me to run from you. That night was my biggest mistake yet, never again will I turn my back to you, ever. Anyway, Florence almost thought I was papa, I certainly treated her more like a Papa than her real dad."

"I see. Do you really regret running from me that night I went to pick you up?"

"Yes and no. Yes, for the reason I stated, as well because I injured Tom. I wish I hadn't. No because if I didn't, I never would have met Bashlay, he was such a sweet shorble."

"Well there you go." Valquee replied after setting down her tea. "It's your turn. Ask me something, anything at all, and I will answer it with as much honesty and truth as I can."

Ian thought hard, what was something he deemed appropriate but not overly personal. There were hundreds, no, thousands of things he wanted to ask, he had to pick just one, something easier said than done.

'What'sss your family like?'

"Scorch!" Ian scolded.

'Only trying to help.'

"You are—" Ian caught himself. 'Thank you Scorch.' He instead thought. "What was your family like?" Ian echoed Scorch's question.

Valquee smiled. "Well like you, four of us there were in my immediate family: my brother, me, and my parents. My mother always loved to bake, pies and pastries mostly, using elvish delicacies of exotic fruits. My brother and I were quite spoiled. Not a day went by that we weren't pampered with love and sweets. Father loved the sound of music. Often he made musical instruments with extraordinary sound. A passion my brother adopted. When papa wasn't making them, he was playing them. He was one of those funny dads, had a raging sense of humour which always made us laugh. Both of them died in the Great War fighting side by side along with me and my brother. Mother, she died by an arrow through the heart. Dad, he died after a castle wall collapsed on top of him. It was hit by a trebuchet."

"I'm so sorry to hear. What about your brother?"

"Died the same way as dad just last year. He was sweet and caring. No one could ask for a better brother."

"A castle wall collapsed on top of your brother last year? Where? When?"

"End of year last at Ackles Academy, he was caught in the Great Collapse. I should perhaps tell you Teargo was his name."

"Teargo? The Teargo that I attended the funeral for?"

"Aye. Now it's my turn." Valquee jumped in. They talked for many hours that night, only stopping when Ian's jaw appeared to have split into two from such a gaping yawn. Only then did Valquee usher him off to bed.

"What about Scorch?" Ian asked.

"He can sleep in your room for now. When he no longer fits through my door, we'll have to send him to the dragon's quarters. Hopefully by that time he'll have learned to fly, else he'll spend many nights with the elves. Trust me our ground is not created with comfort in mind." Ian and Valquee laughed merrily as they drifted down the hall to their allotted bedrooms.

Chapter 40
Trainings and Tongues

"That was an interesting class wasn't it Wok? I mean who knew there was a plant that helps in the production of molten." Florian was rather enriched in the class he had just endured. His interest, however, quickly faded from memory seeing the crowd of students coagulating around a poster hung sloppily on the wall. Florian pushed to the forefront of the crowd.

'Welcome,' it read. 'Second and third grade students needing to fulfill their challenge can submit their application. Include your name, transcript and reason why you feel yourself worthy for this challenge. Whomever is chosen will be receiving further details upon notice. Submission closing date is December seventeenth. Any submitted after such date will not be considered. Must have a minimum of eighty percent grade point average.'

Florian cocked a brow. 'Perhaps,' he thought, 'that would be a golden opportunity.'

Lunch that day consisted of a quick bite in the mess hall before slipping off to his dormitory to gather the required paperwork. This was, of course, after he explained himself profusely to Hivell. He wasn't the only one, however, preparing the paperwork; across the dormitory, Thyle was filling identical scrolls but for greatly different reasons. He saw it as a chance to slip off to seek training in the Yotar theory.

Travels were rough on the stretch of land between the Dural Glades and Oursjour. Snow whipped off the mountains which meant sheer whiteout conditions for the travelers. If it wasn't that, the rocky rough ground slowed the wagons and carriages. Why the Occluder's men were traveling so far east was beyond doubt, but no one ever questioned master's rule, not without fatal consequences.

To run a normal errand of the Occluder's with a select number of men wasn't so bad. In this particular case, however, trying to mobilize an entire army with all their equipment always seemed slow. Endless complaints reverberated in the ears of all, and tempers grew short.

"Come now, boys! This war is of great importance to master, we'd be right fools to mess it up for him." Many reluctantly agreed. So far, this was how travel from Sardon had become, and so it seemed would remain for days to come.

Valquee led Ian to the courtyard the next morning after a big breakfast. Along the way, however, they were met with resistance in the form of Xsealiadd.

"Valquee, where are you taking him?"

"To the courtyard, Ian must catch up on his training. He has missed so much from the academy."

"I object!" Xsealiadd shouted as he repelled Valquee's actions. "Being our new peacekeeper, Ian needs over six hundred years of training to perform, properly, the function of the title. And being that my life is perishing quicker than I would like, I would think I should get priority!"

"How would you like it if Ian showed up at the academy next year, leagues behind his classmates, how would he feel?"

"Those teachings are mindless drivel compared to what I must educate him!" Xsealiadd rebutted.

"Well then it's settled!" Valquee reported.

"What?"

"We'll both teach him! You can have him during the sunlit hours, and I get him when the moon is high." Valquee stated.

"But, I need to sleep!" Ian protested.

"There will be no need for that!" Valquee interjected.

Xsealiadd frowned. "You know, that's highly unnatural Valquee."

"It is the only way, if we expect to teach him all we can."

"If it must be, then it is settled." Xsealiadd's frown deepened. "Come Ian, we must get started."

"What was that about?" Ian asked.

"At the end of every session I will cast upon you a spell that forces you awake, keeps you from wanting sleep."

"What! That's not fair! I like sleeping; I like not having to think."

"Sorry Ian, this must be done." Embracing him around the shoulder, Xsealiadd steered him in the opposite direction. "You know, Ian, when you train with me, we train in the library. Can you guess why?"

"Because my language skills are lacking." Ian drawled.

"They must be, or else you wouldn't be addressing me in common tongue!"

"I'm sorry master, what language would you like me to attempt today?"

"Black tongue!"

"Here, in Rulan!"

"Well, we have to do it sooner or later, and here's as good as any. Uga!" Xsealiadd had switched over.

"Uga soodie, sorry, I mean crackai." Ian struggled.

"Atta boy! You'll get the hang of it, eventually. You will be pleased to know, however, once you master these tongues, the hard part of your training is done. After which you read, read, read." Xsealiadd informed, guiding Ian to an upper floor in the library.

"Here, read these aloud and tell me what they're about." Xsealiadd instructed.

"I'm sorry I missed that." Ian asked, they were still speaking in black tongue and Ian had missed the entire sentence.

Xsealiadd didn't mind as he graciously repeated the direction. Patience was so crucial, Ian quickly learned, when trying to teach such a vast amount of languages.

Ian was doing well reading the many scrolls as he was expected. The language of shadow is a very guttural tongue. This was Ian's greatest struggle; trying to keep the aks and chaks deep in his throat. Some words even got him so tongue-tied he couldn't even begin to pronounce them. Those he simply pointed at for Xsealiadd to go through the enunciations with. After several redundant soundings of the words, Ian would continue awkwardly.

"Good!" Xsealiadd praised, his black uttering's deep in his throat. "Tell me what it means." Xsealiadd asked as Ian had just concluded the readings of a rather lengthy scroll.

Ian stared at it for a long time trying to pick out any familiar words.

"It's talking about the evolution of trolls and their contribution to Sardon. What they did I could not say." Ian attempted.

Xsealiadd's face lit up. "Oh bravo, simply superb!"

Again and again Ian had to read different scrolls and works and do his best to sound out their meanings. He kept going as best he could until his head flopped on his desk with mental exhaustion.

"Okay you're done for today! Xsealiadd commented back in common tongue. Now Ian, please be aware that I am about to place a spell upon you which will strengthen you with vigour for Valquee. Upon your next visit with me when we first commence, I will do it again and henceforth afterwards, morning and night, until Valquee tells me otherwise."

Ian nodded, yet he was unable to subdue a groan. After a great string of phrases foreign to Ian's ears, Xsealiadd dismissed Ian to Valquee who came to the library to pick him up. Ian felt he could run a race, he was so invigorated.

"Otarre osherree anna!" Valquee smiled.

"Oh no." Was all that Ian could say.

"When you're with me, you speak in Rukkian Ian. We need to brush up on those language skills of yours. So along that subject line, I believe you meant to declare, outan gana! Oh no in Rukkian."

"Hmm..." Ian began. "I'd wonder where I heard that one before." He looked to Xsealiadd who grinned broadly.

"Wait! Xsealiadd before I go, I have a question that has been troubling me lately."

"Be quick Ian, you're cutting into Valquee's time. You are you are!"

"Being peacekeeper, if I were to die what would become of the blade?"

"The blade, m'boy, would, in normal circumstances, shatter and all that you have known in this world to be good would be gone, however, being the chosen one when I had sworn you in as peacekeeper. I had taken such precautions as to reiterate old vows, to ensure the blade's safety. Being young in heart I do not quite expect you to fully understand. How about you question me upon the matter when you are a few more winters advanced in age and perhaps I will elaborate a little more fully. Besides, time we at the present moment do not possess. You are cutting into Valquee's lessons... away with you now, away with you."

Ian gulped. "Thank you master, I will see you again when the sun rises."

"Uralle appan na. Neki otarani sumban ee nay!" Valquee rambled as she swept Ian away.

"What?"

"Rukkian Ian." She reminded as the library doors slammed shut in their wake.

The moon had swelled to its full potential by the time Ian and Valquee reached their chosen training site. Scorch was already there. They were nestled in a clearing far more west of the city where no one seemed to be.

"This is where we train from this point forth." Valquee informed in her Rukkian tongue. "Tonight I am going to begin teaching you how to kill different animals; hopefully you won't ever need this skill. I will be teaching you things such as, if you were to kill a centaur, what are the key points to attack to sever a major artery? There are seven of them. Another prime example would be, on a six headed sloth, which is the most efficient jugular to sever? And yes there is one."

Ian was utterly confused.

"I don't know Valquee." He said as best he could in Rukkian.

"That's why I'm going to teach you. Oh yes, and there is one more surprise."

"Really, what's that?" As Ian asked it, a blood red dragon he recognized to be Blazzan, Valquee's dragon, landed before him.

"Blazzan has kindly agreed to assist by training Scorch for a while. He is camping here, keeping a low profile from the villagers. Though dragons are welcomed in Rulan, they are not appreciated, it's best that we respect that. Blazzan's first priority is to get your little squirt airborne."

Blazzan nuzzled Ian in the breast.

Valquee smiled. "He congratulates you on becoming a rider."

"Gee thanks, uh, Blazzan."

The dragon cooed, his scales shimmering and chiming as he ruffled them in the moonlight.

"At the beginning of every training session, we will spar each day using a different weapon." Valquee instructed, her Rukkian as smooth as silk.

Ian's chest tightened with nerves, he hadn't sparred in months, he knew he'd be rusty. Valquee stood opposite him adjusting her gear. Ian was more focused on getting in the right mind set. Shaking his arms and head, he loosened his muscles and cob webs as best as he could.

Ian nodded, "Okay, I'm ready." He informed, his Rukkian nowhere near as fluent in comparison to Valquee's.

Valquee's sword flew through the air in a series of blows. Two, she landed on both of Ian's shoulders and one on his scalp.

"Perhaps you are not as ready as you think."

"Ugh! You're just too good!" Ian scoffed, walking in a circle to ease his frustration.

"I am not too good, you just try too hard. If you have to think whilst you spar, you will get hit. It's all spontaneous reaction. Don't think!" Unexpectedly, Valquee lunged. Ian out of instinct, deflected the blade away with the shaft of his war axe. "Very good. Now prepare yourself for another round."

Once more, Ian got into his niche. Swinging his axe like a baseball club several times he gave Valquee a quick nod. She sprang upon him like a feline. Ducking from the first blow, he barely got his axe in the way of his pelvis, to save him from the quick succession of blows Valquee unloaded towards his midriff. The third time, before Ian could even react, Valquee touched her blade at the base of his neck.

"Dead." She commented simply in her Rukkian tongue.

Again and again Ian was bested at the edge of the blade.

"I am awful! I'm never going to get this!" Ian slumped against a boulder. Tears reared their appearance which he quickly wiped away with a hand back, praying that nightfall would blind Valquee from them, though he doubted otherwise.

"Ian! Have you failed to remember what has been told to you last year?"

"What?" Ian honestly couldn't recall.

"Even the slowest elf can best the quickest man with ease. You will never beat me, though you can provide a fair challenge."

"Well, that was wonders for the depression, thank you very much Valquee! So in other words, I'm wasting my time! And here I thought you were to support me through times of trouble."

"I am, I mean, I do. Look, if it's any consolation, the longer I am with you, the greater your improvements. Day by day I see it, your swordsmanship improves immensely."

"Do you really believe it?"

"I do." Valquee replied causing Ian to rush over and embrace her.

"Thanks Valquee."

"My pleasure, now, how about I train you better in those enchantments you still so struggle with."

Ian groaned, a universal sound in every tongue, one all could understand. With obligation, he followed Valquee indoors.

"Now now Ian, no attitude towards your mentors."

Ian had been training for not yet twenty four hours and he was already growing irritable, the inability of being allowed to communicate in common tongue he missed immensely.

The day dragged on painstakingly slow, the only thing that kept Ian's spirits from sinking entirely was his brief meeting with Scorch before dawn where they quickly reviewed with each other all they had learned. After which, Scorch went off for breakfast and a rest whilst Ian was whisked off to train furthermore with Xsealiadd. In Ian's eyes, this time could not come soon enough, as he had at long last found himself to be making his way to Scorch and his rendezvous point.

Scorch was just in the midst of showing Ian all he'd learned on the wing when Xsealiadd broke free of the bushes.

"Here." The wizard interjected in the tongue of the dwarf as he handed Ian what he recognized as a colloiden roll, Ian's breakfast. Ian sulked as he gave Scorch a longing look. How he'd love to just make off with his dragon to some cave and sleep the day away.

"We're pursuing the dwarven language today?"

"Aye, oh and I almost forgot!" Xsealiadd exclaimed as he uttered the incantation that kept Ian from getting sleepy, except this time, he did it in the dwarvish tongue. "You see my lad that was to show you that a spell is not a spell for the words that are spoken, but for the intent and meaning behind those words; despite the tongue in which it was weaved."

"Huh?" Ian was confused.

"You'll learn my lad, all in good time, all in good time!" Xsealiadd exclaimed ensnaring Ian round the shoulders and whisking him off to the library.

Chapter 41
Happenings and Tellings

∞

Florian was unsure just how Thyle could be so relaxed when he himself sat in the principal's office just so nervous, his heart pounding in his throat.

At the current time, the principal's office was empty, however, somebody had requested their presence at this time and day; or maybe that's it, maybe it wasn't today at this time, maybe he had gotten the time and place mixed up. He couldn't have or else Thyle wouldn't be beside him, two couldn't possibly make the same blunder, could they? No, no it had to have been the principal, he messed up the appointment time, that's why he's was not here, or perhaps this was a big joke. Do they even have a new principal to be present in Rennaux's stead? No one had really seen any new occupant in Rennaux's chair at meal times in the mess hall. Perhaps there wasn't a principal at all and the academy was leaderless. Maybe someone just set Florian and Thyle up to make them look like fools.

"Oh help me!" Florian blurted out into the pressing silence startling Thyle who responded with a dirty gaze.

Florian cowered.

Just then the door flew open and a scrawny figure rushed in looking irritable.

Thyle leapt to his feet at once.

"Cano!"

"Thyle what a pleasure!" This Cano fellow plopped into the principal's chair.

"Who killed dad!?"

"Some elf that snuck into the Occluder's secret service. The Occluder himself is out there trying to hunt her down, probably as we speak."

Thyle remained quiet.

"So can I help you?" Cano asked.

"We were requested to be here." Thyle replied, exposing the notification report for Cano to see.

"Oh that's right! Of course. Bring it here, and congratulations both of you, you did very well—"

"All we did was submit our name—"Florian was confused.

"HUSH! I will get the warden to arrange everything."

"Thank you Cano, so what's this about?"

"Right I suppose you wish to know. Well, if you haven't guessed, this is a challenge. But a different challenge, it is—"

"How?"

"Silence! You have each other yes. But no mentors allowed. Instead, you will travel in the company of my men who will accompany you to a village. There you must steal for me one item. Not just any item, one I have aspired, for a great long time." Cano's eyes gleamed with greed.

"And what is this item?" Florian cut in.

"My men will explain everything, now, if there is nothing else, please leave."

"Yes sir."

"Not you Thyle, I meant the other one." Cano glared at Florian, who, at a loss for what to do or say, got up shaky kneed and exited the room. Upon his face, a look of total and complete disdain.

"What do you want of me?" Thyle asked, also growing sour. He knew to never denigrate a friend that way, why didn't Cano?

"The Occluder wants you to be the new principal."

"What!" Thyle roared in complete and utter shock. "But I thought you were the new principal."

"I am only here to guide you."

"But I don't want to deal with things."

"That is fine. Label you principal, I do your dirty work. Would you accept on those terms?"

Thyle hesitated, he hated getting himself into unexpected things. "How can I not?" He responded at long last, slowly and with care.

"That's m'boy!"

Once again the door flew open unexpectedly, this time it was Wok the toran who busted through. "Why am I not going on this challenge? I put my name down just like they did. Why wasn't I picked? I don't want to be left behind when all my friends are going! I should've left when Ian did!" Wok screamed in an outrage, flailing his pudgy hands before Cano and nearly unseating an unsuspecting Thyle.

"Sorry Wok, you were not chosen because you're simply just too stupid." Cano responded a sneer etched confidently on his thin lips.

"I... am... not... stupid!" Wok huffed barrelling at Cano. In two great bounds he had upturned the desk and had Cano dangling by the throat.

"Oh dear." Thyle was at a loss of what to do. "Anyhow, thanks for choosing me Cano." Thyle rose to his feet, excusing himself from the room.

"A little help!" Cano wheezed.

"Sorry, can't. You'd be a right fool to mess with a savage like Wok, he's a tough brute." Thyle smirked before vanishing from the room.

Three days it had been already that Ian had endured his training. Already he had learned to refine his enchantments, though still none had prevailed. On that topic, Ian was growing weary of hearing Valquee talk all about good composition and a passionate heart. The two elements in which she believed Ian's issue lay, when it came to not creating the magic of the spell. She claimed it was because he had never had an experience in his life that would shape him into a more compassionate person.

"Just you wait!" She told him. "One of these days, something's going to happen to you, something big and unexpected that will make you open your eyes and see how fragile life truly is. Only then will you completely understand. And that, that is when you'll become a pro at those fine idiosyncrasies that make up a working enchantment." Though it hasn't happened yet, Ian was frightened to experience it when it did.

Every night he would go out at the start of his and Valquee's training session, and would spar with anything from swords to flails, something he still failed miserably at against

Valquee; who was still a formidable opponent. On their second session, Valquee had started refreshing his skills in archery and was attempting his hand with an elvish bow.

Tonight was different however, Valquee and Xsealiadd had switched shifts for a night, something Valquee was not pleased about; for in order to get back on their nightly schedule, they both would have to train Ian, each on a twenty four hour schedule.

"Yeah!" Ian blurted on first encounter with such a plan. "It's amazing how okay it is when the student must go night and day without sleep, but the moment the professor must do it, oh my, the world must end, I don't get my pillow!" Ian sassed.

"Enough attitude Ian!" Valquee barked. "I'll see you tomorrow, same time same place." With a scowl she vanished to the bushes leaving Ian with Xsealiadd.

"I get you for one night, so I will make it special." Xsealiadd commented after performing the spell that kept Ian alert. "Please follow me." Xsealiadd led Ian to the clearing in Rulan where normally meetings were held. There awaiting them were two identical bed rolls and pillows.

Ian was ecstatic. "Does this mean it's nap time!"

"I sure hope not." Xsealiadd replied, watching Ian dive to a bed roll and gain comfort.

"So what are you going to teach me that can't be done when the sun burns bright?"

"I'm to teach you all I can about the heavens and prophecies. I will do all I can do let myself take you from Valquee one night a week so we can begin such an important topic."

"If we must, then we must." Ian smiled as he gazed blissfully to the stars.

Xsealiadd joined him on the remaining bed roll. "Not to waste time or anything, but what you see up there are not just stars but a tanglement of meanings, like a puzzle wanting to be unravelled. You see that..., it's that's called a constellation. Every time you see distant suns grouping like so, that's what they are called; each has a name, individually they have a meaning, and together they tell a story. Depending on the time of year, the story changes with the seasons which progressively, night by night, change and distort the constellations you see. New ones arise from time to time, and old ones fade. You must always keep an eye to what they are saying. Marvellous events have been foretold in their telling, like your birth for instance. But contrary to what you believe, I shan't burden you with their names and meanings; that is what books are for." Xsealiadd heaved a monstrous text seemingly from nowhere and dropped it onto Ian's chest, knocking the wind from him. The book had to have been at least two thousand pages. "This book lists every star, its name, every meaning, and of course, every constellation. Most importantly, it helps in the unravelling and telling of ancient stories and prophecies. You may also find this a help." Xsealiadd plopped a smaller book on top. "Reading the stars is as complicated as learning another language. You must promise me Ian. Even if we cannot have any more nightly sessions, you will lie beneath the heavens at least once a month and plot the locations of every star; and more importantly, any new stories they may tell."

"Yes master," Ian responded letting the massive book fall open. Illustrations of stars connected by lines and arrows riddled its pages. Even Ian, with his young eyes, had to squint to read its fading script.

"But this is all in, all in..." Ian tried to depict the unusual symbols.

"Do you remember nothing of our teachings these past months?" Xsealiadd winked, tapping the cover of the small, leather bound pocket book.

Ian pulled back the cover of the indicated book "*The Language of the Gods, a beginner's translator for the aspiring spell weaver.*" Ian read the title aloud. "But Xsealiadd?"

"—you keep those books, cart them around wherever you go, plot the stars each month, and when you see me, whenever you see me, you give me your heavenly documents."

"—but your books, I can't keep them!"

"Relax dear lad, I have no need for such rubbish any longer. I am no longer peacekeeper; I have no desire to learn anymore, and this is something you greatly need to know. Besides, should I ever feel the desire to look something up, the library is just around the corner."

"Just around the corner? But Xsealiadd, your home near the academy, do you mean not to return?"

"My bones are wearing, I am no longer fit for travel; I plan to live out my days here in Rulan, unless of course, something draws me away. I cannot ignore the fact, however, that serenity and peacefulness surround the village of Rulan in such abundance."

"But the students, won't they need you?"

"As a peacekeeper, it was my duty to shield and protect the peace folk, like a queen overlooking her drones. Being no longer a peacekeeper, I see no obligation to remain in such a dreadful place."

"Then, being a peacekeeper, it must be my duty to be near those students."

"Yes and no. As a peacekeeper, it is your duty to be where you are needed most. Those students face an element of danger each day they risk facing classes. There are, however, a great number of skilled fighters who are there solely to protect those students. Why else would there be mentors. Even if you did return to protect them, what would you do should the day come when you must stand up and face danger?" There was an awkward silence as Ian became at a loss the best way to answer. "The truth, dear lad, there is nothing, nothing you could do. Not now, you are not ready." The silence pressed in on them for a great long time. At last, Xsealiadd sighed. "Well, I suppose I should teach you how to read the stars." He stretched his neck. "Now, open that tome to page one thousand, three hundred and fifty one. Tonight you are going to learn a tale of a pressing nature; of a young king who loses his way, turns dark against his people."

Ian drew alert. "Didn't this already happen with Farrizon?"

"It did. But this prophecy is fresh suggesting it to happen again in our very near future."

"Who? Why?" Ian grew nervous, a lump forming in his throat.

"No one knows, not yet anyway, we must wait for the stars to tell us more. That is if they tell us." Xsealiadd explained.

Ian gulped. "Have - have the stars ever lied?"

"Never. Never in my lifespan anyway. Soon, history will rerun itself."

Chapter 42
Obligations and Festivities

A rhythmic pounding like the beat of a thousand drums sounding as one resounded in the near. Shouts and cries lifted above all else, including the strong resounding beat, sending shivers down the spine of any who heard. The potency of the racket kept Florian from his focus.

"Why did I enlist in such a debacle?" He thought, shaking his head hopelessly, but not before he stole a nervous glance from the window. Sliding from his stool after ensuring Hivell's and the professor's attention were elsewhere, wayward on some other point of interest, he crawled to the tiny classroom window, where he wanted a better look.

At least a thousand humanoid figures, no larger than a pinkie nail stood framed against the rising sun. Perhaps about half of those who traveled, stood in uniformed formation; line upon line, row upon row. The others were a mass of confusion. Scattered throughout, crammed into the tiny clearing at the eastern edge of Ackles Academy's vast grounds.

"They're ready for us now." A voice spoke hurriedly, just above a whisper. Florian, however, failed to acknowledge the speaker.

"Florian."

"Hmm?" Florian jerked from his vantage point by the sill, nearly toppling as he executed a startled leap. Something equally as unnecessary as the hand that was placed on his shoulder.

"Come now." Thyle reached his hand from Florian's shoulder to where Florian could easily grasp it. With a bob, he urged the distraught Florian on.

Slowly, Florian followed Thyle to the door.

"Wait!" Florian paused, slipping between the desks and fellow classmates. He stood himself very near Hivell's shoulder, parting his lips, he meant to speak. The words never came, instead, dying somewhere in his throat.

"I'll miss you Florence." Hivell softly spoke, not even turning to acknowledge a now weeping Florian's presence.

Silent tears spilled his eyes as he just stood there motionless, his heart crying, longing to stay next to Hivell, a place, ever since Ian had parted, where it felt safe. Hivell had become Florian's best friend. Suddenly, and unexpectedly, Florian flung his arms around Hivell's neck in such an embrace, he wished it to never end.

"You as well." Florian replied simply as he unravelled his arms shakily a long time later. Turning his back to the only known comfort remaining, he refrained from the one thing his heart begged him to do; go back to Hivell and never part.

Following in Thyle's wake, Florian made for the hall. Once that door was closed on the classroom behind, Florian simply froze with emotion. Every feeling he had ever experienced in his lifetime boiled up inside, rendering his body useless to operation.

"Come, they are waiting." A gentle voice broke his mindset, accompanied by a strong arm wrapping around his shoulders.

Teary eyed he had no choice but to place one foot before the other as he listened to the chanting of the drums rise in volume, rise in excitement.

About to part the grand entrance doors, they burst forth before Thyle's grasp, even before he ever had a chance to reach for the dragon handle.

Before any could acknowledge the happenings, what felt like a thousand hands reached in and pulled Thyle and Florian deep within the excitement.

Their time had now come.

Once again Ian had the spell of energy cast upon him as he was dragged off to another session with Valquee.

"This is not right!" He complained, "I miss sleep! I miss not having to think, I miss white linens and a fluffy feather pillow."

"Don't worry Ian, I have had a little chat with Xsealiadd these past few days and we have decided you, from this point forth, will get weekends off. Personally, I think it's a waste of time, you can do whatever your heart longs to do. If it be sleep, I will find you a bed with all the dressings. I can even talk Xsealiadd into putting you into such a sound slumber, both Scorch and you shant be disturbed, even at the angriest thunder or loudest clatter of cookware." Valquee's Rukkian rolled off her tongue like wind through the trees.

"Bless you Valquee." Ian yawned widely.

"Yeah yeah yeah, now where were we? Oh yes, tonight I am going to teach you how to harness excess energy from your dragon to work stronger, more stable magic; tonight will be the first night Blazzan and I teach you and Scorch as a proper dragon and rider." This ensnared Ian's attention.

"Sounds like fun!" He commented loosening his muscles.

"Fun no, interesting, perhaps." Valquee interjected, also preparing herself. "Now, the key to becoming stronger is to connect to your dragon by means of your souls. Remember, you are a team now. You best start fighting as one."

Ian eyed Scorch who was bounding about, nipping at Blazzan's tail. With a growl, Blazzan tucked it beneath his stomach, causing Scorch to go in seek of it like a big game. Ian doubted strongly he and Scorch would ever fight as a team.

"I seriously doubt that Valquee, he is too immature. Besides, you said it yourself: The age of the rider is over."

"Do you not remember what I have spoken to you? You are the first of the forthcomings. Though most don't wish to accept it, there will come a time when once again, dragons and riders must reunite, you will see. I am trying to train you for that time. Just don't expect friendliness when it comes."

"What do you mean?"

"I mean, most don't welcome the concept of the forthcomings, most do believe the time of dragon and rider are done. Now, no more excuses, you are training as one and you will simply learn to do it."

Ian sighed. "Well, you know lil' dude..." he looked to Scorch who cocked his head. "You're maybe young at heart, well I'm young in skill, so let us grow together."

"That's the spirit Ian. Now to start, I have brought forth tonight with me a little surprise."

"What!" Ian was nervous.

"Behold, this is what we call a saddle. Though men, and even some elves choose not to use it, we are trying to enforce them as a safety precaution ever since that one rider toppled from his dragon. Also, with them we have found that we are able to do more complex manoeuvres. One of these days I will teach you how they're made but it is a lesser skill to learn."

"Oh, so does this mean I'm flying then?"

"No, Scorch is barely ready to fly himself. He's only just learned. You are riding him as if on a horse, just to get the feel of a dragon back. I will be joining you on Blazzan's backside; he will also join in on guiding our young Scorch here."

"He's too young. I doubt he could support me."

"Oh he can, I haven't been telling you but in secret I have had Xsealiadd help me strengthen him with enchantments and spells. He is not ready to be airborne, but on ground he will be fine."

"Okay. Wait, before we start, maybe you can take me on a ride on Blazzan, just maybe to experience..." Ian flushed, he hoped in the dimming light Valquee did not see.

"Oh!" Valquee was surprised she did not expect that of all things. Blazzan must've said something because Valquee's tone suddenly grew worrisome. She was silent for a long while, evidently she was conversing with her dragon in private.

"What was that about?" Ian asked.

"Blazzan insists you go up alone to see what a real rider experiences."

"Oh no! No, no, no! I am simply not ready." Ian tried to talk his way out of it.

"Blazzan thinks you are, so come, I must equip you with some eye shields and strap you in a saddle. We'll use Scorch's, as I truly don't wish to waste time searching for Blazzan's. When I create them, I make them adjustable to expand with your dragon's growth." Valquee explained strapping on the saddle.

"Here." She commented, handing Ian a pair of goggles.

Ian eyed them warily before putting them on. He immediately began to sweat once the eye gear was in place as they were made from a leather which wouldn't allow his flesh to breathe.

"Why do we have to wear these?"

"You ever try traveling at high speeds with no windscreen? You just can't stop blinking. It just dries your eyes out. You're not going to be a good rider when you can't see."

"Oh."

"Now get up there!" Valquee grew impatient, ushering Ian up Blazzan's foreleg.

Ian's stomach churned. He suddenly didn't want to do this. To worsen the situation, was when Ian looked to Valquee: she was green as a frog.

"This isn't going to be good, is it?" Ian asked. Valquee, however, did not respond.

"He's in." Was all she said, patting Blazzan on the hide.

Blazzan shot skyward like a bullet, Scorch keeping tight in his slip-stream. Apparently like geese, dragons fly in a "V" formation when traveling together.

'I'm here for sssupport.' Scorch's thought interjected.

"Thanks," Ian replied. "Blazzan, I should really tell you, I have traveled with a dragon before, dangling from the maw. Needless to say, I didn't enjoy it!" Ian shouted over the wind.

'Thisss issss how a real rider fliessss.' Blazzan's thoughts, though strong, were still choppy in such extreme situations. A downfall of being a great harker, Ian was quickly learning, was that you missed a lot.

"Get ready." Was all Ian heard before Blazzan was spiralling, corkscrewing, flipping, rolling, diving, falling, and rising as he showed off his aerial acrobatics; catching thermals and updrafts as he flew.

Ian was nearly sick. Over his shoulder he could see Scorch practicing his own aerial manoeuvres, he was definitely improving.

Ian could faintly sense a flurry of colour and emotions bounce between the dragons as they spoke in their native tongues. It was only then that Ian realized, Blazzan must be teaching Scorch flying lessons.

Once Blazzan levelled out, Ian could at last appreciate the beauty of flying, he could see the vast expanse of trees as far as the eyes gaze. Mountains spanned far to his left, and over his shoulder beyond the trees, a great number of men seemed to be mobilizing.

"What's that? Blazzan, can you fly south? Turn around, please, take me south!"

Blazzan somersaulted, flew upside-down before at last, levelling off once more heading in the opposite direction. The closer Ian got, the more it was confirmed, a large army amassed at Hucklandish's southern borders.

"Quick Blazzan, take us to Valquee, we must spread the word!" Blazzan landed as stealthily as a mouse, Scorch less so.

"Valquee! Valquee! An army! There is an army amassing just south of here! I can only guess their intentions!"

Ian had barely got his straps loosened when he was scrambling out of the saddle and slid down Blazzan's slippery leg.

"Is this true?" Valquee asked. Blazzan must've confirmed it, for she suddenly turned inward. "Ian, please remain here a moment while I speak to the King." Before Ian had a chance to respond, Valquee had vanished through the trees.

Chapter 43
War is coming

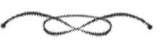

When Valquee returned she was in a huff. It seemed the entire Rulan was stirring in her wake.

"Well Ian, it's a perfect time to start thinking as a fighter does."

"Wait a second we're still training at a time like this?"

"Of course."

"But..."

"Enough! Rulan is not ready we need help from all we can. Now, to fight well you require many attributes. First, you need stamina. Let's see how you fare, jog on the spot." Ian began to tire after an hour. "Hmm, very disappointing. Quick hands make you able to react when something comes at you." Out of the blue, Valquee whacked Ian with her blade, he didn't even flinch in reaction. "How terrible, after all I've taught you. Stealth is also crucial." Valquee commented, as just then Ian stumbled, landing on a pile of green ware which smashed and cascaded everywhere. "I see my work has been cut out for me." Valquee grew cross. "No matter, even a lousy fighter will fare fine if he relies on his dragon. In times of terror remember this phrase: vugar ak othnak. Should you be forgetting our Rukkian tongue it means we are one. Say it with me now: vugar ak othnak."

Ian echoed the phrase. His world warped and scewed, suddenly every detail was sharp and vibrant. Trees seemed brighter and he could see farther.

He was faintly aware of his wings chafing against his scales and his palms sweaty, he could feel the soft, cool earth, on the underside of his talons and the leather rim of his goggles, which he forgot to remove, tickled him with sweat.

"Wait a second!"

"Yes Ian, you and Scorch are now one. Pick the hardest spell you know, one you have never been able to achieve. Say it now."

"Valquee no!"

"Trust me Ian, just do it."

"Befirriate!" He shouted. The forest of Hucklandish started to burn. Ian was upset and exhilarated all in one.

"Vugar ak othnak! Oukersh!" Ian heard Valquee cry. The fire had perished. "Vugar ak othnak!" She cried again. "Say it once more to break connection with your dragon." Valquee instructed which Ian did immediately.

"Wow! That was awesome!"

"You see Ian, use this in battle if blade fails you. Being a rider has its perks."

"Indeed." Ian agreed, as he grew distracted by how alive Rulan was this morning. "So what does this mean for your Rebirthing Party?"

"Oh, nothing would ever get in the way of our festivities, if we have to stay and fight then we will, but nothing would ever get in the way of our celebrations."

"Ian did not like the sounds of that one bit, though he didn't show it. "Wait a second. Where's Xsealiadd?" Ian asked.

"We have conversed and have both agreed my training will be far more useful in this upcoming battle."

"But what about sleep for both of us."

"Well, as for you Xsealiadd will be along shortly to reinvigorate you and as for me, I'll tell you a little secret?"

"Sure."

"Elves don't sleep. Not as you know it anyhow."

"Oh, this is going to be a long training session."

"Not particularly. We break for festivities in a couple days time, now pay attention for you have much to learn." Valquee scolded as Ian grew distracted once again by a wagon full of elvish wine being pulled into the village.

"You all know your roles; it's time you go to your stations." The Occluder's voice was tense, yet quiet as he bathed the land in an icy chill.

"I'm not going anywhere unless I can leave with mama and papa!" Florian chimed stubbornly. Ever since he discovered his parents were in charge of hygiene of the army and manning supply trains he had hardly left their sides.

"Silence! This is the eighth time I've had to scold you, pip squeak, about talking out. You would think my men would have sense enough to choose students who can follow directions. We are supposed to travel mute unless we are at rest in one of those designated safe zones we discussed, and this is not one of them!" The Occluder himself was attracting attention as a herd of centaurs not a hundred yards away pricked their ears.

"Our stealth has been compromised men! Bring them down!" The Occluder's voice screamed in the minds of his archers. Obediently their bowstrings creaked with tension as their arrows sped into the twilight.

One by one the centaurs fell. Others scattered but were quickly subdued. It was then that the Occluder blessed his decision to bring some quick footed befoullers along.

"Now get in position, we are wasting time!" The Occluder snarled. This was easier said than done. Being at the edge of Hucklandish where snow is non-existent and a muddy slush reigns supreme at the brink of transitioning from snow to green space, supply trains and people grew stuck in deep sopping grounds.

The deeper into the woods they pressed, the more tired they grew as more and more frequently they stopped to rest. The only thing they had in their favour was the Renaissance Celebrations were underway and no one seemed to notice anything peculiar happening in the elvish woods. Vegval had clouded their minds and dulled their senses. A fear Ian had possessed for over a year now.

Chapter 44
Party Crashers

The festivities looked tempting from Ian's vantage point atop the watch tower's roof. The watch tower itself was constructed shortly after the last siege on Rulan. Xsealiadd had weaved spells to emit spectacular fireworks that he said would last all week long. Enchantments were being sung causing Ian's heart to grow fuzzy, dancing and elvish music also was underway seemingly to never cease. Wine and elvish fruit delicacies were about in abundance, something that made Ian's stomach gurgle with hunger.

Ian, however, once he heard the Blade of Amity was being held in secret in Lord Guwhyon's chambers, promised himself he would not have a repeat of last celebration. He was going to stay bright, alert and clear minded. He was not going to give in to the scrumptious elvish wine.

It had been a week since Ian's first flight on Blazzan, and since then, Xsealiadd had been doing all he could to strengthen Scorch's wings so he could bear Ian in battle.

His first flight on his dragon was rather frightful. Being thrown astride, Scorch had leapt off the cliff of Rulan only to fall like a stone. Poor Ian, who was not strapped in, tumbled head over foot to the spiked topped trees below. Luckily, Scorch's reflexes were sound as he bolted beneath Ian and gently fell to earth, easing his landing.

This was even after Ian took care in explaining that he could not fly, so should he be dropped, he would splat to earth.

This was something even a week later Scorch still had not forgiven himself for, even with Ian's countless words of positivity. Ian forgave the dragon, but Scorch could not excuse himself. What a difference even a week made, Scorch could now bear Ian short distances here or there, long enough, according to Valquee, to carry Ian from danger.

Scorch's latest taxi was to carry a fully armoured Ian and himself, also clad in dragon plated protection made by the elves in which Valquee insisted he shield his scales with. It made, however, his flight very difficult as Scorch struggled to bear the weight of his armour, not to mention a plated Ian as well.

So here Ian was, miserable as can be, upon the watch tower with Scorch, the only other, it seemed, who still knew war to be coming; as well as the sole ones who truly were prepared.

"Well Scorch, at least we have each other. Can you sustain a flame yet?"

'No.' Scorch's thought interjected.

"You can't breathe fire yet! Well what good is a dragon who can't breathe fire! We need all the weapons we can get!"

'Well, I'm sssorry it'sss jusssst the firebane tassstess foul, it doesss. I just can't ssstomach it. Bessidess, I have a bite and ssslassh more deadly than you can imagine; one that improvesss every day.'

"I suppose, I just don't think we will win this you and I."

'Have faith, you sssstrongly underessstimate your ssskills. Asss long asss you remember all that you have been taught, we will do fine. Remember, when all elssse hasss failed, jusssst ssay vugar ak othnak.'

"Thanks Scorch I needed that!" Ian ensnared Scorch's neck. "I know our start was rough, but we will always be one you and I."

'Asss long asss I'm alive, we will be one! I will feed you life until my dying breath and dragonsss live a long time, like a flame that never diesss.'

"A flame that never dies! Yours has not yet sprung to life!" Ian joked. This caused smoke to furl from Scorch's tiny nostrils.

Darkness fell in an eerie way, plunging Rulan to an inky blackness. Surrounding trees reached their branches high, their snaking limbs stretching their best to blot out the moon.

Whether it be the darkness that made Ian's mind cloudy or the potent enchantments permeating from the merriment below, or even the lack of sleep and nourishment, whichever be the reason, Ian was strong on a notion that the trees were growing before his gaze. 'Hmm, must be my imagination.' Ian thought, his eyes beginning to droop.

Staring absent-mindedly at the fire crackling and burning in the clearing below, Ian did not even grow aware that sleep had ensnared him. Xsealiadd's spell had long worn off. It wasn't until Scorch had nuzzled him in the ribs that Ian grew alert to his blunder.

'What, what is it?' Ian thought to Scorch.

'Over there in the bussshesss!' Scorch jabbed his maw to the air in the direction he was indicating. His eyes sharpened, his nose was raised to the air. Even his barbed, forked tongue lashed out between a small gap in his lips, sensing the surrounds.

Bolting upright from his seclusion of the nook of Scorch's armpit, Ian squinted hard against the pressing darkness.

"I cannot see a thing!" Ian thought with frustration.

'Become one, Ian, sssee asss I do.'

"Vugar ak othnak!" Ian cried as his vision quickly sharpened. He was faintly aware of his tongue whipping the air before him and the gentle pressure on his side where his back was resting, he could feel the heaviness of the armour binding him within; he could feel the burn in his eyes where sleep lingered on the edges of his consciousness. He could feel the chafing of his scales pull on his armour. None of this mattered, what was most relevant was the bush that was stirring perhaps two hundred feet before him.

Something was there, something with unknown intensions.

"It is certainly something we should fear." Ian replied after withdrawing himself from their telepathic connection. "Perhaps we should get a better look."

'With caution.' Scorch replied. Mounting his dragon they preformed a quick fly by before Scorch's wings tired.

Many torches dotted the forest below.

"Hurry, before we are seen! We must warn the others!" Ian cried.

'Then watch your toesss lil' ssssquirt, it'sss about to get hot!' Scorch warned as Ian folded his feet before him, clutching Scorch's frill spikes like reins for balance. And what an entrance Scorch made as he landed right on the elvish ceremonial fire in the clearing below. The fire hissed to oblivion as it touched Scorch's cold armour.

Ian leapt from Scorch's back, rushing to confront all he could find. He did his best to spread the word. Grabbing a dancing elf upon the shoulders, Ian halted him in his tracks. "Danger stirs in the north, we must prepare for battle!" Ian nearly screamed in the elf's face within the din of the merriment.

"Hey relax kid! Have some wine." He smiled and handed Ian a goblet full of Vegval before dancing off.

"Will no one listen to me?" Ian cried after the numerous failed attempts at ensnaring someone's attention.

Fireworks erupted overhead as Ian came to his senses.

"Fireworks? Xsealiadd! Scorch, we must find where those fireworks are coming from!"

'Then hop on!' Scorch signalled lowering to a crouch to ease Ian's mount.

The moment Ian was on and had clutched the horn between his hands, Scorch took off like a bullet. Running he may have been, but was weaving between the crowd like water flowing through crags.

Sure enough, Xsealiadd was sitting with Valquee on Teargo's front stoop, the house Xsealiadd had inhabited since his arrival in Rulan. Both were conversing over Vegval and every so often, Xsealiadd would emit awe inspiring fireworks.

"What, what is it?" Xsealiadd asked seeing Ian's face in a panic. He leapt to his feet in a hurry, spilling the wine.

Valquee, also sensing trouble, aped Xsealiadd's motions.

"Trouble in the north, evil is stirring!" Ian panted.

"Are you sure Ian?"

"Yes, I saw many torches moving through the trees. I doubt any elves would be roaming now given the circumstances."

"Very well, stay here with Scorch and don't move!" Xsealiadd was stern as he and Valquee took off in a flash to spread the news.

Elves darted in utter chaos clad in elvish veils, garments which appeared like see through night dresses, bearing goblets filled with wine. None carried weapons. Some elves ran stupidly, screaming down the winding streets, others guzzled their wine ignorantly trying to absorb last minute festivities.

"My God, no one is ready, there is no way to survive this war. We need readied men, I cannot fight alone..." Before Ian could finish his thought, Xsealiadd had reappeared from nowhere and ensnared him by the collar.

"To the cliff top! Shoot all you can!" Xsealiadd barely shouted when a wave of enemies poured through the southern tree line, the paw of Sardon on their breast. Xsealiadd was caught up with the flow of enemies, like a broken levee they flooded Rulan, engulfing all in their path.

Chapter 45
The Raising of Blades

The climb down the rock-face was excruciating. Banged, bruised, tired, and achy, Thyle and Florian inched their way down the cliff face, their fingers cramping.

Behind them they left a coagulation of men, archers who were shooting into the bustle of Rulan below. Florian did his best to block out the dying screams of the elves as he concentrated on the task at hand. A feat, though optimistic at the start, seemed hopeless now. Florian's biggest worry was how to hold on until the bottom for his fingers were in such cramps, he was sure they were to give out any moment, yet inch by painstaking inch, the ground crept up to meet him. 'And here I thought crossing Rulan's river swell was hard!' Florian thought as he, at last, dropped the last six feet to the ground where an anxious Thyle awaited.

Both were clad in black with charcoal on their faces, dressed to suit the job they were sent to do: steal some sword from the house fourth south from the cliff. They were almost there.

The door to the house in question burst open and a distraught elf came bustling forth. Suddenly an arrow whizzed by Florian's ear and struck the elf in the chest. With a painful scream, he fell motionless to the ground, bleeding rather profusely from the arrow wound in his breast.

"We killed the King!" Great shouts resounded on the cliff behind and a great war horn punctuated their victory.

Florian tore his attention from the cliff and noticed Thyle to be at least ten feet in front of him. Scurrying to close the gap, they crept rather stealthily into the open portal of the King's house.

The house was black as pitch as any drop of the moonlight which survived the hungry trees' grasp and fell upon the city of Rulan was killed by the walls of the structure. Florian had no choice he had to light a torch.

Unburdening himself from his pack, he rummaged about. Soon a torch sprang to life.

He let its dancing light fall upon the room. Its orangey glow touched tattered books and trinkets of unusual fashion. Florian danced and weaved about these objects like a dancer deep in tune with his music. Constantly, he let the torch light sweep over the objects that surrounded him.

There, concealed at the back of the house behind a pile of books was a polished elegant sword in a display case. 'There, this must be the one.' Florian thought spinning about. He quickly realized Thyle had vanished; deserted him for a more noble cause.

Ian didn't expect there to be a barrage of opponents on the cliff top, nevertheless he discovered it in the most difficult way as they were showering him with arrows mid-flight.

Scorch got Ian to the ground safely but landed rough, his wing membrane torn by an arrow wound. Ignoring it as best he could, he whimpered as he rushed to meet the confrontation of men charging out to greet them. Snapping and slashing wickedly, his wing held in an awkward stance, Ian felt sympathy for him but only for a moment as he himself was surrounded by foes caught up in the fray.

The noise was deafening as Ian's axe clashed against pike, spear, hammer and sword. Armour and helms screamed as they were greeted by unfriendly hunks of steel, Ian needed help. Above him, vultures circled hungry for fresh meat. And Scorch, well he was dealing with his own set of problems: his wing, already wounded by an arrowhead, now had an angry gash from where blade met flesh. As well, his chest plate was dented so badly he could barely breathe without pain. Blood trickled from the generous collection of wounds he was receiving and he was overwhelmed by the vast numbers of men.

'Ian we cannot hold them!' Scorch's thoughts were strong but fearful.

"When all else fails we become one!" Ian reiterated. "Vugar ak othnak! Rendunal!" He shouted the first piece of magic that came to his mind with naught a moment of hesitation.

Thunder clapped in the sky and lightning pierced the heavens, illuminating the ferocity of the raging battle all around. Below, even the experienced elves seemed to struggle to subdue the Occluder's wrath.

Amongst his own reign, men began to flee and it didn't take Ian long to find out why, once again, he had set the Forest of Hucklandish ablaze, and for Ian and Scorch, there was nowhere to run.

'Ian, I cannot fly you off thisss cliff. My wing...'
"Then what are we to do?" Ian grew panicked.
'Leave it to me!' Scorch replied. 'Mount!'

Immediately and with haste, Ian climbed into the saddle. 'Don't ssstrap yourself in!' Scorch ordered. Before Ian was ready, Scorch leapt off the cliff and opened his wings which billowed and swelled catching the wind and slowing their fall.
Scorch howled in agony as the wind hammered at his wounds, pulling and tearing the already wide gash in his membrane.
He landed heavy, and quickly stilled as his wings fell like a blanket to his side, draped across the earth.
Ian carefully got off to assess the damage when Xsealiadd appeared out of nowhere yet again, metal clashing naught twenty feet away.

"I saw you fall." Was all he said, "Heliar umpey!" Xsealiadd swished his staff widely before bringing it down upon Scorch. Immediately the dragon's wounds mended, the arrow from his wing clattered to the ground. Ian immediately scooped it up for his quiver.

"Circle above, shoot with your bow, Valquee will soon join you."

'I don't have the ssstrength.' Scorch pushed his thoughts to Xsealiadd.

"Well then, interriar lagganne!" Xsealiadd once more tapped Scorch with his staff. Immediately the dragon grew bright eyed as he stood erectly.

"Bear me as long as you can. When you tire, land on a roof-top, we'll shoot from there." Ian instructed Scorch as he clambered back on to fulfill Xsealiadd's order.

'I can't fly with thisss breasssst plate Ian, look at itsss dent.' Scorch protested.

Without hesitation and with fumbling fingers, Ian began unclasping the armour which, soon enough, thudded to the ground.

They had just become airborne as a group of torans rushed over to present a challenge; Ian's main concern was flying arrows.

"Remember, stay out of arrow range!" Ian instructed nocking one of his own as Scorch grew in height.

It wasn't Ian that spotted the shadowed figure lurking in the heart of Rulan but Scorch. Confronting it, Ian realized it to be Florian who immediately defended any word or physical attack with his blade.

Unfortunately for Ian, he was forced to spar. They were fairly evenly matched, except Florian clutched a box, veiled by a cloak under one arm, which slowed his defence and disabled his shield.

Something cold, hard and feeling to be on fire stabbed heavily into Ian's back, dropping him to his knees he crumpled in agony. Expecting Florian to finish him, he was surprised when Florian fled, though he quickly reminded himself, Florian was really his sister, Florence.

Without further ado, Ian lay earth bound, his vision hazy. His mind flickered with thoughts of impending doom as he wallowed in self-pity. 'I'm down,' he thought. 'Does this mean I'm finished?' Off in the distance, Ian caught a glimpse of a man, his stabbing arm severed, blood squirting from the stump on every beat of his heart. In his left hand, he clutched a flail in which he madly, savagely attacked his enemies.

"I suppose not." Ian answered his own question, pulling himself back astride Scorch.

As silent as a mouse, Scorch took flight just in time for Ian to catch a glimpse of Florian running through the night.

One by one, Ian began emptying his quiver when Valquee, astride Blazzan flew up to join them. She had somehow managed three quivers full. Where she found so many arrows Ian could not guess.

"I doubted any would notice me up here on dragon back, which is why I chose to help you; besides, your archery skills lack seriously, no offence!" She shouted over the void of space between them.

"None taken!" Ian groaned as he quickly quieted, the arrow wound paining him. Joining Valquee, Ian began shooting foes from their heightened vantage point, though he nowhere near matched her skill level. To worsen things, every pull of the bow caused injury to his back where the arrow had struck.

"Their armour is weak around the neck!" Valquee informed. Ian cackled, "I'm lucky if I hit them at all!" He commented but quickly silenced from the pain. Even from this high up, Ian could hear Xsealiadd's voice rise above all else as if amplified, he was chanting some form of magic.

Light shone from seemingly nowhere bathing the entire Rulan in warmth.

Much of the army fled, snorgs who feared the light.

That was all the help the elves needed as they began gaining the upper hand.

Ian recognized the spell of Foomantacilla Erezerenté being echoed again and again as one by one snorgs faded into nothing.

"It is time Ian!" Valquee shouted.

"Time? Time for what!"

"It is time we show those Sardon folk. Show them what you've been chosen to be! Come on Blazzan!" Valquee ordered, slapping her dragon on the rump which dropped into a streamline dive. Ian vaguely heard the familiar cry vugar ak othnak! As she bolted by. Immediately, Ian did his best to match her skill. The moment Ian became one with Scorch he was once again filled with energy, he had to let it out as he belted out every spell he knew.

Ian wavered as Scorch suddenly shot back upwards after toppling many soldiers, something that apparently didn't go unnoticed by Valquee.

"Don't forget!" She shouted advice over the battlefield. "Grab five inches below the lowest neck spike for optimum balance, then lean low for streamline aerodynamics."

Ian struggled to pry his white-knuckled fingers from the saddle-horn but assumed the position, nevertheless, just to please her.

"Atta boy!" He heard her shout though it was quickly lost in amongst her sea of enchantments and spells.

Something happened then even Ian could not recall, he had just pulled out of some complex manoeuvring when he suddenly grew cold. All his happiness abated him and he could feel his grip loosen; growing slack, he slipped from his dragon's saddle, plummeting nearly two hundred feet to the ground below, though landing he could not remember.

When Ian at last awoke, he found himself to be resting on white linen sheets, again. Next to him, Valquee was nursing both his and her own wounds with some salve and a dampened rag. In the distance, Ian could hear frantic cries though the clashing of metal seemed to have ceased.

Opening and closing his mouth several times, Ian was going to ask what happened before deciding in opposition to it as he stilled his jaw.

Valquee, however, seemed to answer it for him.

"You're lucky you have friends on the battlefield Ian Cosswell."

"Sorry?"

"No matter, once you were protected, we took you here to the seclusion of my home; when it was safe to do so of course."

"What happened to the battle I mean? Who won?"

"Nobody, the army retreated on the Occluder's word, the elves are furious."

"Why would they retreat?"

"Because they got what they came for."

"What!"

"Yes Ian, this war had a purpose. They left with Nighdrake's scale, Xsealiadd and the Amity Blade."

"The what, what, and what!" Ian couldn't believe his ears.

"Yes Ian, the elves are, if not now, soon going to plan our revenge. First however, we must appoint a new chief of Rulan."

"Do you know who it will be?" Ian asked with curiosity.

"Oh, you are just right full of queries aren't you? It will be Athrin. He was Lord Guwhyon's son, it is only fitting that he'd be next to the throne."

"Oh, uh, one more question?"

"Just the one?"

"Scorch how and where is he?"

"He is doing quite fine. Mad at himself for not being there to catch you but he'll mend. Right now he and Blazzan are out hunting something, you should do as well."

"Hunt?"

"Eat, there is a small banquette being held at Lord Guwhyon's former residence. We are meeting there to have a pick-me-up snack and discuss our next course of action. You're welcome to join in if you'd like."

Ian grunted as he shifted in pain and stiffness. All his battle aches were coming back to haunt him. "You go on ahead I'll find you in a bit."

Valquee did not wish to leave but after much persuading she, at long last to Ian's wishes, left him in solitude.

Chapter 46
Captives

Thyle doubted his skill. He was not the least bit confident he'd be unable to slip away undetected. Yet here he was free from his pledge, free to do as he pleased, all he needed now was to resist the summoning, then and only then would he truly be a free man.

Unfortunately, however, he must find his way free of Hucklandish Woods, a forest which made him tired, weary and oh so lost and alone. Night still pressed potently upon his surrounds, and the land marks he could faintly see all looked the same.

Thyle felt hopeless, with nowhere to go and no one in whom to trust, he slumped against a tree and before he knew it, the forest had robbed him of his remaining strength. Allowing his head to droop, he had soon fallen asleep.

"What did I do to deserve this? I am just an old man. Must you drag me across the countryside?" Xsealiadd pleaded.

"Silence! You will do as you're told!" One of the torans, who was dragging him along, snapped. They had been listening to Xsealiadd's whining since they had departed Rulan; it had grown irritating.

"No, you know what? I don't think I will listen to you anymore." Xsealiadd chimed.

"You will because you must..."

Xsealiadd was frozen, statuesquely inbound within the earth, as if someone had turned him into an ice sculpture. His mind, however, was anything but stagnant: it swam constantly with what was called unspoken incantations. Chanting to the gods, he kept himself occupied.

The Sardon folk were at a loss for what to do with a stiff, routed to the spot, wizard. Needless to say, the Occluder wasn't too happy with the matter either. After learning the situation, he repeatedly tried to break Xsealiadd's mental defences. Only then would he be able to observe what spells the wizard was weaving and be able to counter them with his own black magic. This was easier said than done; mind shields were strong.

Florian panicked as he scrambled about the woods, he was lost, alone and didn't want to get caught; that was his biggest fear, getting captured.

Of course that was before he tripped in a gopher hole in the black of night and sprained his ankle; then he wanted to get caught, just not with the blade.

Lucky, or unlucky for him depending on how one looked at it, the elves were angered as they hunted the fugitives; cowardly Sardon men who still lurked in the forest.

By the time Florian was found, the blade was well hidden. Slumped against a tree he was near asleep when he was confronted by the scowling elvish folk, seeking rebels that may harm their men.

A delicate thin blade touched below Florian's chin; its cold steel plunging a feeling of vulnerability deep into the marrow. Florian opened his eyes, but didn't dare move for fear of leaning into the, no doubt, sharp blade.

"Name!" The elf interrogated.

'Should I lie?' Thought Florian to himself, but thought against it, the elves were nice people. "F-Florian." He replied nervously.

"Florian! Florian Boreaigge? You spent the summer with Hivell in Rulan, am I right?"

"Aye." Florian groaned, his ankle pained him.

"What brings you here? Shouldn't you be at school?"

Florian thought quickly, "I'm here as I was completing a challenge. I was supposed to deliver a message to the King of Rulan, however word has touched my ear that he has passed into shadow; I was just turning back to the academy to tell the principal the message was unsuccessfully delivered when I got lost in this vast forest and tripped. Now I hurt my ankle and can't walk." Florian informed, shifting awkwardly.

Immediately, the elf turned his attention to the wounded ankle in question. "Well Florian," the elf began, pausing to heal the swollen joint. "You will be pleased to know a new king will be crowned at sunrise, so if you'd like you can pass the message to me and I shall carry it proudly to the bearer of the new crown."

"Uh, okay," Florian began, he wasn't prepared for this as he thought hard and long.

"You don't have a message do you?" The elf questioned suspiciously.

"I do! I do! I've just, sort of, forgotten it? My mind has been elsewhere these past days that's all." As he spoke, a thought popped in his mind, something he heard while traveling with the Sardon folk. "I was told to say..." he began speaking slowly and with care. "The war that will, or has already befallen Rulan, allowed the Occluder to gain a piece of a complex puzzle of his own; also that when the two pieces are joined, one he already has, that a body will form; one fuelled by black magic and is for the Dark Lord himself. This war was to gain that piece."

The elf cocked a brow. He could see through the lines, he suspected foul play.

"And did you get him that piece?"

"What! Me? No!" Florian screamed, shocked at the accusation. "I was, it wasn't my job to steal anything, it was taken along with the wizard, Xsealiadd."

The elf didn't look convinced; this left Florian with little choice. With quick hands he revealed a dagger concealed beneath his cloth and stabbed hard and fast.

Though elves are quick, when caught off guard and unsuspecting, it is difficult to react. By the time he countered, it was too late: Florian had crippled him and was bolting into the night; his ankle healed. He ran through the darkness and well into the morn; by the time evening had come, he had slumped in a place unknown, welcoming in the night with falling tears.

The Prophecy

Chapter 47
The Proposal

The room seemed far too small for the amount of people crammed into it. The moment Ian entered the door he felt claustrophobic. He was at one of those gatherings where he couldn't even stand still without getting bumped or jostled. After many repetitious excuse me's and pardon me's, Ian found the hors d'oeuvres. He had just picked up a square laden with berries when a booming voice broke the din.

"It is normally customary for the prince to speak on behalf of the king, however Athrin being in his current state of mind, I think you would all agree to be highly unfit to face public appearance on this solemn day of mourning. He is not alone. On this day we all grieve for those who are lost, ones who gave their lives as a sacrifice while shielding our beloved, sleepy village of Rulan.

"Though it was a tragic time when we lost so much, we must not forget about who and what we stand for. Hope, freedom, peace and harmony. Something the Amity Blade was to deliver, but has struggled with these many years and now has failed entirely, as it was ripped from our hands. Why, you may question... for the individual's gain to achieve childish dreams in world domination. Why is there always one who desires to better themselves against the rest? One who spoils life as we know it to gain control, to achieve foolish, folly plans at the expense of others. Others whose lives have been ruined as a loved one fell from the heart. People like Athrin and so many others of you, who have lost those they love who were protecting our lands. I think it's only appropriate we take a brief moment to honour the dead who have fought and died for world unity. Hail the deceased. May the light always shine and may hope always remain."

"Hail!" The room responded as one before plunging into a respectful silence.

After several great moments of quiet passed, the voice rose once more. "Under the circumstances, I feel it only fitting that we appoint Athrin the next head of council. He would make a fine ruler in his father's stead and in his heart, wants to chase the hope and peace we all dream about. Should any object they should do so now."

The room plunged to an eerie silence before at last erupting into applause "Hail King Athrin!" The room once again spoke in unison and all as one, sunk to their knees.

From an adjacent corridor, Athrin appeared; he was ghostly white except for his eyes which were red and swollen from his great number of tears.

"I thank you all for such a great honour." Athrin began, his voice shaky. "And I do hope I can lead my people to see better days. Days where the sun always shines, illuminating the best in all of us. A time when we can all be as one. Until this time, by my blood and blade, if I can protect you from further tragedy, I will. The road to serenity is long and unfortunately many shadows still stand in our way. As your new King, I am going to complete what father started, something that has been put off for far too long. As your new King, my first task is to seek revenge on those who have stolen the lives of my father and your loved ones. We will march as one, our hearts beating for our cause, into Sardon. We will win or die avenging those who have been savagely killed for the greed of one. Who's with me?" Athrin roused the crowd which exploded in triumph, all except Ian who grew outraged at the thought. Climbing on the hors d'oeuvres table to make himself vocal, Ian was agitated.

"You plan a war upon his armies? My liege, your people are weak, you cannot face them on your own. If nothing else, please call for aid."

Athrin stiffened. "This is our war. We fight it alone."

"Why must you be so blind-sighted and headstrong? If you march upon them solo, your people will die, every last one of them. The time of the elves will perish."

"Well is that such a bad thing. Perishing for a worthy cause? We have walked this earth, our time must end; why shant we end it in triumph and in glory, filling our hearts with pride; glory for the people who gave their blood, confident in our beliefs? My heart is set on our cause, I will not waver."

"Please, you are hurting now, your mind is not thinking clearly; it is clouded with pain. Tell me, what good is triumph if not rejoiced? What good would it be to fight for an age you won't live to see? All I'm asking is for you to call for help. If we band together and fight as one, shoulder to shoulder, breast to breast, forget and throw aside our difference; not only will we be triumphant, we will form a bond amongst our friends so strong, it shall never stray. We will survive to see the new day, our hearts pounding the same rhythm beneath our chest, regardless of race."

"Friends? What friend would welcome a guest with pain and suffering, torment a dragon into misery? What friend would turn against us in the cold war?"

"The Occluder is not your friend, he never was our friend."

"I'm talking about the dragons!" Athrin roared. "What dragon would betray their rider? No, we're not as fortunate in our friendships as you may believe."

"You may be surprised just who is out there willing to offer a blade. Look, if you won't call for aid, at least allow me a chance to comb Ellezwrainia, from the west to the east, drawing out any who wish to fight. You once said to me you're forever in my debt. You can begin to repay me by allowing me to do this. Look, Valquee told me I'm never supposed to say this, but I'm going to anyways. It won't be the first time I have said too much. I am the first of the forthcomings." Ian pulled back his long sleeve revealing the bite wound to the room. "I am a rider. I have a dragon who apparently would risk his scales for me. A dragon who wants to be bonded at heart. Whether you like it or not, things are in motion that can't be stopped. Times are changing, soon we must all reunite, even dragons and riders. Why deny it, embrace it for it's coming. I will go solo, by flight. Please, let me at least try." Ian fell silent; he didn't like the look on Athrin's features, a scowl that seemed to never fade.

"You have exactly three months to the day and then we march for the stone walls of Sardon. May the rain never hinder and may the wind carry thee forth." Athrin frowned as he made to leave the room, tired of all the fuss.

"Thank you, I depart at dawn may my provisions be prepared." Ian shouted to his vanishing back.

The whole room glared at him, drilling into his heart, almost surveying his intentions. Ian felt awkward as he stood silently. Hopping off the table he made to leave the building.

It must've started raining sometime during the meeting, because once Ian got outside he became drenched quickly, it was pouring.

"What have I just done?" Ian asked himself before jogging distraught down the winding streets at last coming to rest against the side of a building; he was tugging at his hair.

Moments later Valquee joined his side. "Ian?" She asked concerned.

"Aaargh!" Was how he replied, he was extremely upset with himself and others.

"What is wrong?" Valquee questioned. And for the first time ever, Ian broke down and cried in front of the one he loved, or at least, thought he loved.

Valquee embraced him.

"I... don't... know..." He took a deep breath to calm himself as Valquee slowly released him. "I don't know what came over me, I can't do this, not alone anyhow. Could you come?"

"I am sorry Ian. I am needed here with my people in Rulan. My past experience, though awful, will aid in the preparation for battle on Sardon. You must believe in yourself. You can do anything that you believe you can."

"I can't, I can't."

"Yes you can." Valquee comforted.

"I can't! Okay! I have no belief, I have no faith!"

"You say you don't have confidence in yourself, this is true, you don't. Look how far you've come and you still frown at your own image. Here, stand here, look there." Valquee ordered, positioning Ian before a rather large puddle.

"Now tell me Ian, is that reflection an image of weakness and failure?"

"I don't even recognize myself."

"Uh huh, you have come far my lad. Not many would possess the courage to head across the countryside with minimal training, or even confront the King with your idea for that matter." Valquee boasted.

"Well, I most certainly wouldn't call myself courageous, only a fool."

"To be foolish is to be strong, it shows you have faith in your own choices. You have chosen your quest, now it's time to let your star guide you."

"You don't understand Valquee. I love you, like the love you read in fairy tales, you are not just a mentor to me anymore, you're something more, much, much more. I don't want to leave for fear of never coming back. For my heart anyway. It has happened once, I don't want it to happen again. You can't imagine what it's like, not being able to go home; home where I was born, home where peace and simplicity was all I knew."

"Yes I do Ian!" Valquee exploded, "yes I do! You do not know me! Don't even begin to think you know me! I've seen more than you could ever imagine in your wildest daydreams!" Valquee backed off a few paces, she was hurting, something was troubling her though she never explained what. "That love you feel, it's not real. There is no such thing as true love." Valquee interjected, she was still pacing in reverse. With one final look at Ian, she ran as elves do, through the rainy streets of

Rulan. Ian hesitated for a moment, unsure of whether to follow.

'Follow my heart. That's what Valquee told me, well, mine says to go to her and I will.' Ian thought before pursuing Valquee and her troubles.

Ian found Valquee about three streets away. Evidently it was her turn to cry as she sat on the roadside weeping, tears falling into the rain.

"Can we talk without shouting? Please?" Ian tested.

Valquee sniffed. "Sure." A weak smile flickered through her misery and pain.

"Now, speaking as civilized adults here," Ian informed, "you could not be more right, I don't know you, I haven't even begun to uncover your many layers, because you won't let me. And it's rather unfortunate that I don't know you better, 'cause I wish I did. Life is a short thing you know, you can be here one moment, gone the next, and yes I know this is coming from someone who, in your opinion, has not experienced life. Well you know what? If this is what life is, I don't know if I want to know it. Life has fouled me! I want to live a life less complicated, one where friends talk about troubles, face them head on instead of running away. I am leaving tomorrow, I may never come back, the least you can do is tell me your feelings; the ones deep in your heart, maybe then I'll understand. I can't love what I don't know and if it's anything like the tip of the Valquee iceberg, I want to know every bit of it should I never return. I want to truly understand the person that has touched me for so long in so many ways." Ian fell silent he had just realized how much he'd been rambling.

Their pregnant pause was brutal. At last Valquee spoke. "That is what scares me most."

"What?"

"You never coming back. Too many have I seen march off to battle and never return. The man I once loved died at the edge of a knife." Valquee withdrew a dagger from her boot and unsheathed it. It was stained in blood on both sides, Ian noticed as she turned it over. "I never got it cleaned, this was his blood. We were going to bear young, him and I. He was not the only death I've seen. Again and again, ones I have loved died in battle; students I've trained, mother, father, brother, they're all gone. I made friends to help cope with the losses, most of them left me too. You're one of the few I have still with me. I love you Ian, just maybe not how you see it. Love is one of those awful delusional things; it makes you dizzy, it makes you unsteady, and if you don't find solid ground, you may find yourself falling quicker than you may expect. Too many times have I loved, too many times has fate parted us; never again will I allow myself to be subjected to such pain and torment. I would rather be tortured in Sardon over and over before I allow myself to be loved like that again. It's not the love that dissuades me, it's losing them in the end; that's what hurts the most."

Ian sighed, he was foolish to offer advice on something he'd never experienced, but he sure as well was going to try.

"How many people have you lost in your life?" He asked.

"Too many," Valquee sniffed, she was beginning to sob again.

"Then you should know that feeling, when the person died, you wished you had spent more time with them."

"Everybody gets that Ian, it's called regret."

"Exactly, well by not allowing yourself to open up and love another makes you a little self-centred and headstrong, just like Athrin was being."

"How do you mean?"

"Well..." Ian sighed, this was a difficult subject for one who thought like a fourteen year old to discuss with an adult. "By not allowing others to enjoy your company, makes you a bit selfish doesn't it?" Ian faltered. "Sorry, I can't explain it any better. Look, you don't have to ponder on it now but, perhaps when I'm gone and alone, and you look to the full moon, if you think of me, remember what I said, okay?"

Valquee smiled weakly. "Okay kiddo. Look, you should get some shut-eye, dawn is only a few hours away and you must be alert if you are to set out into the wild beyond."

"What about my provisions, and Scorch? He doesn't know yet!"

"Don't worry Ian, I will inform him the moment I spot him flying in. Remember Blazzan is with him, if nothing else, Blazzan will announce their arrival, now it's time you rest."

With a gaping yawn, Ian dismissed himself for the last night in a while on a white linen bed with a fluffy feather pillow.

Though short lived, it was as he had hoped a restful one...

About the Author

Breanna LeLiever was born in Toronto Ontario and moved to the small town of Stirling at age three. Surrounded by nature with her pet parrot Kiwi, and writing as far back as she can remember, ideas flowed together and inspiration offered aid in the most unusual ways. Taking concepts when they came, Breanna was building The Amity Blade; The Prophecy while writing The Birth of a Hero, but it never became a serious project until the completion of the first novel
The Amity Blade is a proposed seven book series, with unusual and thrilling adventures.

Breanna draws insight from highly unusual sources and is constantly on the lookout for new ideas, characters, or monsters to put in her works.

Characters you Meet

THE AMITY BLADE

Aak

Altane

Annestha

Arienna

Auzze

Baljune

Banthumn

Brako

Broxxan

Cano

Dreal

Dugan

Etar

Evaz

Grunkle

Hyashi

Jeban

Leeran

Lord Branil

Lord Danahi

Master Udkaa

Ming

Nalo Tyklonne

Ocenna

Orik

Oshrinne

Paddo

Quartzel

Sam

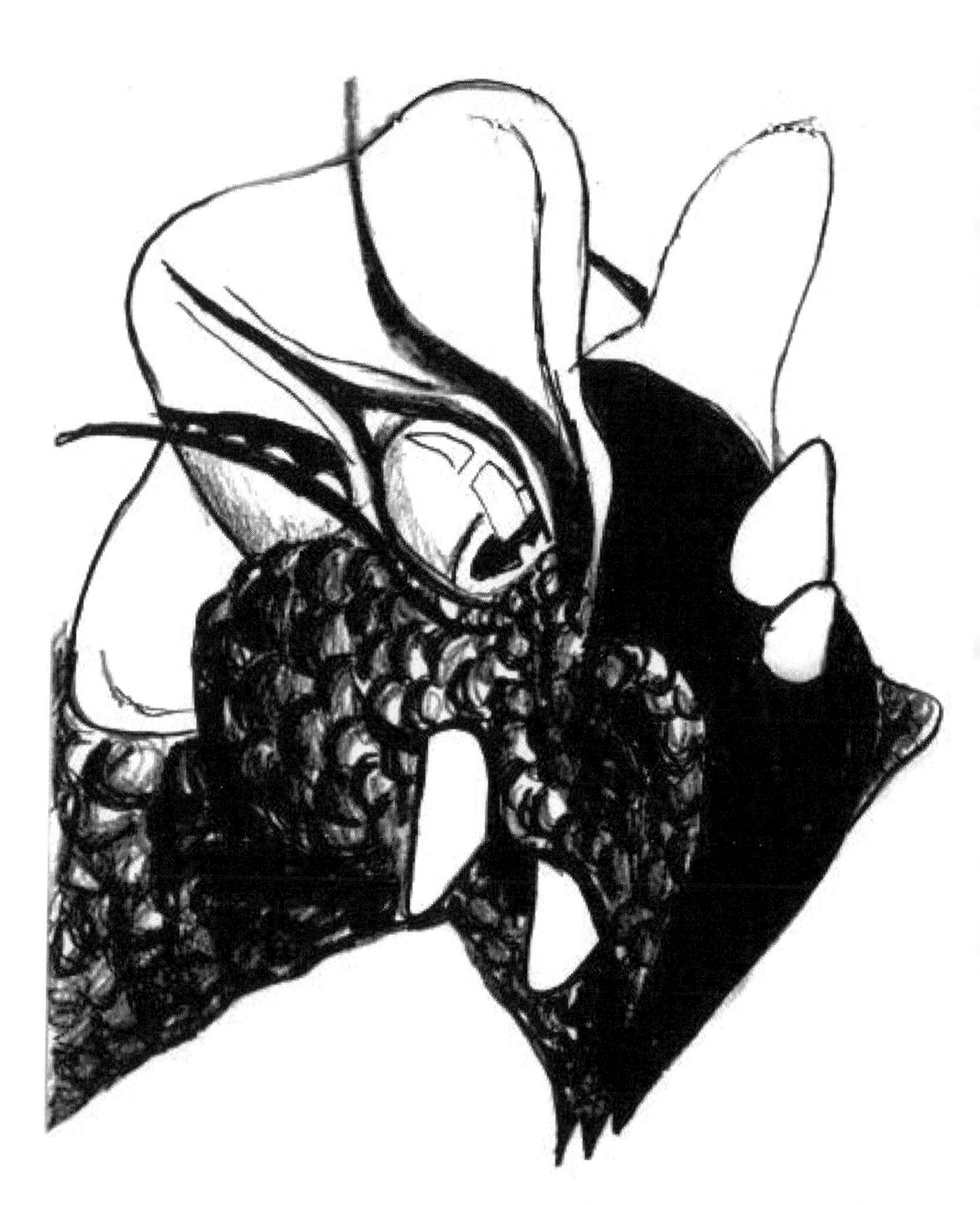

Scorch

Spayuhddeus

Streaks

Thayuss

The Moustachioed Man

Treggle

Trinaris

Ursulfeenia

Viovess

Characters You've Already Met

THE AMITY BLADE

Abboton Frier

Ackles

Artani Boultier

Athienne

Athrin

Baldin

Banthumn

Bashlay

Befouller

Belron

Blazzan

Charilakkie

Dingy

Dowler

Drexel

Eemile

Elorash

Florence

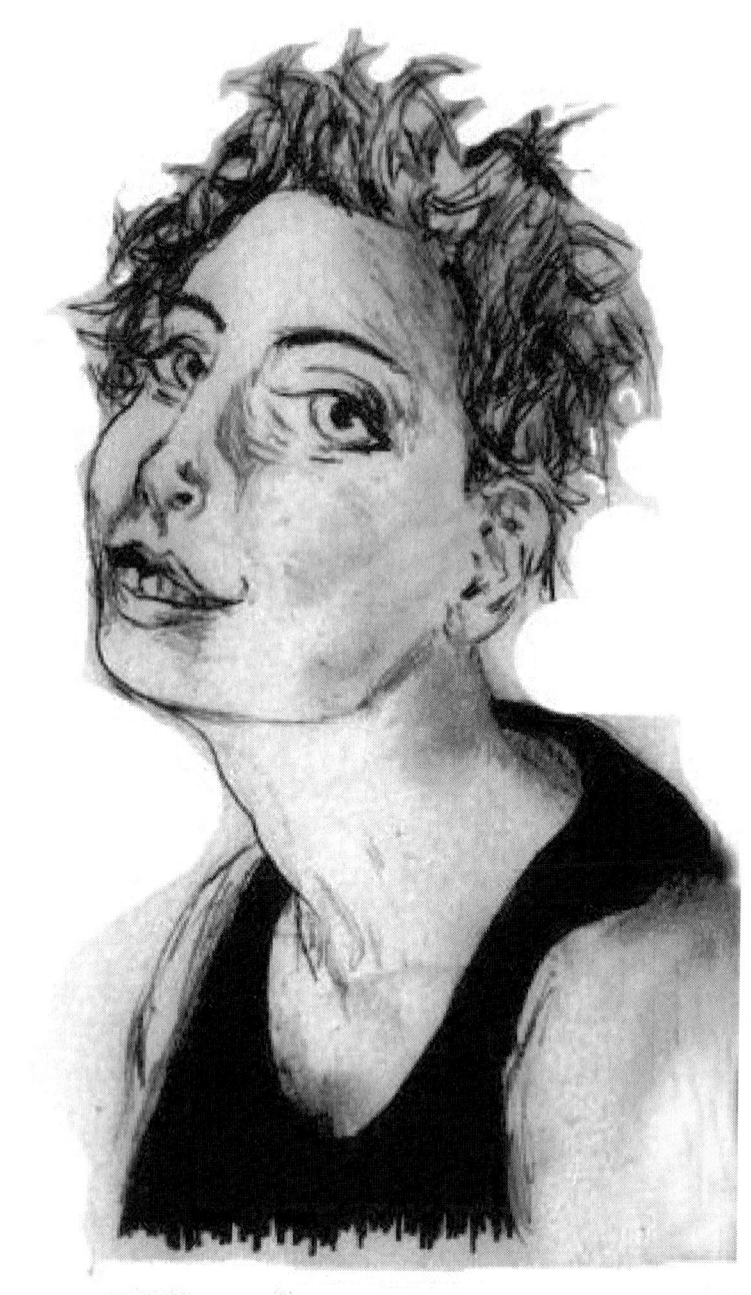

Florian

Fraxron

Garash

Gardo

Gerritude

Gizmo

Gorby

Genevieve Green

Habbar

Hamish

Hamman

Hancer

Hivell

Ian

Irk

Largo

Lord Guwhyon

Magnon

Mme. Davis

Mme. Dumpling

Mozel Gant

Nighdrake

A Nymph

The Occluder
(Larke Dray Farrizon)

Orto

Othorrow

Oulle

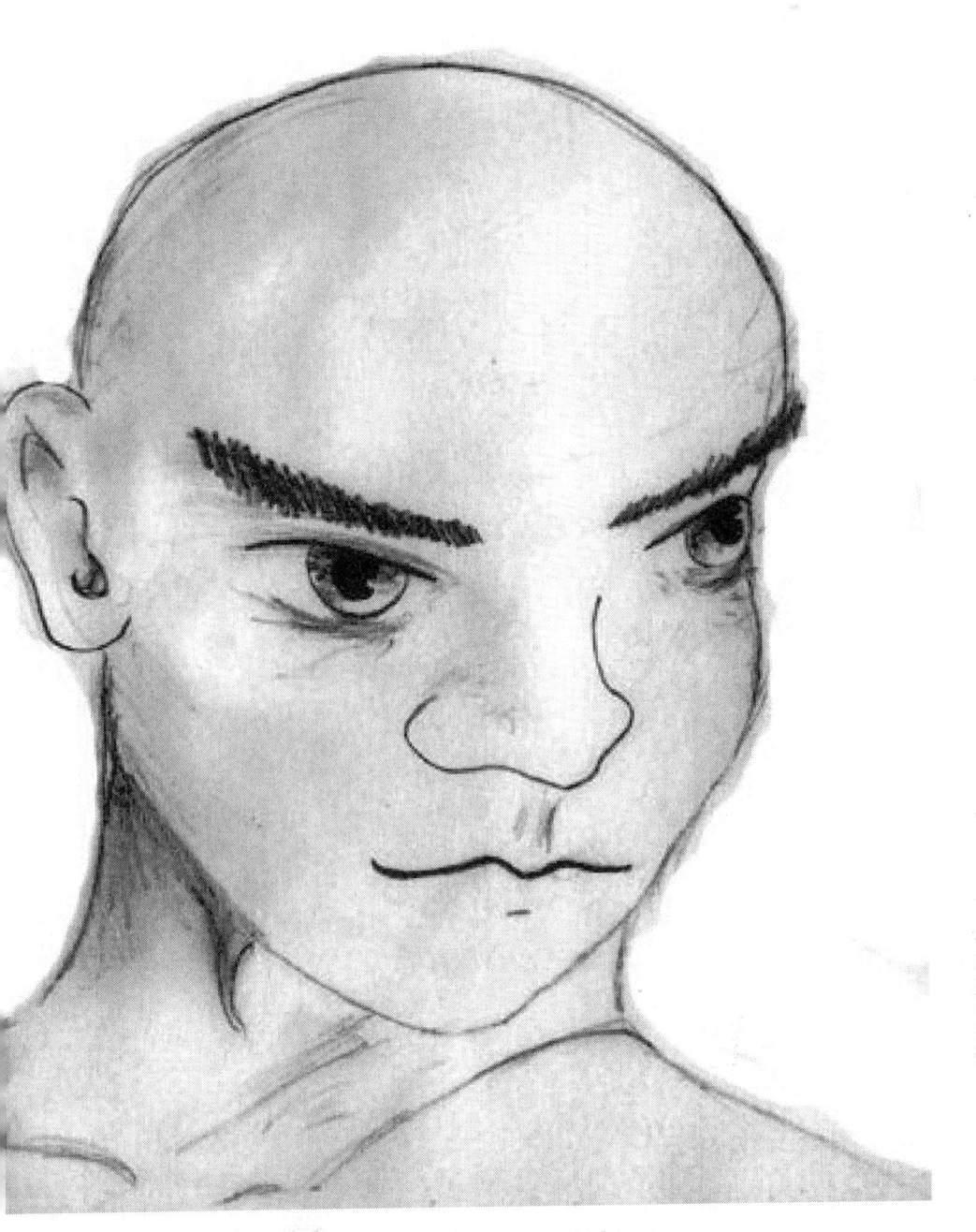

Rennaux

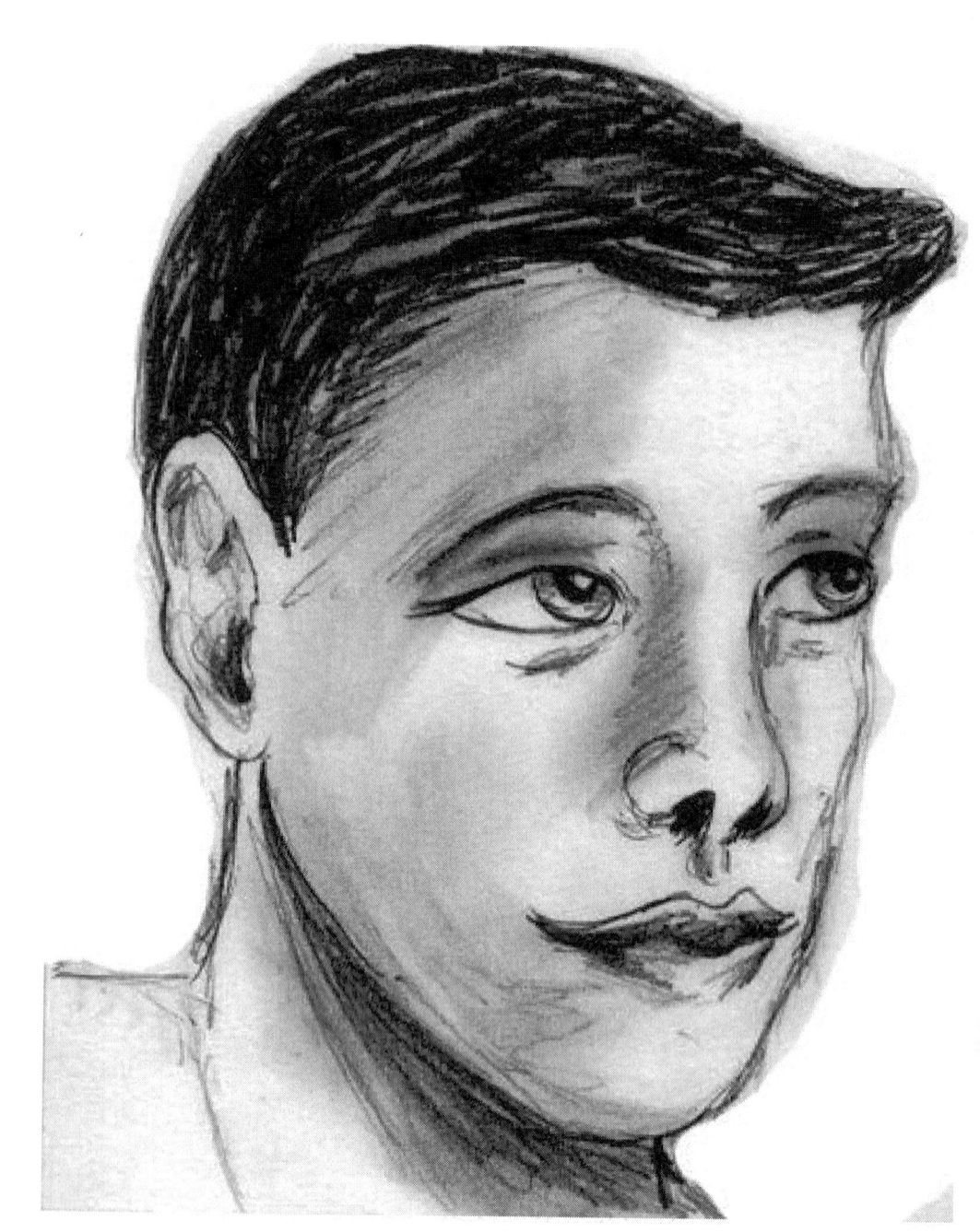

Rubén Hokant

Sauvan

A Shorble

A Snorg

Stanzer

Tathienne

Teargo

The Golden King

Thyle

Tom
(The Stableman of Solan)

A Toran

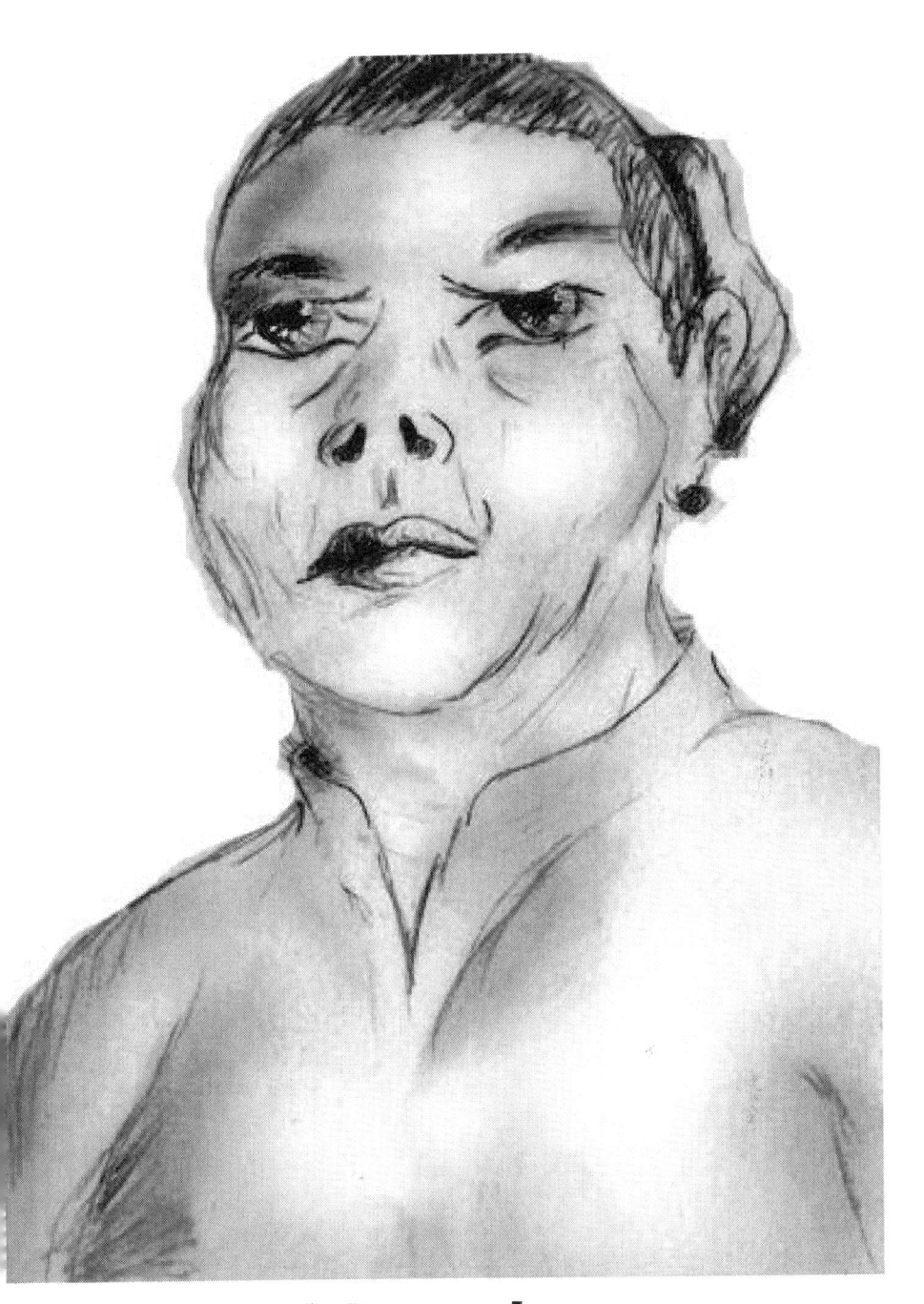

Ursula

Valquee

Wok

Xsealiadd

Made in the USA
Charleston, SC
18 October 2015